BEASTS BENEATH THE FLESH

EYE OF THE SERPENT: BOOK 1

JOE COLOMBAN

ISBN: 978-1-7341447-0-3

This is a work of fiction. The characters, incidents and dialogue are drawn from the author's imagination and are not to be construed as real. Any resemblance to actual events or persons, living or dead, is entirely coincidental.

Cover art by Boris Vallejo

Edited by Philip Athans

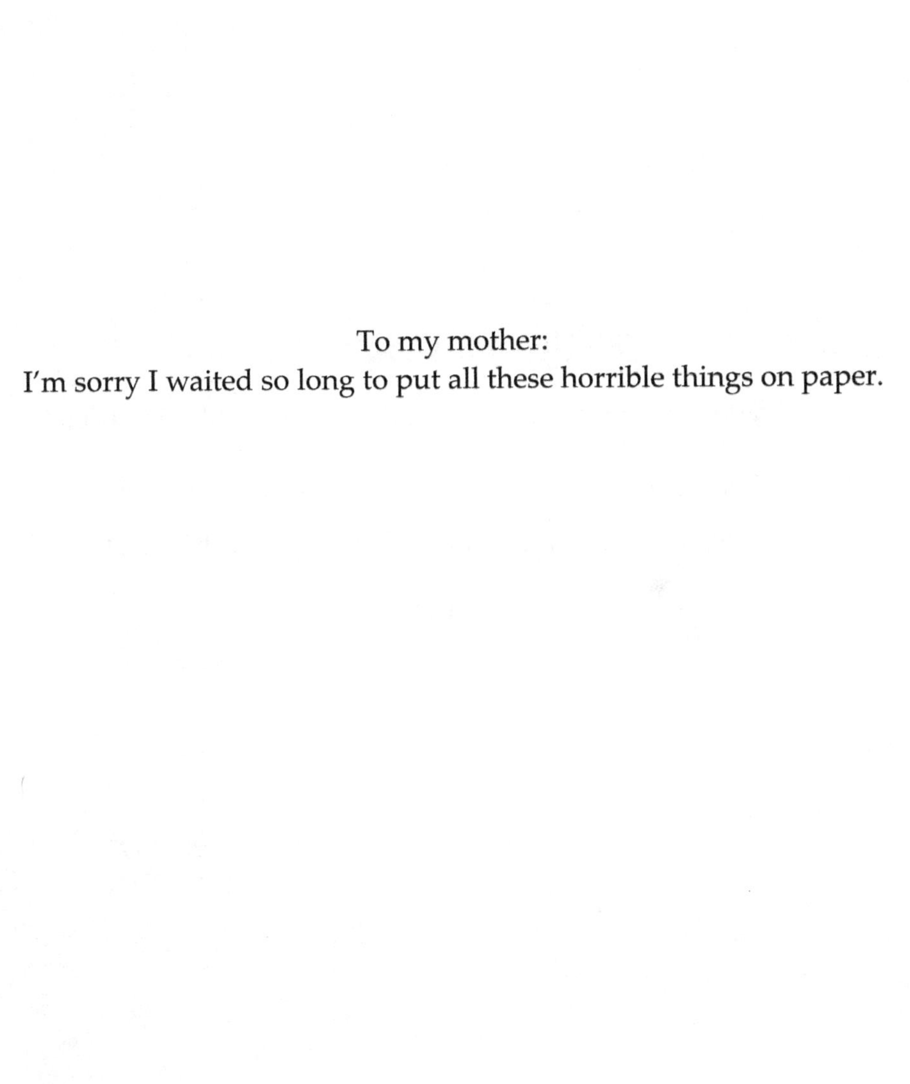

To my mother:
I'm sorry I waited so long to put all these horrible things on paper.

Special Thanks

Thank you to everyone who made this possible. My friends, for feeding my inspiration. My editor, Philip Athans for helping make a coherent narrative. And Boris Vallejo for the beautiful cover art.

BEASTS BENEATH THE FLESH

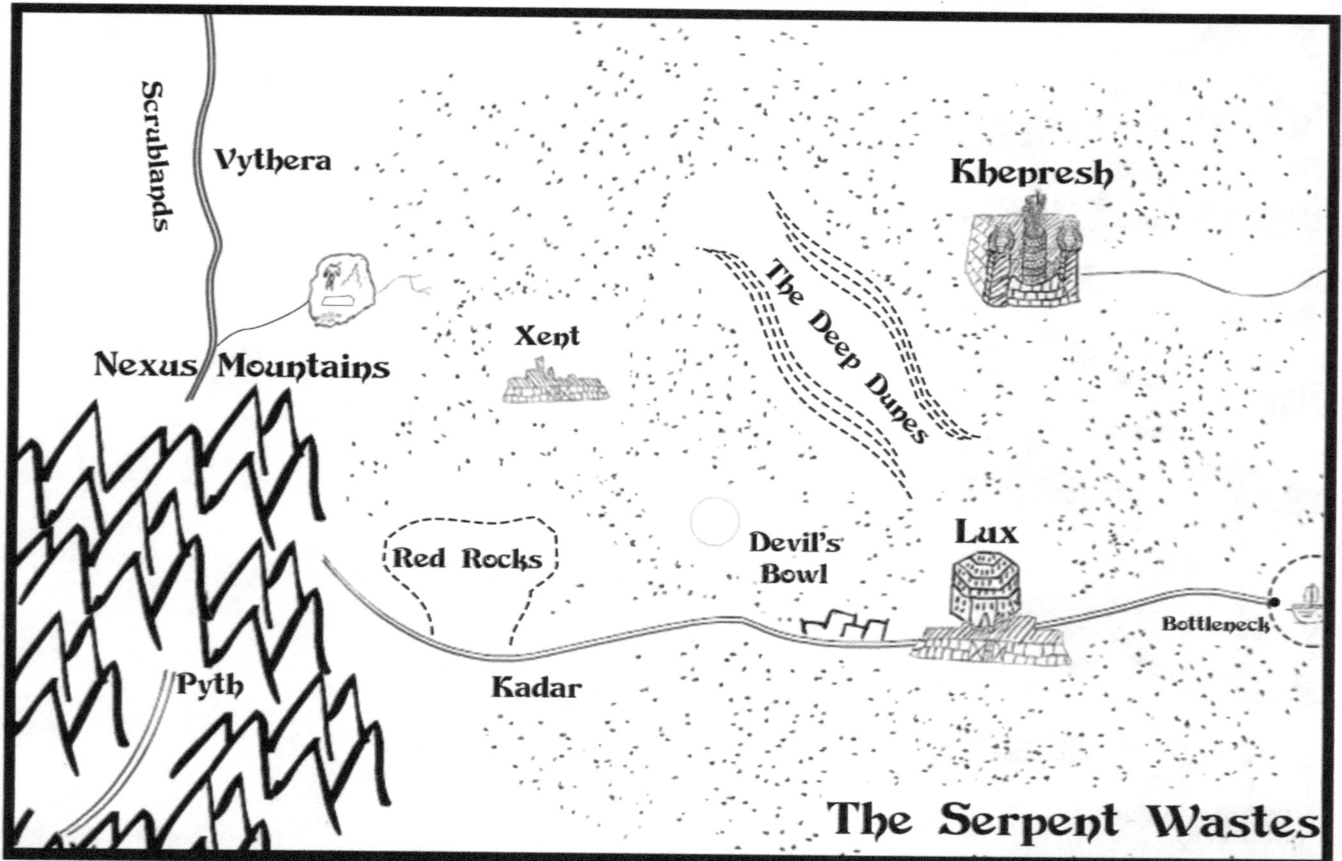

Scrublands
Vythera
Khepresh
Nexus Mountains
Xent
The Deep Dunes
Red Rocks
Devil's Bowl
Lux
Bottleneck
Pyth
Kadar
The Serpent Wastes

The distinction between man and beast is an arbitrary one. Often, gods themselves can't tell the difference. Still, men play their games, blind to whims beyond their comprehension. In these lands only two things are certain. The moon is red, and those beneath it cruel.

—Inscription on the Tomb of Cainus V
First Primus of the Second Ecrecian Empire.

CHAPTER
1

Willem was done with the Legion.

But desertion was an offense punishable by death. Standing in the shadow of a serpent breaching a quarter mile high, that was a negligible concern. Silhouetted against the midday sun, the image burned his eyes.

Angua subterra, leviathan eels of the sand. It snapped at the Legion's airship, a second pharyngeal jaw extending from its mouth nearly piercing the ballasts. Musket fire peppered the serpent to no avail. The salvo shook flecks of dirt from the subterra's hide. A fold of flesh peeled back, revealing a purple eye, the pupil alone bigger than a man. The pupil sharpened to wedge focused on the men beolow. With its assault on the airship a failure the beast fell back over the legionnaires below.

A great number of legionnaires stood paralyzed. Their training covered a vast assortment of scenarios. They'd studied simple matters ranging from slave hordes, cavalry (of horseback or reptile variety), and they'd even drilled on how to ambush serpent-man sorcerers—though that was more theory than craft. Unfortunately, the subterra breaches weren't something they could simulate.

Still, unit cohesion won out. The legionnaires rallied against the avalanche of scaly flesh, their spears thrust upward in defiance.

Willem ran.

Panicked and rebellious screams rang out from every direction. The subterra's shadow grew larger with every passing moment. The impact was akin to a natural disaster. A tidal wave of sand cascaded across the canyon. Legionnaires lucky enough to escape the subterra's hulking frame found themselves scattered. Half of them lay buried in sand from the aftershock. The subterra landed on the cohort left of center, crushing more than half of them.

Willem pushed himself back to his feet. Sand filled his every orifice. His nose stung as he huffed in a plume of dust. He knew that running was an empty gesture. Still, the Legion beat enough stubbornness into him to not let the snakes have their way. Willem spotted a horse that was still moving. He forced his body forward.

The remaining two hundred and fifty men began to regroup. The cohort formed a spear line, gambling that cavalry would follow the breach. If the legionnaires were lucky the cavalry would be of the horseback variety. A balisk's jaws were strong enough to sheer clean through Legion armor.

The spear line stood ready to counter whatever attack waited over the horizon. A minute passed, then another… nothing. Except for the subterra retreating back under the sand, the desert was still. Was it just some hungry animal looking for a meal?

Another minute went by in silence. Still, nothing came over the dunes.

No signal came from the scouting ship above. The ship was too small for anything beyond reconnaissance or a strategic powder keg drop. The glorified balloon bobbed in the desert wind. Tiny dots of crewmen scurried about the railings.

The quiet persisted.

Willem's mind raced. If the attack was over he'd need a good explanation for breaking ranks. He was as good as dead unless he course corrected back to the cohort before anyone realized. Clutching his flintlock in one hand, Willem grabbed a spear in the other and turned back for the cohort. It was his first month in the desert and the cohort was already halved. Willem adjusted his head wrap, leaving only his cold eyes exposed. His armored jerkin chafed at the lean body hidden beneath it. He trudged back toward the cohort. He was preparing to spend the next six months on latrine duty when he noticed the sand churning beneath him.

A distant voice screamed, "Something's coming!"

Plumes of sand erupted throughout the cohort. Legionnaires screamed in terror. Sand snakes of a man-sized variety tore into their ranks. Metal pops punctuated the legionnaires' screams when the snakes' jaws tore through their armor. For every legionnaire with a gut full of teeth, two more were bludgeoned by the tails of the writhing beasts whose fangs eviscerated their comrades.

A sand python breached the sand under Willem. He managed to raise his musket, putting it between his face and the sand snake's. The force of the beast's ambush knocked Willem flat on his back. The python didn't waste any time coiling around him. Willem braced the butt of his gun with his knee and elbow, affording him room to breathe. The snake's coils tightened around his body. The hard oak of the musket dug into Willem's arm. He gritted his teeth, desperate for a way out.

Through a combination of desperation and adrenalin, Willem managed to free his hand from the python's coils. He had to work quickly now. Willem took one last breath before the snake snapped tight around his torso. The python was squeezing the air from his body. He fumbled to undo the bolt on his musket bayonet with his free hand.

Blade in hand, Willem used every ounce of strength in his body to plunge his bayonet into the python's eye. The iron struck behind the eye socket, repeatedly.

After a minute of frantic stabbing, the snake's grip loosened. Willem let his head drop to the ground. Life came back to him with every breath. Satisfied with his work, he started untangling himself from the heap of scaly flesh.

He managed to wriggle his left arm free, then his waist.

Then he spotted another of the damned things headed right at him. His rifle was empty. Absent any other options Willem pointed his rifle at the snake. He rolled onto his knees and jabbed the gun back and forth, keeping it between himself and the snake's dagger pointed jaws.

Willem rocked back onto his feet, juggling his bayonet and flintlock. He knew this was a guessing game where he'd have to keep picking right. Otherwise, the snake would strike him dead. He weaved back and forth, doing his best to keep an eye out for a third beast.

After a minute of this deadly game, the snake grew frustrated. It snatched Willem's rifle in its jaws. Wrenching itself up, the python tore the weapon from his hands. With Willem's only defense gone, the snake coiled into itself, ready to hurl its full weight at him.

Willem readied his bayonet and braced for the torrent of flesh and teeth.

Before the snake could strike, a flash of light blinded Willem. A bolt of searing heat passed over him. When his eyes adjusted the snake's top half was a cauterized stump. His rifle reduced to little more than a pile of molten iron and charred wood with globs of snake flesh seared to it. Patches of sand boiled and melted into glass.

Looking past the scorched remains Willem spotted Centurion Vanrikker reloading a scrawler pistol, a stopgap for the Legion's lack of sorcery. A marvel of engineering, those things. The centurion thumbed a shell covered in red runes into the chamber. No telling how Vanrikker got his hands on one. There were a few hundred such weapons across all Ecrecia.

The gun's muzzle crackled and sparked to life as it released a gout of flame. More than half a dozen snakes caught fire, reduced to twisted hunks of flesh. A tinge of sulfur wafted through the air intermingling with the overbearing smell of burnt corpses. For the moment a tenuous peace resumed.

Willem retrieved a loose horse, hoping to maintain some facade of discipline as he returned to the remaining cohort.

The centurion cracked open the action of his scrawler and inserted another shell into the breach. "Don't think I didn't see that, boy."

"Sir?" Willem feigned.

"Breaking ranks for a beast of burden during an ambush. Your priorities need rearranging."

"Yes, sir," Willem said, relieved the centurion only assumed he was incompetent and not a coward.

"Better learn fast, otherwise you're going to be teaching."

Willem swallowed hard, thinking back on the flayed recruit they'd left blowing in the wind earlier that morning.

The airship lowered a green flag, signifying an all clear.

The centurion flagged down another legionnaire. "Send word to the airship. Centurion Vanrikker wants them to find a solid surface we can make camp on."

The legionnaire saluted and ran off.

As Willem took back his place in the cohort's formation, he couldn't help but wonder about the Elder Serpents, the Damu'yhig. If the wildlife were this dangerous, what would the people be like?

CHAPTER
2

There was something about the foreign traders that set Batal on edge. In form, they were far closer to men than the Serpentine overlords. Yet somehow they seemed just as alien. They hid their angular features beneath heavy cloaks. Their hoods bent at odd contours, ears or horns of some sort hidden beneath.

Bat only got a brief glimpse of one's face as they passed by a torch. It was pristine, attractive even. A trick of the light gave its skin an unnatural tone.

Bat rubbed his scalp, irritated, still fresh shaven. He adjusted his armor, a layer of tanned balisk hide hidden under a linen cloak. In Xent, armor was forbidden to anyone not in the service of the serpent-men. That wouldn't matter much longer.

The traders' leader was speaking with Zaeim, a man of good stature, and thanks to his ability to speak the trade tongue, invaluable to the cause. Zaeim's own garb matched Bat's, spare a more luxurious cloak.

It had been six months since Bat joined the cause. Until then, he'd never seen a serpent-man feed. In his naivety, he'd thought it'd be a dignified process, or at least quick.

That public feeding all those months ago still haunted him. The thrashing, the sound of cracking bones, the bubbling texture of flesh injected with venom. Now Bat understood. Under the rule of serpent-men they weren't subjects, they were food.

Outside the walls was no better. The horrors of man, beast, and things in-between wandered the dunes. Those who lived long often joked that the difference between prey and cattle was bravery. That would all change soon.

The tallest of the traders pointed to a pile of crates. "Do as you will." They stumbled over the unfamiliar words. Their voice was still smooth, elegant even in the way they mispronounced it.

Each crate was the size of a man, their panels scorched and blackened. It was likely to hide the mark of origin. Scuff marks and splinters covered the floor.

Bat pried open a crate to reveal rows of gray metal, swords, and spearheads.

"They call it steel, say it's tougher than bronze," said Zaeim.

Bat noticed that one of the spear head's edges shined brighter than the rest. He laid the blade flat in his hands, the metal was heavy for its size, cool to the touch.

"Shiny edges much good, give best fighters," the trader said.

Bat set the blade down. His hand was bleeding from a cut that matched the blade's outline. Bat didn't even realize he'd touched the edge. No natural metal should be that sharp.

Bat looked up. "How are we paying for these?"

Zaeim waved his hand. "We will grant them certain considerations once we're in power."

The trader uttered something in their native tongue. Each word flowed into the next like poetry. Their language seemed a more complex version of the trade tongue.

Zaeim said something back, and the two shared a laugh.

The traders slipped out of the storehouse and into the darkening streets of Xent.

Bat clenched his fist, blood leaking from his palm. More came with his quickening pulse. A hand gripped his shoulder.

"It won't be long now, Brother," said Zaeim.

"All that's left is to pass out the steel."

Zaeim frowned. "There is one more arrangement we need to make."

Bat swallowed. "Brother, how many debts will Xent owe by the end of this?"

Zaeim gazed off into the setting sun. "As many as needed."

The sun finally set on Xent. The streets were empty, spare the occasional drunk. Bat sat next to Zaeim. Their wagon rattled the cobblestone roads. A handful of their strongest brothers sat nestled between the crates. They'd stop every few blocks, meeting another pair of brothers who'd take a crate of the foreign steel and secret it away in a nearby building in which more men waited.

Bat took a sip of wine to calm his nerves. He offered the wineskin to Zaeim who gladly accepted it. The wineskin was much lighter when he returned it.

They were entering the oldest part of Xent. Bat didn't notice until they drove past the smashed remains of a statue. It was likely that of a god in opposition to Anu Sidoth and his children, the Damu'yhig. This part of the city wasn't near anything necessary for their rebellion.

"What is this arrangement, Brother?" Bat asked.

"The City Master's sorcery would end our plight in moments. We have to snuff it out, fast."

"I still don't understand. What out here could aid us?"

The wagon lurched to a halt in front of an abandoned building. Chunks of adobe lay strewn across the street. In the absence of moonlight, the doorway blended into the dark facade. The doorway only became apparent once a figure emerged.

It was a pale man of slender build in an open tunic. A thick chain hung from his neck. The chain was set with a fist-sized piece of amber, a black martial embedded within its core. "The dreams are vivid tonight." His voice was shrill.

Zaeim bowed his head. "Acolyte."

Bat's blood went cold. He looked to Zaeim. "Brother, the others were suspicious enough of the traders. You'd consort with heretical magics?"

"We became heretics the moment we thought of turning on

the Damu'yhig."

"So you trade one dark god for another?" Bat felt a sharp pain across his face. He tasted blood.

Zaeim rubbed the back of his hand. "What we do tonight will never leave this circle."

Bat whirled on the others. They said nothing, only the slightest nods were visible in the dark. "What will this cost us?" he asked.

"He wants one of the old temples. What's one building weighed against our lives?"

The Damu'yhig might be cruel masters, but there was predictability to their cruelty. That was more than he could say for this acolyte. Zaeim was right, though. In their months of planning, they still hadn't thought of a way to overcome the City Master's sorcery.

"It's already in motion, I suppose," said Bat.

Zaeim looked back to the acolyte. "What would your ritual demand of us?"

"It's already done. Be sure to complete your business before sunrise."

The acolyte bowed and disappeared back into his hovel.

With a crack of the reigns, the wagon was moving again. This time for the City Master's home.

"Are there any other outsiders you struck a contract with?" asked Bat.

"Just the two," said Zaeim. "We will attend to the acolyte when the time is right."

This gave Bat some level of relief. He'd never been comfortable with the idea of sorcerers. The temperament of those who could bend strange forces to their whims did them no favors either. The inescapable fact that some cruel thing could always hold power over him sickened Bat. But if what they did here tonight succeeded it could send ripples through the dunes. It was a reminder that sorcerers and gods could only go so far before someone lashed out against them.

Zaeim pulled the cart over. The City Master's mansion was a short ways away. Instead of the adobe used to build the rest of the city the mansion was made of sandstone. In total it towered three stories high. Palm trees swayed in the breeze inside the wall.

A single guard manned the gatehouse, human.

One of the brothers handed Zaeim a bow. Zaeim lined up his shot and loosed. The arrow hit the guard's torso below the arm.

The guard collapsed to the ground, screaming in pain.

Batal and the others rushed the injured man. He and two others buried their spears in the guard's chest, silencing him.

A voice came from the garden. Bat whirled on his heel, chucking his spear. The steel pierced the man's chest and sent him reeling back, splashing into the garden pool. A second guard accompanying him, however, remained unscathed.

The guard turned heel and ran for the mansion, shouting an alarm the entire way.

Bat rushed over to the pool and retrieved his spear. It'd be a matter of minutes before the guards roused the City Master. Regardless of what the pale acolyte might have done, he didn't want to face the wrath of an Elder.

Bat and the others dashed forward. The guard was halfway through the front door when they ran him down, along with two others. Their spears tore through the men as if they were little more than water. After a few more thrusts Bat and the others forced their way into a lavish foyer.

Oakwood furniture covered the room. Rugs were woven in exotic colors Bat had never even seen.

Two pathways led upward: the servants' stairs, and the City Master's personal ramp.

Another pair of guards came down the steps carrying crossbows.

Without thinking, Bat sprinted for the ramp. A bolt struck his armor a glancing blow. The cries behind him meant someone else wasn't so lucky.

The ramp was steep enough for an awkward climb. He made it to the second floor without resistance. It must never have occurred to the guards that anyone other than their master might use the ramp.

The crossbowman took turns firing at them from the floor below. If Bat could take them the floor would be theirs.

Between Bat and the crossbowman stood a man clad in

bronze plate mail. Each plate bore engraved patterns of coiled vipers. The helm was shaped like the hood of a cobra. Scaly flesh showed through the gaps in the armor. It was a coldblood, the byproduct of a human mating with one of Sidoth's spawn. They weren't as deadly as their parents, but still nothing to take lightly.

The coldblood carried a long double-bladed ax with turquoise inlays.

The only advantage Bat had now was his speed, that and the steel. He bolted forward, screaming like a madman.

The coldblood brought his ax overhead, ready to cleave Bat in two.

Bat leaped forward, thrusting the spear with every bit of strength in his body. The spear struck dead center, meeting no resistance.

The coldblood swung his ax.

Bat watched the spearhead punch through the bronze. There was just as little impact when the spear burst from the coldblood's back. He felt a brief moment of joy before the ax's haft struck his skull.

Bat fell back, pinned under the coldblood, his spear lodged in its chest. The hallway was fuzzy.

He tried to push himself to his feet when a bolt ricocheted off the coldblood's armor.

One of the crossbowmen advanced on him. The guard drew the string back and placed a fresh bolt in his weapon. He rocked back and forth trying to get a shot at Bat's vitals.

Bat squirmed behind the armor, keeping it between him and the crossbowman.

The crossbowman lowered the angle of his weapon and fired again.

The bolt grazed Bat's thigh. His screams echoed in the hall.

The crossbowman reloaded, again aiming for his leg.

Bat closed his eyes and braced himself, but the next bolt never came. He opened his eyes to the sight of the man crumpled on the ground with Zaeim's sword through his neck.

Zaeim rolled the coldblood off of Bat before pulling him to his feet. "You're a special mix of brave and stupid, Brother."

"Isn't that why I'm here?" Bat said.

The others stormed past them, onward to the third floor. Bat leaned over to grab his spear. With a puzzled look, he eyed the blade, glancing back and forth between it and the armor.

Bat hobbled over to the stairs with Zaeim. By the time they reached the top the rest of the guards, as well as a few servants, lay sprawled out across the floor. No sign of the City Master.

A brief search revealed a single undisturbed room. Zaeim put his ear to the door. Everyone waited with bated breath. Zaeim mouthed the word "asleep."

Did he misunderstand? It wasn't possible that someone slept through that.

Zaeim pushed the door open.

Bat clenched his spear. ready for a wave of sorcery to sweep them away.

Nothing happened.

The bedroom alone was larger than most homes. From corner to corner there wasn't a single stretch of stone unadorned by decoration. On the far end of the room sat a massive canopy bed, the drawn curtain obscuring the occupants. Underneath the bed was a rack of red coals glowing in the dark.

Bat and the others spread out in the room, each making their way to the bed. No one dared break the deathly silence.

Zaeim peeled back the curtain to reveal a mound of sleeping forms in various states of undress.

At the center of the pile was the City Master. The Elder's only link to humanity was his muscled set of arms. Otherwise, he was identical to a cobra but twice the size of a man.

Despite everything that had happened the City Master's slumber endured. His chest pulsed in rhythm with his breath. A trail of black liquid leaked from the corner of his eye, the same for his bedmates.

Zaeim circled to the far side of the bed. Every one of their brothers took a place around the serpent-man. They readied their spears. Zaeim gave the signal. Every one of them plunged his spear into the City Master.

The hail of blades pierced his flesh. The City Master's eyes went wild. They came to rest on Bat, drifting off a moment later, vacant. His body went limp. A foul odor leaked from his cloacae.

Bat let out a sigh, only to snap back to attention when one of the City Master's bedmates screamed. The woman dug through the sheets and drew a knife. Before she could make use of it the brother next to Zaeim skewered her through the back.

The woman collapsed onto a broad-chested man who lay next to her. A wave of panic rolled over the harem, each awakening more panicked than the last. Two more reached for blades and met the same fate as their master. The pack of naked, sweaty people fled the mansion, tumbling over each other.

"Leave them," said Zaeim.

"What if there are half-breeds among them?" one of the others asked.

"The crowds will choose their fate. Should they live, they'll be our messengers. A warning is best delivered from a broken soul."

Bat limped to the window. Steel and screams echoed throughout the night. A guard tower burned in the distance. Raids like this where happening all over Xent.

Bat looked at his spear, its edges stained by the black ichor that leaked from the dreaming City Master. The city would soon be theirs, but at what price?

CHAPTER
3

Thazgarr stalked through the remains of his village. His movements were deceptively quiet for his body of thick corded muscle. In one hand he carried a studded war club, in the other his javelin.

The Ebonthorn laid to the west beyond the forest. To the east the scrublands—that's where the devils came from.

He ducked behind a mound of corpses. Two marauders and a balisk no more than ten strides away. Neither carried bows, only swords… and the balisk.

Thazgarr noted the dried blood on a corpse's nose, some foul poison or acid released into the wind. Thazgarr didn't know if the serpent-man raiders could invoke such bizarre magics again. An acceptable risk. Thazgarr crouched behind a larger man he used to train with.

A raider mounted the balisk.

Thazgarr knew he had little time. He placed his arms on the top corpse of the pile and pushed. The body tumbled to the other end of the mound. The sound of flesh against flesh was heavy in his ears. The tumbling body got the scale-skin's attention.

The guttural hissing of their foreign tongue frayed at Thazgarr's patience.

Thazgarr braced himself against the corpse mound, lower this time. He listened for the creaking of metal and leather as a raider drew near to investigate. Their footfalls grew louder, haphazardly negotiating the necrotic terrain.

If Thazgarr's timing was off the history of his tribe would end here. He listened for anything that might betray the scaled devil's location. The moment passed in silence then Thazgarr heard a dismissive sound in that alien language. It was on the other side of the pile.

Thazgarr pushed the corpse mound forward using every ounce of strength in his body. Gravity did the rest.

The raider panicked when the wall of corpses toppled over on him.

Thazgarr came bounding over the corpses in the confusion. He hurled his javelin at the balisk. The shaft struck its leg joint, sending both it and its rider tumbling. Thazgarr snapped his eyes to the raider trapped beneath his feet. He crushed the his head with his club. Brain sprayed from the eye socket.

The balisk thrashed on the ground, its rider trapped beneath it.

Thazgarr drew a second javelin from his quiver, lined up his shot, and plunged it into the balisk's throat. The beast went limp, the rider still trapped beneath.

Thazgarr made his way to the pinned raider at a deliberate pace. The scale-skin would be more talkative if he had time contemplate his situation. Thazgarr dropped into a crouch within arm's length of his foe, his club pinning his foe's free arm.

"Scale-skin," Thazgarr said in his low rumble of a voice, "when your people were slaughtering mine I heard them chanting the name Sidoth. Who is this that inspires you?

The raider coughed "God," in a labored moan.

"Would your god not shed his enemies blood in your name? Would he not avenge them?" Thazgarr gestured to the broken serpent-men bodies that littered the camp.

"Sidoth makes his miracles through his children."

"And who are his children?"

"We are all his children, for Anu Sidoth is the progenitor. He sired the first of his children, they sired the next generation, and so on. Praise Anu Sidoth."

Thazgarr's eyes narrowed. "One more question and I will release you. Where rest the greatest of your god's loving thralls."

"Our great cities to the east, in the dunes. They house those closer to Sidoth than I could ever hope to be."

"Thazgarr crushed the raiders's head beneath his club. The skull rippled and cracked. One of its eyes popped out, still dangling from the nerve. "I release you, scale-skin."

Thazgarr pulled the javelins from the balisk.

No sign of life remained, every voice silenced. Only the wind remained.

Tied to the balisk's back was a standard. The sigil of the one responsible for this. Thazgarr gathered whatever supplies he could from the village and began walking east. He had no clear destination or plan, only a goal. "All the serpent-men must die."

Sraac peeled a patch of dead skin from his arm and tossed it to his balisk. The beast snapped the flesh from the air, hissing in approval. His deep blue surcoat billowed in the wind, his face hidden behind a featureless ivory mask. He gazed at the midday sun.

Captain Uwais should have been here hours ago. When he trotted over on horseback, he offered no apology or explanation.

Sraac's mask was the only thing hiding his annoyance. "You're late," he said, maintaining an even tone.

His contact, the heavyset mercenary leader of the Kestrels, chuckled before answering, "And you waited for me, Cutter of Men. What will I be doing for a chest of your gold this time?"

"How familiar are you with the slave rebellions in Xent?"

"Last I've heard they're decorating the city walls with the heads of snake-men and their thralls. Not the most unsightly decision.

Sraac made a habit of ignoring the Uwais' casual antagonism, a fair trade for how cheap his fees were. "The massacres are a negligible loss. The issue is that the rebellion endangers the local farm fields. We want this quashed so we can reestablish production."

"Such a fine box of gold over some grain and fruit shrubs? Are your masters running short on wine this season?"

It was never clear if Uwais was being coy or dense. "The food shortage itself isn't the problem, it's about what fills that demand. Should the commoners get hungry enough it opens a door for foreign interests."

The sellsword nodded. "And what mysterious incursion will I be saving you from this time?"

"Kasair. All they would have to do is make port with a few tons of fish and they'd have a foothold on our soil. A favorable tariff negotiation before we'd be wearing their clothes and keeping our gold in their banks. Within a decade they'd start pushing to initiate low-borns into their religion." Sraac booted his balisk's head when it started for the Uwais' horse. "That's what my superiors deemed an acceptable reason to give you gold."

Uwais scratched his beard, a mocking gesture. "I don't know. I rather like kasair silk. Spending my time on a barge eating exotic foods served to me on top of a perfect ass… Gold is always nice, but to sacrifice such a future is unconscionable. I'd need twice as much gold for that kind of sacrifice."

Uwais almost seemed eager to tell him that. "What are they offering you to defy Sidoth?"

"I haven't the slightest idea what you're talking about. No one's invited me to turn on your god, yet."

Through great personal effort, Sraac resisted the urge to put a crossbow bolt through the sellsword's head. "You forget your place, human."

Uwais snarled. "My place? Your blood is as warm as mine. Whatever you hide beneath that robe, you're as far beneath the Elders as you think I'm beneath you. Convince me why your boot tastes better than an ash nymph's, Warmblood."

Sraac spent several seconds in silence. The Elders gave him a meager budget for quelling an insurrection, relatively speaking. He could end the threat to Sidoth's domain quick or cheap, but not both.

"I'm waiting, scale-skin."

"Are you a gambling man, Captain?"

Uwais shot Sraac a suspicious look. "You're not the type for games, Warmblood. What are you proposing."

"A wager to see if you're worth the gold. I'll bring a handful of my men to Xent, and you bring yours. If your company manages to slay more men than mine I'll double your fee. Less work, more profit."

The sellsword ran his fingers through his greasy beard. "And if you slay more?"

"I keep your payment, and you learn to respect the Damu'yhig."

"Why would I agree to such a gamble?"

"I'll bring no more than ten of my Otomi, all warm-blooded half-breeds like myself, a few of Sidoth's… less gifted creatures and nothing more. With all your Kestrels you'd still outnumber us more than twenty to one if I'm not mistaken."

The sellsword went quiet, picking at his beard.

Sraac folded his arms. "I'm flattered that you feel threatened by a game that's twenty to one in your favor. Most men would be confident enough to think it a sure thing." Sraac hid a smug face behind his mask. The captain's ego was bound to get the better of him. "Of course I'm sure your men would understand. There's no shame in denying a hundred some odd men a fortune if you don't think they're up to it."

Uwais shot Sraac a sharp look "You have a deal, Warmblood. By the end of next month, I'll be swimming in rebel blood… and your coin."

Sraac extended a gloved hand to the mercenary. "May Anu Sidoth, and Kadar the Hooded Death, smile upon our contract.

He took Sraac's hand in a firm shake. The gold bands that decorated his wrist jingled. "I'll meet you at the Eastern Gate of Xent with my Kestrels."

Sraac and the captain parted ways.

While Uwais was gathering his forces, Sraac would need to find the other half of the fortune he'd promised. That, or a way to avoid paying it. At least he had time to plan.

Something was off, though. The captain was oddly specific in his knowledge of kasair debauchery. Those were hooks that he needed to pull from the dunes another day.

CHAPTER
4

The wind swept through Arri's short muss of white hair. Under the midday sun, her ash blue skin seemed silver against the rich purples and blacks of her leathers. Her pointed ears twitched with the every change in the winds. The sharp, angular features of her face did little to hide her boredom.

A man dressed in exotic furs stood at the edge of her ship, a bag over his head, hands bound behind his back. He was a short one, only a quarter head taller than her, and she was often dwarfed by damned adolescents.

Shipping out last month, someone offered her a bag of gold to strand the bastard halfway across the sea. Wasn't too specific, said as long as it was somewhere bad, he'd be happy.

Arri's fingers hung over one of the pistols strapped at her waist. It would have been easier for everyone if she put a bullet in him and left him for the sharks. Poor bastard didn't deserve the Serpent Wastes. Too bad that's where she was heading, and the man with the gold seemed like he'd get prickish if he found out she half-assed the job.

"Oy, Baghead!"

The man went ridged.

"This is an informal marooning instigated by the cash payment of a third party." Arri rolled her eyes, reciting the rites from memory. "In compliance with the free intermediary act of the Ashborne Fleet's Third Naval Supremacy Concords, I'm hereby obligated to allow you a counter offer payable in the currency of your choosing. Your belligerent paid us a sum of thirty gold…" Arri held a piece gold out in the light. "The fuck is it you stamp on your coins? Some kinda bird?

"It's the proud emu, you sea-bitch."

"Right, got thirty some odd of those ya willing to part with?"

"Will you take a promissory note?"

Banks complicated everything, still it was his right. "What's yer trading company?"

"Goldshire and Goldshire."

"Anyone know if G&G has a branch out here?" Arri shouted to the crew.

A voice bellowed from the deck, "Don't think so, Captain. The serpent-men try to keep their gold in their own vaults. Might be a week or two north."

"I ain't sailin' that far for the extra coin." Arri pulled out a knife and cut the man's bonds. "Closest shore is an hour due south. Can't say the coat's a good idea."

"I'm good for the money." The man's hands were shaking.

"Ya think you're the first to try and fuckin' spit roast me between a trade factor and a creditor so ya can slip at in the confusion? I'd take that as an insult if the other prick didn't put ya over the barrel the way he did."

Arri booted the man over the side of her ship.

The man let out a half scream, half insult as he plummeted, crashing into the rowboat below.

She glanced over the ledge. "May your sins stay hidden beneath the ashes."

Arri turned back to the deck of her ship, the *Whale Hound*.

For all the fleet's bragging, they still had problems sourcing new ships. The flotilla was an awkward cluster of whatever the Ashborne could get their hands on. Gathered around the remaining dreadnaughts were hovels in the wake of floating castles. But when a new ship built in the classic Ashborne design launched it was a sight to behold. Only last year did Arri lose the ability count the launches she'd seen on one hand.

The *Whale Hound* was a refurbished whaling vessel of Ecrecian make. It was by no means a perfect ship but it did just about everything she needed.

Made of a deep brown oak, the *Whale Hound* had a standard three mast design, and an open deck plan. The last owner modified it with a few well-placed compartments for contraband.

The artillery mounts were a retrofit, swapping the canons for ballistas. Stockpiling enough black powder for anything more than her pistols was a nightmare. The Ecrecians, even their outlaws, were skittish about trading the stuff to outsiders. It didn't matter too much. Without a qualified gunner, it'd only be a matter of time before they blew themselves to chunks. Couldn't even reel in a cannonball.

The heavy lift gear was welcome when it came to hauling cargo—the legal kind. It was also fantastic for hauling plunder from the depths: "salvage," as they called it. Arri often wondered how much of the wealth on Ashborne ledgers came from dead hands. Best not to look too hard at where the gold comes from.

The crew looked at Arri expectantly. They were a motley gang, drifters from every corner beneath the moon.

"We got some gold burnin' a hole in our pockets. Anyone gonna fight me on making port in Bottleneck?"

A round of fist pumps and cheers came from the deckhands. The crew scattered, save Quartermaster Farrell, a heavyset kasairan man in a loose black shirt.

"The fuck is it now?" asked Arri.

"We still need to complete the rites of stranding" Farrell unfurled a bundle of incense.

Arri frowned. The incense smelled terrible, a mix of lavender and rotted fruit. "I doubt the Strahlian gives too much of a shit." Arri gestured to the rowboat shrinking in the distance. She could still hear a string profanities in the distance.

"The ritual isn't for the stranded Captain Adfir. You're familiar with the standards the Admiralty Board holds its captains to, provisional or otherwise."

"Are threatening me on the deck of my own ship?"

"It's foolish to assume they don't have eyes on you. Kasair or otherwise." Farrell leaned in and whispered, "You're setting an example as the first captain of spotted lineage."

Arri's eye twitched. "What does it matter? It's one fucking grandparent, none of them had sorcery and it did wonders for my jawline."

"That doesn't matter to them. You give them a reason and anyone in your boots won't see a captaincy for at least another century."

Arri bit her lip. Farrell had a point. All the successes she had in the last half decade was an afterthought. Regardless of how much gold she pulled in it wouldn't mean shit if she didn't toe the line. "You win this round." She put her fingers to her lips and whistled.

The crew lurched to a halt, all eyes on her.

"Yah thought I'd let yah go about yer business without doin' the rites, yah little shits? Gather in."

The crew let out a series of half-hidden groans.

"Don't yah be fuckin whingin' about the Crow!"

"Do you always need to be this difficult?" whispered Farrell.

"On my own ship, fuckin' absolutely," said Arri.

The crew not performing important tasks gathered around Farrell. Each of them dropped into a low kneel.

The quartermaster lit the incense and started chanting in the old tongue.

Arri wondered if he understood his own chant. She only recognized a handful of words herself: ash, cleansing fire, renewal. All were regular in sermons of the Ashen Crow.

One crewman held back a gag when a particularly thick cloud of smoke passed over him.

Arri could understand dragging the other kasair into the sermon. Yet there wasn't a single reason to make the humans sit through it. The lot of them looked like children kept from play. Men hid grimaces as they listened to the quartermaster drone on in a language they didn't know.

Of course, you also had the converts and sycophants looking for extra favor. Everyone in the front row had crude metal birds hanging out from their shirts. Those were the ones that annoyed her.

The winds shifted and smoke enveloped Arri. The rotting stench flooded her nose, her eyes stung, she could taste the rotted fruit mixed with ash. She folded her arms and endured.

The rite was finally wrapping, Farrell reverted to a common tongue. "What lays hidden within the ash?"

"Cinders," said the crew.

"And the cinders beget?"

"New flame."

"A glorious blaze!" He dug his hand into the fire and pitched a fist full of cinders in the air.

"And so it will be done." Each crewman returned to their position.

Arri took a position on the aft deck where the breeze was strongest. The bitter scent of incense lingered, clinging to her ghost white hair. She shook her fingers through her bangs in an attempt to rid herself of the putrid smoke.

Farrell approached, rubbing ointment across his burned palm. "You don't need them to love you. You're their captain, not their mother."

"Fear alone makes 'em sneaky. Yah also gotta make 'em feel like shit if they cross yah."

"Did your mother teach you that?"

"Think anyone makes it this far without bein' a manipulative bitch?"

"Fair point."

Arri tugged at the cord around her neck, exposing the vial hanging from it to the sunlight. Loose ash shifted around inside the glass. Supposedly it was a vestige of the Ashen Crow. Molted bits of wing shed mid-flight, the rain of ash that followed in its wake. The glass was warm to the touch, as always.

Arri peeled her armor forward and tucked the ash back under her blouse. "I doubt there's any more converts in this lot."

"I agree," said Farrell. It may be time to recruit some fresh faces."

"Well, yah keep drivin' away the good ones every time you make 'em sit through a damned pre-meal sermon."

"A crew needs to act as one and faith builds discipline."

"Not the same way metal wizin' past their heads does."

"Regardless, could you play along until you get their approval? The board is lodged too far in their own ass to admit when they make a mistake. Then once you're in, anything short of the Crow couldn't gainsay you on the deck of your own ship."

Arri frowned. "I guess."

The quartermaster bowed his head. "Thank you, Captain."

Arri wrapped her arm around the ship's helm. The coming winter would mark her fifth year of playing captain. How many more winters could the admirals stretch this out?

As much as she wanted to, Arri couldn't blame them. It was only in the last decade that the kasair's population climbed back into the hundred thousands. The Ashborne were a mere fraction of that. The others scurried back to the crater or scattered amongst the other nations.

Then there was the embarrassment that was Quarthast. Shit, if she was born in time, she'd have loved to see it. At least before the Ecrecians put it to the torch.

If they'd learned anything watching the other races, it was the danger of subversives.

Much like water their time in the ice flows made them hard and sharp, unbending. The warmth of the sun might soften them eventually, but it was taking far too long for her liking.

A whale spout erupted not a hundred yards ahead of them.

Arri looked over at the quartermaster. "Yah think Bottleneck is hurtin' for some fresh meat?"

"I'd say that'll net us five thousand gold easy."

Arri whistled. "What's that, like a hundred twenty a share?"

"Before the vultures take their cut."

As delicious as they were Arri didn't much care for hunting whales. The prey above the water was much more satisfying. Still, she had a crew to think of. Those who might stay in Bottleneck deserved a respectable severance pay.

CHAPTER
5

Batal felt sunlight wash over his face, morning already. He'd hardly moved from the seat he took after the attack.

One of his brothers whisked past him carrying bizarre treasures from the Master's horde. Bat made a game of guessing the value of the items. Carved metal trinkets, foreign rugs, and furniture, all luxurious.

One man carried out a slave garb that consisted of a pair of leather binders and a matching collar. There was a length of chain threaded through a metal ring behind the neck for a leash. At the end of the chain dangled a hook tipped with a metal ball the size of an apricot. Bat had once seen a similar piece with traders like the ones who gave them steel.

Hopefully, the gold collected would be enough to rebuild, establish new allies. It was only a matter of time before Lux and Khepresh organized a counterattack. Fortunately, Xent had the best silt and could outlast either in raw attrition.

Zaeim stepped out from the office carrying a phallic shaped crystal wine glass in each hand. The price of such a cup was more than Bat could make in a full year of farming.

With every passing trinket, Bat questioned how much the City Master favored his own desires over his duties to Xent.

Zaeim handed a glass to Bat. "How's the leg, Brother?"

Bat chugged the wine. It had a pleasant burn. He pushed himself to his feet. His thigh ached. "I'll manage."

"Good, we still have work to do."

During their siege of the estate, Bat failed to appreciate how lavish the courtyard was. The garden walls were a polished white sandstone with a black and bronze trim running along the top. Countless semiprecious stones Bat didn't know embedded the walls, forming murals. Each mural depicted a different beast facing a jade cobra in battle.

The only creature Bat recognized at a glance was a basilisk. The other beasts were either of foreign origin or combinations of other creatures.

Off in an isolated corner was a lone pomegranate tree. On the opposite end of the yard sat a patch of blue-green bulbs topped with rigid yellow crowns. Both seemed like afterthoughts compared to the splendor of the garden's pool. Matching rows of palm trees formed paths between each feature of the courtyard. Each of the paths converged on the central water feature.

The pool was the same white sandstone as the walls. Lotus flowers and grapevines encircled the water's edge and their warm hues danced along the water's surface. The bottom of the pool was a set of layered turquoise tiles. Had he not speared that guard the water would have been a vibrant blue.

The pool tempted Bat, its cool embrace a sweet release from the burning sun. Later, there was still a great deal he needed to do.

Bat, Zaeim, and the others piled into the wagon. Their plunder replaced the spear crates sitting in the wagon bed. A shoulder-high pile of treasures spilled to their ankles at the slightest shift of the cart.

Zaeim laid the severed head of the City Master across his and Bat's laps. Blood still leaked out the serpent-man's neck.

"It's getting on my cloak," said Bat.

"You can have the end with venom soaked fangs if you want," said Zaeim.

Bat chose not to press the issue.

They passed a number of homes in a similar state to the mansion. Blood caked adobe, broken doors, dead coldbloods, and lesser serpent-men littered the streets.

When they came to an intersection Bat could see the Eastern Gate. A group of twenty or so of their brothers were mounting pikes along the wall. The corpses of the overthrown wasn't a terrible backdrop for declaring a new ruler. If a tad brutish.

Another wagon passed by them when Bat felt the weight in his lap lighten.

Zaeim tossed the City Master's head to the other wagoner. "Do something creative with that one, Brother."

He nodded and continued toward the gate.

Bat looked at Zaeim. "You're not going to make a claim for leadership, Brother?

"Not yet." Zaeim pulled on the reigns, turning opposite the gates.

Bat tapped his foot. It wouldn't be hard to get the rest of the citizenry on their side, but they'd need to be quick. Any meaningful discussion of who'd take power resulted in splinter groups. More than once, such squabbles had killed a coup before it was born. Zaeim should know that every second mattered. They'd need to be as one before the serpent-men returned. What could be more important?

He spotted a broken statue, his hairs stood on end. Bat spent the next several minutes talking at Zaeim. It was foolish to trade subservience from one unnatural force to another.

Zaeim's only response was that he didn't plan to carry this debt for long. He repeated this in increasingly annoyed variations.

Bat hadn't noticed last night, but the old part of Xent was silent. Even the telltale signs of squatters were missing. He knew the old ward's population was sparse, but he never knew it was outright deserted. It didn't make any sense considering the overcrowding in other parts of the city.

Maybe the Acolyte only wanted solitude. Until his night in the mansion Bat had undervalued space. Bat frowned. If the City Master's slumber was the Acolyte's doing a building was too simple a whim for a sorcerer.

The wagon pulled into the square, and before them stood a temple. Unlike the rest of the crumbling adobe buildings, the temple was a solid piece of sandstone. Stained glass windows adorned the pristine walls.

Zaeim led the others inside.

Waiting for them was the Acolyte, perched on a stone bench. The light from sun colored windows tinged his skin a sickly yellow. The old man pushed himself to his feet, his cracking knees audible from across the room. "I take it your night went well."

Zaeim bowed his head. "The temple is yours."

The Acolyte smiled, the few teeth he had gleamed a brilliant white. "Very good. Now if it isn't too much trouble I'd like some assistance removing those unsightly things." The Acolyte motioned to a set of statues depicting Sidoth and his first brood.

"Of course, but first, I have another proposition for you."

The Acolyte raised the part of his face where an eyebrow should be. "I am open to further arrangements. But be warned, depending on what you seek, my compensation will likely be more…" the Acolyte paused, searching for a palatable word… "abstract."

Again Zaeim bowed his head. "In time, friend." Zaeim motioned to the back offices. "Shall we discuss this somewhere a little more proper?"

The Acolyte, Zaeim, and one of their other brothers head to the back room.

Bat gripped the hilt of his sword. This man would be the death of them. Compromising this early would doom them to fail.

Zaeim should know what horrors a sorcerer would commit in service to their magic. Innocent lives secreted away for use in dark rituals. Nightmares hidden from the view of mortals until it was convenient.

Bat would put his people to the sword before leaving them to unnatural beasts.

His leg still burned and Zaeim was the better swordsman, but he had the element of surprise. He took two steps forward, the oiled hide of his scabbard rustling only a little as he drew his blade.

Before he took another step Zaeim drew a dagger and drove it into the Acolyte's back. The Acolyte collapsed into Zaeim's arms, and Zaeim locked his arm around the Acolyte's jaw.

"The door!" Zaeim shouted.

Their other brother sprinted ahead to a heavy stone door. He dragged the stone slab open with both hands. The low rumble of stone grinding against stone raised the hair on Bat's neck. Inside was a staircase leading into darkness. A chill leaked into the temple accompanied by a rotted, musty foulness.

Carved into the door was the image of a skeleton with a city nestled in its ribcage. It was a passage to the catacombs.

Zaeim took a second knife and buried it in the Acolyte's stomach.

When the last of the old man's strength faded Zaeim hurled him down the stairs. The sounds of flesh and metal clanging against stone echoed and warped into an unnatural howl.

Zaeim resealed the door by dropping a bronze bar across the frame, wiped the sweat from his brow, and said, "Now we can claim the city."

Bat stood in silence, his sword dangling by its pommel between two fingers. "Were you planning this the whole time, Brother?"

Zaeim shrugged. "I said I didn't plan on carrying that debt, didn't I?"

"Why didn't you tell the rest of us?"

"I didn't know if the Acolyte could see beyond his surroundings, physical or otherwise. Word and thought could be vagaries at most."

"Did he know?" Bat pointed at their other brother, a man named Musa whose back was still braced against the door.

"I knew Musa would react most in line with what I needed to be done. A knife to the old man's throat would have been nice though."

"What if the Acolyte managed to call on his sorcery?" Bat said.

Zaeim frowned "We'd be dead and he'd have his temple. Either way, the City Master and his guard have been dealt with, someone else would take our place and lead."

Bat scowled. "You'd risk all our lives like that?"

"Would you prefer if I'd risked them on a coherent Damu'yhig?

"I suppose not," Bat said.

"Good." Zaeim snapped his fingers. The rest of their brothers filed out into the temple square, returning with armfuls of loot. "We'll leave the goods here, keep a supply cache ready."

"Shouldn't we share those with the rest of our brothers?" asked Bat.

"I want something we can fall back on if the others are less than receptive to my proposition."

"So now we're plotting against our own brothers."

"Only if we have to. Hate for the serpent-men is what binds us. Without them, we'll misplace frustrations and turn on each other. We need to snuff those flames out now."

Bat nodded. As much as he didn't want to believe it, the logic was sound. The serpent-men who lacked their blessed sorcery often compensated for it with cunning. Despite their inferior numbers they held power for millennia. Playing commoners against each other was no small part of that legacy.

He didn't like the idea of stockpiling the temple either. Regardless of how isolated it was, it drew the Acolyte's attention for some reason. What was he even an Acolyte to?

The trip back to the Eastern Gate was much more pleasant. Between the fresh air and sunlight Bat was almost able to forget about the Acolyte. Still, there was a great deal of work to do.

More pikes had been raised since they last passed. Alongside the City Master and his coldbloods were their human collaborators. Guardsmen and city officials all hung, traitors to their own people. As they drew closer Bat spotted the treasurer, the slobbering fat man skewered by a dozen shafts.

While it was by no means a happy scene, Bat couldn't help but indulge a certain catharsis.

A crowd was forming at the display. Gasps accompanied excited pointing as they picked out faces hanging from the wall.

Zaeim handed Bat the reigns. "Circle around to the front."

Bat did so without protest.

Zaeim stood to face the crowd, bobbing with the wagon. "People of Xent, we bring you freedom!" Zaeim spread his arms wide before the crowd. "For far too long we've lived as cattle for the Damu'yhig. But now I make you a promise."

The crowd fell silent, hanging on bated breath.

Bat stopped the cart in front of the pikes.

Zaeim faded into background noise. It wasn't that Bat didn't believe what was being said. He'd already heard it dozens of times when Zaeim would practice on new recruits. Sections came and went, changed order, the final version had been ready for over a month.

Bat rocked back and forth in his seat. Between dramatic pauses and cheering the speech was dragging on longer than he'd like. He tried passing time by seeing if he could recognize particular heads skewered on the pikes. While Bat didn't recognize anyone in particular, he did notice one of the heads was only dangling by a strand of cheek meat.

Through the rebellion, Bat had learned the weight of a severed head. It wasn't something to leave hanging precariously over a busy street. He spotted a ladder to the battlements. Re-skewering the head wouldn't cause too much trouble.

A climb later and Bat was ramming the skull back on the blade. The corpses were starting to smell. Bat pinched his nose, wondering if it was laziness or ignorance that allowed such a shoddy job. No matter now.

Bat turned back to the ladder. When he looked beyond the walls he froze, panicked. The wheat fields were dead, withered and warped to a sickly grey. Months of food gone.

Bat's cries were lost among the cheering crowd.

CHAPTER
6

Willem looked over the mangled remains of his flintlock. Heat melted the barrel out of shape and the striker was missing. Where the wood wasn't burned, cracks ran all the way from the muzzle to the stock. Completely unsalvageable.

If he was lucky the last round of casualties left the vanguard with more rifles than soldiers. He wouldn't mind the relative safety of a spot on the rear firing line. If the vanguard was still light on rifles they'd hand him a spear and send him to the front row to repel cavalry. A less appealing proposition. His best bet would be to grab a working flintlock off a dead man before the logistica collected them to be redistributed according to some nonsense criteria, or bribery.

Another option pushed its way into Willem's head again for the second time that day: desertion. He ran his hand over his Legion mark. The lives that awaited deserters where short and violent. When it came to deserters, the Legion was exceptionally creative with their executions. In concept the practice was simple: if a soldier failed to learn, he would be an example so others could. And so far, the sound of a man burning alive in a giant bronze statue had been effective at dissuading desertion. At least it was prior to the campaign in the Serpent Wastes. He glanced at a pair of medics dragging away someone missing half his face. Snakebite.

There were few places the Legion couldn't go, and any place beyond their reach was that way for good reason. Staying with the cohort wasn't an appealing option either. As the medics passed Willem's gaze strayed toward the edge of the camp. A pair of boys had been strung up for "conspiracy to mutiny," a crime that amounted to getting caught stealing extra rations.

Willem's eyes drifted to his satchel. He'd pruned away the nonessentials, turned it into a rudimentary go-bag. Should desertion become the best option that bag would be his only lifeline. That and whatever else he could carry away with him. He took his bayonet, wiped away the dried snake brains, and pocketed it.

After hiding the bag under his bedroll, Willem made way for the edge of camp. He passed by some legionnaires gambling for a spot on the airship.

Everything was falling apart. They hadn't spotted a single serpent-man settlement since they entered the desert. The wildlife already halved their numbers. Despite the incident with the subterra, the centurions were insistent on pushing forward. From the rumors floating around, it sounded like nothing would change their minds.

None of this was worth it. He and everyone around him were getting torn to pieces, and for what? The copper to build some new toys? Their lives amounted to little more than numbers on a balance sheet. Goggle clad academics were always on about revolutionizing the empire. The next time an engineer needed special metals for a project, Willem was going to leave a powder keg in their shop.

To Willem's surprise, he found a group of legionnaires crowded a sentinel at the edge of camp. "What's going on?" he asked.

"Someone's out there," said a legionnaire. "We sent out riders to take a look."

"Let me see." Willem grabbed the spyglass for himself,

despite protest from its owner.

A single silhouette stood atop a hill a hundred yards out. Something about the figure unnerved Willem. It looked like a man, but something wasn't right about it.

The breeze kicked up. The figure's robe billowed against it in the wind betraying awkward proportions. The tip of the hood was parallel to its shoulders. The chest was broad and the arms muscular. The rest of the body tapered into a narrow waist, too narrow for a pair of legs to match such a robust upper body. When Willem realized what he was looking at, his mouth went dry.

Carved malachite and bones threaded through thick copper strands. They weighed down the creature's green and yellow robe. In one hand the figure held a censer on a chain, in the other a torch. It ignited the censer. The flame burned a deep green. Cast against the alien light Willem saw its face. Staring back at him wasn't the face of a man, but a hooded cobra. Unlike any of the serpents he'd seen before, this one had something in its eyes. Not the bestial hunger of a wild animal, but a cold, malignant intelligence. The spawn of Sidoth, a Damu'yhig.

Willem lowered the spyglass. "It's a real one."

"What?" One of the other soldiers looked at him in confusion.

Willem spun on his heel and made way for his tent. "Up until now, we've been dealing with wildlife and peasants. Whatever that thing on the hill is, it's planning something. Better raise an alarm."

"You still have my spy—" A violent eruption in the dirt beneath the legionnaire's feet cut his protest short. He froze in shock, expecting a sand snake to bury its teeth in his groin. Nothing happened. The legionnaire let out what started as a sigh then turned into a wet cough, then a wet cough with blood. Willem watched as the legionnaire began to convulse. A pink goo flooded from his mouth and nostrils.

"Gas! Poison gas!" Willem shouted. He ran for his tent.

Gouts of an emerald fog erupted from the dunes. Soldiers began dropping to the ground, faces contorted in agony. They bled from every orifice, choking on their own viscera.

Willem clamped his elbow over his face as he ran, blocking

his airflow. By the time he reached his tent, more than half the camp was on their knees. He felt like his chest was about to burst.

Willem tore into his things searching for a rag. With his free hand, he shoved it into his pants. Warmth flowed through the rag not a moment later.

Willem mashed the piss-soaked rag against his face. His eyes and nostrils burned, but he could still breathe. Willem grabbed his satchel and ran. He had to reach the horses before the gas did. It was only a matter of time before the serpent-men took the cohort. As bad as gas or subterra were, they paled in comparison to whatever the serpent-men did to their prisoners.

He didn't have time strap on his armor. He made way for the stables. The fog was getting thicker. Willem could see at most twenty paces into the mist. An unnatural quiet fell over the camp. Everyone was either hiding or dead. Willem kept moving.

Willem cut through the center of camp. He stopped to wash out his eyes when the burning sensation became too strong. The contorted forms of legionaries littered the camp. The dead lay in pools of their own liquefied innards. Each of their faces had an expression of confused agony. What set Willem on edge were the legionnaires with arrows in their backs.

Willem dropped into a low crouch. Something was moving in the fog.

At the edge of his vision, he could make out a group in thick robes. Willem darted behind a tent. He peeked out to get a better look at this new threat.

The robed figures casually strolled through the camp, oblivious to the gas still thick in the air. Each of the figures carried a bow. They moved between the dead and dying loosing an arrow into each one they passed. Once they shot a legionnaire they'd move on to the next without breaking stride.

With only a piss-soaked rag between him and painful death, fleeing was the preferable option. Willem ducked between a pair of tents and gave the serpent-men a wide berth as he passed. Pressing on to the stables Willem kept an eye out for any signs of survivors. Silence endured, only disturbed by the rhythmic sound of arrow shafts piercing flesh.

By the mercy of some god, the horse pens were upwind of

the gas. Free from the venomous cloud Willem doused his face with water again for good measure. The lingering smell of piss hung on his lips.

Willem scanned through the horses and picked one. Engraved on its stall was the name Reckless. The name had nothing to do with Willem picking that horse. Reckless just happened to be the biggest horse by more than half a head.

Only after he'd finished tacking Reckless did it occur to him. A horse of this size and quality must have belonged to a centurion. Despite the situation, Willem couldn't help but picture Vanrikker hanging him from the airship for this.

He'd completely forgotten about the airship. Someone up there had to be alive.

The airship hung in its usual spot high above the camp, safe above the vibrant green of the venomous gas. There were no alarms, no riflemen. The ship's crew seemed completely oblivious to the massacre beneath them.

Willem drew his new spyglass and surveyed the crew. The airship riggings were completely empty. They should have been preparing some type of countermeasure by now.

Willem stood there puzzled.

The ship began to dip on one side, rolling into a descent. With the ship's bow exposed Willem saw an arrow peppered corpse slumped over the helm. The ship spun further, revealing the shredded gas sacks on the starboard side. The ship dropped deeper into a sideways spin. The gondola tore away clean from the balloons as they dropped into the gas cloud. There was a cacophony of metal and wood smashing into the ground.

Willem hauled himself onto Reckless and gave the horse a kick. All he could do was ride, ride and hope that the raiders went up in flames with a powder keg explosion. After a few minutes Willem felt the pressure wave of a detonation behind him.

He didn't look back.

The *Whale Hound* had barely docked and a crowd was already forming. Some to gawk, others looking to buy whale.

The beast was a third the size of the ship. A smooth gray with a white underbelly, it was only stained where hooks bound it to the ship's hull. The carcass reeked in that special way that only a dead whale could.

Arri leaned out from the rigging. "Meat's three silver a pound. Yah want something special, make a bid."

The crew emerged wielding picks, saws, and lengths of serrated chain. Soon the butchery was underway. They sheared slabs of meat from the whale's flesh with exacting precision. A line for simple cuts formed off to the side. They'd handle special requests as they cut deeper into the whale. It started with tanners bidding on swathes of hide. Next came the blubber, set aside for oil.

Once the bones and offal appeared the gawkers began to clear. Artisans bought bones, looking to carve tools and finery. A fat, rich-looking jackass made a dramatic show out of buying the skull. Rib by rib the bones disappeared from the dock.

Arri double checked her pistols.

They were coming for the organs. That was the draw for those who fancied themselves apothecaries and sorcerers. Figures hidden beneath dark hoods skittered out from dark corners of the docks. They each carried bizarre sets of tools, of which Arri could only guess the purpose. They chattered back and forth in unintelligible gibberish, motioning at parts of the whale.

Their orders were strange enough, but those paled in comparison to their questions. What color were the eyes of the first man to draw blood? Where were the metals used in the harpoons mined from? Was the whale facing east when it died?

The gold was plenty but still Arri knew from their eyes they were fleecing.

The mountain of meat had whittled to little more than entrails now. Only the heart and stomach remained. The stomach would be easy enough, if nothing else it'd be good chum. Hearts, on the other hand, were a hassle. The flesh was valuable but not to the kinds of people who'd be wandering by the dock, not the kind with enough gold.

"Howellin can find us a buyer," said Farrell.

"Aye," Arri said, taking a drag off a wineskin. "Can't pull in this much gold without the warden lookin' for his pound of flesh." Arri was about to hop off the deck when someone caught her eye.

A group of five, dressed in riveted bronze ring mail and jade cloaks, were heading toward them. Coldbloods. Only they were stubborn enough to wear something that heavy in this heat.

Each coldblood had a khopesh at their belt, a spear in hand. The other bidders fell silent, opening a path for their superiors. Not a few moments later a trio stood at the base of the ship.

Arri hung from the rigging, making sure she was out of reach of their spears. "Can I help you, gentlemen?"

The lead coldblood lowered his hood, revealing a face of golden brown scales and green, slit-pupil eyes. "One hundred gold pyramids for the heart."

Arri grinned. "Any counter offers?"

The rest of the crowd was silent. The chemists and petty ritualists were dispersing when someone shouted, "A hundred and fifty." A black and yellow banded serpent-man dressed in leather emerged from the crowd.

Arri noted a handful serpent-men in the same type of leather drifting through the crowd. Her grin reversed.

"One seventy-five." The coldblood locked eyes with the one in leather. "Know your place, half-breed."

"Two hundred." The one in leather stared back. "My contract comes from the ziggurat, same as yours. You willing to gamble your master is higher than mine?"

The rest of the crowd gave the serpent-men a wide berth.

"Three hundred," said the coldblood. "They'd send their own if they were of equitable status."

"You think you know all the goings-on of your master?" The one in leather let out a mock laugh. "Four hundred golden pyramids."

"Four and fifty." The coldblood leveled his spear. "I'll not bid again."

The other drew a pair of long daggers, his men poised at the edge of the crowd. "Five hund—"

The crack of Arri's pistol made a good part of the crowd flinch. "I am not fuckin' havin' this." Arri dropped onto the dock, positioning herself between the two serpent-men. "Normally I'd be more than happy watching you two gut each other. However, since

I can't toss the dead one in the bay and be done with it, I have a vested fuckin' interest in you two not startin' shit in front of my ship."

Both serpent-men were speechless.

Arri re-holstered her spent pistol, leaving her hands hovering over a pair of loaded ones. "I liked the number five hundred. How 'bout yah both give me half that. I'll fuck off for a bit while you strapping gentleman go find a back alley and stick each other senseless. Then whichever one of yah staggers back'll get the heart."

"I don't hate that proposition," said the one in leather.

The coldblood's eyes fixed on Arri, scanning over her form. It was counting her pistols.

"I still have more shots than yah do men, if that's what yer wonderin'," she said.

One of the other coldbloods pointed his khopesh at her. "You dare threaten the Damu'yhig?"

"Get yer fuckin' bronze out of me face." Arri's right hand drifted from pistol grip to the hilt of a cutlass.

The serpent-man flicked his tongue. "I'll carve your ears from your skull and—"

Arri swung her cutlass. In a blur of motion, she struck the flat of the blade, hard. The khopesh warped and bent at an odd angle. As pretty as the bronze blades looked they'd always fallen short of the rare metals. Not that steel blades fared much better.

Arri heard the sound of crossbows racking behind her. "My crew's only a little more patient than I am."

The one in leather tossed a bag of gold at Arri's feet. The coldblood stalled a moment before doing the same.

The one that threatened Arri was bending his khopesh back over his knee. "We'll not forget this, ash nymph."

"I'm sure it'll give yah plenty ah sleepless nights."

The serpent-men retreated back into the town.

Arri sheathed her cutlass. That was one of the better outcomes. Had the they come to blows it would have been a nightmare. They'd detain the crew. Their gold would have been seized along with the heart, disappearing into who knows where. Worst of all they'd be in the sights of whoever the coldbloods worked for.

The ire of a guardsman was by no means convenient. Still, it was better than getting tangled between whoever was pulling the strings. She hoped that the one in leather would win.

Arri looked back to her crew. "Everyone who had the stones to pull a crossbow is drinkin' on my coin tonight."

Willem lay sprawled across the dirt, collecting his thoughts. If there were any other survivors they'd execute him on principle. If he managed to make his way back to the border on his own they'd assume desertion, or worse, treason.

If he was lucky he could spend the rest of his life in a penal colony like the Crag. More likely they'd chain him to the wheel of a dynamo to power an aristocrat's toys until his body failed. There was no going back now.

It wasn't fair. Of all the regions they could have sent him it had to be the one that's gods were real. And unlike Nocturna Primus or whatever the chimera worshiped, the serpent-men gods were listening.

There were so many places he could have been instead of this hateful desert. A beach on the Northern Isles guarding a research expedition. Down in the Strahl Protectorate repelling chimera and sampling exotic meats. They could've stationed him at one of the sea forts fighting temptations of colorful wenches. Even if he was dealing with the vampires they'd have good wine. But no, dry deserts, snake bites, and now lung melting fog. That or getting flayed alive for having an appropriate sense of self-preservation.

Willem checked his horse for a pulse… nothing. Ecrecian horse breeders had a bad habit of breeding for speed instead of endurance. The unfortunate beast must have dropped dead from heatstroke on the spot.

This was the first chance Willem got to inspect his commandeered steed. The name was familiar. Beneath its Legion brand was the insignia of a prestigious stable. He couldn't remember the name. But he did remember winning a bag of silver on a racehorse with the same brand on his eighteenth birthday. That wasn't more than a month before they shipped him out.

Whoever it was that bred these horses charged an absurd amount of money for them. It must have cost the Legion four years of a vanguard's pay, eight for a normal legionnaire. They could have bought forty some-odd stable horses for what this one cost. And some of those wouldn't have dropped dead in the desert heat.

The Legion made a habit of expensive and impractical solutions. Reckless was only one example. Willem's friend in logistics told him how expensive that smoldering wreck of an airship was. For the same price, they could've outfitted a tenth of the vanguard with scrawlers.

Willem had no idea if scrawlers could stand up to a real sorcerer, but they were bound to fair better than the airship did. He could say the same about for the rest of Ecrecia: price before practicality.

No sense in crying over toys he didn't have. He sat up and began digging through his satchel. For the foreseeable future, all he had to rely on was in that bag. There was a handful of silver coins, hardtack, spare knife, a powder horn but no gun. He also had most of a waterskin, half a jar of spices, a spyglass with some liquefied lung on it, and a roll of linen bandages.

He took a length of linen from his bag and wrapped it around his Legion brand. The extra layer chaffed, uncomfortable in the desert heat. Still, it was preferable to being identified as a foreign soldier. Or worse, a deserter, if he somehow he ran into other Ecrecians. With a sweep of his knife, he cut the excess linen from his bicep.

Foliage danced on the horizon to the east. Trees silhouetted against the outline of that blood-spattered moon. The dirt between Willem and what he hoped was an oasis looked well packed, less risk of an ambush from beneath. He carved a fresh piece of meat from his horse's thigh and marched into the unknown.

CHAPTER
7

Thessalia's pale skin glimmered like ice as she stalked the black basalt halls of Lux's ziggurat. Slaves and half-breeds fled the corridor at the sound of her gold and malachite sandals clacking against the floor. Anyone without a room or well placed closest to hide in did their best to avoid eye contact. Luckily enough for them, Thessalia had a singular focus.

Her golden slit pupil eyes locked onto the room at the end of the corridor. She managed to reach the end of the hall without accosting a single soul.

Thessalia reached for the silk curtain blocking her view of the room. She froze, her black stiletto nails brushed a curtain embroidered with a pattern of the Anu Sidoth falling from the heavens.

She couldn't be angry in this conversation. Thessalia took a deep breath. She adjusted her headdress, assuring that nothing poked out from underneath. She straightened her turquoise dress, smoothing over the beaded mesh. Next, she made sure her modest bust sat symmetrical with her broad collared necklace. The piece was interwoven copper strands and malachite, the family colors.

Thessalia turned to her slave, the girl following two steps behind her. "How do I look?"

"Immaculate as ever, Mistress."

Thessalia smiled. "You spoil me, dear." Anissa was a kind girl. She always knew the right thing to say.

Thessalia returned her attention to the silk curtain. Nothing good had ever happened to her in that room. She brushed her fingers against the curtain. An ivory coil of muscle whipped out and dragged her in before she could raise any meaningful resistance.

She found herself bound in a torrent of pulsating muscle. A sinewy pair of arms and a tail mashed her face against a bare washboard abdomen. She felt a chill run down her spine as the creature spoke in its honeyed, taunting voice.

"Dear sister, it's been ages," said Nysra.

With no small effort, Thessalia wrenched an arm free from her sister's coils and returned the hug. It was all she could do to deflect the half-veiled display of dominance "Sister," she said with some effort. Thessalia felt the air return to her lungs as Nysra loosed her death grip.

When resting on the base of her tail Nysra stood a head and a half taller than Thessalia. The harsh angles of her face obscured a serpentine lower jaw split at the chin. Spare some strategic jewelry, she left her torso bare to flaunt her perfection. She was the ideal the Damu'yhig aspired to. Below the navel her form tapered into the monstrous cord of muscle and bone she called a tail. Her alabaster skin matched Thessalia's, mixed with patches of emerald green scales.

"Have a seat, dearest Thessalia, tell me what brings you stomping into my humble lair." Nysra slithered over to a shelf laden with ornate bottles, taking one carved of bone. "Wine?" She'd already grabbed a second cup.

Thessalia overlooked the veiled allusion about her legs, or rather her absence of a tail. Nysra's game was simple. She would try to goad Thessalia into an outburst she could retaliate against. It was a game they had played since they were children.

While Thessalia was adept at not losing, she'd hardly ever consider dealings with her sister a victory.

Thessalia leaned against the rim of a large copper bowl, the metal digging into her hip. Designed to accommodate the Damu'yhig physiology the seats were less than comfortable.

"No, but I would enjoy a cup of whatever it is your pouring." That was their other game. Nysra would attempt to feed her the disgusting oddities of far-off lands. It was generally safe when Nysra poured herself a glass too.

"Anyway, I commissioned the collection of a few… curiosity pieces. Display items, some creature parts to experiments with, nothing that would interest you. I sent an envoy to collect my parcels and he never returned. Coincidentally, guards in our family colors were down by the docks today." Thessalia did her best to avoid a condescending tone. "You wouldn't happen to know if Father, or one of our other siblings, collected it by mistake, would you?"

Nysra ran her slender tongue around the rim of her cup. "It's no matter as complex as that." Nysra handed her sister the goblet and returned to her copper bowl. "I took it."

Thessalia stood dumbstruck. She planned a long-winded and arduous line of questioning. She'd hoped to extract an answer without having to face a confession. Nysra skipped the usual passive-aggressive foreplay to get straight to the antagonism.

Thessalia stalled by taking a drink from her goblet, it was a mixture of wine and blood with a peculiar aftertaste. "Ah, why?"

Nysra let out a mock giggle. "Dear little Thessalia, It hadn't occurred to me that this was something you could feasibly acquire on your own, given your modest standing within the temple. I assumed it was a gift from some foreign suitor looking to broker an alliance with us. You've always appealed to the tastes of lesser species." Nysra adjusted her posture, stretching her tail overhead. "You should be thanking me. If I hadn't found it first surely it would have caught father's attention. Do you think he'd be more disappointed that it wasn't a dowry, or that you were hoarding a whale heart all to yourself?"

Thessalia could feel the heat washing over her face. The bitch plucked away at her insecurities like strings on a lute. She had saved, scrounged, and embezzled for years to afford that whale heart. Biting her lip, she felt a warm plume of blood in her dry throat. Why was she so angry? She had better control than this.

Nysra drained the last of her goblet. "Is the manticore blood too strong for you, dear? The merchant said trace amounts of the venom lingers it the blood. It stimulates the veins, excites the heart. It's not as potent as a barb, but still enough to get the blood flowing."

"Where is the heart now?" Thessalia struggled to keep an even tone.

"Well, I couldn't spoil the surprise by letting Father stumble onto it. I hid it where no one of consequence would ever consider wandering."

Thessalia took a deep breath. "Which petty warmblood did you displace for your little game?" The Damu'yhig built their temple with their hierarchy in mind. Members of more refined breeding occupied the upper floors, Sar Emush Amon Thule at the top. Father and the other Elders were beneath Thule, and so on and so forth, all the way down to the ground level. At the base resided those more man then serpent, but still worthy of acknowledgment. Thessalia herself occupied the first floor. Through painstaking efforts, she occupied the suite closest to the second floor access way.

Nysra licked wine from her cheek. "Think deeper."

"The catacombs?"

Nysra pointed her clawed forefinger at the floor. "Almost."

"Ilupagru?" Thessalia felt herself twitch at the word.

Nysra gave her a predatory grin.

Thessalia felt a flash of cold run through her. Sidoth left his children with few explicit commandments. One of the few they bothered upholding was to never infringe upon the Ilupagru's border.

The name's meaning had died along with its host language generations ago. A common assumption was that it translated as "the void beneath," or something of that nature, a parallel to the abyss that existed between the stars, the void above. It wasn't an appropriate analogy since it implied the eldritch place beneath the catacombs was empty.

From what Thessalia had read, it was a labyrinth, not wholly compliant with the laws of nature. Given the heretical nature of expeditions beneath the catacombs, no formal documentation existed. Of course, that was without reading between the lines of certain family histories. To Thessalia it was obvious. An excursion into Ilupagru could ruin or secure entire bloodlines for generations.

Nysra would never risk her position with Father to inflict such petty cruelty. She planned to use the heart for her own ends, and could be baiting her into a trap. Thessalia needed an answer, one Nysra wouldn't willing admit.

Thessalia braced herself and set down her goblet. "I guess it can't be helped then. Do as you wish with the heart. Perhaps you can win the affections of Father, or one of the other males you've had your sights set on."

Nysra smiled and poured herself more wine.

Neither implied incest nor her lack of a suitable mate riled Nysra. Thessalia needed to pluck a more sensitive string. "You could make an offering to Anu Sidoth, or Kadar. Such sacrifice is bound to get their notice."

Nysra set her cup down. There was the faintest twitch in her eye. She was getting closer.

"If you used it in one of your sorceries, I'm sure the results would be amazing. That's what I was planning to—" Before Thessalia could finish half a ton of scaled flesh collided with her chest.

The room was fuzzy. A ringing noise drowned out whatever Nysra was saying, if anything. In her disoriented state, Thessalia couldn't make any sense of her position. Her sister's face came back into focus. Nysra's tail coiled around her chest and, her feet dangled in the air.

Thessalia felt a slight bob as her sister lowered her to eye level. The pressure on her chest made it difficult to breathe. Nysra's face loomed mere inches from her sister's, waiting for her senses to return.

Nysra glowered at helpless Thessalia. "Let me make your position inescapably clear, Sister. I allow you to wear the family colors. I allow you to stomp through the temple terrorizing the other half-castes. I even allow you to continue living in the polite fiction our mother has weaved around you. What I will not allow is you conflating your own aberrant magics with my sorcery." The manticore venom must have been affecting her too.

"Jealous," Thessalia said, her breath labored. For all Nysra's talent, she was at best semi-competent in sorcery.

Nysra's eyes narrowed. "Jealous of you, the byproduct of our mother indulging in a carnal novelty? Your words are almost as insulting as your life."

There were several things Thessalia would have liked to say if she had the ability. Mother always said her human traits were a deformity of birth. Nysra's accusations were never spoken aloud, but they had always lurked in the back of her mind.

Thessalia choked out what little resistance she could. "Liar." As the word escaped her lips Nysra's clawed digits wrapped around her neck.

Nysra leaned in, her face a hand's width away. "You are an emblem of betrayal. Every redundant limb, every excess bit of flesh an insult against our bloodline. The lines of your face are hardly that of our mother, and they're certainly not of my father." Nysra punctuated her statement by carving her thumb through Thessalia's collarbone all the way to her temple.

A hot streak of pain erupted in her face. Rivulets of blood formed along the surface of the wound. What Thessalia wasn't prepared for was her sister's tongue.

Nysra ran her forked tongue along the wound, savoring the taste of blood, sweat, and tears.

Thessalia recoiled into herself. She lapsed into memories of that tongue. Throughout their childhood, Nysra's tongue was a favorite amongst torture implements. She used it much in the same way a human child would dangle a bead of spit over a helpless sibling. Often she'd claim she could taste Thessalia's fear.

Nysra swallowed the mixture of bodily fluids as elegantly as one could, letting out a faint moan. "Now, are you going to be a polite little betrayal and sit patiently until we can arrange a suitable place for you?"

In a mix of anger and desperation Thessalia smeared her hand through the bleeding wound. Had she breath to spare, she'd taunt her sister for forgetting the basics of blood as a catalyst in transmutation. She grabbed her sister's wrist and began rasping out an eldritch chant.

With every subtle inflection of tone in her throat Thessalia's blood changed. The blood rippled in her hand as its elements realigned into those of an acid.

There was a sizzling noise, followed by a smell of burning mixed with a hint of sour.

By the time Nysra realized what was happening her wrist was a warped yellow. She let out a screech, her jaws wide enough to swallow a man whole.

Thessalia enjoyed a full breath of air as her sister unhanded her.

Her relief turned to terror when Nysra's tail tensed around her.

Nysra whipped her sister through the air with the full strength of her tail.

Thessalia went soaring into the hallway. She connected with the basalt floors of the temple, tumbling like a rag doll. Struggling to regain her footing she felt the gentle hands of her slave, Anissa, guide her to her feet.

The sounds of inarticulate rage rang out from her sister's chambers. Objects were being smashed upon the floor.

Anissa braced her mistress's side, propping her up. "Where would you like to go, Mistress?"

"Anywhere but here,"

CHAPTER
8

On his fourth day of walking, Thazgarr came across an oasis. The sound of sloshing water gave him a chill. A boulder, many times the size of Thazgarr's old hut, jutted out from the sand on the edge of the oasis. If he could scale it, it would be perfect for getting his bearings. But other matters took priority.

Thazgarr drank deep from the oasis's pool. His olive skin glistened in the desert sun. He had been traveling for days and was beginning to think that the scaled one had lied to him, not that it mattered.

Dying alone in the dunes was only a little worse than dying alone in a field. The memory of Thazgarr's people would die with him. If he had any say, he would burn it into the collective consciousness of the serpent-men. He'd carve a long and bloody path through their lands. That was the only suitable epitaph Thazgarr could think of. A massacre so grand even their god would have to give pause to their actions.

Thazgarr scratched his chin. "Sidoth does his miracles through his children." What did the scaled devil mean by that? Was the slaughter ordained by their Sidoth? Were they compelled to this madness, or was it of their own making? The sorcery they wielded meant something unnatural was at play. Sidoth sent mortal subjects instead of willing Thazgarr's people dead himself. There must be a limitation to the god's power. Perhaps this Sidoth had a weakness to leverage, a way for Thazgarr to slay the scaled devil.

Maybe the god was indifferent. The notion of an apathetic god angered Thazgarr more than a tyrannical one. He made a promise to himself. If he couldn't wipe the serpent-men from beneath the moon, he'd force their father to smite Thazgarr himself.

The foliage to Thazgarr's side rustled.

Thazgarr drew a javelin. "Show yourself."

No response came from the reeds.

"Show yourself. I won't ask again!" Thazgarr raised the javelin to his ear, ready to throw it at whoever was hiding from him.

The reeds remained silent.

Thazgarr took three steps and hurled his javelin into the grass. There was a bestial cry.

The javelin reverberated, embedded in something out of view. Then the javelin began swaying back and forth. A lizard emerged from the reeds, the javelin embedded in its hide. The best way Thazgarr could describe the beast was similar to the balisks he had killed but bigger. It was taller than a man on a horse and had more legs, more rows of teeth. The beast plucked the javelin and snapped it between its jaws.

Thazgarr planted his feet wide and let out a defiant roar. The creature mirrored Thazgarr's posture and answered the challenge with a roar of its own.

It occurred to Thazgarr that this creature wasn't a serpent. Risking his life to kill it would do nothing to further his war against the scaled devils. Upon this revelation, Thazgarr sprinted for the boulder on the opposite end of the oasis. Given how little damage the javelin did he doubted his club would do any better against the creature's armored hide.

The creature was thick and clumsy, the kind of beast that overpowered their prey on even ground. If Thazgarr could get to the boulder he'd be safe long enough to figure out his next move.

He could feel the tremors of the lizard chasing after him.

With a running leap, Thazgarr grabbed hold of the rock. Smoothed by wind and time, the boulder face had little to cling to and the sun-baked stone burned Thazgarr's hands. Pushing through the pain, Thazgarr hoisted himself up, one arm over the other.

Thazgarr pulled himself higher, the beast getting louder with every moment. He could feel it drawing closer. The boulder trembled beneath his fingers. The beast planted its forelegs on the stone and lunged at Thazgarr. Thazgarr looked ahead, the summit was another twenty arm lengths.

Thazgarr resumed his climb. The frenzied roars beneath him were a reminder of what would happen if he fell. The first length was about as difficult as the last. He had plenty of strength, but the awkward curve of the rock made it hard to grip.

The stone continued to burn him. For the next few handholds, his progress slowed. He became more deliberate in his movements, allowing his hands a moment of respite from the scalding surface.

Thazgarr refused to let his journey end this soon, in the belly of a lizard.

The last few handholds were torture. Every time Thazgarr pulled his hand from the rock it left a patch of seared skin behind. Thazgarr reached the landing and swung his shoulder over the ledge. The pain he felt in his hands spread throughout his arm. It was as if he was a child grasping a hot skillet.

The barbarian bellowed a hateful scream of agony, defying every nerve in his body telling him to let go. He pulled himself past the ledge to the safety of the surface. Multiple hands pulled him forward. Three men: a short man in a tattered leather jerkin, a fair-faced foreigner wrapped in a fine pelt, and a cold-eyed westerner with a bandage cinched around his arm.

Thessalia stepped into the lounge. Clusters of bowl-shaped seats dotted the third step common area. Various cliques sat scattered about the room, their territory marked by eclectic decorations. There were statues of gods and the skulls of exotic beasts, plenty of other garish displays of wealth. The younger, less refined groups favored large cushions or pillows.

The floors were warm to the touch, heated by some sort of furnace system routed beneath the stone tiles. A layer of segmented purple mats covered the surface. Their modular design made them easy to replace as needed.

A pair of tapestries depicting Sidoth's first daughter Pyth concealed the far corner of the room. The goddess was vomiting a torrent of snakes into the sea. Between the intricately woven fabrics, Thessalia spotted a tangle of undulating pythons. It was the back of Ydriss's head. Thessalia made a line directly for her sister.

Had it not been for Ydriss's manifestation of rare gorgon traits her standing would be no higher than her own. She took Ydriss's pity as a personal insult, but it did have its benefits.

Nearing her sister's hideaway she caught glimpse of some new device. A glass cylinder filled with purple smoke swung from the ceiling. Wax hoses dangled from the main chamber.

"Is it ready, Syron?" said Ydriss, her tanned form fit snug inside a dress made of jade sequins.

The well-sculpted kasairan wore a purple vest of silk that left his abdominal exposed. He handed Ydriss a hose capped with a silver mouthpiece.

Thessalia watched her sister take a long drag off the hose. Ydriss held her breath for a moment before letting out a cloud of purple smoke that trailed from her nose. Her pythons writhed in pleasure as the chemicals flowed through Ydriss and into them. Ydriss handed the kasairan a coin purse.

Syron bowed his head and turned to leave. As he passed, Thessalia caught her eyes drifting to the dagger-eared ash nymph's exposed chest. Her eyes snapped back forward in time to catch him wink at her. She tightened the strap on her headdress.

Ydriss finally noticed her approaching. "Thess, try this." Ydriss pushed the pipe to her face.

"Why is there a ash nymph in the ziggurat?"

Ydriss frowned "You realize that he can hear you?" With ears like those how could he not?

"That doesn't concern me. Why is he in our home."

"Work summons. He was installing the smoke pot." Ydriss continued prodding her with the hose.

Thessalia rolled her eyes and took a puff. Smoke rolled over her face. The fumes tasted like fruit. The tension in her back melted away. Her heart slowed to the calmest it had been since her confrontation with Nysra. "Yes, your new toy is very nice. I need to ask you something."

Applause came from behind Ydriss. A group of high caste spawn gathered along thick cushions under the cylinder. Thessalia shrunk at the sight of her sister's peers. Any one of them could melt her with little more than a thought. A large number of humanoid jawlines among them, though, only one had a fully serpentine head. The bloodlines were deteriorating at an alarming rate.

Thessalia did her best to ignore their audience and handed back the hose. "Nysra stole something from me. Did she mention anything to you?"

"She hasn't spoken to me in days. I assumed she went west with Father."

"Have your spies found anything?"

Ydriss gave her an odd look. "You think I use spies to keep tabs on our sisters?"

"I do not take you as a fool, Sister." Thessalia never could determine how sincere Ydriss's lackadaisical nature was. "Regardless, there's no way this could completely escape your attention."

A giggle escaped from their audience. Thessalia turned to see a pair of siblings from the Enshassz line. The brother and sister whispered to each other. They were the grandchildren of the overseer of treasuries. One of their aunts married a wealthy human for the short term gain of their line. They seemed to have learned the wrong lesson from that arrangement. In the arm not wrapped around their sibling, they each kept a matching human pleasure slave. Their poor spawn would have to live without a drop of sorcery in their blood.

Thessalia bit her tongue, the pain was enough to shake her from the smoke's stupor.

Ydriss's delicate fingers guided Thessalia's face back to her own. "You know Mother gets uncomfortable when you're here, Thessalia." Ydriss leaned into her ear. "She can't protect you from the Elders here."

It was true. The Elders were unwilling to debase themselves by entering the warmbloods' domain. It was her best shield from their wrath.

"A whole whale heart," Thessalia said.

Ydriss's eyes widened. "Seriously? There's no way someone wouldn't notice."

Thessalia nodded.

"If you need any help finding it… I know you don't exactly do too well outside the temple," said Ydriss.

"No, she told me exactly where it is. I was hoping it was a bluff." Thessalia bowed her head to the others and started for the door. She made it halfway across the lounge before Ydriss's footfalls caught up with her. "You can't be thinking that."

"I will not put in that kind of time and effort into something just so the bitch can steal it out from under me," said Thessalia

"This is serious. Why do you two have to be like this?"

"Because my existence disgusts her."

"Because you're always challenging her!"

Thessalia whipped back on Ydriss. "If you had bothered to challenge her once in your life, if she ever had to deal with a single tangible threat to her position, maybe she wouldn't be like this." She took a deep breath. "Enjoy your new toy."

Thessalia slid past the curtain and back into the hallway. Ydriss had taken the easy path, lounging away with the others. She sat idle, assuring no one paid her any mind, feasting on scraps and letting life pass her by. Her lack of ambition was only rivaled by Nysra's lack of discipline. It was a less dangerous but equally infuriating waste of potential.

She felt a hand wrap grasp her shoulder. "I don't want to hear your pleas to reason," said Thessalia.

Ydriss pushed her to her knees. "Thule."

On instinct, Thessalia put her forehead to the stone. Jade sequins rattled as Ydriss did the same.

Sar Amon Thule made no distinct sound when he moved. Only the discrete rustling of scales against fabric. Thessalia had no idea how he actually moved, nor had she ever seen him with her own eyes. All she knew was many had made the deadly mistake of not noticing his approach.

The sound of countless slithering appendages scraping on stone reverberated across the floor. A cool breeze washed over the hall. The rustling of scales grew louder.

In the corner of her eye, Thessalia saw yellow-brown appendages sweeping across the floor. One of the cold things brushed across her fingers, then another, heavier one across her back. Sequins rustled as the appendage passed over Ydriss.

A small tentacle drifted over Thessalia's neck. The tip curled under and started probing at her jugular. Her heart was in her throat. The probe hung there a moment longer before moving on.

A masculine voice let out a howl that instantly fell silent, followed by a wet thud.

Thessalia waited there for several minutes before raising her head. She caught a mass of intricate, pulsating black robes disappearing around the corner. The closest thing Thessalia could liken him to was a living storm cloud.

Walking behind Thule was a pair of nulls, his personal servants. Their breeding was comparable to coldbloods, thick muscled humanoids with cobra hoods. Their eyes were black, empty of anything. They had a grey scale coloration and no overt sex characteristics or autonomy of their own, hence the name. It might have been more appropriate to call them drones as they served Sar Thule with unparalleled efficiency. No one knew who they were or where they came from. Only that they were deadly loyal and had the sorcery to serve their master.

A ways down the hall was half of a corpse. The chest and everything above it was missing. A single set of jagged teeth marks ran along the wound.

Ydriss brushed some stray bits of dust from her forehead. "You can't expect me to waste my life trying to win the favor of that thing."

"No… I couldn't. I apologize." Thessalia leaned over to get a better look at the corpse. "Does he do that often, wander down here to eat servants?"

Ydriss folded her arms. "It's not always servants." The

pythons growing from her head stirred in agitation.

Thessalia feigned curiosity. "And no one protests this blatant theft of property and loved ones?"

"You're too smart to have been ignorant of this. Whatever it is you're planning, don't get yourself killed."

"I'll consider it. Do keep well. Despite everything I say to the contrary I'd prefer if you didn't get your head bitten off."

Ydriss smiled. "You have such a warm heart."

The four drifters relaxed the best they could atop their stone isle. Unable to sit on the rock without burning themselves they squatted against a tree that managed to push its way through the boulder somehow. Willem gazed at the tree, the spotty shade from its branches the only respite on this stone shelf. In a way, he had a twisted sort of respect for the stubborn hunk of wood.

Willem turned his attention to the bleached skeleton curled up at his feet. Whoever it was, they choose thirst over the beast below, an undesirable fate. Willem sloshed his waterskin. It had grown light in the last few hours.

The basilisk patrolled its pond. If the academics back in Ecrecia were correct it shared a common lineage with the smaller balisks. At some point the species diverged, favoring size over a pack structure. While it wasn't smart, it was territorial. An apex predator, how it survived on such meager scraps was a mystery.

One of them would have to think of something. Willem began appraising his fellow stranded.

The one in finery, Dylus, had a fair face that clashed with his accent. A native of Strahl, he didn't look like he spent much time in the wild, much less in life or death situations.

Thazgarr, the thick-bodied wild man, looked capable but hardly said a word. Best not to provoke him. The legions had a long and messy history with his kind.

Then there was the small one, Ricard, odd name for a wastelander. He sat there napping, his shadow intertwined with the tree's. He had a certain quality about him. He was a survivor—maybe at the cost of others.

Willem wiped the sweat from his brow. If he wanted off this rock he was going to have to do it himself.

The greenery beneath was taunting him. He couldn't help but think there was a cruel irony in dying of thirst this close to an oasis. He didn't march out into the desert to find an idyllic little gravesite.

Willem gave the tree a second look. The wood was strong and dry, workable. Willem climbed into the tree, bayonet between his teeth. He picked out a long branch about the diameter of his wrist and started cutting. The teeth of the bayonet ripped at the wood. Sawdust flitted onto the others.

Ricard looked at him. He waved off the stray bits of sawdust that landed on him. "You know the tree isn't going to kill you in your sleep. You are gonna miss that shade, though."

"Making a bow," Willem said, his voice labored.

"I don't think a little bit of wood will do anything to a lizard that big."

"Little bit of wood, no. Broadhead arrow dipped in something foul…" Willem gestured to some rotting fruit. "Maybe it'll think twice about chasing us."

Ricard scratched at his beard." How many bows worth of tree you got there?"

"How much longer will the water last?

Ricard shook his waterskin. "Assuming a cool night, half a day's worth."

"Two, maybe three, but then we'd be light on arrows."

Ricard looked over his shoulder. "Can either of you aim worth a damn?"

Thazgarr raised his hands. They were bound in balls of linen.

"Same idea as a crossbow, right?" Dylus said.

Ricard looked back to Willem. "I'd say two and a short bow with lower draw weight."

Willem nodded.

Ricard brought his boot on the skull. He took the bone fragments and started sharpening them.

Dusk rolled over the oasis. Willem looked over their meager arsenal. Stripping the tree of its branches afforded them a pair of longbows, a short bow, and a total of fifteen arrows. Each arrow had a head of sharpened bone. The bowstrings and fletching where made from leftover linen of Thazgarr's bandages.

The plan was simple. Once night fell they would sneak down to the oasis and fill Everything they could with water. Once they topped off they'd escape into the desert before the basilisk noticed. It wouldn't stray too far from its territory, and if it did they'd use arrows to dissuade it.

Dylus suggested that they retreat back to the rock and wait until a better option presented itself. There was no guarantee someone would wander by before they starved. They'd grow weaker the longer they waited. Still, they needed a destination.

"Nothing good between here and the northern shore," said Dylus.

"Same to the west," Willem said. He hoped the others had a less than firm grasp of geography.

Thazgarr stretched his knee to his chest. "Going east."

"Care to elaborate?" Willem asked.

"Scale-skinned devils to the east. I intend to kill them."

"And you know this because…?"

Thazgarr cracked his neck. "Dead scale-skin told me."

"Well, I'm following the man who's twice my weight in muscle," said Dylus.

Ricard examined one of his arrowheads. "There is a city a few days east, mostly human, but they have their share of scale-skins. Either way, I'm going with one of you I can outrun."

Willem shrugged. "Okay, I guess we're going east." Willem didn't like the idea of marching straight into serpent-man territory. He didn't like being alone out here even more.

Each of his new companions had something he could use. The wild man looked like a skilled fighter, most valuable at the moment. Ricard seemed to have an understanding of the culture here. While Willem didn't say it out loud he agreed with Ricard. He'd only need to outrun one of them if the lizard was hungry.

Willem thought back on how the Legion always touted the value of superior numbers. That principle would be under review once news of the gas attack reached Vestinus.

One by one they descended the boulder. Ricard went first, his landing muffled by the sand. With no sign of the basilisk,

Dylus and a canteen laden Thazgarr followed in quick succession. Willem took the rear, bow ready. The four made their way into the oasis, the territory of the beast.

The silence of the cold desert night felt unnatural. Without the chirping of crickets or owl cries, the only thing to break the silence was wind slipping into a howl. The four reached the edge of the pool.

Thazgarr fiddled with the cap of a waterskin. The wet linen around his hands kept him from getting a good grip.

Willem felt his heartbeat reverberate through his chest. He and Ricard stood, arrows nocked, ready for the basilisk.

Willem scanned the oasis. The gap between him and the reeds was twenty strides away, too close for his liking. Last time he ran before even setting eyes on the beast.

Something rustled through the reeds. He snapped back to attention, drawing his bowstring to his cheek. Ricard and Dylus did the same. Several seconds went by in silence. Willem's shoulder felt sore. He let off the tension on his draw. Another gust of wind buffeted at the reeds.

"Dylus, help Thazgarr with the skins. Less time here is better than an extra arrow ready," Willem said.

Dylus grabbed a pair of waterskins hanging from Thazgarr's neck and started dunking them in the pool.

Willem asked Ricard, "This going to be enough for the four of us to get somewhere?"

"Fresh water like this is too good to pass, even with the basilisk. Something is bound to be a day or two out, a trading post if we're lucky."

"Have a way to boil it?"

Ricard looked at Willem.

"Waterborne illness." Willem looked back to the reeds.

"You westerners have sensitive stomachs?"

"I've seen a man die of diarrhea. It's not pleasant."

"Pretty or not, everyone shits themselves when they die. Your friend just had a head start." Ricard grinned.

Willem returned the expression.

Hissing from the reeds cut their catharsis short.

"There's no way it heard that." Ricard raised his bow and

took aim.

"It's downwind, must have smelled us. How are those waterskins coming?" Willem drew his bow back.

"Two-thirds filled." Dylus corked a waterskin and retrieved his own bow.

"It'll have to do."

Dylus and Thazgarr broke into a run. When the beast's head emerged from the reeds Ricard and Willem loosed a pair of arrows and joined the retreat. Behind him, Willem heard primal anger.

The four raced along the dunes tripping over each other as the sands gave way beneath them. Once they passed the rock Willem looked over his shoulder. The beast was still in pursuit, an arrow stuck in its foreleg.

Ricard nocked a second arrow. Monetarily breaking stride, he loosed the shaft. The arrow bounced off the lizard's armored skull without effect.

Willem did the same, aiming for the creature's knee joint. The creature stumbled but continued the chase, wood gnashing in its knee.

The chase continued for another hundred strides. Ricard loosed the third arrow, again with little effect. The basilisk was closing the gap.

Adrenaline was beginning to fail them. Dylus stopped running. The other three continued unabated. To survive they only need not be the slowest. Willem couldn't help but look back at the fate he'd avoided. To his surprise that's not what he saw. The fair-faced Dylus pulled out an arrow and knocked. He planted his feet firm and drew his bow in a fluid motion. The beast hobbled toward the motionless foreigner.

Willem trailed to a halt, watching the standoff. When the beast was a mere fifteen strides from his prey, Dylus loosed his arrow. The shaft flew straight, striking the basilisk's eye. Dylus about faced and resumed running in terror. Willem fell into step as he passed.

The four continued their flight long after they realized the beast had given up. The next time he looked back it was returning to its oasis.

"You couldn't have done that sooner?" Ricard demanded.

"Short bow didn't have the power to do it from any farther out." Dylus slung the bow over his shoulder, taking a sip of water.

"So you can shoot out eyes like it's nothing, but you can't keep a longbow drawn?"

"Exhibition archery back in Strahl. Don't have to hold the draw with a crossbow."

Ricard opened his mouth twice before responding, "Well okay then."

For the first time in weeks, Willem was genuinely happy about being wrong.

CHAPTER
9

Sraac's slid his pick between the cracked adobe of Xent's outer wall. With each swing of his picks, he pulled himself closer to the battlements. Mud flakes peeled from the bricks and clung to his mask. The wall hadn't received maintenance in decades.

Had the city's leaders grown lazy? He wondered. Did their heads decorate Xent's walls, not because of wild-eyed upstarts, but rather their own apathy? This opened the way for more troubling possibilities. Was this the beginning of a pattern? The noble blood was going stale in his home city of Lux, too.

When Sraac reached the battlements he buried a pick in a watchman's spine. He stepped over the guard's corpse and made his way for the gatehouse. He knew his focus should have been on the task at hand but he couldn't help but dwell on Lux's future.

Lux had plenty of half-breeds like himself wandering its streets. But only a handful of respectable sorcerers had been born in his lifetime. Minor talents and other aberrants surfaced every so often. Those couldn't shoulder the weight of a city, let alone the country.

Sraac unsheathed his khopesh. His curved blade, forged

from bronze, had a hilt made of ivory with a pommel carved like a snake's head. Sraac raked his sword across an unsuspecting guard's back. The guard reeled back as Sraac kicked him over the wall. He continued for the gatehouse without breaking stride.

Had the Elders become incapable of producing viable heirs, or were they choosing not to? None protested Elder Thaxiss taking his own sister as a mate, despite the effects such a union would have on the bloodline. Was it insecurity in their heredity? Were the Elders unwilling to relinquish their power to the next generation?

Either way, it was costing them sorcerers. It spelled catastrophe for all who dwelled in the dunes. Sidoth's blessings had kept his Children beyond the reach of the Legions and the Ashborne fleet. Without the blessed sorcery, that gap would narrow. It would be another generation before anyone openly acknowledged the breeding crisis.

Sraac made a set of hand signals. A pair of arrows flew from unseen vantage points, striking both gate-men in their throats. One man clutched at his throat trying to keep his blood from spilling out onto the battlements. The other fell from the wall, splattering on the road below. A moment later a third arrow struck the bleeding man in the eye, killing him.

The gate's locking mechanism was a simple tension spring, released with the flick of a finger. All Sraac would need to do was release it and the Kestrel horde would have free reign of Xent. Sraac laid his hand across the switch only to pull it back. Even though the mercenaries were more than willing to sell their loyalty, he could never own it.

Captain Uwais' slip of the tongue hadn't gone unnoticed either. If they hadn't already the kasair were about to make him an offer. The landless ash nymphs wielded far more influence than he'd like.

Regardless, their relationship seemed to have run its course. Sraac stared at the gate release. If he opened gates the Kestrels would put the rebels to the sword in a matter of days. Xent could begin rebuilding within the fortnight, but the Kestrels would still be a risk. If the gates stayed shut the rebels could do some respectable damage to the Kestrels. Maybe even put them back in their place for a while. However, Xent would remain a resource sink for several months. The Damu'yhig couldn't afford that.

Sraac released the locks. The Kestrels would flee back into the dunes before any real harm came to them.

Sraac retrieved a bag of green powder from his robe and emptied it over a torch hanging in the gatehouse window. When the powder struck the torch a bright green flame erupted. In the distance, bloodthirsty war chants. Not much later the sound of hooves pounding dirt joined the chanting.

The Kestrel raiders came into view. They looked more like a horde of barbarians than a mercenary band riding through the gates. The Kestrels cut down or trampled anyone unlucky enough to be on the streets. Sraac imagined a similar scene happening in Sidoth's other cities. He could slay every foreign power looking to cleave a piece of this land for themselves. He'd still have the enemies already within their borders.

Sraac spotted the captain lighting a market stand on fire then he turned to find a pair of figures standing behind him. Their uniforms reflected his own garb, only their robes were a greenish brown in color. Each wore masks of cloth instead of ivory.

Sraac nodded. "Mont, Dakar."

The pair of half-breeds nodded in unison. "Was hiring the Kestrels a wise choice?" said Dakar.

"No. No, it was not. Where are the others?

"They broke off from Elder Thaxiss's intervention out west two days ago. They infiltrated Xent earlier today under Doz's command."

Sraac nodded. "And the one with the Beast Mother's blood?"

"Doz decided to allow Khazra to hunt… unsupervised."

For a moment Sraac almost felt sorry for the rebels. "Good enough. In the meantime I want you two to raid every alchemical lab in the city." Sraac handed each of them a scroll.

"Is that all?"

"For now."

Each half-breed bowed and left through the window, dramatically leaping between rooftops as they fled into the night.

Sraac saw this as a waste of energy.

Strolling down the stairs Sraac looked off into Xent. The Kestrels' mayhem echoed in the dark as they spread into the city proper. This mess would have been much smaller if Thaxiss could be bothered to make a slight detour on his trip back to Lux.

Along the city walls, Sraac spotted the head of the local City Master, a Child of Anu Sidoth killed in the initial uprising. The massive cobra skull sat skewered on a makeshift pike, its neck corkscrewed around the shaft, shredded bits of tongue dangled from the end of the throat.

Such a sight defied all logic. A Damu'yhig of such exceptional breeding should have enough sorcery to melt the rebellion. It would take less time to light a candle. Yet here he was, as dead as the city officials. Sraac averted his eyes from the grim sight. It wasn't his place to second guess who Sidoth deemed worthy of his gifts.

Sraac stepped over the gate-man. He doubled back to examine his weapon. Rather than bronze, the spear had a tip of steel, a foreign metal, rare in the dunes. Outside interference or not, he'd quell the rebellion, no matter the cost.

The half-breed fled into the dark alleyways of Xent.

The sounds of slaughter rang through the city. The Kestrels painted Xent with its own blood, rebel and bystander alike. They cut a red path through the streets, a crude imitation of the moon above.

"Praise Anu Sidoth."

Bat stood two strides behind Zaeim. He and his fellow conspirators crowded around the City Master's table. Bat had dreaded this meeting for months. Delegating who would take on the duties of the City Master was the tipping point. It would dictate the flow of all future infighting. It wasn't playing out anywhere near the way Bat thought it would with the crops poisoned.

Zaeim stood there absorbing every challenge shouted at him.

"It was the damned traders!" shouted one of them.

"We've provoked Sidoth!" said another.

"Taking the aid of outsiders was a mistake," said a third.

It took every ounce of discipline Bat had not to draw his blade. His counterparts for the other three were the same. Both reluctant but ready to shed one another's blood for the sake of their brothers.

"Silence," Zaeim said. "Without the steel, our revolution would have ended that night. If our grain was the trader's price, so be it."

The man across from Zaeim squinted. "What are you suggesting?"

"The merchants wish to negotiate from a place of power. We should make it painfully clear how little we need them. With strict rationing, we still have enough grain to last the better part of a year. Lux will be in bad shape without our grain. When the serpent-men's thralls see us marching on empty fields their spirits will break. If we apply enough pressure they might even dessert. Once their siege fails, we offer barter."

The table was silent, each of them mulled over Zaeim's plan.

"You think we could outlast them in attrition?" one of them asked.

"Longer than they could endure, no. Longer than they're willing to endure, I believe it possible."

One of the men held back a laugh. "Only you could wield a weakness like a weapon."

One by one each man took his bodyguard and left. Zaeim and Bat were last.

The City Master's mansion was buzzing with activity. Since that first night, it had become the rebellion's central hub. It was the closest thing to a throne they had to take.

Messengers came and went at every hour, reporting the minutiae that went on in Xent. It wouldn't be long before they were scouring every corner of the city for signs of the serpent-men to come.

Behind the fortified walls, rebels wallowed in the garden pool, an oddity rarely experienced except by those wealthy in gold or breeding. The only interaction Bat had with the pool so far was skewering a man in it. He decided to keep quiet about that, no reason to ruin the other's hard-won respite.

"I'll have a bigger one built when I'm crowned City Master," said Zaeim.

Firelight danced over Bat's face in the cool night's air. "Suppose we'll need something to look forward to if we're going to win."

"We're going to need some new holidays, too. At the next meeting, I'll suggest the revolution's anniversary."

"We may be getting ahead of ourselves. The common folk might not abandon the old festivals so easy."

Zaeim's smiled faded. "They're a reminder of the old ways, it'd invite nostalgia or worse. A clean break would work best."

"The old ways run deep. If we push too hard they'll push back."

"Fools. Necessary, but fools nonetheless. They'll drag us all down if we aren't careful." Zaeim itched at his beard. "The fact that our own are willing to assume Sidoth himself was responsible for the crops is an insult. The traders will burn for that."

Bat said, "You seemed more forgiving at the meeting." Zaeim never desired as much but he refused to look weak in front of those he had to regard as equals.

"There's no telling how far the merchants hear."

Bat bit hits cheek. Infighting was one thing, but aligning with outsiders against their own was detestable treachery. Then again Bat thought they'd done the same until the Acolyte was tumbling into darkness. Who's to say this supposed traitor to Xent didn't have similar plans?" Bat wanted to think better of his people. He shrugged. "I'll let you worry about the intrigue. Give me a direction to point my spear."

A messenger burst through the gates. "Kestrels!" he shouted.

Zaeim grabbed a spear, passing another to Bat. "Fortify the gates."

"There already within the walls," said the messenger.

Zaeim didn't say it, but the look on his face screamed: more treachery.

Bat, Zaeim, and their brothers weaved through the

alleyways of Xent. The mansion was secure enough but sitting idle would brand them cowards in the eyes of the people. If they were going win support the people would need to see them fighting in the streets.

The Kestrels timed their attack with the guard change. Men were still strapping on armor as they ran to meet the Kestrels. Bat's eyes were only half adjusted to the darkness, he couldn't imagine the others were much better.

The others formed a blockade in the souq. The battle lines were broad, plenty of obstacles to keep the horses from trampling them outright.

Spearmen took refuge in market stalls, skewering riders as they passed. The battle-hardened Kestrels were quick to recognize the pattern. Half a dozen of them fell before the stalls were beset by arrows and firebombs.

Light from the burning wood rippled across city streets. The distinction between mount and rider blurred in the dancing lights. Flames reflected in glassy eyes. Bloodthirsty cries of man and beast swirled into a storm of gleeful slaughter. Blades cleaved through flesh like hungry beasts.

The Kestrels were masters of mounted combat. It was a discipline Bat never thought he'd have to face in the narrow streets of Xent. Even with their steel spears, the rebels were struggling. On open ground, Kestrel sabers cut down five men to their one.

Bat hid behind a stack of crates on the outer rim of their defensive line. The ground shook with every pair of hooves thundering by. With every passing rider, he thrust his spear, leaving gashes on anyone he could. He lost count of how many times he thrust his spear. His hands ached, flesh tore from his fingers and stuck to the shaft of his spear. He did not slay a god's favored son so his people could fall here.

Exhausted, he thrust his spear again. The blade went low, punching clean through a horse. The beast tumbled, ripping the spear from Bat's grasp. The rider flew headlong into a crate, his neck bent at an unnatural angle.

Bat drew his short sword. If there was a break in the stampede he could retrieve the steel. None came.

On the opposite end of the souq, the Kestrels were flowing

in the opposite direction. They had let the raiders encircle them. The Kestrels. a whirlwind of blades slicing deeper with every pass, carved into their forces.

The souq was a lost cause. Men stumbled over each other in the confusion. Contradicting orders echoed across the unwieldy mass. Bat pushed his way through the battle lines back to Zaeim who was coordinating a spear line to some effect.

An arrow struck Zaeim, dropping him to one knee. The shaft struck him at a steep angle, too high to have come from a horseman. Outlines moved along the rooftops.

Zaeim wouldn't last long in this condition. Without thinking, Bat hauled his brother over his shoulder. He shouted at Musa. Through some miracle, he managed to hear him.

The burly man and a handful of followers pushed their way over to him. Bat pointed to an alleyway. Musa nodded.

A crate sailed into the body of their forces, crushing anyone in its path. The Kestrel horde halted, leaving an opening at the opposite end of the souq.

A great shadow rose across the adobe bricks that marked the far end of the souq. A low pitched, half hiss, half growl rumbled through the air. Even the Kestrels seemed unnerved by it, enough to miss their horses drifting beneath them.

There was a gap in the Kestrels' circle, narrow but enough. Bat pushed his body forward with everything he had. Swords swept clean past his face.

Musa and the others forced their way onto his flanks, creating a buffer between Bat and the Kestrels.

The rest of the Kestrels realized what was happening and moved to block the hole. The line broke in other places as the massive beast tore into the souq, knocking men into the air like toys. The Kestrel slew Bat's brothers as they fled, flooding through whatever gaps they could find.

Anyone who could help Zaeim was on the other side of the Kestrel horde. They were cut off from supplies or refuge. Bat gritted his teeth.

Thessalia sat curled up in her bath, wine cup dangling between her fingers. The slash mark running the length her delicate features had closed yet Nysra's cold spittle still clung to her face. She hated that tongue.

Nysra's tongue had always been her most prized weapon. For Thessalia, hardly a day went by without that tongue giving her some kind of problem. Her sister's antagonism had started playful enough. But over the years, like any well-nurtured seed, it blossomed and spread.

Thessalia dug her nails into her calf muscle. It was all because of her bizarre birth defect. She was at no fault for her lack of the organs necessary to make full use of her sorcery. No fangs, no tail, at best a vestigial venom gland that left traces of the ichor pulsing through her veins. Through painstaking effort, Thessalia had managed to develop a form of blood magic. She could only drain herself so much in the service of her sorcery. Even with years of refinement, she was no match for the gifts her sister squandered.

Father continued to distance himself too. For some reason Nysra mentioned dowry. Did she know more than she let on with that last taunting? The idea of getting traded away for an alliance with outsiders disgusted her. Such a dishonor reserved for the half-breeds and the un-sorcered. Thessalia had left the temple twice in her life. Stuck on a ship and sent to a foreign land she couldn't pronounce the name of. That scared her more than anything her sister could inflict.

She needed that heart back.

Nysra had to be bluffing. There's no way she'd endanger herself by passing the threshold into Ilupagru. Thessalia wracked her brain thinking of somewhere else the heart could be. Any storehouse within the temple would attract the attention of her father or the Elders. Nysra wasn't stupid enough to store it off grounds, where humans or warmbloods could get at it.

It could be a half-truth, not within Ilupagru but on the fringe of the catacombs that border it. The deeper catacombs were both seldom traveled and large enough to house the heart. Once the wine haze cleared, Thessalia would begin her search.

Anissa waited, jug in hand, already refilling her wine for the fifth time that evening. Worry was in the girl's eyes, A non-comprehension of what she had seen earlier today.

Thessalia drained her wine. "Speak."

"Mistress?" she asked, faint hesitation in her voice.

"You're hiding a troubled look behind that wine jug, dear." Thessalia extended her cup.

Anissa refilled the cup again. "Mistress, of all the reasons to finally go to blows with your sister, why an exotic foodstuff?"

Anissa was a more than adequate confidant. Yet a frustrating part of that was her ignorance of the matters of which they often spoke. She couldn't reveal what she didn't understand, especially not after her seventh cup of wine.

"Do you have any concept of what a whale is, Anissa?"

The slave girl shook head.

"I'm told its size and power are only second to the leviathans. It's the sea's approximation of the ones that stalk the dunes. Such a beast would have a heart to match, the size of this bath chamber."

Thessalia took another sip of her wine, allowing Anissa to grasp the scale of what Nysra had stolen from her. "While whale heart is a delicacy, the I acquired it for ritualistic purposes." Thessalia's cup felt light for having just been filled. She held her cup out for more.

"Wh—what do you intend to ritual, Mistress?" Again Anissa filled the cup.

"I'm going to conjure Kadar. The firstborn son of Anu Sidoth values strength, something the heart is symbolic of. Such a sacrifice should be enough to draw his attention for an audience."

"What? Mistress, why would you risk such a feat?"

"To renew the blessings of Sidoth," said Thessalia.

Anissa betrayed another uncomprehending look.

"Right, so it's believed that there are two ways to achieve sorcery: blood or direct contact with a source. By blood I mean the gift is hereditary. The Damu'yhig is a more literal title than most would assume. It's believed Sidoth was… enthusiastic about seeding his domain with life. Thus we have a disproportionate number of sorcerers to the other races."

Anissa nodded.

"The specific properties of one's sorcery correlate to whatever entity the blessing came from, their source if you will.

Father and I descend from Sidoth by way of the demigod Vythera, hence father's ability to transmute great quantities of venom. Had he been from one of the other lines we'd wield the gaze, or command hordes of our wild brethren. I imagine it's the same for how different vampiric houses manipulate their body chemistries, or whatever it is the ash nymphs do."

Thessalia took another sip of her wine. Anissa was quick to refill the cup this time.

"The other method is contracting directly with a source. That's what I was planning to do. Every few centuries some soul will attempt to conjure a source entity. Documentation is vague. If the summoner is successful it can elevate their power to levels seen in our earliest generations. The ones that secured our place beneath the moon. When a family achieves such a feat the others will go out of their way to please them."

Anissa seemed to grasp the broad concepts. "But Mistress, why does it have to be you?"

Thessalia sank deeper into her bath. "It's been an exceptionally long time since such a conjuring happened. The blessings are… thinning within the blood."

"Thinning, Mistress?"

"Anu Sidoth is one of many ancestors. Thousands of mundane bloodlines between us and him have diluted his blessing. For example, if Father used you as a host for his brood, the offspring would be of negligible value, warmbloods. If he were to take one of my sister or myself…" Thessalia winced. "The resulting children's blessing would remain undiluted."

"Oh," Thessalia tilted her bed back to meet Anissa's eyes. "This should go without saying, but if you tell this to anyone, I'll rip your heart from your chest and feed it to you. Then I suppose I'll tear out your entrails and eat those myself."

"I'll summon your evening meal, Mistress."

Thessalia smiled. "You know me so well, darling."

The temple was the same as they'd left it. Besides Musa, there were another five men, none of which he recognized. He could only hope that the others survived the rout.

He set Zaeim down on a bench. His breathing was shallow.

When they peeled away his armor the arrow came with it, leaving behind a cut on Zaeim's chest. The wound itself was black and festering. The area around it showed discoloration.

"Find an antivenin!" Bat pulled out a knife and cut into Zaeim's chest.

Bat pressed his face to the wound. "It's already circulating, you'll get yourself poisoned," said Zaeim

"You'll be fine, you've survived snake bites before."

"A snake bite is not the same as an arrow dipped in a concentrate." Zaeim coughed. "For all we know they mixed in fermented shit." He forced a smile. "Glad I stopped you from trying to suck it out now, aren't you?"

A vase crashed to the floor as the others dug through the City Master's horde.

"Bring me something to drink," said Zaeim.

Not a moment later Musa rushed over with a bottle. Painted on the glass was a red flower Bat didn't recognize, nor did he care.

Zaeim drank a quarter of the bottle in a single drag. "Good wine, definitely worth murdering the City Master." Zaeim handed the bottle to Musa. "Drink, things like this is why we fight."

Musa drank deep and handed the bottle to another. The process repeated over until the wine reached Bat, where it hung in the air.

"You can't die," said Bat.

Zaeim propped himself up on his elbows. "I made peace with my death the day we chose revolt. Everything after that was a gift."

"What should we do?"

"Whatever you think is best for our people."

Bat took the bottle. "Brother, we'll be lost without you." He finished the last of the wine in a single gulp.

"No one can hold the reins forever. I just have to hand them off at a bad time. Make the serpent-men pay a steep price for anything they take, Brother." Zaeim rested his head on the bench, drifting into slumber.

The moon was halfway across the night sky when his heart stopped.

Musa was busy answering questions about the supply cache. The City Master's horde lacked any practical warfare supplies. The others seemed placated by the idea that they hid the treasure here for emergency funds.

Bat didn't care. With Zaeim dead the others would tear each other apart in their lust for power. If any of them survived the attack.

He wouldn't know the extent of the damage until they could reach the mansion. Someone had to have succeeded in defending territory. Such coordination meant someone on the inside aided the Kestrels.

No, the beast from the souq meant the serpent-men had come. Unblessed coldbloods at most, but they were still serpent-men. And they killed his friend.

Even if they repelled the coldbloods and their horde, the serpent-men would return. Next time they might even come with a sorcerer. Bat knew they wouldn't survive another blow like that one.

Maybe the best choice would be to flee into the desert. He could disappear into one of the countless tribes that stalked the dunes. Living beyond the walls couldn't be worse than the wrath of Sidoth. Of course, not everyone would make it. A whole city couldn't disappear. Anyone who stayed behind would be at the Kestrels' mercy or worse, made an example of by the Damu'yhig. They'd wipe even the facade of humanity from Xent.

What was best for our people. That was Zaeim's dying wish. He'd see this through to the end.

Musa and four others were digging through the loot, looking for tools of sorcery or something to help. "Wait, weren't there seven of us?" Musa gestured to the door. "We posted a guard."

The temple door hung open, devoid of life.

One of the others approached the door. "Taking a piss, I'd guess.

A blur of motion whipped past the door and skewered him through the face. From the back of his head protruded a pale white blade made from a material like that of a beast's claw. Where Bat's brother's face had once been, the blade connected to a serpentine appendage, a tail of some sort. Bat had never seen any kind of serpent-man with a stinger.

The tail ripped itself from the skull and disappeared back outside. It was gone before the body crumpled to the floor.

Bat and the others unsheathed their blades. They'd not lose another to whatever beast was about to come charging through the door.

None came. The only thing to cross the temple steps was the pale light of the moon.

Glass shattered behind them. Bat spun round to the sight of a broken window.

Religious furnishings and loot littered the hall, plenty of cover for the beast. One man climbed atop a bench, whipping his head back and forth. "It's here somewhere!" he shouted.

The tail coiled out from under the bench and slashed his tendon. He let out a wail of pain. The man tumbled into the aisle. He clutched at the wound, blood spraying from between his fingers, more than it should for a cut that size.

Bat sprang to help him only for Musa to grab his shoulder and snap his back.

Another from the spear line rushed to aid his brother. A broad-bladed dagger flew from the darkness and pierced his temple. His body crashed into a bench with a thud.

Bat's grip tightened. It had lured them. This was more than a simple beast.

The tail reappeared by his brother with a slashed tendon. The scaly tentacle wrapped around his neck and dragged him flailing out of view. His choked screams ended with a crunch, and again the temple fell silent.

"There's nothing… nothing between us and the door," Bat whispered.

Musa nodded, as did the other. Spears thrust into the darkness. Step by step, Bat and his brothers backed out of the temple.

Bat trained his eyes on the darkness, looking for the faintest hint of the thing stalking within. A low growl came from a few paces in front of them.

A bench blasted forward, it shattered, spraying rubble

across the temple steps. It crushed the man opposite him.

Bat and Musa bolted into the dark, running side by side. Their boots clattered against cobblestones. The cacophony that echoed down the road made it impossible to hear if anything followed them.

Bat looked back to see how close the beast was.

A figure hidden beneath a sand brown cowl, carrying a body in the coils of its tail, stepped out into the moonlight.

Bat looked to Musa. "Back to the mansion. The others must know."

Musa nodded.

The two turned a corner. A moment later there was a wet crunch behind them. Bat looked back to find the body splattered against the side of a building, half of its head crushed against the wall.

Bat weaved past every corner possible to keep sightlines short. He knew outrunning the creature was a fool's gamble.

Turn by turn, block by block, Bat and Musa ran. They ran so long they could see the shifting age of the adobe alleys.

Bat couldn't take anymore. He doubled over, his chest burning. He didn't care if the beast killed him. At lest then he could rest. To his surprise, nothing carved into his flesh as he stood there panting.

It seemed they lost the beast, or it lost interest in them.

Sounds of the Kestrel war band echoed in the distance. They were drawing near.

"They'll take the temple," said Musa.

"Let them have it. The City Master's curiosities will do them no good."

Bat and Musa eluded Kestrel raiding parties deep into the night. Hardly an hour went by without them checking rooftops for a coiled tail, ready to strike. With the first rays of dawn, they finally reached the mansion.

Bodies from both sides littered the streets, a fresh coat of blood over the layer left by the serpent-men.

Boys hardly into their teens were gathering weapons from the dead. If they were going to win this they'd need every piece of steel available.

Civilians pushed bodies to the side of the road, making way for wagons. People fled for the gates. Bat didn't blame them.

The mansion was intact, spare the warped metal of the gate. The entrance was narrow enough to force a bottleneck, and kept the Kestrels out for now.

Inside was a flurry of activity. Men having their wounds disinfected and stitched. Men doubled over in pain, vomiting. Bat cringed, remembering what Zaeim said about coating weapons in shit. Killing blows didn't matter when infection would do the job.

Bat pulled a messenger aside. "What news do we have of the other members of the inner circle?"

The messenger shook his head. "None yet." He pushed past Bat and out into the city.

Bat suspected the others met the same fate as Zaeim.

Musa looked to Bat, mirroring his expression.

Bat knew that every moment they weren't moving against the Kestrels was lives wasted. "Someone has to lead."

CHAPTER
10

Willem and his new associates trudged through the desert. The sun was extra brutal today. Any area of exposed skin had taken on the hue of a roasted red potato.

Willem was actually happy that he had to leave his armor. Until now he'd been kicking himself for leaving the metal behind. The unbreathable leathers would have been bad enough. Had he the time to secure his lorica he would have succumbed to heatstroke before reaching the oasis. It didn't matter much. A wild snake would have torn through the metal anyway.

A self-destructive safety blanket.

Since their departure, Willem had taken to measuring the abilities of his new companions.

Thazgarr, the wild man from the west seemed the most capable in raw power. Judging by the skin peeling off his shoulders he was just as unfamiliar with the wastes as Willem. His hands were still damaged from his climb, too. There was also the matter of his personal war with the Damu'yhig. Such a suicidal goal would make him unsuitable as a long-term ally.

There was also the matter of Legion history with the wild

men. Expansions of Ecrecian territory came at the cost of native populations. Had Thazgarr such violent inclinations, he wouldn't react well to Willem being Legion. Willem tightened the mock bandage around his Legion brand.

Ricard trudged alongside Willem, striking sparks with a piece of flint he found in the sand. "Your arm all right, Will? If it's some kind of corruption it's probably too late to cut it off."

"It's fine," said Willem.

Ricard was still an unknown quantity. He knew the wastes, had an understanding of the culture, and he wasn't a bad shot either. Definitely the most useful at the moment. The red flags didn't escape Willem's notice: Ricard's gear mismatched, scavenged. It didn't look like he stuck with anything for too long. If a better deal came along he'd sell them out in a heartbeat. Best to cut ties once they reached some type of civilization. Best do the same for Thaz.

Dylus had already surprised Willem once. Without a doubt, he had the most long term value of the three. He claimed he was from the Strahl Protectorate. His clothes and mannerism matched. He was too well dressed for common folk. To be stranded on another continent without supplies or minions, he had to be someone of consequence. A black-bagged noble, he guessed.

Willem would press him on that later. Even with Dylus's aim, he was the least useful right now. He refused to discard a considerable amount of redundant weight. He said his jacket was a rare pelt, manticore or something. Whatever that was it sounded valuable.

Willem would have to keep his new friend alive if wanted to see any dividends, though. The protectorate wasn't the worst from what he'd heard. A good blend of civilization with a lack of Ecrecian oversight. If he could just get the Dylus to a port city, he might have a way back to civilization. A way that didn't involve summary execution.

A breeze whistled through the dunes. Willem trekked through the wastes, hot grains blasting in his face. He pulled his scarf over his face. Once the sand was in it would be impossible to get it out. He felt his weight shift as a bank of sand gave way beneath his feet. He found a pair of bows, Thaz's war club, and his own bayonet aimed at his feet.

Several seconds went by. "Bad step," said Willem. They returned to marching.

They kept to hard packed dirt the best they could. But traveling through the loose dunes where subterra prowled was unavoidable. Ricard assured them that four people couldn't make enough noise to attract them. They treaded light anyway. Plenty of beasts smaller than the angua subterra still prowled the wastes.

The logistics of this ecosystem troubled Willem. How did anything survive in these lands? The only water they'd seen in days belonged to a lizard the size of a carriage. Balisks hunted above the sands while pythons and subterra stalked beneath. It was like the land itself was working against the Legion.

Did the Damu'yhig truly have a god on their side? Not once had Willem seen a balisk turn on its rider, nor a serpent-man devoured by a wild serpent of any breed. The Legion, by comparison, dealt with plenty of infighting and treachery. It didn't matter now that the Legion was well behind Willem, it was still unsettling.

Then it occurred to Willem that as far as he knew, he'd managed to penetrate deeper into the Serpent Wastes than most cohorts. And he'd done it with only four men and minimal equipment. He'd accomplished what warcraft theorists had spent countless man-hours and gold on. He doubted there was much more he could do on his own but the sentiment was nice. Then something else occurred to Willem.

The Damu'yhig only unleashed their sorcery en masse. Once the they broke their enemy, they reverted back to mundane means for clean up. Like the archers in the fog. Was there some limitation to their otherwise superior sorcery? Compared to the hundreds of serpent-men, the other race's sorcerers numbered in the dozens at most. Most were only capable of child's play before the Damu'yhig's feats.

The kasair supplemented their magics with naval supremacy and trade. The humans augmented theirs with technologies like the scrawler. But the serpent-men had no such fallback. Did they ever need to rely on something else?

Willem and his companions reached the peak of another

dune. A silhouette crossed the horizon.

Willem pulled out his spyglass. It was a group of riders. They looked human. At least they were on horses. They were clad in loose linen wrappings, scimitars hung from their belts, bows on their backs. They rode in tight formation to obscure their numbers.

Willem cursed under his breath. Between him and the others, they had ten arrows left. If the raiders attacked every shot would have to count. Thazgarr had enough javelins to form a spear line, but without cover, they'd be easy picking for the archers. While the raiders' exact numbers weren't clear there were enough to run them all down.

Willem unslung his bow. "Aim for the horses if you have to. Easier target."

Ricard did the same.

Dylus examined an arrow fletching. "A few horses would be nice."

Willem trained his eyes on the raiders. "Good to hold a weapon, Thaz?"

There was no response.

"Thaz?"

Thazgarr had walked several yards out in front of them.

Willem's mind raced, wondering what the barbarian was planning. If he called him back now it would reveal their disorganized state to the horsemen.

Thazgarr raised his war club. The wood was a dark oak contrasted by shining metal studs that glinted in the sun. The wrap of the weapon's hilt blended with Thazgarr's bandaged hands. At the right angle, Willem could see a spattering of dried blood on the aged wood. Dangling from the club was Thazgarr's waterskin.

Willem didn't understand the gesture. The best he could guess was that the barbarian was threatening to drink their blood. He could be saying he'd beat the water out of them. Willem emptied his mind when the horsemen started moving toward them. The horsemen approached them not at a charge but a light canter.

They stopped twenty strides out. The one in front, their leader, dismounted and continued to Thazgarr on foot. Both men stood ten paces from their respective group. What was Thazgarr planning, some kind of honor duel?

Willem's blood went cold when he saw Thazgarr hand his war club to the marauder. He was surrendering. The blood-lust driven wild man of all people was surrendering. Willem's mind raced, thinking of ways to escape. Being taken prisoner might be acceptable for the others. After centuries of bloodshed between the Legion and the natives, it wasn't an option for Willem.

The desert tribes had some creative forms of retaliation. The image of getting buried to his neck and left in the dunes crept into Willem's mind. Left to boiling away under the sun. Wildlife would tear away pieces of his face while he was unable to do anything but bleed out.

Then the tribesman handed Thazgarr his scimitar. Thazgarr waved them over. The tribesman did the same for his followers.

A puzzled sense of relief washed over Willem. "What just happened?"

Ricard brushed past Willem. "Thaz invited them to trade."

Willem felt his eye twitch. "Just like that?"

"Well, it's easier than getting shot at when you want something."

Willem slung his bow. For the second time on his march through the dunes, he was happy to be wrong.

Thazgarr handed Akhil back his scimitar. He struck Thazgarr as well kept for a native of the Serpent Wastes. His sun-kissed skin peaked from beneath a fine inlaid scarf and turban. His beard was deep black and well trimmed, every item on his person looked placed with intent.

Akhil returned Thazgarr's war club. "A fine piece of woodworking, a rare sight out here. So what do you wish to barter, my western friend?"

"Water and knowledge. The location of the nearest scale-skin village, and supplies to reach it." Thazgarr unloaded the few items on his person. A light travel load had always been Thazgarr's preference but it left him under prepared for bartering. Unwilling to trade his war club, all Thazgarr had was his javelins and waterskins.

"My traveling band will have more goods," said Thazgarr.

"We shall see," said Akhil. "While we wait, a few days

farther east is Xent. It is a place where they value walls above freedom. They perceive the serpent-men as less a threat than nature. Not a place I much care for. What knowledge would you share of the west, my friend?"

Thazgarr nodded. "You know the oasis to the west?"

Akhil frowned. "Many of my people have gambled their lives on that place and lost. This is nothing new to us traveler."

"We maimed its guardian, it's blind in one eye and an arrow in the foreleg slows it. Not weakened enough for my four, but an opportunity for your people."

Akhil smiled. "I'll remember that, friend."

Willem and the others walked over to Thazgarr. Three of Akhil's followers did the same. Thazgarr gestured to his javelins laying in the sand. "Bags open, bartering for water."

Dylus shed a coin purse followed by his bow and arrows. Ricard tossed in a nonsensical pile of trinkets. Among them were leftover skull fragments from the arrows. Willem's hand was firm on his bag.

Thazgarr looked at the meager pile, then locked eyes with Willem. "Next water is days away. We're bartering."

The pair shared an uncomfortable silence as Akhil's men set out a spread of desert plants and tools. Willem stepped forward and placed his bag next to Ricard's pile of flint and bone fragments.

Thazgarr kept Willem in the corner of his eye, feigning interest in some metal picks. The man was crafty, whatever he didn't want coming out of that bag could be a problem. But they still needed water.

Dylus was playing with an iron hook strung from a length of rope. The little foreigner frowned when he heard how little value his coins carried out in the dunes. Any appeal to such frivolity was less water for the journey.

Thazgarr turned again to the tribesman. "Akhil, your wares are fine, but we travel light, and only can afford the water."

Before Akhil could respond, the sounds of spitting interrupted him. Everyone's eyes locked on one of Akhil's men. He was hovering over Willem's bag, holding a carved horn. The rider scraped a black mush from his tongue. "You westerners have the worst spices I've ever tasted."

"Yes, we do." Willem's eyes never left the horn. "That has sentimental value, would you prefer to trade for something else?" Willem reached into his bag and tossed a shiny brass cylinder to Akhil.

Akhil turned the cylinder over in his hand.

"Look through the small end."

Thazgarr remained silent. Best not to interfere.

The tribesman placed the cylinder to his eye. His expression turned from suspicion to fascination. "No wonder you guard these treasures, westerner. This more than covers the water."

"Throw in a spear."

"Done." Akhil signaled for his men to bring the goods. "Does this conclude our business?"

"Not quite." Thazgarr walked over to Dylus at a slow, deliberate pace. He stood over the foreign-born man, letting their difference in size sink in. In the same low rumbling voice he used on Willem, Thazgarr said, "Please give me your rare pelt, small exile."

Without protest, Dylus handed Thazgarr his manticore hide. Thazgarr tossed the jacket to Akhil. "This pelt belonged to a great beast, not of this land. A fair trade for a few of your sun cloaks." Thazgarr punctuated his statement by tearing a piece of red flesh from his shoulder.

"More than fair for you, my friend," Akhil said with a grin.

"Then might I ask one more thing?" Thazgarr tossed Akhil a rolled piece of canvas. "Which of the scaled devils rides under this banner?"

Akhil's eyes went wide as he unfurled the blood red piece of canvas, revealing a dark sigil. Smeared in coal was the visage of a cobra head with its fangs thrust through a man's skull. "This is the standard of Warmaster Ur, of the northern city. Where did you find this?"

Thazgarr scowled "Among the remains of my people."

Akhil tossed the banner back to Thazgarr. "My friend, those who seek Thanok Ur will only find ruin. He is the teeth of the Damu'yhig. Whatever he did to you, I bid you, find peace before he can do more."

"Thank you, friend. While I won't heed your warning, I will respect its weight. Now our business is complete." Thazgarr raised his arm to Akhil.

The tribesman returned the gesture, and the two men grasped each other's forearms. "Walk softly and swing hard, Thazgarr."

"And may the blood that stains your blades bring profit, Akhil."

The two groups parted ways with one final skyward pump of their weapons.

CHAPTER
11

Thazgarr caught his eyes drifting toward Willem's bag again. Molded glass eyes made by the domesticated men were a treasure valued far more than any spear or water. It was worth more than the memories of a carved spice horn, especially from such an unsentimental man. Something in that bag was more valuable than a glass eye—or more dangerous.

The other two men were simple: an exile and a drifter. But the one from beyond the mountain, likely from the domesticated tribes. There was a discipline in him, a discipline and a craftiness that would make him dangerous, or useful. For some reason, he also walked the wastes. Could he be an ally against the scaled ones? Only time will tell.

The sky washed into a brilliant orange as the sun dipped beneath the dunes. For a time they traveled in silence. From his periphery, it was Willem's voice that broke the silence.

"How did you know they wouldn't kill us?"

Thazgarr took a sip of water, using the time to choose his words. "A battle avoided is better than a battle won. Akhil would know that."

"They had superior numbers, weapons, and horses it would have been a slaughter."

"But not one they'd emerge from unscathed. When a tribe is small, losses outweigh gains. Your molded glass will be of great value to them, but only if they have riders to guide with it. Our kind doesn't have the uncountable numbers of the men beyond the mountains. That is why they live when the armies die in droves"

Willem seemed to consider this for a moment. "Then you understand the futility in trying to slay all the Damu'yhig on your own."

"My ideal is not one of reason. I likely won't slay their gods. Still, I will try."

Willem folded his arms. "How would you plan to do that?"

"The scaled devils have already fallen for the trap that is civilization. They align in name, but not will. Like the men beyond the mountains, should the right pieces fall, the rest will tear each other apart as they return to their natural tribal states."

"And you believe this is the fate of all civilizations?"

"Domestication is a whim of circumstance that softens both will and body. Those who grow drunk on their ancestors' valor doom themselves to having it stripped from them. Have I given you much to think about until we next speak?"

Willem was silent.

Dylus fussed with his new, less luxurious cloak. "I don't see why it had to be my jacket you traded."

"You will thank me someday, exile."

"And another thing—you keep calling me that, why?"

"Did you willingly leave your homeland with nothing but the clothes on your back?"

"Lawful exile under articles of the Strahl Protectorate require the signed affirmation of no less than… Are you even listening?"

Thazgarr's apathy drowned out the exile's ravings.

"More accurately, they marooned me," said Dylus.

"Shall I call you a maroon, then?"

Dylus settled into a quiet rage. If the soft foreigner was going to survive the Serpent Wastes he'd need to face every available bit of harshness in preparation for what may come.

"So who had you marooned?" asked Ricard.

"Not sure. Either a wealthy businessman or a wealthy politician." Dylus adjusted his cloak.

Ricard blinked. "That's specific. Any reason you narrowed it down like that?"

"Well, if it was a someone of lesser affluence I wronged, they would have just stabbed me."

Ricard motioned for Dylus to continue. "That only explains why it wasn't someone else, why was it a rich man?"

Dylus bit his lip in hesitation. "I… may have been seducing the heirs to a few fortunes."

"Well, that makes sense. Wait, why were you so touchy about the manticore coat if you have mountains of gold waiting for you?"

Dylus scoffed. "Have you ever tried seducing a rich man in filthy rags?"

"How shapely is the flesh beneath the rags?" said Ricard.

The two went on bickering. While he remained silent, Willem seemed to be paying close attention.

Thazgarr pulled his cloak tight as the sun sank beneath the dunes.

Sraac sat with his feet crossed on a table studying a fresco that wrapped around the antechamber. It was a curious contradiction of heresies. Depicting Anu Sidoth with other gods was sacrilege, demanding the piece's destruction. Yet defacing the image of Sidoth was an even greater heresy, thus the mural remained. The simple piece of art must have been a bureaucratic nightmare.

The effort put into the depictions of the lesser gods, while commendable, its motive was an enigma. At the top of the fresco, hanging above Sidoth, was the moon. Whatever pigments the artist used gave the blood stain an iridescent red glow. Anu Sidoth towered over the other gods. His form was a massive hooded cobra with his body weaving throughout the room.

To Sidoth's right was the Red Harlot, a demoness with a swollen belly. She was a goddess of fertility, debauchery, and other assorted human impulses. Sraac questioned the goddess's placement next to Sidoth. Had the fresco been in the main hall he could dismiss it as an attempt to draw in the more lascivious crowd. In a secluded back office, it was either the personal request of a priest or the unchecked wiles of an artist.

Moving on was a silver man with wings and a dog head, one of the many death gods. If Sraac was remembering right this one was Xohloto'bas. Death cults were always fighting over which of their gods was the real one.

The artist couldn't seem to decide on a particular sea god, so they used a few different leviathans as well as the Dreaming Wake. The ocean itself was as powerful as anything that dwells beneath it, he supposed.

Hanging above the entrance opposite Sidoth was the Elder Roots. It was a vestige of some kind of tree that touched everything beneath the moon. It was a central fixation of mad druids and skin-walker survivors. Neither group was common enough in the dunes to poison the minds of regular people. So it was a questionable addition to the fresco.

Starting the loop back toward Sidoth was some mountain beast. Probably there more for contrast with the leviathan than any theological value.

Next was the Ashen Crow, a god the kasair brought back when they returned from the ice floes. Whatever the Ashborne Fleet worshiped before, they'd lost to time. Sraac would gamble it involved the same thing that drove them from the mainland in the first place. The image of a giant bird molting ash had a certain gravitas to it. Regardless, it was another intrusion on Sidoth's domain.

He came to Nocturna Primus, the vampire god from the western continent. The figure depicted was a pale, naked man with red eyes and bloodstained claws. The vampires Sraac had dealt with in his line of work were more elegant than this crude depiction. Given how tight-lipped the nobles of Valok-Nur were about their god, this guess was as good as any.

Personally, Sraac thought that the Beast Mother would be a better fit than the Red Harlot. The artist ignored plenty of more fitting gods in favor of the beastly pantheon assembled. Of course, this begged the question of why surround Sidoth with a menagerie of beasts? Aesthetic grandeur had been the patron's priority. The piece aspired to no meaning beyond impressing guests. The fresco's patron understood that art was valuable, but not why.

Sraac wondered if the commissioning priest allowed such art out of ego or ignorance. Neither was comforting. If a holy man had such a hollow understanding of his own heritage, what did that say about the rest of the theocracy? Their lapse in faith is what brought about their ruin. Hopefully whoever they sent to assume control would learn from their predecessor's mistakes.

The rebels were collapsing under the pressure of Kestrel raiding parties. Only pockets of resistance remained. Soon the serfs would be back under boot and normal crop production could resume. It would be a rough year, but if the Elders agreed to a farming initiative in Lux they wouldn't need to make any concessions to the Ashborne.

The sound of breaking glass and drunken revelry echoed through the halls. A stray Kestrel followed survivors from the souq massacre to the old temple. Unfortunately, Khazra gutted the rebels before they could do the same to the Kestrel. Now the whole band was running amok through the supply cache.

No major incidents had occurred yet, but with their particular blend of bloodlust and greed, it was only a matter of time. The Kestrels had performed better than expected. The rebellion exhausted itself in its bid against the City Masters. The Kestrels hadn't lost as many men as Sraac would have liked. Soon they'd be looking to collect the extra gold he promised.

Dakar hadn't returned from his supply raid yet either. Without the necessary alchemicals, the situation would get complicated. Sraac ran through a series of fallback plans in his head. One of the more cathartic options involved opening the catacombs in the middle of the night. Xent's necropolis paled in comparison to Lux's but there was never any telling what might find its way to the surface.

Captain Uwais staggered in. There was an ornate wine jar dangling from his fingers. Sraac gave a faint nod. "Captain."

Uwais belched. A putrid smell. "You're a sore loser, half-breed master. You might only have killed the four at the gate—doesn't mean you can't celebrate. Call your patrols back and join us."

"We aren't finished yet. There's still plenty of rebels to slay," said Sraac.

"Always wringing blood from a stone." he grinned. "So I talked to the men and they feel bad since you never stood a chance. We're willing to make a deal."

Sraac glared at him, his scowl hidden behind his mask.

"You can keep that second share of gold you promised, and instead we'll take what's left of the city folk."

Sraac sat in silence for a moment. "You want the Damu'yhig to give you control of the city?"

"No, we'd take survivors with us."

"And what would you do with them?"

Uwais shrugged "Sell them, trade them, train them in the ways of the sword, make some heirs. What else would we do with them?" The captain waved his hands in the air. "I promise we won't eat them. We generally don't do that."

Sraac's gloves creaked under the pressure of his fist clenching. "We will discuss this when you have your head about you. After the rebels have had the boot put to them. As for the wager, I still have a few tricks up my sleeve."

The captain set his wine jar on the desk, gave a mock bow, and sauntered out.

The moment the door closed Sraac grabbed the wine jar and pitched it across the room. The clay vessel crashed into the Elder Roots section of the fresco. Chips of colored plaster bounced across the floor. Drops of red wine clung to every ridge of the mural.

Sraac wondered if the captain knew how self-destructive his taunts were. The Kestrel leader had to know he was threatening to undermine the entire point of the operation. He was short-sighted and impulsive, but he couldn't be that stupid. Sraac slumped back into his seat. "Captain Uwais has either lost perspective on our relationship or sold his loyalty to the kasair. Don't kill him yet, though."

Dakar stepped out from the shadows, surprise in his eyes. "How—"

"The timing was appropriate. You fail to conceal your flair

for the dramatic by leaping from rooftop to rooftop. Report."

Dakar nodded. "Mont has discovered the rebel stronghold, he has a scout watching it as we speak. Kill-teams started at Xent's center and are and are moving out in a spiral cover pattern."

"And the alchemicals?"

"We've acquired sufficient quantities of the substances you requested. May I ask what their purpose is?"

"Did master Thaxiss offer a reason for not assisting in Xent?"

"He deemed it… beneath him."

"There you have it. We're making do without his sorcery."

Dakar began to speak, then thought better of it.

"Join with a kill-team and assure that no one launches an attack until we're ready."

Dakar bowed and took his leave.

Sraac rose from his seat and went out into the hallway. The sounds of breaking glass and cheering echoed from the main hall. The Kestrels were celebrating their last victory with a round of day drinking. Leaking the rebels' location to the Kestrels wouldn't be too hard. All it would take is a misplaced paper or a scout wandering by the right street. Assuming they're sober by noon they'd finish the rebels off a few hours after dusk and collect their reward. Sraac had plenty of time.

Sraac turned in the opposite direction of the revelry. He passed by what he assumed was the catacombs tunnel, based on the size of the crossbar. He slid the wooden bar a few inches to the left, unhooking the wooden jam on one side. The pathway still looked sealed but one good push and the door would come right open. Sraac understood the petty futility in such a gesture, but impulsiveness had already taken him. Best to get it out of his system now.

He stopped at the door at the end of the hallway opposite the Kestrel debauchery.

Sraac drew a polished knife and held it parallel to the door frame. It reflected the hallway back into the knife. He placed his other hand on the latch and stood there, leaning on the door. He gazed into the reflection and waited.

His muscles started to grow sore when he spotted a figure

stagger into the knife's reflection. The lone Kestrel froze, afraid Sraac had seen him. He opened the door and slid inside the room, paying no attention to his would-be observer.

The lone serpent-man looked over the storeroom, spotting a table in the corner. Stashed beneath it were a pair of bound leather cases. Sraac placed the cases on the table, careful not to disturb their contents. He undid the various ties and fastenings on the bags, revealing an assortment of viscous fluids and powders. The bait was set, now he needed a hook.

"Praise Anu Sidoth."

Thessalia felt a throbbing sensation force its way into her skull. She considered trying to follow it back to the whale heart before realizing it was the wine taking its toll. A smell hung in the smothering darkness, luring Thessalia on. She crawled to the edge of her bed covers. When she lifted the covers a dimly lit room and a bowl of pig flesh greeted her. Anissa was laying out a fresh set of robes, the sweet girl.

"The wine didn't compel me to any action unbecoming of my status, did it?" Thessalia said before biting into her breakfast.

"Nothing that won't go unnoticed, Mistress."

"Good." Thessalia rose from under the covers and a chill washed over her bare skin. She must have been brought to bed right after her bath. "How much of that wine is left?"

"I can have a fresh jar within the hour, Mistress." Anissa's eyes drifted toward an empty corner of the room.

"Tempting, but no. There's pressing business to attend to." Thessalia made her way to a fresh set of robes, passing in front of Anissa.

A shade of red washed over the girl's features. "May I ask what we will be attending to, Mistress"

Thessalia covered herself in her robes. "*I* have pressing business," she said. When the robes slid across her back Thessalia felt a wave of static discharges, setting her hairs on end. "You may take today and rest. Do whatever it is you do when I don't require you."

"You're too kind, Mistress," Anissa said, aiding her with fastening the copper clasps of her robes. One final arc of static discharged as a clasp brushed against Thessalia's waist.

"Think nothing of it. I actually do have one task for you now that I remember." Thessalia produced a scroll tube from her desk and handed it to Anissa.

Anissa took the tube and looked it over for the name of the recipient. There was none.

"The contents of that scroll are for you. If I've not returned by tomorrow night I'll likely be dead. You've been loyal in the many years you've served me, so I'm leaving everything to you."

"Mistress, I—"

"I want you to place the largest possible contract on my sister's head."

CHAPTER
12

Arri took a seat at the back of an open-air theater on the outskirts of town.

Bottleneck encompassed an estuary for the Kadar. Despite its shortcomings, Arri had a fondness for the place. The town was isolated enough to keep away most authorities who could gainsay her. But not too far as to deprive her of assorted vices.

As its name implied, Bottleneck was the chokepoint that kept anything too threatening from sailing upriver into Lux. For a good deal of modern history, it had served as the serpent-mens' bulwark. But in the last century, the Ashborne had finally promised enough wealth to open a port. The kasair did what they do and Bottleneck became the closest thing the eastern side of the continent had to a trade hub. The new prospects drew in all sorts who were dumb or greedy enough to be curious about the serpent-men. As with anything else, they had varying degrees of success. And the best part was that the Ashborne took a cut from it all.

The Strahlians tried hocking plenty of shit: wheat, exotic pets, bizarre plants. Ashborne frigates could always rely on them for steady work.

Not much from Valok-Nur. Occasional whispers of a vampire passing through. Must not care for the weather.

Arri herself had considered recruiting a sorcerer for the crew a few years ago. The temperamental pricks put that idea to bed right quick.

Ecrecians were sparse. Their fixation with conquering the continent put them in an awkward spot here when it came to trade. Still, their novelties still found their way here.

Arri took a sip of wine, holding back a giggle when the cat circus's ringleader hit the stage face first. It was a beautiful mess. There was a grey and white calico intermittently licking and clawing at a cat missing an eye. Another, larger cat walking across a rope leaped into the audience to chase a rat. A pair of a local breed sat behind a set of cowbells swiping at each other. The rest of the cats wandered around the stage aimless as they pleased. The Ecrecians had to have known what they were doing when made these types of acts.

She'd forgotten the unpleasantness from earlier. That was until she felt the bench shift beneath her.

Sitting beyond arm's reach was Howellin. "Miss—Captain Adfir. I trust the delivery went as planned." His thick muss of white hair was bound into a ponytail. He wore a matching red silk waistcoat and jacket with silver embroidery. Given the right circumstances, his little smile could bloom into a shit-eating grin.

"Crates were in your boys' hands by sunrise, just like you asked. Thought you moved the warden's office to Lux by now, easier access to the Damu'yhig," said Arri.

"A crewman who will remain nameless worried about the incident from earlier. They stopped by the local branch, they had a message rushed upstream, and here I am."

Arri despised the way he overproduced every little syllable. "Suppose you're also here for yer cut." Arri reached for her gold pouch.

Howellin waved his hand. "No, I'm sympathetic to your generation's opinions on who is or isn't entitled to part of their earnings. Though I'm hurt you didn't think I could have gotten you a better price for such an exorbitant catch. We'll keep this our little secret."

"Damn decent of yah." Arri took a sip of ale, setting the flagon on a tray next to her wine. "Well, yah didn't come all the way out here for a look at my pretty face. Out with it."

"Straight to the point as always. One of the many things I enjoy about you."

Arri bit her tongue.

"Are you familiar with poppies?" he asked.

"Can't say I've ever touched the stuff, had to let a cabin boy go when they got the better of 'im."

"I won't bore you with the details but the serpent-men have developed a taste for the stuff."

" 'Bout time somethin' stuck. Lemme guess. You a want fresh shipment snuck under the noses of the guards." It wasn't a difficult task, but Arri was less than happy about having to make another month-long trip to Strahl after only a day in port.

"Unfortunately it's not that simple. The damned poppies have taken root in this forsaken place. Within the Damu'yhig's private gardens no less. I need you to do something a little more… preventative."

Arri scowled. "Yah want to send me on a suicide mission over yer fuckin' rent money?"

"Goodness no, that's pocket change compared to what you're worth."

Arri squeezed her bench. "I'm listening."

"Legally, the poppies are now a blockade to the Ashborne's expansion in this region. Removing them would be a deed worth ordaining you as a captain."

"Ordained?" she said.

Howellin smiled. "A contingency from the early days. The acting commander of territory in conflict can field promote those who offer distinguished service to the Ashborne. It never specifies the particular nature of the conflict. Think of it as a loophole."

"And the admirals will take that laying down?"

"That particular ruling was from the first Concord, inked with the Crow's own ash. If the admirals defied it they would undermine a good deal of their own authority."

Arri stared at Howellin for a solid minute. The offer made sense, if only it hadn't come from him. The bastard was only honest enough to keep her guessing. His benefit was clear, but was it the only one? "Why are you all the way out here if you so damned good at this?"

"I imagine it's much the same reason you're here. In the flotilla I'd be little more than a shark, out here I'm a leviathan." Howellin rose, patting dirt from his coat. "May your sins stay hidden beneath the ashes, Captain."

Arri leaned back on her bench. She wanted a reason to turn down such an appealing offer. Howellin might be a snake but he was still on her side. That must have been why the fleet stationed out here in the first place.

An ordained captainship the Admiralty Board couldn't say shit about without defying a god. She did like the sound of that.

Howellin had to be working some angle, though. In all their exchanges Arri had never seen him so much as bless a sneeze. Yet somehow he was now an expert on pre-secular law.

"How the fuck has he not been stabbed?" she wondered.

When Howellin was ascending the staircase, Arri caught sight of an oblong piece of metal under his coat. It was too big to be a normal pistol.

A Scrawler.

Arri's attention snapped back to the cat circus when the stage caught fire.

For days Willem had been turning over what Thazgarr had told him. Civilizations are doomed to destroy themselves. It was uncomfortably accurate to what he'd seen in the Legion. Ego and reputation outweighed the value of life. If the wild man was right they might even fall in Willem's lifetime.

His only comfort now was knowing humans could survive in the wastes. It made this ordeal feel less impossible.

Better options were still on the table. Willem's eyes flashed to Dylus. If the Strahlian was half as important as he dressed he was by far the best choice. Bodyguard to a wealthy man of a far-off land sounded appealing. All Willem had to do was get him to a port.

The next thing that stood between him and that future was the gates of Xent. The massive wall cast a shadow over Willem in the morning sun. The black silhouette of the city before him betrayed no details of its nature, spare the dry cracks of age ingrained in the walls.

The battlements were devoid of any guards. No noise came from over the wall.

Willem didn't understand. Were the Damu'yhig so secure in their power that they felt no need to guard their own walls?

Ricard stepped forward. "Honorable Masters of Xent, We are a meager band of tradesman seeking work, may we have permission to enter your gates?"

Ricard's declaration met with silence.

"Guess they're sleeping in. We'll try the Eastern Gate."

The group began their trek along the south wall. It wasn't long before Willem started noticing other signs of concern. The deficit of noise and sentries became more apparent as they walked. Not much later Willem realized they were passing along a wilted grain field. The sun no longer in his eyes, he caught a plume of smoke peaking from beyond the wall.

"Something happened." Willem felt a cold sensation in his stomach. "We should leave."

Ricard brushed past Willem. "Nah, I'm looting the place."

Thazgarr continued past him without a second glance. "Nowhere else to go."

They were right, the last of their supplies got them to Xent. Leaving without more water or a destination would be suicide. Willem pulled out his new spear and continued forward. Hopefully whatever did this had already moved on.

As he walked, Willem attempted to piece together what had happened. Wild men couldn't be responsible. Were the Damu'yhig turning on their own? But if that was the case, how were they still repelling the Legion? Were they that much stronger than the Ecrecians? There still wasn't enough to go on. The Eastern Gate might have an answer.

After an hour of walking the gate came into view. The gate lay open, inviting if not for the pair of rotted, feces-stained corpses beside it.

The one that impressed Willem was an overweight man, dressed in what were once nice robes. He was likely a city official of some sort. A dozen pikes supported the bloated corpse. His spine had given out under his weight causing his body to dip in the middle. Someone had slashed his belly open. His rotting intestines were flapped in the wind. The stomach had torn wider under its burden, pushing ribs through flesh. A valued member of the community by any measure.

Willem looked to see if this display inspired anything in Thazgarr. The wild man was unresponsive. His eyes locked on something else among the dead. Coiled around one of the pikes was a cobra head. It was like the one Willem spotted at the Legion camp.

The men stared at their age-old enemy presented before them. The Damu'yhig's eyes had a hypnotic quality to them. Willem thought back on how something like this did so much damage, yet here one was, head on a pike like a lowly dissident.

Willem's eyes fixed on the severed head. "So they are killable."

Thazgarr grunted in approval.

Willem and Thazgarr broke from the trance when they heard Ricard. "They already got the good stuff." The little man rifled through another corpse.

Passing through the gates Willem and the others finally got a good look at the city. Smoldering remains of market stands reeked of burned fruit. Splintered wood and jagged shards of clay littered the streets. Dried patches of water intermingling with blood stained the ground. Bodies clutching farm tools or rudimentary swords lay trampled along cobblestone paths.

"Cavalry," said Willem.

The city streets were long and well lit. Willem switched back to his bow and allowed the others to take the lead.

Ricard made his way to a body that stood out from the others. In garb, they were closer to Akhil than the city dwellers. After pocketing a few other items Ricard held up a hunk of bronze. "Kestrels."

Willem squinted, he was able to make out the shape of a metal bird pin in Ricard's hand. "Another desert tribe?"

Ricard shook his head. "Sellswords, but something like this is far above their type of work."

Willem dropped into a crouch. There was a chance the Kestrels were still nearby. He made the Legion hand signals for "quiet," followed by "keep moving." Blank stares were all he received. He pantomimed a shushing motion and pointed to a side street. The group nodded and moved down the alleyway.

Willem felt like an idiot. Luckily, the wild man didn't recognize Legion hand signs. The barbarian recognized the spyglass for what it was, though. He had some familiarity with Ecrecians. With familiarity often came bad blood. No telling how long his singular focus on the Damu'yhig would last.

He'd have to be careful with what he revealed going forward. But he'd also be putting himself in more danger by withholding tactical input from the group. Willem's hand drifted across his satchel. He'd already sacrificed his spyglass to keep his gunpowder. Could he even make use of it out here? The sound of straining wood brought him back to reality.

Willem spotted Ricard and Dylus trying to shoulder their way through a wooden door. Most of the buildings they passed so far only had a curtain obscuring the entrance. Whatever was behind that door was worth protecting.

Ricard thrashed against the door. His burglary technique lacked nuance. The assault was loud, while the door yielded a little there was no sign of it giving way anytime soon.

"What are you doing?" Willem asked.

"Breaking in," Ricard huffed before ramming the door again.

"What if someone is waiting for you inside?"

"I stab them."

"What if they're waiting to stab you the second you get through?"

"Do you have a better way?"

When it came to urban targets, Willem was confident that no one knew how Ecrecians executed raids. Thazgarr stood against the wall beside the door, war club ready. Ricard took a position opposite Thazgarr, bow in hand. Both Willem and Dylus were a few steps off the wall, bows trained on the door.

Willem nocked an arrow. "Ready?"

Once he received three affirmative nods Willem drew back

his bow. "Now."

Thazgarr struck the door over the latch. The door swung inward with a spray of splinters. The latch tumbled end over end into the room, clattering against the stone floor. Thazgarr retreated back behind the wall.

No one in the entryway. "Clear!" Willem shouted.

On Willem's signal, Ricard pivoted around the door frame and into the room. Thazgarr followed, then Dylus, and finally Willem. Had anyone actually been waiting for them the breach would have likely succeeded.

Ricard slung his bow. "All that for an empty warehouse?"

Willem switched back to his spear. "The idea is to be the ones doing the ambushing, get the first attack off."

"We're not doing all this every time we go through a door."

"Entrances and rooms with light shining through."

"Deal."

The interior of the building had a sandstone floor. Wooden support beams intermingled with stone reliefs. A system of narrow walkways hung above the main floor. The floor was empty, the only clutter a few cursory jars scattered about. On the far end of the building, Willem spotted a set of heavy double doors.

Ricard inspected one of the jars. "Storehouse from the looks of it."

"Looks like the Kestrels already cleared it out." Willem sighed. "Anything in the jars?"

"Cheap wine." Ricard dipped his head over the rim.

Willem scowled. The storehouse was a dead end. Without food or water, they were no better off here than out in the wastes. Of course scavenging now carried the risk of running into trained mercenaries.

Without a plan, they'd be stuck in this ghost city until they could find a new destination. Akhil had mentioned the grounds his people prowl to the south. Even if they could scrounge the supplies, it was only a stop, not a destination.

Willem pinched the bridge of his nose. There'd be no end to his exhaustion, mental or physical. Fleeing into the wastes was a mistake. He lost count of how many times he'd thought that now.

Willem's thoughts went back to the poison fog attack, the

agonized look in his dead comrade's faces. With every passing day, he was getting closer to the creatures that caused that pain. Was he so afraid of the Legion that he'd take the Damu'yhig over them—monsters instead of his own blood? He tried to banish the bleeding faces of the other Legionaries from his thoughts, but to no avail. Willem was likely the only one who would know what happened to them. For a moment, Thazgarr's war on the serpent-men didn't seem so irrational.

Willem was about to move on when he spotted a staircase leading below ground. Looking down he saw refraction dancing along the wall. As Willem descended deeper the signs grew stronger. His nostrils felt smooth. There was a faint echo of sloshing. Bits of condensation clung to his forehead. He rounded the corner, and for the first time in months, he smiled.

"Water!"

The cistern was filled to his waist in water. Willem fought the urge to dunk his head in the pool. He'd had enough gambling on parasites after the oasis. He did indulge in splashing the lukewarm liquid across his face. Every splash felt like he was washing away years of fatigue.

The others joined Willem and within minutes they had a boiling fire ready. The four sat around the fire, discussing their next move.

Ricard started. "All right, Xent's a dead end. I say we grab a cart, stockpile whatever isn't nailed down, and head south for the river."

Willem switched a bucket of boiling water for a fresh one. "Why couldn't we do that when we left the oasis?"

"Too far out, but given a cart full of supplies we could reach the Kadar in a little more than a fortnight."

Thazgarr looked up. "Explain this 'Kadar.' I've heard the scaled devils chant its name."

Ricard took a sip from his wine jar. "According to the locals, Anu Sidoth fell from the heavens and landed in the Nexus Mountain Range out west. There he sired his first children: Pyth the Endless Maw, Kadar the Hooded Death, and Vythera the Mingler of Venoms. Scattering into the ocean, each carved one of the major rivers that begin at the Nexus. The one to our south is

Kadar's. It flows east all the way to Bottleneck. The river has enough water and fish to keep us going until we find another settlement."

Thazgarr nodded "I accept this path."

"You're not going to try to kill the river too, are you?"

Thazgarr scowled at Ricard.

Willem fed the fire. "There's still the matter of finding food and a usable cart. Given how fresh the bodies look there's still the risk of running into the Kestrels."

"Well, if the Kestrels are still in town they're bound to have carts for their own loot," said Ricard.

"We're not fighting any group big enough to put an entire city to the sword."

Ricard frowned. "The Kestrels might not be smart, but they're thorough. They'll already have sacked anything worth taking. As you've already seen, whatever they don't have room for, they torch."

"It's a whole city. There's no way they got everything. We should check before engaging."

Thaz and Dylus nodded.

"You're no fun," said Ricard.

"No, but I'm alive."

The Lux catacombs were a warm orange under the light of Thessalia's torch.

She attempted counting the skulls as she passed, countless as the rows were. It would only take simple math to get an estimate of how many of her ancestors rested here. As the hallway stretched on she began to wonder if one day her skull would rest within these walls. She wasn't in any rush to join them, but it was a nice sentiment. It would be proof that she belonged here, that she wasn't the product of betrayal many assumed her to be. At least it would drive Nysra mad if she outlived her.

Traveling the halls felt like traveling back in time. No two skulls were quite the same. Back toward the entrance ramp, the skulls were more human. Traveling deeper they began to bear unfused lower jaws and oblong shapes.

A pattern began to emerge. Over the generations, the skulls

would transition from human to serpent. Then the next set of ancestors would look human again. These were likely the generations that had renewed Sidoth's blessings. She felt something of warped kinship with the dead renewers. They were the weakest of their generations, yet they accomplished the greatest feats.

Thessalia ran her fingers through the vials of blood hanging from her neck. Conjuring sorcery from fresh blood was a taxing experience. So as with her many other shortcomings, she found a way to cheat. The process wasn't perfect. It took several days of redrawing and distilling her blood to produce a vial of adequate potency. They didn't stay fresh for long, either. Still, the process was preferable to carving into her wrist anytime she needed to draw on her sorcery. She still carried a knife, though, should she need more than the three vials she had.

If she had a few more days Thessalia could have had a fourth vial ready. She didn't trust Nysra to understand the conditions necessary for the conjuring of Kadar. Admittedly, neither did she, but at least she bothered to learn the theorycraft. Ideally, the ritual would be under a red phase moon, also referred to as a Sorcerer's Moon. In most of the her native lands, a Sorcerer's Moon was only a quarter annual event. Nysra, being the hasty bitch she was, wouldn't be willing to risk the heart rotting before the moon was ready. That was assuming she bothered to calculate if the moon was entering a desirable position, which it was in the next few days.

It was a waste. So many places ignorant to sorcery received monthly or even bi-monthly Sorcerer's Moons. There were whispers that the kasair knew swathes of ocean that received them on a weekly basis. If they did trade her to the ash nymphs like Nysra implied, she'd have that at least. That and access to one of those wild-eyed madmen they called astronomers.

Thessalia rounded a corner that descended to the next level. At the mouth of the ramp stood a guard. Two legs, arms, independent lower mandibles dripping with venom, semi-adequate breeding. Likely here on Nysra's behalf.

"Azto, I assume who have a reason for obstructing my path."

"Lady Thessalia, the lower catacombs are closed on order of Lady Nysra."

"Yes, very good. You're relieved of duty." Thessalia stepped to the left.

Azto wouldn't have any actual grasp of the hierarchy beyond, above, or below him.

Azto drew his sword. "Your sister left explicit instructions to forbid you entry. She said it's for your own safety."

"And if I were to try and overcome you?"

Azto, while capable was simple for the Damu'yhig.

"I'm to strike you dead as an act of mercy."

"And you think she'd protect you from my mother if you struck me down?"

"She gave me her word."

He really was as dull as he looked.

"Azto… What did she offer you? Gold, status, cloacae?"

Azto remained silent.

Thessalia sighed. She placed her delicate fingers along Azto's shoulder. "I'm sure she isn't the only one whose rewards appeal to you."

Azto's sword arm relaxed beneath her touch. She stepped in closer. She traced her fingers along his neck, letting her thumb dangle precariously along his lips. It was a curious experience, being the carnal aggressor, fulfilling. In the past, suitors would often lay out their propositions like business offers. Temple slaves would bare their throats at her mercy, dull and pathetic.

"Your sister said I could keep any bribes I'm offered," Azto said.

Thessalia didn't waste any time to interpreting what that meant. She gouged her thumb into Azto's mouth, penetrating his venom glad. His glands were fully developed. But he still had a considerable amount of human dilution. Venom would leak into his blood, a perfect vector for transmutation.

She chanted in the arcane language of transmutation.

Azto let out the beginning of a scream, cut off by the sound of crackling ice. Radiating from his skull and down his body, ice crystals tore through his veins and out his skin. The crimson crystals formed an ornate latticework along his body, beautiful in its own way. A bulge formed in his chest, likely the flash frozen fluids expanding through his heart.

Things would be so much easier if she could transmute at range like Father.

Thessalia pulled her thumb from the corpse's mouth, wiping it clean on his collar. "I doubt you deserved that, Azto. But you were too honest for this place."

Azto tipped to one side and struck the wall, a crack sheered along his head.

Thessalia stepped over the corpse and continued along the hall.

Halfway down the ramp, she looked back at Azto's body. He was one of few Damu'yhig who never held her birth defects against her. Never shunned her the way the others did. And now he lay dead, cold and alone, because of her.

No, Nysra chose to use him. His death was on her hands.

Thessalia stepped out onto a sandstone overhang. Beneath the catacombs was a spacious pit, the void. A vast mirror array redirected beams of light all the way from the surface through dust glinting in the air. The lights bounced around the massive chamber, illuminating its every corner. The harsh lighting established a border between the catacombs above and the void below.

Ilupagru.

In rhythmic bursts, the scent of rotten eggs would drift up from the darkness. Then the event would retreat as the airflow reversed itself.

The practical stonework of the temple gave way to a labyrinth of alien geometries without symmetry or reason. Parallel lines seemed to intersect when the eye wasn't focused on them then snap back when attention returned.

Some paths were wide enough to accommodate large groups. Others were so narrow only a child could cross. Scale was further convoluted by distance and perspective. On closer inspection, the massive path was only inches wide and feet beneath the overhang. It didn't help that the geographic distance of objects seemed to shift with every new detail.

Dozens of stairways coiled through the void in any assortment of irrational axes. Any that rose past the threshold back into the catacombs lay smashed to pieces. There was no way she hid the heart down there.

Thessalia scanned the overhang. Off in the distance, she spotted a wooden crate with crow sigil burned in the side. It was the same mark as the group she contracted for the heart.

Thessalia circled the crate several times, thinking of a way to remove it. There was no way she could lift the carriage sized piece of meat on her own, much less fit it back through the catacombs. How did Nysra bring the heart here? No crane hung from a higher passage. There were no wood scrapings in any hall she'd traveled. They might as well have built the crate here.

Water seeped from the crate's bottom. The packing ice was melting. Thessalia undid the latch and opened the crate. Inside was a mound of ice shavings, but no heart.

Thessalia felt a sharp pain in the back of her head. Her vision blurred. Something knocked her off balance, face first into the freezing ice. The light shut out behind her. The wood vibrated beneath her as she struggled to regain her footing.

She grasped for a vial of blood. Before she could begin a transmutation she lost balance, falling back into the ice. The box was tipping.

Everything became weightless. A slushy mess lifted into the air, enveloping Thessalia. The box struck something, sending its contents tumbling out of control. Thessalia spun end over end. Loose ice was the only thing that kept her from splattering against the inside of the crate.

Light strobed through fist-sized holes, more opened with every impact. Outside was a blur of motion, stairs, overhang, dirt, stairs, white figure, stone.

The crate crashed to a halt, more splinters than box.

Thessalia crawled from the wreckage, soaked and disoriented. She dropped to her hands and knees and unleashed a torrent of vomit. Once her nausea cleared she noticed her ring and pinky fingers had dislocated. The pain traveled through her arm like a slow-burning fire.

Tears welled in her eyes, half pain, half rage. She thrust her head high toward the overhang. Her voice cracked. "Bitch! Have fun with your harem of slave boys tonguing your cloacae, and telling you how clever you are. Because it's going to be the last pleasure you'll ever have!" Tears cascaded down her face. She continued her string of obscene threats until her throat was sore. She was met only with silence.

Thessalia tore some cloth from her robe and bound her fingers as best she could. She placed her hand in the mound of slush—best to ice the swelling while she had the chance.

Where did Nysra even get ice? And why waste such a luxurious novelty on a death trap? It wasn't important, likely the packing for the real heart. The only answer Thessalia had for the second question was more upsetting. The shaved ice was cushioning, Nysra wanted her to survive the fall.

Crushing her windpipe and getting dumped into the void was too merciful a death for her. Nysra wanted her to suffer. It was a fair gamble something in there would accommodate that. Nysra could only ever set her mind to something when it caused her sister anguish, it was a shame. If she applied that time and energy elsewhere she might even have had the capacity to match their father.

Thessalia looked at the smooth walls separating Ilupagru from the catacombs above, then at her contorted hand. The chances of anyone finding her here were as laughable as climbing out.

She could leap from one of the stairways. If that failed she'd still deprive Nysra the satisfaction of casting her into the void. That was also assuming Nysra would ever bother returning here and saw her body. The last option hung in Thessalia's head longer than she would have liked.

Supposedly, those who managed to return from Ilupagru never came back the same as they left. They returned with aberrant biologies and twisted insights. Many theorized that the Thule bloodline had discovered a lost science here. That it was the key to their current supremacy. Sar Amon Thule was the last of his bloodline and lived in self-imposed isolation. That had to mean something. Anytime Thessalia had asked her parents about Amon Thule they'd dismissed her outright.

Maybe a quick death was desirable compared to whatever waited for her in the void beneath. It wouldn't be too different from casting impromptu sorcery. She'd just slash along the vein instead of across. Easier still, she had the blood vials. She was only a transmutation away from a combustible.

No, the anger was stronger than fear. She could take her own life at any time, might as well try and spite her sister's efforts first.

The ice was melting into a puddle of water. She scooped the remaining ice into her mouth. The cool liquid soothed the soreness of her last tirade.

Without any particular plan, she descended into Ilupagru.

CHAPTER
13

The souq, as Ricard called it, lay in ruins. Stalls were overturned. Shredded tarps flapped in the wind. The Kestrels spared no effort in sacking the market.

Thazgarr rolled a hunk of wood that was once a wagon back on its wheels, only to have it crumble. The axle had snapped in half and the cargo bed was missing.

"No good," Thazgarr said for the fourth time that day.

The Kestrels Ricard spoke of were methodical in their pillaging. They'd smashed every cart Thazgarr and the others found. This wasn't an honorable plundering. Done correctly, they should leave survivors behind to rebuild and be pillaged again. It was much like reseeding the forests after taking their wood. The Kestrels showed no such forethought.

Many things about this siege struck Thazgarr as incorrect. The entrance was too clean. Attacking a city of this scale the Kestrels would have had to pay a much higher price at the gates. A normal raiding party would have fled back into the wilds long before the corpses began to rot. Adorning the enemy's own battlements with their dead was unpractical. Thazgarr could only come to one conclusion. This wasn't a raid, it was a cleansing. Much like his own village, something wanted these people erased.

Thazgarr ran his hand along his war club. Sidoth's treacherous children were bound to be behind this. Snakes weren't beyond eating their own young. The Kestrels may have slain the Damu'yhig who's head rested on the wall, or they may be avenging it. Either way, they are complacent in the scaled devils' rule. Thazgarr didn't understand why humans would turn against their own in favor of these beasts. It mattered little. Should they cross his path the dogs would meet the same fate as their masters.

Thazgarr pulled another wagon from a pile of wreckage. The back half was completely severed.

"Well if nothing else they're persistent," said Ricard. "I'm telling you, our best option is to find their camp and steal a cart out from under them."

Willem shook his head. "We're only risking that as a last resort. There's still plenty of carts we haven't checked."

"So you're going to search through every broken cart in the city because you're afraid of a little fighting."

"Yes, Dick. I would like to avoid dealing with large groups who leave heads on pikes. Fighting when it's avoidable is a genuinely fucking stupid idea."

Thazgarr rolled his eyes at the bickering.

Willem scratched at the layer of stubble he'd grown over the last week. "We can patch something together from the leftover wrecks."

"We still need to find a solid axle if the wagon's going to be anywhere near desert worthy. But I'm telling you the Kestrels already torched anything valuable. Depending on how long they've been here—a couple weeks based on the severed heads—they've already made a full sweep of the city. Outside of that little cistern, they have everything left that's worth having.

The group stood in silence for a moment.

Dylus cleared his throat. "Is served head rot a common measurement of time out here?"

Ricard smacked Dylus upside the head.

Thazgarr was about to step in when he spotted a cloaked figure watching them from the edge of the market. He drew his war club. "Who stalks us?"

The petty squabbling disappeared when the others drew their weapons.

Without words, the robed one unfurled a braided whip and began swinging it overhead in a wide circle.

Thazgarr approached the cloaked figure, war club ready to deflect. He edged closer a step at a time. Just outside of the whip's reach he noticed the slit pupil eyes beneath the hood. "This one dies."

Thazgarr heard Dylus and Ricard's footsteps somewhere behind him.

Willem flanked to the right, spear in hand.

"I thought you too much a coward to fight," Thazgarr said.

"A four-on-one fight is better than the rest of them learning about us."

The serpent-man shifted from side to side, keeping wreckage between himself and the archers. He didn't advance but wasn't backing away either. With a flick of a wrist the scale-skin cracked its whip. The loud snap echoed through the air.

Thazgarr heard the reverberations of something shuffling out of sight through the alleyway. "Something else is coming!"

It occurred to Thazgarr that whips were weapons of terror, not war. He'd only seen them used by pit fighters and slavers himself. They maimed, but slaying was difficult, particularly when used alone. But the tool had other applications.

A lumbering beast emerged from the alley behind the serpent-man. A scaly, sword-like claw reached out and grabbed the corner of a building, pulling itself into the light. Each finger left behind gashes in the stone.

The creature stood at least three heads taller than Thazgarr. It had a pair of thick, scaly legs hooked with talons to match its claws. The torso was broad, spreading outward into a muscular set of shoulders. A pair of shriveled vestigial breasts dangled from the chest jutting between the scales of the otherwise smooth torso. The neck resembled the body of a python prowling beneath the wastes. At the end of the neck hung a fleshy head, more human than serpent. The face had feminine features, a pair of eyes vacant of everything beyond a hint of sorrow.

Thazgarr lowered his war club, unsure what to make of the creature.

The serpent-man readied his whip. The beast stepped in front of its master, its claws splayed. The master continued his awkward side step, keeping the market stalls between himself and the archers.

Thazgarr saw Willem retreating off into the market. The scale-skin was also distracted by the fleeing Ecrecian. Thazgarr took the opening. He rushed in, taking a swing at the creature's head. The club connected. It was a glancing blow, thanks to the flexibility creature's scaly neck.

The master retaliated with a lash of his whip. The corded leather bit into Thazgarr's shoulder. The beast lunged forward, swiping at the barbarian.

Thazgarr hopped back, keeping out of reach. The master swung his whip again. The leather caught Thazgarr's wrist, leashing him. Thazgarr felt the whip tighten, pulling him toward the beast. It wasn't enough to move him, but it would keep him off balance. He planted his feet and readied his club.

The beast made a wild slash at Thazgarr.

Thazgarr swung back, aiming not at the beast's head but at its claw. The claws and war club clashed. Thazgarr felt a momentary resistance followed by release. Alien blood spattered across Thazgarr's face.

The beast's claws dangled by stray bits of flesh. All that remained was the jagged bone of fingertips. The creature let out a shrill howl. Thazgarr felt it beneath his skin.

The master flicked his wrist twice, sending a loop through the whip.

The loop hit Thazgarr's brow and rolled around his neck. He felt the hot leather tighten around his windpipe.

The master threw all his weight against the whip, trying to pull Thazgarr off balance.

Thazgarr tensed his neck. He could still breathe, but the scaled devil had leverage. Thazgarr's head bobbed forward under the strain of the whip. His arm still tangled, unable to move without strangling himself.

The beast was returning for a second attack, looking for

revenge. Thazgarr pulled with every ounce of strength in his body. The force of the whip around his neck made it impossible to outmaneuver the beast.

The beast raised its remaining claws for a killing blow.

Thazgarr pulled with everything he had. It felt as if his eyes were about to pop from his skull. He fell back. The tension against his neck was gone. Thazgarr felt the tip of the claw graze his scalp. He crashed into a market stand behind him.

Thazgarr hauled himself through the stand, putting whatever he could between him and the frenzied beast. A storm of splinters of hot breath sprayed in his face.

Thazgarr rolled out of the far end of the stall. The barbarian freed himself of the whip, tossing it aside. There was no sign of the master.

The beast let out another scream as it tangled itself in the tarps of the market stall. It kicked stones through the air, thrashing in rage, the barbarian out of reach.

Thazgarr stood back. He couldn't strike at the frenzied beast without taking a lethal blow from its claws. He sprinted back to the other side of the market stall. Finishing the master first would be simpler.

Thazgarr gave the beast a wide berth as he ran back to the alley. When he turned around the stall he found the master dead, an angled arrow high in his chest. Thazgarr traced a line back to the arrow's point of origin.

Willem stood perched atop a stack of crates at the edge of the market square. Somehow in that little time, the Ecrecian had found himself a vantage point.

The coward had his moments.

Shreds of cloth flew through the air as the beast freed itself from the tarp. It approached Thazgarr again, bloodlust in its eyes.

Thazgarr spotted a pair of figures weaving behind the beast: Dylus and Ricard. He retreated, leading the beast back into an open space. Thazgarr jabbed at the beast with his war club—not hard enough to come within reach, but enough to keep its attention.

The beast switched to grabbing at him. It didn't like what Thazgarr did to its claws.

Thazgarr weaved between the desperate gouges of the beast, waiting for an opening. His stamina was beginning to waver. How much longer would they take?

An arrow struck the beast's ankle. The sting of the arrow tip threw the beast off balance. It fell forward. The beast planted its good hand against the ground, catching itself. Its head undulated back and forth, ready to snap at Thazgarr.

Thazgarr planted his foot and raised his war club to his shoulder. He swung at the creature's elbow. There was a wet crack as Thazgarr maimed the beast for the second time.

The beast's arm snapped in half underneath its weight, sending it crashing to the ground. It dug its feet into the stone trying to right itself, to no avail. Its long neck was working against it now.

With the beast against a solid surface, Thazgarr saw his chance. He raised his war club overhead and brought it down on the beast's skull. The beast shuddered and spasmed, but continued to move. Thazgarr swung his club again, this time in the creature's neck. The screeching stopped, but the spasms continued. Thazgarr let out an ear-shattering war cry as he clubbed the creature again and again. When Thazgarr regained his senses all that remained of the creature's head was a chunky pulp of brain and bone. The purple innards of the creature covered everything above Thazgarr's waist. Thazgarr took a seat on the carcass, catching his breath.

Ricard leaned out from behind a derelict stand. "Thaz… You okay there?"

Thazgarr nodded.

The smaller man approached Thazgarr. Dylus followed, pocketing the serpent-man's whip as he passed.

Ricard took a seat next to Thazgarr on the corpse. "Are we going to have to do that every time you find anything vaguely serpentine?" Ricard asked.

"Yes."

Before the conversation went any further cries of alarm echoed in the distance. Voices shouting back and forth. "I heard something over there!"

Dylus and Ricard turned to flee. Out of the corner of his

eye, Thazgarr spotted Willem climbing a roof, moving in the same direction. Thazgarr rose to face their pursuers, war club in hand.

Ricard shouted, "There's too many to fight head on."

Thazgarr remained.

"Thaz, the Kestrels are humans. Think of all the serpent-men you'll never kill if you die here."

Thazgarr gritted his teeth. The tiny man was right. He took one last look at the remains of the scale-skin and his monster. Good enough for today. Thazgarr turned and joined the others in their flight.

Thazgarr ran at a comfortable pace. Every step sent dust swirling into the air. The echoes of dogs and horses bounced around the adobe, hiding how close their pursuers were. Weirdly enough Thazgarr enjoyed the way the serpent blood cooled his skin.

Ricard was keeping pace with some effort. At a glance, he was sure the Ecrecian was following on the roofs above. Dylus would fall behind at his current speed.

"Keep pace, exile."

There was no retort. He glanced over his shoulder again to see if something had happened to the urbanite. Dylus was gone, no sign of Willem either. Branching paths filled the alleyway, the crafty ones had taken advantage of that.

Thazgarr and Ricard ran snaking between different paths. Their flight took them from the marketplace to cracked and brittle hovels. The passageways grew narrow, claustrophobic. At most they could fit four men shoulder to shoulder. Still, the Kestrels hounded them.

"Let me ride on your back, Thaz," Ricard rasped.

"Why?"

"Your legs are longer. You can outrun a horse better."

Thazgarr was keenly aware of the increasing tempo of hooves pounding behind them. There were too many to count through the echoing. The Kestrels would trample them in such a narrow place. It would take no more than a horse or three.

It was foolish of them to send so many riders into the narrows. The wild man drew a javelin from his back.

"Thaz, if you stop to throw that you will die!" Ricard

shouted. "Even if you hit one, the rest will smash you into the dirt like that monster's head,"

"Quiet."

Thazgarr raised his javelin over his shoulder. The dirt beneath his feet was inconsistent, hard in one spot but soft in the next. The best Thazgarr could guess was that they were by another cistern. There was moisture lingering in the ground. Water softened all things.

Thazgarr raised the javelin, locked in his iron grip. Without breaking stride, he plunged his weapon into the ground, embedding it in the dirt. The shaft leaned at an angle, braced and ready for the Kestrels.

The thundering of hooves behind him was overtaken by the sounds of men baying their mounts to stop. Then came a cacophony of noise. Flesh crashed into flesh. Dirt kicked into the air. Weapons rattled against each other.

Thazgarr looked back. The riders had avoided skewering themselves on the javelin, but in the narrow space they had little room to maneuver. Once the first pair of horses collided the hunting band turned into a stampede. The leaders of the band were trampled by their followers.

Ricard let out a mocking laugh, making a gesture over his shoulder.

Thazgarr almost let himself smile before he realized their new problem. They had reached a dead end of the alleyway. All that waited before them were adobe walls, smooth and without purchase. Thazgarr's hands had improved since the oasis, but he was nowhere near able to climb a flat surface. Even if he could scale the wall the remaining Kestrels would riddle every inch of his body with arrows.

The Kestrels were beginning to climb out of the mountain of mangled horseflesh. Doubling back wasn't an option either.

Thazgarr looked at the Kestrels then back to the dead end. The wall was in terrible shape, loose dirt stirred in at its base near the cracks, some kind of air flow.

"Get behind me." Thazgarr barreled ahead of Ricard at full force. With every step, the wall grew to encompass more of Thazgarr's vision. Thazgarr closed his eyes and thrust his shoulder forward.

He made contact with the adobe and felt a flash of pain. He'd used the shoulder that the beastmaster had whipped open, a poor snap judgment. Next, he felt the impact of bone on mud backed brick. It was the same shock as crashing into any hard surface. The aged adobe gave way to the impact, failing against Thazgarr's strength.

He felt a certain satisfaction in his physical prowess. That satisfaction turned to inarticulate dread once there was nothing beneath his feet.

Ricard's screams echoed off the walls.

They were inside.

Thazgarr landed on a hard surface. He opened his eyes to a room filled with mummified corpses. Unlit pathways led off in every possible direction. "Catacombs," he said

"Don't care." Ricard sprinted past Thazgarr and into the darkness.

Thazgarr sprang to his feet and followed the strange little man into the deathly abyss.

CHAPTER
14

Adobe bricks cracked under Willem's boots. He wasn't a particularly heavy man, but the rooftops weren't built with chases in mind. Whole segments of parapet would sheer off the wall and tumble to the ground. He kept moving, lest the roof collapse beneath him.

The former legionnaire watched Dylus zigzag between pathways, deftly evading the Kestrel horsemen. The foreigner was craftier than he let on, he'd be a boon if they could make it to actual civilization.

He'd lost track of the wild man and the scoundrel. Willem was hopeful they'd escape their share of the riders. Thazgarr had made short work of whatever that creature was.

That beast's face haunted Willem—some product of the aberrant sorcery Damu'yhig practiced on their thralls. There was a twinge of uncomprehending agony in its eyes. Had it not tried to gut him, Willem would have felt sorry for it. It was better off dead than serving the half-breed. The sooner Willem could get off this continent the better.

Willem lost Dylus through a building. He leaped across to

the opposite ledge. Riders flooded through the streets, a river of flesh and metal. Fortunately, it hadn't occurred to the riders to look up. He only had two arrows left and a running shootout was less than ideal. Again Willem lamented the loss of his flintlock, one of the few things he missed about the Legion. He spotted Dylus roll out a window and followed him.

A stray rider pulled out from a side street, cutting Dylus off. They stared at each other in shock for a moment before reaching for their weapons. From nowhere Dylus unleashed a whip. The crack of the whip sent the Kestrel's horse rearing back in fear, keeping the rider's sword arm out of reach. It was at best a stalemate. Soon the rider would prevail.

It was only a matter of time before more Kestrels heard the commotion. Willem drew back his bow and loosed an arrow. The shaft plunged right into the horseman's neck. The man clutched at his throat, trying to keep pressure on the wound. He fell from his mount, landing hard on the ground. His horse took off in a panic.

One arrow left.

Dylus looked up in confusion. He waved in thanks when he saw Willem perched on the roof above.

Willem held out his remaining arrow and pantomimed a plucking motion.

Dylus nodded. He yanked the arrow from the dying man's neck and unslung his own short bow.

Willem cursed under his breath. He wanted Dylus to toss him the remaining arrows. The foreigner was an excellent shot, but close combat with a horseman was no place for a bow. Willem gritted his teeth. He couldn't correct Dylus, not without drawing more attention to them.

The pair ran for several more blocks. At two separate intersections, Dylus had to slay an unsuspecting horseman. Both times he put an arrow through them clean. Other than the sentinels, the sounds of Kestrel search parties faded in the distance.

For now, they could retreat back to the storehouse to plan their next move. If Thazgarr and Ricard were alive they'd still need to find a cart for enough supplies. If it was only the two of them, a pair of horses might work. Willem didn't completely want to abandon the others. They both proved to be of adequate worth out in the wastes, despite their shortcomings. Still, Willem could see them making things difficult in the future. Best to debate that once it became an option and not a hypothetical.

The sun was lowering on Willem's right. He raised his arm to shield his eyes. Focused on the sun, Willem failed to notice the fragmented section of parapet he until he stepped on it. The adobe crumbled beneath his foot. He lost his balance and went tumbling onto the main section of the roof. Before he hit the roof an arrow whizzed through the spot he would have been not a moment later. The shaft snapped in two when it struck the roof.

Willem pushed his back against the parapet for cover. He pulled the bayonet from his bag. Dry blood caked the blade, still, it offered enough of a reflection. Willem raised the blade over the parapet.

Across the street, on the opposite roof, he could make out a figure silhouetted against the sun. It was waiting for him.

The only cover Willem had was the parapet. Anything beyond a foot or two of the roof's edge was exposed. Willem crawled on all fours toward the far end of his cover. He could call for Dylus but he was gone by now, worse yet he'd be pulling him right into an ambush.

Willem got into a low squat, careful not to raise his head above cover. He nocked his last arrow and drew back the bowstring. Last he saw the archer was opposite where Willem fell, near the middle of the roof, sun to his back—a risky shot. Rumors were that the wastelanders could see in the dark. If it was a coldblood they might even see heat. Waiting him out wasn't an option.

Willem forced himself up, back straight, eyes squinted in the sun. The silhouette moved. He must have seen the knife. Willem adjusted his aim and loosed, dropping to his knees once the shaft was clear. An instant later an arrow flew overhead, disappearing beyond the roof. The other archer also guessed wrong. Slim chance it was out of arrows too.

In that split second Willem saw the figure cast against the sun it dredged up dark imagery. Details were sparse. But the way the robes flowed, the size and angle of the bow, the casual shooting posture. They all matched the figures who massacred his cohort. Well-maintained instruments of death. It would have more arrows.

Willem swallowed hard. Every inch of his body wanted to run, wanted to get itself off that roof and away from that serpent-man. He could hurl himself into a side alley and drag himself away. His assailant wouldn't be far behind. If the serpent-man didn't kill him, if it decided to capture him alive… Willem thought back to the abominable creature Thazgarr killed. Again his thoughts lingered back to the Legion camp. It had to die here.

Willem opened his satchel. What did he have to work with? He dumped out the rest of his spices. The legionnaire wondered if trading for more arrows would have been a better deal than the spear.

He set the jar off to the side. Next Willem retrieved the last of his spare linen. He cut the fabric into narrow strips. With slight hesitation, Willem opened his coin pouch. The Ecrecian silver stamped with the grand regent's head had done him little good in the wastes so far. It would likely do him much less in an enemy city.

Finally, Willem reached for his powder horn. Black powder was one of the technical advances that let Ecrecians keep their place beneath the moon. Deprived of the same sorceries afforded to the Damu'yhig, they'd learned to make due. He'd been hesitant in disregarding the powder. He didn't have a way of utilizing it without a proper firearm. But something about this dire situation had afforded him a deeper insight. He had been thinking of the black powder as a means to use a gun. He should have approached the matter the opposite way.

He did a test burn on the cotton. The cloth seemed to burn at an even rate. Willem cut a strip long enough for a five-second burn.

After a thorough wipe of the spice jar, Willem began filling it with powder. For every thumb width of powder, Willem dropped in a few coins. The silver had a good weight to it. Not quite as good as lead, but better than shards of clay.

The difficult part was making a notch in the jar lid to accommodate the linen. Careful not to crack the lid, Willem carved a small opening with the serrated side of his bayonet. The

Legion implemented some kind of convoluted metal latch system on their sealables. A spare strip of knotted linen wouldn't make a sufficient seal alone. The fuse was set and ready to go.

Willem rolled over on his back and raised his bayonet one more time to confirm the archer's position. An arrow flew past his knife. The archer hadn't moved a muscle since their last exchange. He struck his knife against a piece of flint. On the third strike, sparks showered the linen fuse, bringing it to life.

He hurled the jar in a high arc over the parapet. Another arrow whizzed past his wrist, the archer hadn't moved. A moment after the jar disappeared over the ledge he heard a crack reminiscent of thunder. The timing wasn't anywhere close to a five count.

Willem poked his head over the ledge. There was no sign of the archer. Scorch marks blemished the adobe on the far side of the street. Silver coins pierced the walls of both buildings.

Good enough.

He made a mad dash for the back wall of his building. Willem swung his legs over the side, scaling across a pair of windows.

If the archer was only concussed he'd at least have a head start. Willem took off into a back alley to head in the same direction he last saw Dylus.

Shadows grew long in the evening sun. The alleyways were all but enveloped in darkness Willem welcomed.

He had to be getting closer. There were more corpses with arrows in their vitals. He was heading in the right direction. Dylus would be getting low on arrows.

It looked like the foreigner had scavenged what he could. Several corpses bared blood gushing wounds. Others clutched at bows but were missing their quivers. Unfortunately, Dylus seemed to be persistent in his arrow scavenging.

Dispatching the archer took longer than Willem had hoped. If Dylus kept moving at the pace he was he could be a mile away by now. Soon the trail of arrowed corpses would run out and he'd lose the trail.

Willem regretted not explaining what a rally point was when he decided the cistern would serve as one. He considered taking back to the rooftops, but the risk of more archers banished that idea from his head.

Minus the supplies used in the bomb, all Willem had was his spear, a knife, and leftover gunpowder. He could still bludgeon someone with the bow if somehow he lost his spear too.

The entire situation was a mess. Half an hour ago he was adequately equipped and accompanied by a semi-competent group. Now he was back to being alone with little more than a pointed stick.

The tides of fortune seemed to be fickle out in the wastes. Willem grumbled to himself realizing he still preferred this to the Legion.

Willem was about ready to head back to the storehouse, hoping he would find someone there. A whip crack echoed through the alley. Willem followed the noise with caution. There was no telling if it was Dylus or another serpent-man with some kind of beast in tow.

Willem made his way down the alley as the whip cracked repeatedly. He turned a corner that opened into an intersection. His eyes took a moment to adjust when he gazed out into the light.

Everything came into focus. He spotted Dylus surrounded by no less than five of the Kestrels. The foreigner was keeping them at bay, making good use of the whip, but his muscles began to tire. With every swing, the whip crack grew less and less concussive. Finally, the whip began to slump in his hand and a sellsword behind him managed a successful tackle.

Willem knew there wasn't anything he could do. Trying to fight all five of them would be suicide.

A pair of Kestrels dragged Dylus back to his feet. Willem gritted his teeth, waiting for them to gut the man. For some reason, they didn't. A tall one with an ornate headpiece seemed interested in the foreigner. They must have thought him exotic. It wasn't every day a Strahlian wandered through the Serpent Wastes.

They bound Dylus and loaded him onto the back of the horse.

Relief washed over Willem. He still had time.

The Kestrels rode off down a derelict street.

Willem had no idea where Thazgarr and Ricard were, let

alone if they were alive. Even if they had the common sense to return to the cistern there wasn't enough time. If he let the Kestrels get away with Dylus he'd be on his own.

Willem followed after them.

CHAPTER
15

Ricard held the glowing knife over Thazgarr, an unsure look on his face.

Thazgarr crouched, giving the smaller man access to his torn shoulder. He clutched a loose skull in his hand, readying himself. "Do it."

Ricard tapped the knife to the wound and it erupted in a meaty sizzle. As the flesh beneath the knife cooked, Thazgarr wanted nothing more than to scream. He suppressed the urge, squeezing the skull.

Ricard pulled the blade away. The skin warped and charred, but it closed. "Okay, that was a bad idea." The scoundrel waved the knife in the air to try to cool it.

"Better than wandering a crypt with an open wound." Thazgarr looked at his dust-filled hand. In his moment of agony, he'd crushed the skull. He waved his hand, shaking it clear of the necrotic powder.

The body was a fragile thing. If that scaled beast's claws hit, his skull would've cleaved in half. That was but one of Sidoth's devils, one petty enough to keep on a leash. This massive maze stone was only one of their villages.

If their kind thrived in the wastes, along with an army of human thralls. For a moment the giant man felt very small. There wasn't enough luck in the stars for him to win even a thousandth of his battles.

Tribal feuding was a simple affair. It seldom ended with entire tribes wiped from beneath the moon. But the warfare the scaled devils practiced, it was of a scale Thazgarr didn't want to comprehend. They were like the domesticated humans beyond the mountains. They reaped the poisonous fruits of this "civilization," as they called it.

Until now Thazgarr pictured his enemies as a single pillar. He thought that breaking a few stones at the base could send their empire tumbling into ruin. But the scaled devils' empire wasn't a pillar. It was a spider web, intricate and flexible. One could pluck away at its threads, but the rest would bear the load. Then the spider would repair the cut threads and seek to poison its prey. He was but a fly in that web.

The tribal ways would do him little good in the future. He'd have to learn to fight on the same terms as his foe. Thazgarr's mind drifted to the soldier, Willem. The boy possessed a dishonorable wisdom, distasteful but effective. It'd already spared him a gruesome death twice since they met. If he saw the boy again he'd ask him of his ways.

They couldn't stay much longer. A Kestrel brave enough to follow them might have heard them closing his wounds.

The searing pain in Thazgarr's shoulder reached a tolerable level. He rose from his knee, and he and Ricard continued into the darkness.

The catacomb air, while stale, was a comfortable temperature. The passages barely fit Thazgarr's broad shoulders. The low hanging arches grazed the top of his head in the dark.

Shelves of tight packed bones lined the walls. Rather than whole skeletons, the crypt keepers arranged the bones by type. All the skulls were piled in one place, ribcages in another. Thazgarr wondered about the tradition behind this practice. Why bother sorting the empty vessels? Were they stored as supplies for dark rituals?

The rigid curves of arrangements of bone formed hypnotic patterns in the darkness. Some formed the illusion of abstract shapes crawling in the dark.

It struck Thazgarr odd. The entire city reeked of rot, but in a crypt of all places the smell of decay was absent. Once his eyes adjusted to the darkness he realized the bones were in pristine condition.

"Why do the city folk strip the flesh of their dead this way?" Thazgarr said.

"Stew meat, I'd guess?"

"No. The fields outside the walls were large enough to make cannibalism unnecessary. Only a handful of the dead were scale-skins, far too few to feast on all this flesh."

"Fertilizer then."

"There'd be no need for a crypt. They'd bury their dead in the fields. Their meat is being taken for some reason."

"Can we let this be a mystery?" Ricard asked.

Thazgarr nodded and the two continued. Ricard had a point. Whatever purpose behind the Sidoth's death rights was a madness they'd never understand.

The catacombs seemed to stretch on for miles. They might have run the entire length of the city. Another maze of stone to further complicate the one on the surface.

Little planning seemed to have gone into the rudimentary passages. Moisture seeped from the floors, intersections had no rhythm in their placement, pathways curved at odd angles limiting visibility, and sporadic echoes of unknown origin set Thazgarr on edge.

A low hum whispered through the halls.

Thazgarr stopped, raising his hands to silence any questions from Ricard. The sharp-eared wild man listened close.

The sound came again.

What he had hoped was wind passing through a hole to the surface sounded closer to a labored moan. The pair stood back to back in silence for several minutes, weapons ready in the darkness. The crypt returned to stillness.

Thazgarr lowered his war club, relieved. The narrow halls weren't ideal for its heavy swinging. The sounds of bone clattering to the ground cut that relief short. Echoes reverberated all around Thazgarr, depriving him of any sense of direction.

Thazgarr let out a scream in defiance. The noise that came from Thazgarr warped through the walls, turning into a bestial roar. Any natural creature beneath the moon would have had its will shaken. The roar echoed no less than three times before fading into the dark.

A fleshy nub jammed into Thazgarr's back. The fleshy thing felt hot and moist. It probed at Thazgarr's spine. He spun on his heel, ready to strike. He barely realized that it was Ricard's elbow before he caved the man's head in.

Ricard pointed over to a black archway, fifty paces away at the end of a shrinking path. "Open space," he whispered.

Ricard led the way, his small size allowing for easier negotiation of the terrain. The halls grew more oppressive with every step. Packed bones hung from the shelves, brushing against Thazgarr as he passed. The passage continued to shrink, forcing him into a side step. For every inch forward Thazgarr moved that wide room grew more appealing.

The pair continued their shuffling retreat. Thazgarr looked back for any sign of their would-be pursuer. When he craned his head back he caught the faintest hint of… something. A tinge of sulfur and shit hung in the air. Until now the catacombs had been absent either scent.

"Quicker," Thazgarr said.

The passage grew narrower still. Dangling bony hands dragged along Thazgarr's chest and back. Looking back again Thazgarr saw the glimmer of golden light bouncing off the wall. A lantern bearer crossing the last intersection? Who'd be here, though? It was possible people fled here to escape the Kestrels.

The light grew more intense, too strong for natural light. Sorcery.

The archway was close. The light grew stronger still. It bounced off the walls, creating a miasma of images cast against the hard angles of the bones. The light was warm, hot even.

Thazgarr looked again to Ricard. Before he could bid his friend forward a stray finger bone caught him in the eye. He clamped his eyes shut and pushed forward.

The bony limbs tightened around him. Brilliant patterns danced across the inside of Thazgarr's eyelids. He pushed forward with every cord of muscle in his body. He needed to put a corner between him and whatever sorcery the light was about to unleash. It felt as if the hands were grabbing at him, stalling him for the thing in the light.

In the span of two steps all the resistance holding Thazgarr back vanished. He stumbled forward onto a sandstone floor. The wild man sprung to his feet and drew a javelin. He turned back to the bone-laden hall, only to catch a glimmer fading into the passage opposite the one it came from.

Ricard asked. "I miss something, or do you hate tight spaces that bad?"

Thazgarr put away his javelin. "Devils roam these halls."

Ricard shrugged and retrieved a torch hanging from the wall. With a little effort, the torch sparked to life and the room came into view.

The first thing Thazgarr noticed was the drop to his immediate left.

Rather than a proper chamber, they found themselves in a massive stone stairwell. The outer rim had a floor, each side leading off into several passages like the one they came from. A stone column supported each of the corners. Lifelike carvings of serpents sprawled across columns ascending toward the surface.

The stairs themselves interlocked between columns, weaving back and forth over a pit. There were three more floors beneath them, a pit of mixed bones at the bottom.

Ricard pointed at something shining at the bottom of the stairwell.

Before Thazgarr could protest Ricard was already down the first flight of stairs.

Bones clattered every which way as Ricard dug into the pit. Under torchlight, the dull shine of metal brightened with every handful of bones cleared. Ricard dug past his knees in bones before they could see the treasure in full.

Nestled in a ribcage sat the silver idol of a beast somewhere between dog and man. It had pointed ears and bared teeth. The idol's eyes were shining blue gemstones shaped in a predatory gaze.

Thazgarr leaned over to inspect the treasure. Depending on its mixture of metals, carrying the bust could be impossible. To his surprise lifting the idol put no strain on him, even with his bad shoulder.

"Must be hollow," said Ricard. "Still, the eyes should be worth something."

Thazgarr ran his fingers across the idol. The eyes were cold to the touch, no discernible crevice between the gemstone and the socket. There was something oddly comforting in the eyes. "We'll defile the idol another time." Thazgarr made a makeshift harness from his assorted leathers and sun cloak. With their treasure in tow, the pair began their ascent.

Grave robbing was a new experience for Thazgarr. It seemed the idol was an incidental addition to the mass grave, cast among the bones by happenstance. The dead likely had little interest in the trinkets around their bones anyway, or so he hoped. He couldn't afford to disregarded any resource in his campaign against Sidoth. Not even in the name of morality, not if he wanted to succeed. Should the gems fetch a high price Thazgarr's wiser comrades could find some use for the coin.

Thazgarr looked up the stairwell. If any god under the moon was merciful, or at least despised Sidoth as well, this would lead back to the surface. The sun may be harsh but it was a natural harshness, unlike whatever things roamed these cursed halls.

Had that thing either not sensed Thazgarr, or was it apathetic to him? Regardless, Thazgarr's mind strained to identify what that aberrant light could have been. Boatmen spoke tails of beasts from the deep luring sailors to the depths with hypnotic lures. These tombs couldn't house such a creature, could they?

It could be something else, some unknown breed of sorcery. The scaled devils seemed capable of any such abomination. Thazgarr swallowed, thinking how dangerous the sorceries were. Still, there were darker possibilities. There were primal things burned into the edge of man's collective memory.

Shadows danced in the torchlight as Thazgarr climbed. Each column he passed was a devilish masterwork. The carved serpents almost seemed to writhe and slither along the walls.

All the paths converged on a single landing suspended from the center to the stairwell. Hints of fresh air drifted from above, but with it came a rotting stench. Unlike the rest of the catacombs, this place smelled of death.

A wooden bucket big enough to fit a man dangled from a rusted chain. Blood stained the bucket, a necrotic slop oozed from the cracks. A cloud of flies hovered around the bucket, feeding on whatever filth lay inside.

"Think that's what they do with the flesh?" said Ricard.

"Maybe." Thazgarr unslung his war club.

"So whatever it was you think you saw, they're feeding it?"

"No. The city has been in chaos for weeks. No one to put food in the bucket. If that devil wasn't interested in us it's likely something else was being fed. Be silent now."

Thazgarr heard the faintest crumble of stone to his left. Thazgarr spun on his heel.

The body of a giant serpent hung outstretched from the adjacent staircase.

He swung his torch back and forth, the fire obscuring his own vision.

The serpent recoiled, drawing its hood, a cobra. The beast's scales were a mottled black and brown against the fire. Its eyes shined gold. It was big enough to swallow a man whole.

On his backswing, Thazgarr spotted a second set of eyes shining in the dark. He rolled left, dropping several steps. He regained his footing and spotted his second assailant. Another cobra, its neck coiled into the body of the first.

"Two heads!" Thazgarr shouted."

Ricard was silent.

Thazgarr grabbed a javelin in his offhand, keeping it between him and the cobra. He couldn't help but envy Willem's decision to take a spear.

The cobra lashed out. Thazgarr jabbed at the cobra's nose. The cobra reeled back in pain, its nostril torn open.

Thazgarr heard a scream.

Ricard dropped from another staircase onto the second head's neck. He shoved his blade through the cobra's snout and out its chin. He grabbed an arrow from his quiver and stuck it through the cobra's eye.

The cobra hissed, spraying blood everywhere. It reeled back and pitched Ricard from its neck.

The little man landed on a set of steps a level below, but he wasn't moving.

The cobra flexed its jaw twice before it retreated, choosing the easier meal.

"I'm here, devil! I'm the meaty one!" Thazgarr shouted

The cobra paid little mind to Thazgarr's taunt as it slithered downward. The second head kept its remaining eye trained on him.

There was no good path to Ricard. Any route faster than the cobra's would likely end with him plummeting into the pit. Leaping onto the cobra, while possible, would only end with him between the second head's jaws.

The beast was getting closer to Ricard with every passing moment.

With a leap, Thazgarr put himself onto a staircase that led right above Ricard and the cobra. Thazgarr hurled his last javelin.

The pointed wood pierced the cobra, but the beast remained undeterred.

At a loss, Thazgarr took the dog-faced idol and hurled it.

The cobra's second head lunged at the metal. Intending to knock away the trinket and send it tumbling into the pit. The cobra's teeth cracked, shattered even. The idol entered the cobra's throat. The beast bent at an unnatural angle, almost like loose cloth struck by a stone.

The idol continued along its path, the cobra going with it. The beast crashed into another staircase on the way down, smashing right through it. The cobra landed in the pit, impaled on a countless number of bones. The beast lay still, oozing blood into the pit.

Thazgarr stood there for a moment, reevaluating his concept of weight. He only remembered to check Ricard once the small man started groaning. Nothing had broken, but bruises covered everything beneath his right hip.

Thazgarr helped Ricard to his feet. The small man felt

heavier than the idol, yet Thazgarr couldn't imagine throwing him at the cobra and having the same effect.

A short trip back downstairs and the pair were elbow-deep in the cobra's corpse. It wasn't long before Thazgarr felt the cold metal of the idol under his fingertips. He pulled the idol free and set it on a mound of bones, wiping away the guts as best he could. Thazgarr looked at Ricard, then gestured at the bust.

"Pick the idol up."

Ricard shrugged. While small, Ricard by no means looked weak. His time in the wastes had left him lean, free of the redundant fats western settlers had. He dropped into a squat, placing his hands around the idol's chin. He exhaled and attempted to lift the metal. Ricard struggled, managing little more than to tip the idol over. What interested Thazgarr was the way bones bent beneath Ricard's feet.

"Thaz, my right leg feels like it's on fire. You don't have to show dominance with your freakish strength."

"That wasn't my intent." Thazgarr re-secured the idol on his back. "The path looks clear."

Ricard jammed his blade in the beast's neck. "Let me grab the snake heads first."

Thazgarr looked at Ricard in confusion.

"What? I'm not almost getting eaten for nothing.

CHAPTER
16

The pale red light from Thessalia's blood vial shimmered in the darkness. The transmutation was a simple mixture of sulfates and an oxidizer. Once exposed to the air the reaction was luminescent. A sorcerer of superior breeding would scoff at such a petty trick. Of course, they'd keep their own personal torchbearer in such a situation.

The light around her neck cast shadows that danced across the walls in every conceivable way. Many of the shadows took forms like those of jagged-toothed beasts. She convinced herself they were the odd angles of her robes bouncing across the walls. It was enough to keep her calm, though she'd never convince herself that every shadow was her own. Not the ones that drifted at the corner of her vision.

She found it strange there was a pleasant quality to the air in Ilupagru. A breeze pulsed back and forth every few minutes, keeping the air fresh. It wasn't a perfect gift, however. Whenever the breeze blew toward her it stirred a cloud of dust. Thessalia held her sleeve over her face, shielding herself from the dust.

The gust only persisted in the main path. Any of the

hundreds of branching halls within the maze would spare her eyes and throat, but she endured. The airflow might lead back to the surface, an opening in a cliff side. Any escape, even the delusion of it, was better than ending up as a skeleton tumbled along these walls. She narrowed her eyes to a slit as a particularly thick cloud blew past her.

There wasn't much to see anyway. Unlike the sandstone necropolis above, these halls were a single piece of gneiss. There wasn't a single noticeable tool mark along the passage. The stratified patterns within the rock ran uninterrupted for miles, only breaking at wind-eroded corners. But unlike any stone patterns she'd read about, these strata curled in on themselves. The lines of stone coiled together forming a helix that wrapped around the tunnels. It was likely a vestige of the same twisted architecture she viewed from above Ilupagru.

Thessalia felt tiny wandering the ruins. They were ancient, enduring, unchanging. Regardless of what she did they'd continue as they had for an incalculable length of time. *I must be the way one unfortunate enough to cross paths with a god, or another great beast beneath the moon felt.* Though the idea of gazing at the Sky Tyrant's shadow was much different than wandering its gullet.

How long had she been walking? Miles? It felt like she'd hardly descended more than a few dozen feet, She'd be outside the city walls by now. Depending on where this path let out she may even have a new route for smuggling.

The last thing of substance to touch her lips was Anissa's breakfast, yet she wasn't yet hungry. Otherwise, it felt like more than a day since her fall. Paranoia would only do so much to pass the time.

The wind relented for a moment before starting to move with her, beckoning her forward. She lowered her sleeve only to find herself opposite something.

Protruding from the stone was an unknown species of plant. A set of waxy white stalks tore through the gneiss as if it were little more than soil. The stalks supported a thick red bulb, its shape and color reminiscent of a heart. Outstretched from the bud were tendrils probing in every direction. The tendrils were each lined with rows of a type of a hair-like fiber. The hairs, in turn, secreted a metallic liquid from their tips.

At the base where the roots bore into the gneiss lay a mound of bones. Thessalia counted a serpentine head, arms, and a ribcage, all in pristine condition. The back of the specimen's tail was still thick with rotting meat.

Other than herself, Thessalia, couldn't recall anyone of consequence disappearing recently. Not anyone recently enough to have rotting meat left, anyway. Perhaps this man was from Khepresh, some sycophant risking his life for favor with High Priestess Ul Kyzagmi.

Among the thousand silver reflections of the plant, there was a distinct color of gold. A jeweled band dangling from the corpse's bony wrist. Thessalia reached for the bracelet.

The tendrils flexed out at her. The movement wasn't particularly swift, but it was enough to startle her. Thessalia stumbled back, pushing away from the plant. Once she was clear of its reach it reverted back to its initial position.

Thessalia took a moment to catch her breath before rising again. She picked what she thought was a minimal safe distance and held her hand out. Again the tendrils reached out to meet her. She waved her hand back and forth in a looping pattern. The plant followed her every move.

She drew her knife and prodded at one of the metal beads tipping the hairs. The droplet clung to the blade when she pulled it back.

The closest thing she could equate the fluid to was mercury, toxic to the touch. Why a plant would be secreting toxic metal of all things was beyond her. Thessalia glanced back over at the skeleton.

She shook her knife to free it of the metal. The mercury clung to the bronze and didn't budge. After a third shake, she tried wiping the metal against the cavern wall. The blade stuck to the wall. Thessalia grabbed the knife's hilt and planted her foot against the stone. With more than a little effort, she pried the knife from the wall, relieved that stone didn't come with it. Again she looked at the countless barbs tipped in the shining adhesive.

The tendrils sprawled wide, leaving a few inches of clearance on either side. Simple immolation was the easiest option, but that would only leave her with two vials. One was still required as a light source, and there was no end to the tunnel in sight. Sight. The plant didn't have any obvious sensory organs, yet it could follow her every move.

The air flow reversed again. Another wave of her hand and Thessalia was able to rule out scent. She glanced over at the rotted tail on the other side of the plant. The plant wasn't too picky if it was surviving all the way down here.

Thessalia unslung the pair of blood vials hanging from her neck. With a whisper one of the blood vials' contents came to a simmer. She held out both arms, a vial dangling from each hand. The tendrils twitched and drifted toward the hot vial. Thessalia grinned.

With some more of the metallic fluid, the vial of hot blood was dangling by its cord just beyond the tendril's reach. Thessalia dragged herself on her elbows along the corner of the passage. She inched herself forward, the barbs drifting right by her. Without a constant flow of chanting the blood would cool before long. She pulled herself clear of the barbs as a tendril refocused on her leg.

Thessalia grabbed the meaty segment of the tail.

Stood on end it was the same size as herself. With a push, she tipped the rotted pillar of flesh into the tendrils. The tendrils embraced the flesh, dragging it into the bulb.

Thessalia slashed the cord and pocketed the vial. A moment later and she also had the arm that sported the gold bracelet.

The bulb unfurled a series of chitin lined petals and took the tail. Thessalia couldn't see inside of the bulb, nor did she want to. The plant started making sounds reminiscent of one of father's feasts. There was wet smacking, tearing muscle, throat undulating to accommodate piles of meat.

Clear of any immediate danger she indulged in the fantasy of feeding Nysra to the plant. Her agonized pleas for mercy would grow less coherent with every drop of mercury on her skin. Her thrashing body reduced to nothing as it ate through her skin, muscles, and finally her organs. The vacant look in her eyes as she accepted that's how she'd spend her last days.

Of course, Nysra would ruin it all with a breath of acid.

Still, Thessalia regretted not having a way to take the plant with her.

She looked back to see the tail disappear into the bulb. The stalks pulsated as a bulge flowed from the bulb and into the floor. Thessalia was sure there was an interesting answer to were that stalk led, but she had more pressing matters.

Thessalia looked over the bracelet, disturbed by what she saw. The bracelet bore the markings of the Sithrak line. The bloodline ruled Lux prior to Thule, their sorceries well respected and feared. Like any other victor, they grew complacent. Their sorceries weakened along with their blood.

When Amon Thule made his claim for Sarrutum, the Sithraks were less than graceful in relinquishing power. Plenty still wandered the streets, half-breed bastards, products of indiscriminate lust. Any Sithraks worth their family's name had been dealt with. Now they were little more than trophies decorating the lairs of other bloodlines.

This begets the question of why a corpse bearing the sigils of a long dead house would be that fresh. It would take considerable effort to breed a specimen as exceptional as that one in secret. Such a plot would also result in plenty of inferior children to gamble a trip into Ilupagru on instead.

It was unlikely anyone outside of the Damu'yhig could even have such a bracelet. Spare a few trophies the Sithrak treasures were melted for coin. Thessalia only recognized the house's symbol since it emblazoned her mother's paperweight

Another idea crossed Thessalia mind. In an act of desperation, a Sithrak might have fled into Ilupagru during their upheaval. They could have been hiding here for years, biding their time. Of course, that didn't account for how they'd been surviving all this time, nor how timely their death had been. If they had been living here all this time a single plant would have been a negligible danger. That was unless they had not found a way to escape.

Thessalia walked for several more hours. There wasn't a logical circumstance that could have brought that man to the plant.

Lost in thought she was slow to notice that the passage had rounded into a tube. The twists of the path became more erratic. The lines in the rock were hardly strata anymore. They'd become more erratic, twisting in on themselves, coiling in loops and bends.

Thessalia gave up keeping track of where she was in relation to the temple. She'd not gone much deeper than a few floors. Pathways intersected at irregular intervals. The breeze had grown into a gust, the exit must have been getting closer if that's what it was.

She wondered what her mother would think of this whole debacle. Mother did her best to avoid obviously taking sides, but Thessalia knew she'd be much worse off without her kindness. Any other bloodline would have discarded her long ago. Defectives were held in almost as little regard as half-breeds. They were little more than walking ghosts without sorcery or names to call their own. Had mother not spent hours every day helping her find a way to draw upon her sorcery, she had no idea where she'd be today.

Maybe that time was what Nysra was jealous of. Her own sorcery was more than she deserved with the way she squandered it. Still, her sister was capable of more than Thessalia could ever dream. With reagents, a blood moon, and a full runic array her talents were still nothing compared to a mispronounced incantation from her sister.

If she managed to find a way out here, Nysra wouldn't face any consequence, spare the assassins she hired. The accusation of attempted murder would be little more than background noise to her. Mother would still have to accept her as the superior brood.

Thessalia scowled. If only she could pull sorcery from deeper inside herself, something beyond petty blood manipulation. She could feel it during the blood moons, it made her hairs stand on end and excited her blood. Every moment under that red light felt like she was bathing in a pit of needles. It felt as if the power was there but misaligned. Regardless of what Nysra said she was of equal breeding, despite her deformities. If she could barter with Kadar to unlock that force she'd stand head and shoulders above her siblings. Mother could finally admit she was the favorite. And father would finally acknowledge her.

The tunnels went on bending in every conceivable direction. Any sense of depth had disappeared. Flat ground had become little more than a novelty.

Thessalia came to a halt. Her eyes glazed over. The walls were more than gneiss. A pale stalk protruded from the ceiling, coiling along the wall. There was no bulb nor tendril, only a long, pulsating mass that disappeared into the darkness. She was certain she was nowhere near the plant she passed before, much less under it. Unfortunately, the stalk was following the same path as the airflow.

Thessalia timed the pulses of the stalk as she passed. It had a rhythm much like a heartbeat. As other pathways converged with her own, so did more stalks. Each waxy vine pulsed, matching rhythm with the others, resembling an umbilical. Not long afterward the tunnel seemed more stalk than stone.

The stalks began to weave and cross, never tangling. The umbilicals coiled into each other, forming a pale cable hanging at the tunnel's center.

The flora fascinated Thessalia. The pale things were cast deep below the ground, deprived of even the most basic necessities. By all means, they should have been extinct centuries before anyone laid eyes on them. Not only had they survived but thrived. They were a predator, feasting upon those unwilling to see the threat they posed.

They could hold the secrets of this place. Thessalia pulled out her knife and gouged one of the stalks. The plant bubbled and mercury spouted from the hole. With every pulse, more fluid oozed from the wound.

Instead of splattering at her feet the mercury clung to the umbilical, continuing to flow along the exterior.

This was far more fluid than secreted by the tendrils and it seemed to be flowing in the opposite direction. The pulsing continued completely unabated, sputtering more and more mercury along the vines. Curious, but of little value.

The tunnels converged into a single corridor. The airflow focused, what had been a gentle breeze hours ago was now closer to a storm.

Thessalia looked back. Any of the paths she ignored could have hid a mountain of treasures, something to aid her escape. She continued along her path, only mercury and wind to guide her.

CHAPTER
17

Bat stepped out into the courtyard. He wore a bright red cloak that chafed at his neck. He'd gladly trade it back for a simple piece of white linen, but Musa said he needed to look like a leader if he wanted the others to follow him.

Someone was shouting. He turned in time to see a heap of wood fall from atop the mansion. The half-built turret smashed into the ground, almost crushing a pair of guards. They started swearing at the pair on the roof, who returned the sentiment.

Bat approached them. "What's going on here?"

His presence went unnoticed, or worse, they were ignoring him.

Bat put his fingers between his lips and whistled. The tone was enough to halt the shouting match. Each man's attention fell square on him.

Bat repeated himself, more forceful this time. "What happened?"

There was a flurry of pointing and accusations. Both sides were reasonable. Bat had no idea who he should discipline, if anyone. Zaeim never needed to discipline anyone, as far as he knew.

"I don't care. I want it fixed!"

They bowed their head and started clearing debris.

Bat rubbed his temple. This was the third such incident he'd dealt with in the last few days. Seeing both sides now, he liked taking orders more than giving them. Stabbing and deciding where and when to stab were different skills altogether.

No one protested his claim on leadership of the rebellion. Being Zaeim's second granted him that much, likely more weight that it should have. He couldn't help but think there was someone better suited to the role among their ranks.

Most of their leaders met the same fate as Zaeim that night, felled by a poisoned arrow. The one survivor, a large and vigorous man, was bedridden. He was only lucid for a handful of hours these last few days, according to his children. Dissent among the ranks amounted to little now. An accidental generosity from the coldbloods.

They'd taken more than they gave, though. Xent had been in shambles since that night. Communication had broken down. Kestrel bands were roving the streets slaying anyone they saw. There was no telling how many of their brothers still lived, how many of his people still lived.

More were fleeing into the dunes, trying their luck against things that lurked beneath the sand. Beyond the mansion walls, the streets of Xent had grown silent. Bat longed to hear the sounds of life again. The sounds of wheels against cobblestones, merchants peddling their wares. He missed it. The closest he got was the continuous hammering of men fortifying the mansion.

The plan was simple enough. Collect everything they had at the mansion and force the Kestrels into a battle of attrition. Sparing the occasional mishap, the modifications were coming along well.

They'd drained the pool, and a group was scrubbing it clean. Once it satisfied Musa they'd refill it with drinking water for mid-battle relief.

They piled debris along the garden wall as mock battlements. The idea was that they could move while crouched along the wall, spear a Kestrel, then duck back behind cover. In practice, the terrain was uneven, awkward to move across. A man had already cut his foot on a stray piece of metal that found its way into the pile.

It'd still be a while before they could fix the main gate. They didn't have the supplies or the manpower to risk sending out a salvage party, so they did the next best thing. Bat had his men pile garbage at the gate. They'd use the remaining debris to build a gauntlet and force the Kestrels into the courtyard. Spearmen would take position on either side of the gauntlet to extract a toll in the confusion. Thin the Kestrels numbers before they ever encountered a foot soldier.

Bat had learned from his siege of the place that the final line of defense would be the mansion. He had the first floor cleared of furniture, anything the Kestrels could use as cover. Men took picks to the ceiling and filled it with murder holes. He'd man them with spears, arrows, whatever they could hit the Kestrels with. Furniture from the first floor lay stacked at the top of the stairs. They'd barricaded the stairway in case the Kestrels breached the mansion. That left the City Master's ramp as the only means of access. The top of the ramp had two dedicated lines of spearmen and boiling pitch ready to pour.

Non-combat tasks work was on the second floor and above. Those too young or weak to fight helped in whatever way they could.

Thanks to Zaeim's forethought they were able to empty the granaries before the Kestrels hit them. Hand mills were busy day and night grinding the wheat. Among the citizens under their protection there was a miller. For whatever reason, he objected to having the flour ready. He was dramatic about it, too. Whatever his reasons it mattered not. They didn't have the space or time.

The third floor was where they were keeping the young and wounded. The once opulent space looked more like an impoverished street corner with injured fighters sprawled out across the once fine tapestries and rugs. Bat would be surprised to find a single piece of fabric without a blood stain.

Any chance of a free Xent surviving rested with the people on that floor. If the Kestrels took the mansion it would be all over.

Bat continued his rounds, hoping his presence would be

good for morale. Everyone he passed dropped what they were doing to salute him. Bat ushered them back to work the best he could.

They were used to quiet conflict. They'd grown skilled at back alley stabbings and sabotage. Battle was something different. His only real battle experience was overtaking the guards, that and each loss to the Kestrels. Now they were too few to wage a ground war.

The gauntlet was their best option. Going forward they'd need every battle to be on their terms.

The Kestrels might have been the better fighting force but they couldn't have as much to lose. Bat knew his people could endure this, and they'd endure without the bargains of alien forces. Once he dealt with Kestrels he could turn his attention to Otomi.

The Kestrels were a club pummeling him into submission. The Otomi were the razor slicing at his vitals.

Any party small enough to slip by the Kestrels unnoticed had gone missing. They likely met similar fates to that night in the temple.

Bat reached for his blade, the thought of that scaly limb writhing in the dark set upon him. Whatever else was hiding underneath that cloak must have been terrifying. An unending maw of teeth and muscles and limbs.

Bat shook his head. It was subservient to the serpent-men and they died easy enough. All Bat needed was enough men. Put enough steel through it and the beast would die like any other. But that was only one of them.

There was no telling how many of those bloodthirsty half-breed beasts stalked the streets, serving their cowardly masters hiding in the shadows. Breaking them would be the true test.

Bat slid behind a bush into a secluded part of the yard. Once he was sure no one could see him he dropped to the ground, leaning his back against the wall. He was exhausted. Every hour of the day he was plagued with requests, reports. The number of hours he had to rest since the Kestrels' attack could be counted on his fingers. The timekeepers were among the first to abandon leaving clocks empty and bells untolled.

Bat could only guess how long he'd been at this. Every

decision he made took a toll on his brothers. Zaeim made it look so easy. Had he been hiding the same burden?

A runner came bursting through the gate shouting. The Kestrels were gathering on the other side of Xent, getting ready for their big push.

Bat pushed himself to his feet, patting away grass that clung to his form. He stepped out into the courtyard doing his best impression of Zaeim's strut. Attention fell on him.

Bat took a deep breath. "This watch is relieved early. Rest while you can."

The scattered groups of the courtyard filed into the mansion, passing the fresh fighters on their way out.

Bat took a long swooning couch for himself. This would be the last rest he'd have for a while. He'd start his search for a replacement in the morning. If he managed to survive the night, that was. Someone had to be better prepared for this than he was.

Willem tracked the Kestrels back to their base of operations, a temple of some sort. He was hiding in an abandoned apartment down the street. Once the sun set he could risk getting a better look out the window, lest another archer spot him.

No serpent-men stood out from the presumably human main force. The Kestrels were at least semi-disciplined. They had their drunken revelry in shifts so at least a third of them were ready to fight at a moment's notice. The drinking seemed to have subsided a few hours ago. Likely they were waiting for the last of their hangovers to clear. They were preparing for something.

Since they had that beast at the souq market it was a fair assumption they were here at the behest of the serpent-men. That meant someone else beheaded the Damu'yhig on the Eastern Gate. There were other forces at work here. This wasn't a simple pillaging, it was a power struggle. Their hold on the wastes wasn't absolute, as the Legion had thought. Willem allowed himself a little joy at this revelation.

But there were still too many unknowns. If it was some type of rebellion, there wasn't any sign of them. Given the Kestrels' current state they were likely preparing for the final mop up.

It wouldn't be long until the Kestrels packed up and moved on. They'd take Willem's best chance of escaping the continent with them. That was assuming they didn't gut Dylus once they got bored of him.

After the Kestrel's main force headed out for their next battle he'd make his move. With any luck, the remaining sentries would be few enough for Willem to sneak right in and retrieve Dylus.

The Kestrels left their wagons out in front of the temple ready and loaded. If security was light enough Ricard's idea might come to pass. He wondered about him and Thaz. Having them to run a distraction would have been helpful. A small, specialized team had served him well so far. Far better than a cumbersome Legion cohort. The Kestrel could mobilize any time now. This was his only window for the rescue.

The other problem was serpent-men. One of them was already dead, two if the coin bomb worked. If those were the same group that butchered his cohort there were at least ten of them. No matter where they were, they would always be a danger. Willem bit his tongue. He reminded himself, "Survival, not revenge." He wasn't the wild man.

Willem looked over his gear. He found some rags that matched the color of the city's brickwork—suitable camouflage. There wasn't any wood workable for carving into arrows, nor pots with a thick enough seal for another bomb. All Willem had left was his bayonet and the spear.

The spear was cumbersome, less than ideal for stealth. But getting cornered with nothing but a knife was worse. Better to take it as a last resort.

The building was a holy sight of some type. It was likely a secondary entry point, or at the very least something to keep air flowing. He'd avoid the main doorway if he could.

The Kestrels arranged the loot wagons in a defensive blockade. It was smart for dealing with a larger force, less so for a single man.

The whole scenario reminded Willem of a training exercise the Legion ran. They'd split the cohort into two teams. One to attack a wagon train, the other would defend it traveling along a set path. Each team's dinner for the night was whatever they secured from the convoy.

Willem slumped back in his seat. There were few different paths in life he could have taken, plenty less chaotic than this. None of those seemed any better, though. For the wealthy, the Ecrecian capital city Vestinus was a debaucherous paradise. For everyone else, it was a metaphorical, and sometimes literal, meat grinder.

Willem lost two siblings before he was born. One fell into a weaving machine and the other died in a blast furnace explosion. Soot lung took his father around the time he turned ten, disease got his mother not long after. By sixteen the rest of his siblings had fallen into whatever gangs would have them.

Money was always an issue. Vestinus Holdings and their subsidiaries made sure there was plenty of work to go around. Of course, they also made sure that living was expensive enough to keep citizens where they were. Sometimes there'd be enough extra silver for a whore at the end of the month, but not much else.

Willem didn't know how far or even if the accountants looked beyond their ledgers. Their luxurious homes were more than enough insulation from the rest of the city. The newer architecture was cold and uninviting. It paled in comparison to the beauty of the old imperial style the Legion modeled themselves on. That was back when Valok-Nur was a human country. Tensions had cooled between the two nations, but they still weren't getting that continent back anytime soon.

The next time an primus came of age maybe they'd be wise enough to avoid a reclamation war with the vampires. Those never went well.

Two centuries ago they'd sent a full Legion of five thousand men to establish a foothold in the old lands. If the Legion's lecturers were accurate they lasted eight days. That's when the Ten Lords of Valok-Nur rode out to battle, each with ten of their own retainers. Less than a hundred legionnaires returned.

For all the terrible thoughts in its sorcered mind, the grand regent managed to avoid that one. That was if the thoughts in that metal skull were real and not elaborate bureaucratic puppetry.

Everything within Ecrecia seemed generally terrible now

that he thought about it. The colonies looked like a better choice at first. Then Willem heard about the skin-walkers, chimera and the like. That was his impetus for the Legion. They offered an escape to somewhere with the added benefit of training and a firing line between him and the horrors beneath the moon. At least that's what he thought.

Overall the Legion was a hedged bet that he lost. Given the choice to go back, he wasn't sure he'd take it yet. If he could retrieve Dylus he'd still have a chance of disappearing into the Protectorate. Chimera infested as it was, it had to be better than this.

Other prospects still existed, though. This particular uprising had been quelled for a time, but that mindset was infectious. Whatever happened here could inspire another uprising. It was potential for the future, an alliance, or a chance to spite the Damu'yhig. He frowned.

"Survival, not revenge," he muttered.

Shouting started outside. Willem pushed himself flat against the wall, allowing him enough of an angle to view the church. Horses pranced with nervous energy, egged on by riders. Swords rattled in the air.

It was almost time.

In calm, deliberate twists, Sraac attached the last pressure cap to the metal case. The Kestrels had semi-adequate preparation time. He calculated that against the place where Mont scouted the rebels. He grabbed the timer spring and gave it three full twists. Done.

Muffled cheers reverberated through the door. For the last several hours some insipid bullshit preoccupied the Kestrels, probably inconsequential.

Sraac lifted the alchemical device from the sides, careful to avoid the handle. With some strategic handling of the device and the door, he was back in the corridor facing the main hall.

The Kestrels circled around some kind of act. Men shifted and Sraac got a better view. Bobbing heads came into view first, some kind of dancers? Looked like the Captain Uwais was set on keeping the surviving rebels for himself.

As more of the mob cleared Sraac saw they weren't dancers. At the center of the crowd was an exotic man of some sort. What he'd mistaken for dancers was an elaborate juggling routine with severed heads. In total the captive was juggling three heads, two horseshoes, and a lemon. The Kestrels cheered the act on.

The appearance of a foreigner was troubling, regardless of how good his juggling was. Did he have something to do with the rebellion? The factional makeup of Sidoth's enemies may be larger than what Sraac expected. This was something that needed immediate attention. He ducked back into the antechamber.

Seated on Sraac's desk was the captain. "You finally decided to socialize, my friend." He bit into a pomegranate. "I take it that's the toy you were teasing me about earlier?"

Sraac tightened his grip on the metal box. "Can this wait? I need to speak to your new friend."

"The man is nothing, he's already assured me of that. I'm more curious about the thing you're clinging to."

"It's nothing."

"My friend, do you wear the mask because you're a terrible liar? I assumed you always were afraid of showing your face, but now I'm not so sure. It hurts to think you'd lie to me, all to win a bet. I thought we were past that."

Sraac allowed him to bask in his smugness.

Uwais' mock smile faded. "So I asked you, scale-skin, what is the box?"

"It's a weapon, one I plan to defeat Sidoth's enemies with," said Sraac.

"Very good, isn't our relationship more pleasant when you don't try your scale-skin tricks? So what does it do, some kind of sorcery? He ran his hand over the warm metal of the case.

"I have no tangible sorcery I can call my own. Think of this as a type of bottle, used to store the talents of others."

"Ah, so it's sorcery for the common man. I wouldn't mind if you wanted me to finish the rebels with this, send them a message of sorts."

"Do you have any idea how it works?"

"I'm patient enough to let you tell me. You're only a little less human than me. I assume the weapon poses no more danger to me than anyone else who might wield it, scalded or not."

"True. To unleash the box's power you must gaze upon whoever it is you want harm done to and speak the command word." Sraac reached into his pocket and handed the captain a tiny scroll. "The box will do the rest."

Uwais strutted over to Sraac, his belly bouncing with every step. He snatched the scroll with a flourish of the wrist. "I've outsmarted you, Cutter of Men."

In the corner of his eye, Sraac spotted Mont by the skylight, bow aimed at the captain's back. Sraac shook his head. Mont withdrew. Unfortunately, Uwais had also noticed the gesture.

"Was that a no?" He said. "So… I convinced you to put yourself into a situation where you'd have to double my fee. I had my man spy on you, discovering your little plan. And now I have a toy that I'm guessing you're quite fond of. And somehow I haven't outsmarted you?"

Sraac remained silent, giving the little shit plenty of rope.

"And now silence. That's what most annoys me about your kind. You're proud, verbose, and think you're clever, but your egos shatter at the slightest failure. Of course, you have no sorcery to erase your failures. So you sit here in your little room and mope while my Kestrels crush those pesky little rebels for you." He grabbed the box by the handle. He missed the faint click of the device's timer starting.

Sraac stepped out of the the way without protest.

"That's better." The captain walked past him without a second glance. "And next time you need my services the fee is triple."

Sraac took a seat and waited for the Kestrel war cries to fade into the distance.

Once the Kestrels were gone, finally, Sraac made his way to the main hall. There was still the matter of the foreigner. The sellswords left their guest bound to a statue of Sidoth's first daughter Pyth. For some unintelligible reason, they left him hanging upside down.

Up close the man's boots were nice, a little weathered from the dunes but a fine piece of leather. He looked like a man of influence. What was someone like him doing out here? Sraac looked down to find the man studying his own boots.

"Balisk hide?" the foreigner asked.

"Basilisk. And these are drop bear?"

The man frowned "Those are a myth."

Sraac dropped to a crouch to get a better look at the man's face.

"Well then, man of Strahl, may I ask what you're doing so far from home? If you lie, I start prying off fingernails."

The man's eyes went wide and he started explaining. Some roundabout story about getting black bagged and dumped.

What caught Sraac's attention was his use of plurals. He set his palm on the man's chest "We'll come back to that in a minute. Who did you mean by we?" Sraac felt the man's heartbeat quicken.

"Three others: two wild men and an Ecrecian."

"An Ecrecian, you say. Was he Legion?"

"How should I know?"

"Was he marked? Brand on the bicep?"

"I never got a good look. He keeps his arm bandaged."

"Where's the Ecrecian now?"

"I have no idea. Your horsemen separated us."

Typical of the Kestrels to overlook something, like a rogue enemy soldier in their midst. Sraac drew a knife from his belt.

The man shrugged the best he could while tied to a statue. Sweat dripped from his brow. This was the heartbeat of panic, not deception. No spy, no matter how poorly trained, would be this panicked over a few fingernails.

The presence of an Ecrecian was troubling. Was the force Elder Thaxiss attended to a diversion? It wasn't beneath the Ecrecians to sacrifice a score of men to plant a handful of scouts.

"What were they hauling?"

"I was in a box the whole time. For weeks all I could see was fish and poppy seeds."

"That could be any Ashborne freighter."

"I've never even been on a non-pleasure ship before. I'd have no idea what would look out of place."

"Fair enough." Sraac placed an open waterskin next to the

man's face before heading back to the antechamber.

A kasairan vessel was in the area and stockpiling fish. At the very least they were planning around the grain shortage. More likely than not they had hand in it.

The Ecrecian was an unexpected factor. It was possible that they allied with the Ashborne against Sidoth and his people. The Ecrecians would pull all Lux's assets to the west then the Ashborne fleet starts digging in their hooks from the east. The kasair already had a foot in the door. A little more leverage and the dunes would be at the mercy of whatever they could fit in a cargo hold.

The situation wasn't unsalvageable. With the rebels quelled the kasair would lose their foothold. It was all in the captain's hands now. Sraac allowed himself a smile.

Mont was climbing through the skylight when Sraac entered the antechamber.

The half-breed snapped to attention. "The Kestrels are moving on schedule."

"Good. We're leaving at sunrise. Any word from Dakar?"

"Not yet. What are we to do with the foreigner?"

Sraac was airing on the side of fool rather than spy. Still, leaving a foreigner to run wild was an unnecessary risk. "Take him, the Elders will find use for an exotic."

"As you wish. If I heard correctly he had allies as well."

"That's what we'll be attending to between now and sunrise. I want you to gather our scouts once the Kestrels have completed their task."

Sraac went back to admiring the fresco. It was odd, the artist made it so far without anyone striking them dead for heresy. Maybe there was a time when Anu Sidoth allied with the other gods. That didn't matter now.

Thralls of the Ashen Crow, the Ecrecians encroaching on Sidoth's holy land, anything less than a god itself wouldn't save them. Once he finished the rebels he could start on the rest of his god's enemies.

"Praise Anu Sidoth."

CHAPTER
18

Willem crawled beneath the wagon wall. The impromptu defense would have been useful against a coordinated attack, but against a single intruder it only served as cover. The temple stood lit against the night sky. Guards wandered the temple yard.

A lone sentry walked right past Willem. The Ecrecian considered slashing the man's tendon. One less guard, but he couldn't guarantee a quiet kill. Best to avoid attention. The number of men left behind was still unclear.

Patrol patterns were emerging. Two men were always on the front door. At least another four circled the temple, two in each direction. There was creaking in wagon beds above—spotters, he'd guess.

Willem took a deep breath. This was insane. He was risking his life for someone he'd known for less than a week on the prospect they might benefit him.

Dylus had little coin, he didn't know the native tongue, and the Serpent Wastes' culture was as foreign to him as it was Willem. Even if the two of them managed to sneak back into Strahl there'd be conflict with whoever had him marooned in this forsaken place.

There was no rational reason for him to be doing this.

Was there an irrational reason?

He'd hardly looked back since the gassing, or had he? No. Since his escape from that venomous fog, he'd been measuring himself against that day. Every fight, every decision, most of the interactions he had with his new friends. It always came back to abandoning the cohort.

Shit, now he had to save the little prick.

Willem made a full loop of the temple. His elbows stung and his core burned.

No other entrances on the ground level. It would make too much noise if he broke in through one of the stained glass windows. There were only the four guards patrolling, each outfitted with a bronze scimitar and a short bow. Once they crossed an intersection point Willem had a little time before the other two passed. He had to draw them away from their post.

The Kestrels were adept riders with a bit of a cruel streak. They were also mercenaries, so they were looking to profit on this venture.

Willem crawled back to one of the creaking wagons. Boards flexed under the shifting weight above. Willem drew his bayonet, grasping it the way a Legion assassin would. He waited for a full patrol loop, waiting to maximize his time between sweeps. Once the guards were a safe distance he sprung up, ready to stab whoever was in the cart.

To Willem's surprise, instead of a hunk of man flesh, he'd put his blade through an expensive looking pillow. The cart was brimming with luxury goods, treasurers he'd seldom seen in civilized society. The Kestrels were already loading their plunder. It was the perfect opportunity.

He grabbed a gold trimmed bottle reminiscent of a drink his uncle enjoyed. Inside the bottle sloshed an iridescent green fluid. Willem pulled the stopper from the bottle and a familiar burning flooded his nostrils. He doused the contents of the cart with the liquor, and plenty of other flammables from among the loot. With a strike of flint, a fire was underway.

Willem moved along the wagon wall in a crouch walk setting fire to another pair of carts. It wasn't long before the guards noticed. They flew into a panic trying to save their plunder.

Willem took a position on the far side of the last burning cart and readied his spear. He was already gambling with his life. Hopefully this would pay off. It sounded like the patrols were having little luck with the other two carts. Footsteps thundered against the cobblestones. Someone broke ranks.

Through the smoke, he could see a figure on the opposite side of the cart. Willem thrust his spear without hesitation. He felt it strike bone, followed by a man's weight hanging on the haft. Willem yanked the spear back before the haft caught fire. The Ecrecian vaulted over the adjacent cart. The dead Kestrel was carrying a short bow and arrows. Willem grabbed them and made his way for the front door.

The Kestrel short bow had an odd feel to it, different from the one he'd carved at the oasis. It felled the remaining doorman all the same.

Once he was through, Willem jammed the door behind him with a Kestrel's sword. Dylus was on the far side of the hall tied to a statue of a big-titted snake woman. They must've been preparing him for ritual sacrifice.

Willem cut him free of his bonds. The Strahlian bumped his head on the floor but otherwise, he was intact.

The main door lurched inward. Angry shouting came from the other side. The sword held the door for now, but the bronze was starting to flex and slip.

There were no other exits. The walls were smooth, clear of handholds. Breaking through a window would take too long. The back rooms offered little safety against an active search.

Willem passed Dylus a handful of arrows. "Think they know how to breach a door?"

Dylus grabbed his short bow from a pile.

The two men took a position behind a stone bench, arrows nocked.

The sword buckled under the force of the door. The sentinels were coordinating now. "Push!" one of them shouted. The door pulsed, and recessed in a steady rhythm. Another two shoves before the warped sword slipped from between the handles. "Push!"

Willem drew his bow. The sword dangled by an inch. "Push!"

The blade clattered to the floor. The double doors of the temple whipped to the side as the Kestrels stumbled through.

Willem and Dylus each loosed an arrow, felling the first two Kestrels.

The other two realized what was happening and fumbled for their weapons. Before they closed the gap a second pair of arrows came streaking by, striking one man in the head, the other in the gut. No one else charged the door.

"Grab your things," said Willem.

"There's another in the back room. He looked important."

The idea of a vengeful mercenary wasn't appealing. Willem grabbed the remaining Kestrel by the arrow in his stomach and dragged him to his feet. "Let's go negotiate." Willem dragged the Kestrel to the antechamber.

The leader had already seen Dylus's face. Strahlians weren't a common sight out here either. It was better to deal with this now.

Willem held the wounded man in front of him as a shield. Dylus was two steps behind, an arrow nocked.

Willem brought his knife to the Kestrel's throat. "Open it."

The door opened into an office with an elaborate mural. The fresco's line work drew the eye to the far end of the room, where a hooded figure clad in blue robes stood. The figure turned to Willem. Instead of a face, an ivory mask greeted him, a pair of golden eyes peeking through.

The serpent-man stood there a moment. "Ecrecian. I assume the other two are lying in wait somewhere."

Willem's eyes flickered to Dylus.

"Your friend was more than agreeable with a knife to him. So what is it you desire?"

"What do you mean?"

"You stormed the temple alone. Killed what, five men? And now you stand before me. You'd only risk that if you had something to gain."

This gave Willem pause. He hadn't expected a serpent-man, much less one willing to negotiate.

The serpent-man turned to Dylus. "Lower your bow, Strahlian. By the time your shaft hits me, you'll already have been struck dead."

"You're bluffing," said Willem.

The serpent-man made a slight tilt of his head. An arrow came through a skylight and embedded itself in the heart of Willem's hostage. The body went limp, more burden than shield now.

Willem dropped the body. "Impressive. Think your archer can get both of us before we can get you?"

"Gambling your life on spite? I wouldn't expect that from one of your kind."

"You wouldn't expect them to be roaming your cities, either."

There was an uncomfortable silence. It could only have been a few seconds, but it felt like hours.

"True," said the serpent-man. "Your actions so far have led me to infer that you're an intelligent individual. Based on that I'd also infer you understand how little you could do against the Damu'yhig's sorcery."

No way of telling what he was beneath the mask. He felt the need to place an archer, he wouldn't need that if he had sorcery. Still, he had an archer. A vague threat would be best. "Didn't seem to help the one up on the battlements much."

There was an ear-shattering blast. The windows exploded into shards of glass that flew across the room. A layer of dust shook free from the ceiling. A pillar of black smoke was cast against the moon, an orange flair at is base.

Somebody mumbled something.

"What?" Willem shouted, unable to hear his own voice. A high pitched whistling dulled the rest of the sound.

The three stood there in frustration, suspicious of what the others might do. Eventually, the whistle faded and words returned.

"An acceptable demonstration?" said the serpent-man.

Willem nodded. Sorcery or not, testing the him further was a bad idea.

"So we'll return to my question: why are you standing before me?"

This question had to serve some purpose. He was measuring him, trying to determine his allegiance. Willem's answer would determine how he would walk out of here, if at all. "All I want is my men, a cart full of supplies, and a day's head start."

"Petty. You get tangled in all this just so you can leave?"

"I'm only here by happenstance."

"Do you think I would believe that?"

"Absolutely not."

The Masked Serpent seemed to consider this. "Reasonable enough. I'll barter with you. You get your supplies. And in exchange, you do something for me."

"What guarantee do I have that your men won't come after us?

"I swear on my gods that no harm you at my hand until our contract is complete. Kadar takes such matters deadly serious."

Will bit the inside of his cheek. The serpent-men didn't mince words when it came to their gods. "What would you have me do?"

"Go slay anyone who survived that blast. That will show you had no affiliation with any of them and save me a bit of work. Bring me the proof of the captain's death and I'll even pay you the Kestrels' commission.

"And after that, you'll let us go?"

"You will have the head start, assuming you don't break our terms."

Willem frowned. "I imagine the Kestrels made a similar agreement."

The serpent-man ran his fingers across his desk. "They broke terms." He said gesturing at the pillar of smoke.

"Will your beasts abide this agreement?

"They are not beyond control. Regardless of whatever foreign divinity might taint their blood."

You make promises for the spawn of other gods?" said Willem.

"Do you accept the terms or not, Ecrecian?"

CHAPTER
19

Bat pulled himself from the pool. His vision was blurry and all he could hear was ringing. Charred skin rolled off his body. His nostrils burned when he sucked in burning fumes.

The faintest glimmer of moonlight pierced through the rolling layer of smoke above. Dancing firelight gave shape to the black cloud as it wafted over him.

Bat tried pushing himself to his feet only to collapse. He felt stabbing pains all over his body, no feeling past his elbow and knee.

How did he get here? The last thing he remembered was the Kestrels toppling the wall with heavy hooks. The courtyard was a bloodbath. Horsemen ran wild, trampling anyone in sight. Then the man with the bracelets came through the wall holding a box over his head. The next thing Bat knew everything was in ruin, the grounds littered with charred remains.

How? None of Sidoth's aspects related to combustion. He remembered that much from years of sermons.

Again Bat tried to stand. Again he failed. All he had left of his arm was a burned stump, blackened bone poking through the skin.

"Is anyone there?" Bat could only hear a vague echo through the ringing. There was no response.

Bat rested his head against the cobblestones. He wondered what he'd done wrong. More accurately he wondered what he could have done to avoid this. To avoid everyone, everything he'd ever known being consumed in flames.

Bat snapped back to reality when he noticed the dark figure looming over him.

It was a foreign man with rough features unlike any Bat was familiar with. He wore leather and carried a blood-soaked spear.

The man's eyes left him unsettled. In battle the Kestrels had carried a bloodthirsty joy, his own brothers had a passionate rage. The look in this one's eyes was cold, detached. There was a trace of something else but the smoke obscured it.

The foreigner plunged his spear into Bat's chest. The bronze slid right into his heart. The pain only lasted for a moment. The cuts and burns that plagued Bat's body melted away. His eyes lost focus, the foreigner was no more than a shadow now, his spear tones of gold.

If Sidoth was merciful he'd condemned him to the same pits as Zaeim and the others. Once reunited they could revolt against the deadlands. They could make it a just place, unlike these lands beneath the moon.

Like Zaeim said, challenging the serpent-men was a losing gamble from the start. Still, the survivors, the ones who fled, would tell their story. It would even inspire others to raise their blades against the Damu'yhig.

It occurred to Bat that if they wanted to survive their only real option would have been to run. But then the stories would be a disappointment.

Willem planted his boot in the corpse's shoulder and pulled his spear from its chest. The boy that lay in front of him was no older than he was, at most in his early twenties. There was little difference between them and the Legionaries.

They were stupid boys tricked into something much greater

than themselves. They were set against a force beyond their comprehension then made an example of.

It looked like the rebels met the Kestrels in front of a mansion they were using. The explosion blew out the front wall. Anything flammable was little more than cinders.

Willem stepped over the body and plunged his spear into the back of the next one over.

What could we have been? Had none of this happened, what could the countless dead have made of themselves? He wanted to picture explorers or artists. All he could imagine was being choked to death in soot or chewed to pieces in a machine. Not much better than the horrors inflicted by the serpent-men. In a way, they'd won their freedom from the Damu'yhig.

Willem plunged his spear into another body.

At the temple, fueled by adrenaline, he failed to appreciate how unpleasant killing with a spear was. Now he had time to take in every little detail. With the bow, it was a simple feeling of tension and release. Spearing someone was first met with resistance from flesh and armor. Once he pushed through to the bone there was a reverberating shudder. Unless he struck the heart they would gasp, the air pushed from their body.

Most often they'd have a confused look on their faces, unwilling to believe this was how they died. Others had a hateful look, aware of what had happened and resentful. The ones exceptionally mangled or charred from the blast just seemed to be happy it was over.

The smell was the worst part. Ricard was right, everyone did shit themselves when they died. Mixed with the scent of burnt flesh, this place was unbearable.

Almost unbearable. It wasn't enough to cross his employer. Would the Masked Serpent let him leave the city alive? Like always, there were too many unknowns. If the explosion was true sorcery he wouldn't have needed the Kestrels, let alone Willem. It could have been part of some elaborate game of proxies ensuring no one knew exactly what happened. Best to avoid him in the future if possible.

Willem speared another.

It would have played out different if Thaz and Ricard had

actually been lying in wait somewhere. At the very least Willem wouldn't be sticking every shit-stained corpse at the behest of his enemy.

The Damu'yhig poisoned hundreds of Legionaries, bombed their own, and wiped Thazgarr's people from beneath the moon. And here Willem was doing their bidding for a bit of coin and some supplies. If the soul was real this kind of work would stain it. In every sense of the term Willem was a traitor, to his country, to his species, to himself. With every passing body he pierced, Thazgarr's war on the serpent-men seemed less mad.

Willem wiped the sweat from his brow and looked back at Dylus. The Strahlian had been dry heaving since they first caught wind of the dead. "You all right over there?"

Dylus doubled over, gestured for Willem to go back to what he was doing. The sooner they left the better.

But then something occurred to Willem. The rebels were only devastated once they tried holding the city. Based on the dead hanging from the battlements, their rebellion was a success. It was the same as the Legion's encounter.

The Damu'yhig unleashed their power in full when their enemies were many. In skirmishes, they'd resorted to traditional tactics. A small group could attack the Damu'yhig then flee before they retaliated. Rather than one fatal blow, they could bleed the serpent-men to death with countless minor ones.

That was still a numbers game he'd eventually lose. Survival, not revenge. It wasn't his duty to destroy the Damu'yhig. Willem speared another Kestrel.

Dylus waved a blackened skeletal arm adorned with gold bracelets. "Found the captain!"

"Hang on to that."

Willem crawled over the collapsed wall into the mansion. The inside was completely black. The fire must have some kind of delayed burn, turned the entire building into an oven. The room looked like a giant grill, curled bodies for charcoal briquettes. Rubble shifted beneath him. He stumbled and hopped off the mound of adobe.

Willem looked to see what gave way beneath him. There was a burnt hand, no bigger than his thumb, the fingernails smoked, ashes flaking from the bone. He didn't know what he was expecting when he starting digging through the rubble. All he found was the rest of the child's body, burnt, and flattened under his weight. The fire burned away every discernible feature. Erased. As if they had never lived. Never having had the chance to be anything.

The flames were dying out. The once brilliant blaze was little more than a dancing flicker between the ashes.

Willem climbed out from the building's remains. Cinders flitted in the air, reflective against his cold eyes. Ash clung to his clothes, staining them a dull grey.

Willem walked past Dylus, hardly glancing at him. "We're going back to the temple."

Dylus took a hurried step to keep pace. "You're going to risk going back there for a bag of gold?"

"Not for the gold."

"You can't be thinking of making another arrangement with him."

"We aren't doing this again," said Willem.

"So you're a pacifist now?"

"I'm not doing their work for them anymore. I'm still capable of violence if that's your concern."

"Well then why are we going back there?"

In truth, Willem didn't know why he was returning to the temple. It could have been the gold, the stockpile of supplies, but another idea was floating around his head. It was petty and self-destructive, and it would seed future blood debts.

There was something about that smug little snake hiding behind his mask. The dismissive way he sent countless people to their deaths with hardly a glance. Regardless if he didn't know about the innocents or didn't care he should face some kind of consequences.

The only others who knew of the act were loyal to the masked one. Unless some unseen force was willing to balance the scales—unlikely—the task fell to Willem. It was a massive risk without reward. That fat-bellied philosopher may have been on to something when he said surviving and living weren't the same thing.

The temple was the same as Willem left it. The burning loot carts had gone out. Shards of stained glass littered the ground.

Willem booted in the antechamber door, bow drawn. Dylus right behind him doing the same. The room was empty, no evidence the masked one had ever been there, spare a bag sitting on the table.

Willem didn't take any chances. He put an arrow through the bag and sent gold pieces flying across the table. He'd honored his word, and Willem's betrayal of humanity was complete.

After a cursory glance for tripwires or other such mechanisms, he went for the gold.

Between the handfuls of coin shoveled into his satchel, Willem studied his enemy's gold. The bulk of the coins were the broad triangles made of gold, the edges flat and the corners pointed. One side depicted a cobra head, mouth agape. The reverse had lines intersecting at regular intervals. It was likely depicting the stonework of some serpent-man holy site.

Mixed in with the gold were a few rudimentary disc-shaped coins carved from green stone. The stones bore a roughly carved profile of a human face on one side and were blank on the other. Best to figure out the values later.

Willem dumped the captain's charred arm on the table and turn back to the exit. "We'll make a pass of the cistern on the way out." There was plenty of water stockpiled in the main hall, but the cistern was their only chance of finding the others.

Before leaving, Willem scanned the room one last time. Something caught his eye, something he missed last time. Over the doorway, a swath of paint was missing from the fresco. There was an engraving beneath it. It struck Willem odd that the Damu'yhig of all groups would feel the need to cover over a piece of their proud history.

He approached the doorway, spear in hand. With the bronze tip of his weapon, Willem scratched at the plaster tree hanging over the doorway. As he chipped away the paint it revealed an oval shape. Centered in the oval was a smaller circle with a set of four prongs protruding from it. Stone tendrils umbilicaled off the oval back beneath the cover of the mural. Willem scanned the engraving. Below the oval was the awkward curves of primitive lettering.

The sound of grinding stone erupted in the hallway. There was a crash. On instinct Willem half pivoted through the doorway, exposing only his head and spear. The next door over, a heavy stone one, lay along the floor. The warped bronze of the hinges glowed red. The thick muscled calf stood planted atop the stone door. From the shadows, the bronzed muscles of a familiar wild man emerged.

"Couldn't have done that, like, two hours ago?"

Thazgarr whipped his head to the right, war club ready. Up the hall, he saw Will's head peeking out from a doorway. "Today has been a very long and strange one, boy. Do not test me."

"Fair enough." Willem stepped out into the hall. "What happened to your shoulder?"

Thazgarr eyed his wound. The skin Ricard cauterized was black and shriveled. "Closed a wound, seemed like a good idea in the catacombs."

"I'm not a med—a healer, but you didn't do that right. How hot was the metal?"

"It glowed in the dark. Burned out any corruption." Thazgarr glanced back at Ricard. The tiny wastelander was hauling the pair of skulls up the last flight of stairs.

"You don't get a pot glowing hot when you're cooking meat, why—" Willem paused, mouth agape, staring at the pair of skulls Ricard rolled into the hall. His attention returned to Thazgarr. "Your arm's not going to heal right."

Thazgarr tried raising his arm over his head. He managed to raise his elbow to about his chin, his arm wouldn't go any higher, his shoulder began to sting and crack. The war club would be manageable. "How long will it take to heal?"

"A month at least, if you don't use it. Even then some of that is permanent," said Willem.

"I'll make due." Thazgarr looked over toward the main hall. "You've been busy since I last saw you."

"The Kestrels stockpiled all this. They're dead now."

"Your doing? I thought you clever, but not that clever—or brave."

Willem frowned. "It was only in part my doing."

"I'll question that later. Regardless, they should have no qualm with us searching their ill-gotten gains."

Despite Willem's protests the group decided to rest in the temple a while.

At the other suggestion, Thazgarr doused his wound in a potent liquor. The liquid seeped through every crevice of his shoulder with a deep burn. How many times was he burned in this last week? Certainly, more than he would have liked. His hands had healed from the scorching rock, but without a good shoulder a hand only meant so much.

Thazgarr had only slain a handful of Sidoth creations and his body was already beginning to falter. If everything he planned to slay took a toll of flesh, there'd be little left before he was anywhere near his goal. As much as it pained him, he was only one man.

The Ecrecian's tactics could soften the blows a great deal, but that alone wasn't enough. As he said, he was only in part responsible for the destruction of the Kestrels. He needed a weapon he could wield against thousands.

Thazgarr decided to skim the Kestrel's horde. Mixed in with the loot was an armory he could hardly dream of. Bladed throwing disks, daggers that spread open when squeezed, a sword with a blade that flexed like a whip. There were so many fascinating tools of violence. Thazgarr stopped at one weapon, a "crossbow," as the others called it. It was an acceptable crutch until his shoulder healed.

All the weapons here were deadly, but none alone that would allow him to stand against a nation. Thazgarr's eyes drifted toward the many altars of the temple. There were weapons beyond the flesh, the alien ways of sorcery. The eldritch art was always reviled amongst his people, but maybe if they had practiced it they'd still live. How would he even begin that path? Beyond the thing in the catacombs, Thazgarr had never seen sorcery in his life, much less a mentoring sorcerer. The craft would remain a mystery for now.

Thazgarr approached one of the altars, atop it was a statue of a six-armed snake woman. Each hand grasped a different mask with a different expression. The one that rested upon the figure's face bore a devilish, mocking grin. With his left arm, Thazgarr flailed his war club into the statue's head. A few chips flew away and a fine crack appeared in the hair, but the statue was otherwise unscathed. It continued to mock Thazgarr with its grin.

Thazgarr stepped outside. The Ecrecian was loading a cart with supplies. Now was as good a time as any. "A word, Legionnaire."

Willem froze. "You knew this whole time." His arm hung loose, dangling near the knife in his belt.

"The way you carry yourself, you couldn't be much else. Let rest your knife hand, I've no desire to spill your blood."

"What do you want?" he asked.

"To avenge my dead. I thought that was clear."

"No, I mean, what do you want from me?"

"Your mind."

Willem had a confused look on his face.

"There is a wisdom in the way you make war. Dishonorable as it may be sometimes, I'd have died twice already if not for your cleverness.

"Dishonorable." Willem's eyes went dark. "Do you want to know how the Kestrels actually died? The serpent-men burned them, along with who knows how many others. All I did was finish off the stranglers for them. All to avoid fighting one. Is that who you want guiding your hand?

"You consider options I don't even see. You're willing to take paths you find distasteful and survive because of it. This is what I need in my fight against the scale-skins."

"What is it about the serpent-men? Why them and not any of the others that wreak havoc on the wild tribes?"

"Our conflicts with the domesticated humans are natural. We killed each other for livestock and land… reasonable affairs. There was no grudge in the spilled blood. When the scaled devils came, they wiped my people from beneath the moon. They salted the land and retreated back into the wastes. No growth, no plunder, bloodshed for the sake of bloodshed. That I can not forgive."

Willem cocked an eyebrow. "So you're mad that they slaughtered your people for the wrong reasons?"

Thazgarr squeezed the side of the cart. "My wrath is because then they slaughtered them without reason." Wood crackled under his fingers.

Willem placed a jug of water into the cart. "A tempting offer, but no. The first port we get to, I'm buying my way onto a ship and putting as much distance between me and this continent as possible."

Thazgarr helped Willem with the jug. "You fought your way this deep into the Serpent Wastes just to run away? I thought only a man possessed by a burning vendetta could push so far. If you'd fight this hard for nothing, I couldn't imagine how much harder you'd fight for something you believed in.

Willem ignored him and continued loading the cart.

"Then at least indulge me this," said Thazgarr. "At a trading post back west I heard rumors about the Ecrecians. Do your people really have feasting halls where they fill themselves then purge into pots so they can keep eating?"

"That's not a place I've ever seen or could afford to patron, but I wouldn't be the least bit shocked if we did have those."

Thazgarr tossed his silver dog idol into the back of the cart. The wood buckled and snapped beneath it, smashing a hole in the wagon's bed. The rest of the supplies gave way, spilling through the hole onto the ground.

Willem glared at Thazgarr. "We have to load all that shit into a different cart now."

CHAPTER
20

From his corner, Willem could see all the main hall's entry points. Thaz's proposition, while unexpected, wasn't uninviting. It was an impossible goal, though. The Damu'yhig had to have gods on their side. Any coordinated resistance against such a force was hopeless.

Willem glanced over at the statue of the masked snake women Thazgarr lashed out at earlier. It remained smug in the face of her assailant. Willem already had his fill of serpents.

Had the masked one remained at the temple Willem might have thrown his life away by returning. All at the imagined behest of people he'd never met, and the cohort. A stupid risk against a foe he couldn't understand. They had to be the ones sent to cleanse his cohort from their dunes. If gods were backing them there'd be little Willem could do beyond flail at them like Thaz at the statue.

The longer Willem sat in his corner the more restless he grew. The others were playing a dangerous game. The longer they wasted digging through the Kestrel's loot, the more time they'd be at risk of ambush. "Is everyone done picking out their new toys?"

A bronze gauntlet came spinning out of a pile end over

end. A matching gauntlet and breastplate followed. Ricard hobbled over to the pile. His leg was purple and shaky. "That'll about do it."

Willem looked over the armor. Dried blood clung to a hole in the chest. "You're not actually going to try and wear that are you?"

"I plan to sell it. Plenty of people dumb enough to try using scale-skin gear. You tell them this is what the Damu'yhig dress their coldbloods in and they forget all about heatstroke."

"And the snake heads?"

"Boil off the meat and carve a helmet out of it. Think I'll make a set of pauldrons."

"You seem to enjoy your crafts," said Willem.

"Old man was an armorer, left plenty of stuff to tinker with." Without skipping a beat the little wastelander was back to carrying his haul out to the cart.

If they could make it out of Xent in one piece they'd be in good shape. A few days travel south and they'd be on the river. There had to be something near the river. A trading post or a settlement where he could contract a trader—a smuggler, actually.

Dylus walked by carrying an expensive looking rug over his shoulder.

"We're not taking the rug," said Willem.

Dylus spun to face Willem, almost hitting him with the rug as he turned. "It's of a kasairan make."

"I don't care if the kasairan god itself made the rug. Were not lugging that all around the desert."

"A giant bird can't make rugs."

Willem pulled out his knife. "I will tear up the kasairan rug if you're going to be difficult."

"We need trade goods. That thing is worth an entire farmstead back in Strahl."

Willem's eyes widened a bit. Could the disparity in value between a full farmstead and a piece of knotted fabric be that big? Before he could say anything else Dylus was already out the front door.

"Fine, but that's the first thing we dump in an emergency." Willem ran through a list in his head. Food, water, weapons, a few other odds and ends, and the cart was ready. "Last call," Willem said.

"We should stay the night. Start fresh in the morning," said Ricard.

Only now did Willem realize how exhausted he was. It had been a long day running around the city. He hadn't had any real rest since the cistern. A cool room with four solid walls was inviting. Still, there was the masked one.

"No, there's still the risk of serpent-men."

Thazgarr nodded. "And the things beneath the temple."

"The what?"

Almost as if summoned by Thazgarr's words light began radiating through the doorway Thazgarr kicked in. It was no brighter than a torch at first, but with every passing moment, the light grew more intense. With the light came a low pitched hum, getting louder by the moment.

Willem grabbed a handful of arrows from a pile and dropped behind a stone bench. The others did the same, flipping a pair of benches. Arrow nocked, Willem poked his head out from cover.

Light washed over the wall opposite the doorway. Warmth rolled through the room. When Willem thought the light couldn't get any brighter it faded away.

Out from the catacombs stepped an old man, naked and emaciated. Flesh sagged from his distended stomach. His limbs were little more than bone. His lips and throat twitched with what might have been some failed attempt at speech.

Willem rose to face the old man. It could have been a survivor lost in the catacombs. "Hello?"

The bony frame turned toward Willem. Across the man's chest was a massive tumor, oozing an oily black discharge. Willem held back a gag at the sight of the bizarre deformity.

The fleshy surface of the tumor split across the middle and peeled away, revealing a glistening golden orb. Suspended in the orb was an oily black core that radiated streams of fluid. The fluid pooled at the edges before leaking out onto the man's chest. The flesh slid back over the orb then retracted again.

Willem's mind raced to find some way to define the thing

that stood before him. With all his meager education, only one word came to mind: eye. What stood before him was a giant eye embedded in a man's chest.

Willem drew back an arrow. Before he could raise his bow the thing's iris dilated, leaving only a thin rim of gold. A blinding light erupted from the pupil. The low hum returned.

White hot light flooded every corner of Willem's vision. He clamped his own eyes shut, loosed his arrow, and fell back to the floor. His eyes burned with horrible pain. All he saw was white. He tried blinking, There was nothing but vague outlines. "Don't look at it!"

The room was getting hotter. Then there was a hint of smoke in the air, the crackle of kindling mixed in with the humming. The stone bench Willem had his back to was warm to the touch.

"It's burning the room!" someone shouted.

Willem inhaled. The air was hot, and growing hotter. This couldn't go on for much longer.

Willem cursed under his breath. His spear and satchel were sitting in the back of the cart, not that they would do much good, except the black powder. He felt for something he could use and his hand came to rest on a hard piece of flesh. "Please tell me that's your forearm, Thazgarr."

The barbarian grunted.

"Help me lift this bench. There's a frail old man attached to that thing."

"I hope you have a plan, Ecrecian."

Willem felt around for the bench leg. He doused himself with a waterskin, soaking whatever he could into his clothes. He positioned himself beneath the bench leg in squat position. "Lift."

He and Thazgarr pushed. Willem felt the heat hit his feet the moment they started lifting. With tiny steps, the pair slowly raised the bench up on its side. Steam roiled through Willem's clothes, but he wasn't on fire. He shielded himself behind the bench the best he could.

Willem grabbed the leg hanging over his head, gesturing for Thazgarr to grab the other. "Walk it forward."

Willem felt the bench tilt and shift in his hands. Thazgarr

must have been edging his side forward. The bench clattered back to the ground.

Willem pushed with all his strength. He slid his side forward, dropping the bench just past his toe. Every fiber of his body felt like it was about to rip. How was Thaz doing this with one good arm?

They repeated the pattern several times, inching the slab toward the eye thing. The stone was growing hotter with every moment.

"How close are we?" asked Willem.

"A great deal of the room is in shadow. We must be close," said Thazgarr.

"We need to be right in front of it."

Willem felt sweat dripping from his brow. He shambled forward, moving the bench slower with every step. He struck an edge, almost tipping the bench over.

The bench was scalding hot now. How hot was that light? If they didn't reach the eye soon the bench would begin to melt.

"We're at the inner hallway, Ecrecian. The slab is starting to glow," Thazgarr said.

Willem could barely keep his hands on the burning stone. The low hum of the eye thing rung through his ears and pushed out any ability to think. This would either be close enough or they would die. Either way, he'd finally have some peace. Give or take a few seconds of burning to death.

"Tip it forward."

Willem planted his hands on the slab and pushed. The resistance faded as gravity took hold and brought the bench toppling forward.

There was a wet thud followed by silence.

The air began to cool.

The reprieve was short lived. Footfalls and shouting erupted behind Willem. The commotion whisked past him, changing from a charge to the sounds of metal on stone and flesh.

Willem opened his eyes. All he could see was vague blobs of Dylus and Ricard hacking at the body. He shut his eyes again.

"We're leaving."

CHAPTER
21

The pulsating umbilical hung taut at the center of the tube. The rock had reverted back to a flat yellow-orange color more reminiscent of the surface. Had it been days at this point? Thessalia had become peripherally aware of her thirst and hunger. It still placed no great demand on her.

A need to continue overpowered any fatigue she did feel. She felt that if she stopped to rest she would never continue. Tales of treasure seekers read to her as a child always emphasized the agony of thirst. She had passed plenty of desiccated corpses that looked better equipped than her.

This could all be a dying hallucination. She could be bleeding out through a crack in her skull back in the catacombs. Delusion was a powerful thing. It wouldn't be unreasonable for a mind to deceive itself into a happy place in its final moments. If this was a death hallucination, she liked to think it would be more imaginative. An eldritch land beneath her feet and all it amounted to was plants and curved tunnels.

The tunnel ended in a hole. Stepping to the edge revealed a hexagonal room of sandstone. The weaved umbilicals plunged into a pool of mercury built flat against the far wall. Despite the pool's orientation, not a single drop spilled from it.

The drop to the floor below was by no means a long one, still, it was enough to maim.

Thessalia undid the clasps of her sandals. She regretted choosing heels today. The footwear allowed her to stand taller than most of the legged occupants of the temple. It also lessened the gap between her and her siblings, though it was still something they preyed upon.

More importantly, it afforded her a certain convenience during particularly messy social gatherings. Once, in a display of wealth, her father hosted a feast were blood pooled over an inch deep on the floor. It took Nysra hours to have dried blood scrubbed from her lower body that day.

She sat with her feet hanging over the ledge and gently slid herself forward. Once she couldn't lower herself any farther she braced for the drop and let go.

Instead of dropping to the ground she went hurtling toward the opposite wall. She raised her arms to shield her head. Her elbows struck the rim of the mercury well, something popped. She bounced off the stone rim of the well and rolled over onto the wall. The floor?

She lay faint on the ground for a while. Her arm took on a shade of black and burned in an unimaginable pain when she tried to move it. It was the same side as her dislocated fingers.

Once her vision refocused Thessalia glared at what was now the ceiling. The weave of pale umbilicals swayed back and forth as it faded into the dark above. She forced herself back to her feet. She grabbed a bracelet in her good hand and tossed it. The gold ring spun in the air, crested, and dropped back to her feet.

Thessalia's stomach dropped trying to grasp the mechanics of what she witnessed. It was manipulating physics. She could have spent all that time walking deeper beneath the surface. This place was herding her. To what, she had no idea.

The room was empty save for the well at its center. Each wall had a doorway engraved with abstract runes of which she was unfamiliar. The pulsating air had ceased. The only sound was the churning of mercury in the well.

She looked for her sandals, she'd lost them during the fall. With a floor so sparse that only left one option. Thessalia sighed and leaned over to check the well. She caught the last glint of gold as the mercury swallowed her shoes.

She was miles underground with one working arm and now she was barefoot. The mercury started to ripple and shake. If she was the plaything of some alien force, she might as well humor it.

The mercury congealed into a bulbous oval just larger than her own head. The lump split across the middle and opened, forming a faux mouth lined with ridged teeth. Above the jaw a pair of long swept angular protrusions emerged, taking the place of where the eyes would be. They trembled with a faint vibration, reacting to some unseen force. The rest of the mercury animated and began to rise and reshape.

Thessalia took a step back from the pool.

The mercury continued to bubble and shift, rising higher from the pool. The head now sat on a pair of heavyset shoulders, a muscular body and arms forming beneath them. The mercury fluctuated in anatomical accuracy. One moment it was only the vague shape of an arm, the next it mimicked the layered cords of muscle with perfection.

Thessalia was backing away from the thing in earnest now. She yanked off one of her blood vials from her neck and spoke words of power to it. The contents swirled, taking on a turquoise hue. She held the vial, primed to toss, waiting for the mercury to separate from its source first.

Spare the head ornamentation the thing bore an uncomfortable resemblance to her father. Finally, it managed to pull itself from the pool. Instead of a tail the thing slithered forward using dozens of tendrils moving in concrete.

Thessalia pitched her vial at the base of the thing. There was a snap followed by a rush of cold air. The thing stood frozen in place, ice crystals rippling across its surface. The supporting tendrils crumbled and the thing clattered to the ground, shattering into pieces.

It was a momentary success. The mercury was already melting, coalescing.

Thessalia ran.

The halls were short and curved at right angles. She couldn't see more than a few feet in front of her. The sloshing noises of the mercury thing echoed behind her, never revealing its true distance.

Fleeing through the twisted halls Thessalia glanced at a number of aberrant things in her peripheral vision.

A giant malformed head locked in a web of chains spewed purple slime and alien dialects at her as she passed.

She turned another corner to face a tall thing made of bony arms linked together by strands of tar. She slid on her heel and sprinted in the opposite direction.

She ran underneath a mirror bound in red ropes hanging over the path. The reflected hall hosted mob of humanoids she couldn't see occupying the real one. Something in the mirror reached out to her reflection and she felt it brush against her shoulder.

She flew down a stairway and passed a cage with a human-faced horse shouting at her. "Let me out! I can give you any treasure you desire. Release me back into the lands beneath the moon!" The beast had giant eyes and wore a twisted grin on its face.

Thessalia looked back. The mercury thing was splashing down the stairs.

Around the next corner, there was finally an archway showing signs of fatigue. Thessalia grabbed her second vial and chanted to it. Passing under the arch she tossed the glass at the aged stone. The vial shattered and the blood inside ignited. The shockwave knocked her on her stomach, her ears rang and her head throbbed.

The stone was crumbling. Heavy slabs of rock fractured and fell into the corridor, sealing it shut.

Thessalia grinned and returned to her flight. If she was lucky she could find something to deal with that thing. She took another dozen steps before she felt something cold around her ankle.

Thessalia landed flat on her face. Her bad arm surged with pain. She rolled over to see the cascade of mercury seeping through the rubble, an outstretched strand grabbing her leg. The fluid was cold to the touch, with a burning sensation at its edge. She felt her legs go numb as the fluid sank into her skin.

She grabbed her last vial. Shouting into it the light died out, replaced by a turquoise blue. She hurled the vial into the darkness. There was no sound of shattering glass, no snap freeze, only a silver glint streaking through the dark.

Thessalia felt a thick metal hand wrap around her neck. All she could see was the faint outline of the thing a hand's length from her face, the blue vial suspended in its head.

Thessalia pulled out her knife and plunged it into her arm, dragging the blade from elbow to wrist. Blood poured from the wound as she shoved the remains of her arm into the thing's chest. The hall echoed with every conceivable incantation of transmutation. Acids, poisons, accelerants… she tried everything.

The mercury beast hardly seemed to notice the apothecary she was transmuting inside of it.

Thessalia couldn't feel her arm anymore, her throat burned in terrified frustration. What did the thing want with her? She'd already be dead if that was its wish. Cold lines of metal traveled up the veins of her arm.

The mercury around Thessalia's neck expanded. The fluid washed over her chin and clung to her cheeks. It poured itself into her mouth, the metal was tasteless as it slithered down her throat, forcing her to gag. Next, a pair of narrow streams flooded her nostrils, then her ears.

She thrashed helplessly as the metal washed over her face, finally pushing its way into her eyes. Thessalia struggled for a while as the mercury infested the whole of her form. She finally went still as the bitter cold consumed her, fading into nothing.

CHAPTER
22

The sun boiled high above Thazgarr. He was hanging high above a featureless landscape, nothing but sand and sky. Hot blood drenched his arms, flowing down his body. He craned his neck to see what wounded him this time.

Both his arms perforated by a set of thick metal nails. The piercings each ran clean through his bones, pinning him to the side of a massive stone pillar. The pillar had no visible summit, disappearing into the clouds.

Thazgarr looked back in front of him, to his surprise a man now hung on a second pillar opposite him. The man had dark skin and a physique to match Thazgarr's. Painted on the man's chest was the sigil of a cobra piercing a man's skull.

The strange man opened his eyes, revealing a set of slit pupils. The man let out a hearty, mocking laugh.

Thazgarr screamed in rage. He didn't know why. He only knew that man had to die.

He braced his legs against the pillar and pushed with all his strength. His arms tore and popped each time he freed a pair of nails from the pillar. With each nail through his arms he grew colder, but he grew closer to the man. Thazgarr was only inches away from the man's throat, the source of that insidious laughter. His palms finally tore free from the pillar. He lurched forward and wrapped the mangled remains of his hands around the serpent-man's neck.

The pillar lurched. Somewhere beneath that was a cacophony of noise. The pillar listed and fell.

Bitter winds bit at Thazgarr's wounds. his hair whipped at his face as he plummeted to the dunes. All he could do was throttle his enemy as hard as he could.

Finally, the laughter stopped. The corpse had a satisfied look on its face, grinning, eyes rolled back.

The pillar struck the dunes, and Thazgarr the pillar. His shattered body rolled into the sands where it lay limp. Thazgarr looked off into the sky, basking in the silence.

He noticed that the sun was larger than usual, in fact, it was growing larger. The sun filled Thazgarr's vision. A dark spot appeared at its center. The spot grew and began to radiate a black ichor that spread across the sky.

Thazgarr realized the sun wasn't growing, it was getting closer. The ichor writhed in the flames as they neared Thazgarr. The hateful light embraced him wholly, everything was light. Thazgarr clenched his fist and swung it forward.

Ricard yelped and rolled over the side of the wagon, his body limp. Thazgarr awoke to his clenched fist cast against the morning sun.

Ricard staggered to his feet. "I probably didn't deserve that".

Thazgarr gave his arms a once over, searching for the wounds from the pillar. "No… you probably didn't."

Thazgarr found his hand drifting to the cool metal of the silver dog head he found in the catacombs. There was something calming about the bust. Its ice blue eyes, while harsh, offered relief from the reds and browns of the dunes. A piece of abandoned beauty from a bygone age. Yet there was still something not correct with the statute. Only together could the others manage to carry the metal. But to him, it felt like little more than driftwood.

He was over thinking a sorcerer's trinket.

Thazgarr grabbed his club and joined the others for breakfast. Willem had a piece of cloth wrapped around his face. "Not permanent, is it?" Thazgarr asked.

Willem took a bite of orange. "Generally no. Temporary flash blindness isn't uncommon where I'm from. Best case, it'll clear in a day or two."

"Speaking of eyes."

Willem went quiet. Blind or not, his eyes locked on Thazgarr. "What did you see?"

"Bad dream. Killed a man, then a giant eyeball in the sky swallowed me."

"Golden fire and black goo?" Willem asked.

Thazgarr scowled.

"That's what was attached to the naked old man we crushed last night. It paid me a visit too. Had my flesh peeled off by my Centurion. The eye was watching from a torch."

Thazgarr looked to Dylus. "What did you dream of last night?"

Dylus scratched his chin. "First I had a dream about swimming through dead bodies, then one where I was in a tavern run by a talking dog." Dylus went back to eating.

Thazgarr opened his mouth, but words failed him. He attempted this twice more before asking Ricard what he saw.

"I didn't dream about anything, not that I remember. I'm still concussed," said Ricard.

"It was us two that actually killed it," said Willem.

Thazgarr scowled. "A sorcery that transcends death."

"Unfortunately it might be more," said Willem. "We found something in the back room of the temple. There was an engraving hidden underneath a mural. It'd be as old as the temple itself."

"The eye," said Thazgarr.

"I didn't realize it at first, but after staring at the outline it burned into my eyes for a few hours. The resemblance is uncanny."

"Then what is it?"

Willem shrugged. "When I was a boy, there was a crazy old man who would preach on a street corner. One of his favorites was screaming about the secret gods who hid from us. He said there are as many gods as there are stars in the sky. It could be one of those."

Dylus presented a roll of papyrus. "I got a rubbing on the way out."

"Burn it," said Willem. "We should stay as far away from that thing as possible. Let it be a weird thing we agree not to talk about."

Dylus looked to Thazgarr.

Thazgarr shook his head from side to side. The eye was dangerous, but would it actually grow bored of them if they ignored it? Plenty of the gods Thazgarr had heard of seemed content to ignore mortal affairs, Sidoth among them. Sidoth. The divines were a mystery as old as time itself, aberrant and hateful. But it could be a pathway to that devilish scaly god.

Dylus reached into his pocket and pulled out two rolls of papyrus, one blank, one with the rubbing. Thazgarr pointed towards the blank. Dylus cast the substitute into the fire, pocketing the rubbing. The campfire crackled.

Willem's posture relaxed. "Thank you."

Caution, while proving its value time after time in the last few days, would only take Thazgarr so far. If the unnatural wisdoms of those unseen could lay Sidoth's secrets bare before him he would seek them. Slaying everything with a drop of Sidoth's blood may be unattainable. But if the god could bleed after all…

The bodies of the Damu'yhig were strong and countless, but their hearts seemed to be off one. If these eldritch secrets could reveal Sidoth's heart, the heart of his people, Thazgarr may find a way to stab at it. Aspirations for another time.

There was still the matter of his dream. The dark-skinned serpent-man. The battle standard of Ur emblazoned upon his chest. Could that have been Ur or a means to find Ur? Thazgarr committed every detail of the man to memory. The lines if his face, his eyes, his laugh, his dying smile.

Why would the eye show him this? Was it offering him insight? Given that it decided to nail Thazgarr to a pillar, perhaps it was threatening him. The god could be toying with him. They couldn't take the Eye lightly. It had tried to kill him once already.

Thazgarr skewered a piece of meat and dangled it in the fire.

Ricard took a seat next to Thazgarr. "I made you something." Ricard dropped one of his giant cobra skulls into Thazgarr's lap. The inside of the mouth was smooth. A series of leather straps ran through bored holes. "Made a guard for your bad shoulder."

Thazgarr grinned. "This will strike great fear into the scale-skins. I like it."

"Figured I owe you something for getting us out of the catacombs."

"Well met, friend. I'll think of you every time I ram into something." Thazgarr pulled his meat skewer from the fire, the flesh still red.

"Sure you want to risk that?" said Ricard. "The fresh meats we grabbed are borderline at this point."

Thazgarr tore into the piece of flesh. It's sweet flavor danced along his tongue, all the way down his throat. "Suspect meat is a better gamble than trail biscuits."

Sraac studied Dakar's remains. His friend had chunks of his chest and head blown in. The wounds were similar one he'd seen on casualties who fought the Ecrecians. It was likely a product of some western discipline of alchemy.

Dakar should never have been in such a situation. Joining a kill-team doesn't mean going off on your own. Dakar was smarter than that. Disobeying a direct order had led to his death. Sraac adjusted his mask. Dakar's death was a failure of his leadership. It'd be a sin to let such a redundant tragedy happen again.

There were other matters to attend to. Sraac dropped to one knee. He probed at one of Dakar's chest wounds with a dagger and felt the distinct reverberation of metal on metal. With some delicate maneuvering of his knife and a finger, Sraac pulled a metal disk from his friend's corpse. Wiping away the blood, he found himself holding a silver coin with Ecrecian lettering.

Sraac's mind raced trying to find some reason in the act. Was the Ecrecians implying they would destroy the Damu'yhig financially? Were the kasair of some other group trying to cover their tracks? No suitable answer came to mind, no logical reason to kill a man in such an illogical way.

Sraac turned the coin over in his fingers. If he had killed the Ecrecian when he had the chance Dakar might still be alive. By the same token, the Ecrecian and his team might have killed him. It was sheer luck the alchemicals detonated when they did. Four on one wasn't a fight he could win, even with Mont's support.

It was a bold move, attacking the temple with such minimal support. Sraac didn't know if that entire evening was a lucky blunder or a calculated maneuver. There was no consistency to the Ecrecian. He infiltrated the temple, killing no less than four men. Then he wandered into an archer's kill-box trying to negotiate using an expendable as a shield.

Given that the Ecrecian walked out with his ally and a bag of gold it was a fair gamble that he knew what he was doing. He had an unyielding level of field-craft. Sraac couldn't leave such a chaotic man to wander the dunes. Once his head start was complete, Sraac would be hot on his trail, assuming the Ecrecian honored his end of the contract.

A faint burning smell wafted through the air. Mont climbed onto the roof. A charred hand adorned in familiar gold bracelets was stuck through his belt.

"Damn it," Sraac said. The Ecrecian would get his extra day. Lest Sraac dishonor a contract in Kadar's name.

"Khas is dead, arrow to the chest. The lesser child in his charge had its head smashed in."

Sraac had lost his share of soldiers over his career, but he'd never lost three in a single day, much less to the same enemy. "Which way is the Ecrecian's group going?"

"We spotted their cart heading south late last night."

Sraac tightened his fist. "They're headed for Lux."

Lux was the closest thing to a trading hub in all Sidoth's territory. Anything traded in the region was bound to pass through it at some point. And now there was a foreign insurgent heading for it with a small war chest full of gold.

"We don't have time to imprison the remaining workers. Send word to the Damu'yhig that Xent is ready for retaking."

"That's another matter. We surveyed the remains of the rebel hold. Most of the local population was being held there. The bulk of the city's able-bodied farmers died in the blast."

Sraac clenched his fist. The hide of his glove creaked under stress. "How many?"

"We aren't sure, heat fused most of the corpses together. It's also probable that some turned to ash and scattered in the blast. Getting an accurate number will take some time."

"Let me rephrase that. How many do we have left?"

"In our sweep of the city we've found less than a hundred, including children and wounded."

"What about the granaries?"

"We believe the rebels moved their stockpile to their base of operations. It caused a dust explosion when the alchemicals went off."

The grain yields made possible by Xent's aquifer system were a critical asset to the Damu'yhig. The farming efforts in Lux and Khepresh amounted to little more than novelty projects. Things to expand their minds and focus their sorceries. They wasted all that soil on exotic hallucinogens and stimulants from faraway lands. It was the lazy way of freeing themselves from their kasairan suppliers.

Every inch of soil wasted on such frivolities was another conceded to a foreign power. The Damu'yhig were apathetic as long as servants were docile and food was plentiful. If the death of Xent wasn't enough for them to realize how vulnerable they actually were, Sraac didn't want to think about what it would take.

"Ready the horses. The moment the sun passes the horizon we're after them."

Mont snapped a salute and went about his business.

It would take time to retrain a workforce. The kasair would have years of influence at this point, regardless of what Sraac did. He needed to mitigate any further damage from the Ecrecian. Sraac ran his fingers across his dreary eyes. If his gods had the slightest regard for their children they'd strike the Ecrecian dead before he set foot in another one of their cities.

Sraac started over the wall but paused. He looked back at Dakar's perforated corpse. He'd go before Anu Sidoth with metal in his heart. It wasn't the worst death. Sraac pulled a glass vial no larger than a thimble from his belt, the leftover alchemicals. He dumped the glass over Dakar's body. Chemicals mixed with the air and flared to life. Fire embraced to the corpse.

"Rest easy, friend."

CHAPTER
23

Arri appreciated theatrics but even she thought the serpent-men's ziggurat was overstated. They stuck their big black eyesore of a temple on a plateau to the north of Kadar's River. The rest of Lux resided to the south, the two connected by a stone bridge.

The original bridge was a single arch of sandstone carved out by the river. With time the bridge fell into disrepair. The serpent-men had to renovate it with new stonework every so often. Today the bridge was laden with centuries' of gaudy patchwork of conflicting styles.

Arri grasped a granite column, one of a pair. The carved supports looked like a series of upturned snake heads eating each other. The snouts made perfect holds for what was otherwise a dangerous climb.

She clung to the stone when a gust of wind blew by. She hung halfway up the column. Done right, a fall from this height into the water wasn't lethal but it'd still hurt. The wind cleared and Arri continued her ascent.

Howellin was making sure she earned her title, the little prick. First, he says she can't use non-converts because the mission was too important. Next, he goes on about how he couldn't offer help since it would implicate the Ashborne. Maybe he wanted to see her fail. The tragic but expected end of a half-blood reaching too high.

Fuck the captainship, she'd get it done by herself, just to see the look on his face when she did.

Bits of rock dusted Arri where the new work didn't quite fit with the old. The top half of the bridge had three lanes. The sides were white marble staircases meant for servants and half-breeds. The center lane was a ramp made of polished black marble wide enough to fit the *Whale Hound*. It was intended for the legless Damu'yhig, but in practice it was used for carts and litters. Scaling the steps daily would be more than enough activity to keep a normal person in good health. Of course, that was only the case for a select few.

Arri looked out over the city. Lux was laid out like a bird, peasants and paupers to the south by the feet. The wings ran parallel to the river, the docks running along their northern edge. The west wing was home to the assorted markets, skilled laborers, and the human guard barracks, with a healthy number of brothels scattered between them.

The bridge ended between the wings in a part of Lux known as the Scales. It was the ward for the lesser serpent-men and those the Damu'yhig considered useful. Scattered among the Scales were marble towers. Their gilded bronze roofs shined bright, visible from miles. Probably where the city got its name. The district was walled off from the rest of Lux, had its own force independent from the city guard. All coldbloods. That could be an issue depending on where the garden was actually located.

Arri never ventured too far from the docks. Legal or not, anything she needed was never more than a stone's throw away.

She hooked her heel on a stone carved snout and swung to the other side of the pillar. As she pulled herself around a corner the ziggurat came into view.

From beneath the bridge, all Arri could see was the base of the ziggurat. It was a windowless slab of basalt spanning four hundred feet in either direction, a slight taper at the edge. The slab looked about two hundred feet high, smooth finish, impossible to scale. The shapes of more ornate stonework peeked out from the edges but that wasn't Arri's problem.

Beneath the ziggurat rested another hundred feet of smooth plateau. The perimeter lined with ballistas, catapults, and sorcery platforms. Narrow holes dotted the sandstone base, either air shafts or arrow slits. The scale-skins had more than enough time to hollow the damned thing out.

Arri's eyes fell on the set of heavy bronze doors built into the cliff face. Countless years on the river had left them tarnished, cracks running along the surface. At the bottom of the river was a mass with similar proportions.

Arri indulged herself with the fantasy of sailing to the plateau and blasting away. With the proper arms, the *Whale Hound* could have that fortress spread open wider than a two silver whore by lunch. Her dream faded once she noticed a spiked flail the size of a carriage built into the overhang, ready to drop at the pull of lever.

The Damu'yhig definitely knew a thing or two about fortress building, but nothing that looked like a garden. Were the damn snakes stubborn enough to try farming poppies on top of a ziggurat? If Howellin was honest about how much of the stuff they were going through they'd need more space. Arri shuffled over to the west side of the pillar.

That's where she saw it.

Past the west end of the plateau in the floodplain stood a new wall, no more than twenty feet tall. It looked hastily constructed. Water, privacy, and easy access. The perfect spot for a private garden.

Arri swung back to the south side of the pillar, striking the statue's nose with her heel. As her weight came to rest on the stone it gave out beneath her.

Her hands scraped against the rock as she clung to it, her elbows snapped taught. Arri probed for another foothold, easing herself down gently this time.

The snout shaped rock tumbled end over end, plummeting into the river. Instead of a splash, there was a thunderous racket beneath her. Careful not to shift her weight too hard again, Arri risked a glance.

At the base of the column was a fishing boat, a local model they called a dhow, with a curved sail. Water spouted from a hole in the deck. Fishers scrambled back and forth trying to plug the hole.

It wasn't long before another boat hailed them, a third turning in the distance to provide aid. Enough boats circling the column and it'd only be a matter of time before someone looked up.

The penalty for defacing the image of a serpent was severe. Arri understood she wasn't hard to pick out from a crowd. Since neither black powder nor blades agreed with water she'd swam out to the pillar unarmed. Best for everyone she wasn't noticed.

Shadow was her best cover. Arri swung to the west side of the pillar. Here the wind had left its mark on the column, the snake heads eroded to smooth bumps. Arri clutched the rock in her fingertips and began her descent. Bits of sand came loose from the pillar with every step. Wind swirled around the pillar blowing the tiny grains in every direction.

Arri narrowed her eyes, the sand bit at her face, filling every crease of her ear.

Another boat was coming, a barge carrying guardsmen. On the plateau, coldbloods were making rounds. She was right between them and the clusterfuck that would undoubtedly get their attention.

"Shit," Arri whispered under her breath.

Arri pushed away from the rock. She pulled her hands to her chest and braced her legs. The wind rushed past her, whipping her pale mane in every direction.

A two-count later Arri felt the impact in her knees. The river's cold embrace replaced the bitter sting of desert air. Above her, the boats were little more than shadows in the blue. Outlines peeked out over the sides, searching for the source of the splash.

Arri pushed herself deeper, blending in with debris that littered the bottom of the river. She felt the pressure on her ears, a fair sign she was deep enough. She kicked off the pillar for a boost. The currents were stronger than usual thanks to the moon. Anyone smart enough to go looking for Arri would gamble on her heading downstream. Arri cut into the current at an angle. It more than doubled the distance she'd have to swim underwater. Every stroke brought her closer to the wall, but her lungs burned harder. It wasn't far now.

As she stepped onto the edge of the river the trick of the wall became clear. They painted the bottom half of the wall to match the floodplain, the top blended with the dunes on the horizon. Arri could have passed it a thousand times on the docks and been none the wiser. Wouldn't do that without a reason.

Arri scurried to the base of the wall, hooking around to the west end. No alarms sounded. For a while she walked along the wall, counting her steps. The wall ran the entire width of the floodplain curling back into the base of the plateau.

Mismatched sandstone blocks jutted out at regular intervals. Hand holds were narrower than the pillar but they were solid. Arri scaled the wall in seconds.

Poking her head over the wall revealed a garden unlike any she'd ever seen. Rows of freshly tiled silt covered the garden from end to end. Poppies, ergot cultures, mushrooms, things Arri couldn't even name, were all segmented into neat rows taller than Arri, taller than most people even.

The operation put the fleet's hydroponics barges to shame. All this was for a handful of scale-skins? It was too much. This had to be the start of an operation.

A clattering noise echoed above her. A rope lift was descending from the plateau. A pale mass of scales slithered back and forth between a pair of bronze outlines. Arri dropped back behind the wall.

Had they seen her?

Arri bolted for the river. The silt sucked at her boots leaving a trail anyone could follow. If they did spot her it'd be moments before alien forces came pouring over the walls. She dived back into the river.

This time Arri used the current to put as much distance between her and the garden as possible. Her full-bodied strokes carried her along the riverbed with great speed. The next moment, bright orange scales clouded her vision. Arri thrashed, trying to grab hold of the beast, break its neck or something. But no matter how she flailed she only struck water. This had to be some conjured beast commanded to drag her to the bottom of the river. But she felt nothing.

Where did it go? Arri spotted an orange snake no bigger than her thumb wriggling through the water. A moment later it disappeared into the blue.

Arri surfaced under a dock. Gasping for air, she gripped the piling. With every breath she felt her strength return. Arri peaked out from behind a piling. No magics seemed to follow her across the river.

Two close calls in less than an hour, she needed to do better. Coldbloods might be easy pickings, but a sorcerer, not so much. Especially if the shriveled old hags from the fleet were any indicator.

Arri had never been comfortable around the crones, wasting their days away packed in tubs of ash. Hidden deep within their dreadnaughts deliberating over god knows what. Still, the ability to conjure a firestorm wouldn't go amiss right about now. Though whining about what she couldn't do wouldn't get her anywhere, is wasn't a bad base for a plan.

Attention was still on the fishing boat, the barge towing it toward the east end of the docks. Not a regular occurrence, based on the spectacle. Good enough of a distraction.

Arri climbed onto the dock and continued like nothing had happened.

Spare the sinking dhow everything else was business as usual. Boatswains tossed guards bags of coin to overlook certain crates. Guards passed the gold back to dock masters for certain crates to disappear. Deckhands staggered back and forth between taverns and brothels. Children scurried through holes in rotted warehouses. Some with loot tucked under their arms, others with looks of terror. On one dock a crowd gathered around a pair of rat-looking things squaring off in a knife fight. She passed another three fights and a live squid eating contest before reaching her destination, a two-story building.

Arri stepped into Jack's. The tavern was built from the scrapped remains of ships. Sections of mast formed support beams. Walls were a patchwork of different hulls nailed together.

The bar and shelves were a broken keel and a shark jaw bigger than Arri hung from the rigging overhead. The whole place smelled of sea salt with a healthy tinge of booze.

Arri wrung the last bit of moisture from her hair. "Jack, yeh old son of a bitch!"

A bottle came hurtling at Arri from behind the bar, whipping end over end.

She snatched the bottle an inch away from her temple. She pulled the stopper with her teeth and took a drink. "Wait till after I had a few next time. Where's the old man?"

Behind the bar stood a green-skinned girl with a lean build. Years ago Arri made the mistake of joking about her throwing arm. Since that fateful day Arri hadn't been able to enter Jack's without something flying at her head. By now she was certain Glasha only kept those bottles behind the counter so she could throw them. She couldn't complain too much since she usually threw good stuff.

"Dad's around back, I'll get him." Glasha stepped out from behind the bar and disappeared behind a piece of canvas.

She was middle child of the Snars, a trio of sisters in Jack's employ. Exactly why they all called Jack a variation of "father" was a mystery to Arri. Jack never mentioned having children when he served under her mother. Not that they looked anything like him—weren't even the same species. A long time ago Arri decided the answer wasn't worth having anything else thrown at her.

Jack stepped out from the back. Time was finally catching up to him. Gray crept through his neatly trimmed beard and into his blond hair, which had thinned into a V shape at his brow. Lines formed along his forehead accentuating his rugged features. The lingering smell of leather followed him.

"Arriha." Jack's voice was coarse from a life of shouting orders.

Arri hated when people used her full name. It made her feel like a child being scolded. Ironically, years of exactly that was why he got away with it.

Jack took a seat next to her at the bar. "How's your mother?" he asked.

"Still a bitch." Arri took another drag off the bottle and passed it to Jack.

"Same as the day I first set foot on her ship." Jack took a swing before setting down the bottle. He glanced over at Glasha. "I thought I asked you to stop throwing the expensive bottles."

Glasha sulked. "They have a better spin."

Jack rolled his eyes before returning his attention to Arri. "Anyway, I'm sure your mother only means the best for you, probably. So what brings you up river?"

"I need to borrow a rowboat, a nondescript one."

"Ashborne shit?"

"Can't say." Arri didn't like lying to Jack, not that she could.

"It's Ashborne shit."

"Either way I need that rowboat."

"Tell me it's not that little shit who put you up to this."

Arri bit the corner of her mouth.

Jack pinched the bridge of his nose. The decade of practice he had reading her was on full display. "Please tell me you looked over the commission before taking it."

"Promotion to a full captainhood in service to the Crow."

"Your mother pledged service to the fleet. Did you even research the difference?"

Arri shrugged. "Howellin said it was an old loophole."

"An old loophole…" Jack scoffed. "Did it ever occur to you that the Ashborne might have changed the practice for a reason? That Howellin had his own reason to slip this through back channels?" Jack caught himself before breaking into a shout. "I guaran—*goddamn*—tee you he could have had you on the shortlist for captains with half a dozen signatures. If he wanted."

"I need to do this, Jack."

"That's the other thing. Howellin is bound to have his own little group more than qualified to handle whatever this is. So what does he gain from you sticking your fucking neck out?"

"Yeah, he's a damned snake!" Arri snapped. "It's not a question of *if* he's gonna pull some shit, it's a matter of when. I'm not gonna waste my life taking every little fuckin' roundabout because it's safer." Arri made her way to the door.

"The boat will be out back after dark," Jack said.

Arri turned to face Jack. "Thank you."

Jack still faced the bar. "Just be safe. Need anything else?"
"Got any oil?"

CHAPTER
24

Willem watched the vague silhouette of Ricard's hand pass over his face. "Better, but I'll leave them on a while longer."

"Fair enough. If we're attacked try and look intimidating, I guess. A lot of the time a blind man in a confident fighting stance will scare people."

"You ever get tricked like that?"

"No, we kicked the living shit out of that guy. Try and face the right direction."

The wagon creaked as Ricard crawled over all the miscellaneous goods they'd packed in it. While the things they took were plenty valuable they were also slowing them down. Every minute they wasted on gold they might make was another the Masked One could use to catch them. It didn't leave much room for comfort in the cart, either. Willem hardly got any sleep with his face mashed against that kasairan rug.

Not that the sleep he was getting was any good. The others barricaded the temple basement with anything that didn't fit in the cart. That wouldn't do much to keep the Eye out of their minds.

The dream had shown him Centurion Vanrikker. This

meant one of two things. Either the Eye had free reign of his memory and could do as it pleased within his mind, or Vanrikker survived and the Eye was taunting him.

From what history he knew, nothing good ever came from a physical manifestation of the divine. Countless scars marked the lands. The blood spatter on the moon, craters of glass, the titanic bones that littered the seas. There was no way to blame the gods with certainty, but what other force could inflict such wounds upon the lands beneath the moon? These entities, whatever they are were, were best avoided, and the Eye was no exception. Willem hoped the dream was some type of abstract warning to keep away from it, to stay out of its gaze.

"How much longer?" asked Willem.

"A few more days," said Ricard. "We want to stick to the packed dirt. The pythons and subterra have a hard time moving through it."

Today the sun was particularly unbearable. All Willem could do was lay on his gut in the back. Sweat soaked the fabrics of his head wraps.

Either from boredom or delirium, he kept wandering back to that burning building in his mind.

Should he even care? The Eye didn't lift a finger to stop it. Their own people committed similar acts. Even if they didn't, the Legion would commit a similar atrocity if they ever reached Xent. If fate was real those people were always doomed to burn in that fire. There was nothing he could have done. But that same reasoning doomed Willem to whatever horrors were waiting for him out in the wastes.

No, life didn't make enough sense for fate. A god's prompting or not, the serpent-men carried out a crime against their own countrymen. Acts of the gods were heinous and unaccountable. The acts of mortals, less so.

The sun was finally setting. A reprieve from the heat, if only for a few hours. Willem set his head down. Maybe tonight he'd drift off to sleep.

There was howl. He bolted upward, spear in hand.

"Only a coyote, go back to sleep," said Thazgarr.

"Coyotes don't come this far out east," said Ricard.

There was a frantic shuffle punctuated by the sound of a crossbow cocking.

The weight of the wagon rocked as if someone was standing, moving.

"Skin-walkers," said Thazgarr.

"They have those here?" asked Dylus.

"Seems so. Keep the cart moving. There isn't much light left."

The reins cracked, the wagon sped up. Willem wasn't ready and fell flat over. He pushed himself back to his knees and braced the back end of his spear for support. He aimed his spear out at what he hoped was the back of the wagon. Might as well try to look threatening.

The wagon rattled along the dirt. Spare the sound of pounding hooves and creaking wood the caravan was silent. The quiet went on for what for what felt like hours. It felt like the void magnified every little sound a hundredfold.

Willem heard a dry crackling behind him. Then there was scraping along the side of the wagon, ending in another brittle crunch.

No one else reacted. Had they been stricken dead? If there were skin-walkers out there had they coordinated a perfect simultaneous strike? No, they'd already have Willem if that was the case. Something more mundane. "Shrub?"

"Shrub," Thazgarr responded.

Willem steadied his breath. Paranoia might be getting the better of them. Plenty of people disappeared from frontier towns. There was never any solid proof that skin-walkers were to blame, but rumors got around.

Tribes of cannibal sorcerers hiding in their victims' skin. Now that he thought about it, it sounded like a way to keep children indoors after dark. That or a justification to get some arclight towers built out east. There were countless explanations that made more sense, though. It was a shame the man with a giant eye embedded in his chest had to skew Willem's perception of reality the way it did.

"Lanterns," said Thazgarr.

Willem bit his lip. If the sun had only set this was going to be a long night. Willem felt the heat of the lantern on the back of his neck—a token comfort.

Ricard cleared his throat. The wastelander was back and to the right. Thaz mirrored him on the left. That accounted for everyone, assuming Dylus was at the reigns.

The rattling chaos of the wagon went smooth. The horse's hooves muffled to a dull thud, the stressed grinding of wood on wood now a mild creak. They must have hit the sand.

Willem gripped his spear tight. The smoky smell of cheap oil flooded his nostrils. In the absence of natural sound, he thought he was beginning to hear his own heartbeat. There was a *thwack* to his left, followed by the labored grunts of Thaz resetting his crossbow.

"What did you see?"

"Wild dog of some sort."

"Did you hit it?"

"Not sure."

A chorus of howls poured out. The shrill cry seemed to come from everywhere. The howling was so loud Willem could hardly hear the tirade of profanity coming from behind him.

The reigns cracked again and the wagon lurched beneath Willem. He lost balance and fell, landing face first on something hard.

His face was hot with pain. He pushed himself back to his knees and felt for his spear to no avail. They were carrying too much useless shit. Willem shoved his hands into the horde, grasping for the familiar haft of his spear.

The sounds of arrows and bolts whistled through the dark. Dogs howled and barked from every direction. "Protect the horse!" someone cried.

Willem continued his search. He knew how useless he'd be, blindly swinging a spear out the back of a cart. Still, he felt like he needed to do something. His hand came to rest on something cold and fleshy. The unpreserved meat they took.

The flesh was a feast after escaping the Eye. But without any time to salt or smoke the leftovers, it was little more than poison now. Willem tossed the meat off what he hoped was the back of the cart. The sounds of the dogs faded back into the distance. Occasional yelps punctuated the whistling of arrows.

"What did you throw?" asked Ricard.

"Easier meal."

Willem found his spear and took a seat.

They drove the horse for a good while and got some distance from the dogs before resting for the night.

Thazgarr and Dylus were asleep by the sound of it. Ricard was either keeping watch or a quiet sleeper. Willem sat in the center in the center of the wagon, spear in hand, staring into nothing.

The night returned to an unnatural quiet. Willem could count the number of times he'd experienced such silence on one hand. The bustling city of Vestinus, hectic Legion camps… he'd always slept fine. Even in the past few days there'd been enough noise to put him at ease. Tonight there wasn't even a sandy breeze. The wastes had already proved too dangerous for silence to mean safety.

Without that spiteful fireball in the sky, the wastes were freezing. In the black Willem wondered how big the moon was tonight. If there was a sea of pale light, or if he was as surrounded in black as he felt. The sun might have been unforgiving, but it was reliable. Unlike that fickle orb of silver that came and went as it pleased.

The wooden bed of the cart shifted, lowering in the back. Someone must have been climbing out to piss. No, the movement was too subtle. Ricard wouldn't bother climbing off the carts. The others were still snoring. Someone behind him wasn't climbing out of the cart.

Whatever was before him was swift. It hadn't made a sound in this unnatural silence. If Willem tried to raise an alarm the thing would be at his throat before the others woke. Would sound even come out?

The wagon bed flexed again, ever so slightly. It was in the cart with them. Willem remained still, lest he provoke a reaction.

Another step. The creature must have either believed Willem asleep or simply helpless, an easy meal. He'd only have one chance to prove the creature wrong.

Another step. Willem swung his spear wide, imitating the grip Thazgarr used with his war club. The spear cut through the air without any resistance.

Willem keeled on his side, unable to counter the force of his swing. The spear rounded behind him and clattered against something solid.

"What the shit?" Ricard shouted. "You don't need to use a fucking spear."

"There's something here."

The wagon shifted again, likely as Ricard was searching an area. "I don't see anything."

"Neither did I. I felt something moving in the cart."

"And it didn't occur to you that if you pack four grown men into a wagon there might be some movement?"

"It was too quiet." As he spoke Willem realized the breeze had returned. Sand shifted and the sparse cries of wildlife resumed.

"You're delirious. You're on edge after whatever you saw in the temple. Combine that with the whole skin-walker thing and no sleep and you have a firm foothold in insanity. Drink some water, get some sleep, You'll be better in the morning." the wagon buckled as Ricard dropped back into his spot.

Ricard might be right. The Eye was unlike anything else he'd ever seen. Things like that should haunt the forbidden corners beneath the moon, not hide in church basements. The chances of two separate aberrations existing in close proximity to each other should be unlikely, less so among people. Again, the way the serpent-men lived made a little more sense.

A bird of some sort cried out in the night. Did the creature carry silence with it? If that was the case the thing might have been following them for hours. The noise was back. If the creature was real that must mean it was gone.

There was still the possibility this was all a bad dream or the sick taunting of the Eye. The wastes were full of madmen, perhaps he was acclimating.

Willem ran his thumb along the edge of his spear. He paused. It was faint, almost unnoticed. At the tip of the blade there was the faintest drip of a warm liquid, no more than a teardrop worth. "You bleeding?"

"No," said Ricard, before drifting into a light snore.

Willem sat there awake until he felt the morning sun on his face.

CHAPTER
25

"Someone tried to train you on the chamber pot before you were ready, didn't they?" said the stranger.

Sraac aimed his crossbow between the stranger's eyes. He seemed a mixture of human and something else. His skin was a peculiar color, not unlike some of the more exotic clans of kasair. That's where the similarities ended. His hair was an amorphous black mass. From corner to corner his eyes were a dull purple. He carried no obvious weapons and seemed unbothered by the number pointed at him.

Sraac and his Otomi stopped by a watering hole to refresh the horses when the stranger appeared. The man was studying a balisk skeleton no less than a few steps away when Mont noticed him.

"Why are you here?" asked Sraac.

"Water."

"Why are you here in the holy domain of Sidoth?"

The stranger shrugged.

"Nobody sneaks into an encampment without reason."

"There are plenty of things in this world without reason, in all likelihood our crossing will mean little to either of us. As for sneaking in, I was already here, you all just failed to notice me."

Sraac's finger danced near the trigger. "You're doing a terrible job at convincing me not to kill you where you stand."

"I have no say in that."

"How so?"

"You didn't shoot me when you spotted me, nor when I insulted you. You aren't a creature of impulse. Barring any significant change, you've already decided whether or not you're going to shoot me."

"So which do you think it is?"

"Whichever makes you feel more in control."

"You think I'm a petty tyrant of some sort?", said Sraac.

"I believe you latch on to things you can control because so much of your life is either chaos or in the hands of someone else."

Sraac stood quiet for a moment. "You make wild assumptions about someone you only met."

"You aren't that unique an individual. A bit hesitant for someone in your line of work. Something you'd care to talk about?"

"With a stranger I found out in the desert?" said Sraac.

"Who better? We have no idea who each other are and likely won't ever see each other again. Whatever we say will mean nothing beyond the value you give it."

The offer was strangely appealing. Sraac couldn't remember the last time he spoke to someone for a reason besides fulfilling his duties. He lowered his crossbow. "Go check for others." The other warmbloods traded looks before dispersing through the camp.

The stranger took a seat on the ground, producing a canteen. He downed a mouthful before offering it to Sraac.

"I thought you came here because you needed water," Sraac said with a hint of suspicion.

"That's not water, not sure where it came from."

"How do I know that isn't poison?"

The stranger glanced at his canteen. "Hasn't killed me yet."

Sraac shimmied the spout behind his mask and squeezed.

The liquid burned his throat, fumes scorched through his nostrils. He held back a wretch at the vile fluid and returned the stranger's canteen.

"You don't drink much do you?" The stranger continued draining the canteen.

"Only when necessary. Blending into crowds and the like."

"Again it comes back to your work. Tell me, do you find this life rewarding?

"Yes."

"Okay, now why is it rewarding? Do you enjoy special privileges?"

"It's an honor to serve in the name of Anu Sidoth."

"That answer was quick. Now, did you choose this as your life's work, or were you chosen for it?"

Sraac hesitated. "I was chosen for this."

"By whom."

"Another Child of Sidoth."

"And you trust their judgment?"

"Completely."

The stranger tilted his head. "Completely?"

"They are infallible." Sraac thought back on the severed head decorating Xent's gate. "I don't like where you're treading, stranger."

"I didn't think you would. No matter how special you think someone is they can fail like us. In my experience the worst thing you can do is put someone on a pedestal, makes the fall worse," the stranger said.

"They don't make mistakes. To suggest so is sacrilege."

"Well, I can see why it's such a touchy subject for someone in your position. Anything else you'd like to share that won't warrant my death?"

Speaking to the stranger was a mistake. "No… Yes. I made a bad choice, others died for it."

"Bystander, a person you know?"

Sraac thought back to Dakar's mangled corpse. "Both."

"Are you also above reproach?"

"Not even close," Sraac replied.

"Was it only your decision alone that brought death?"

"Some of them would be alive if they listened to me."

"Well, that brings us back us back to where we started. You're tearing yourself apart over what you can't control in a life you didn't choose."

"So that's my problem?"

"You'd take offense if I explained the full breadth of what's wrong with you. Wouldn't listen either." The stranger squeezed the last drops of alcohol from his canteen. "How about this, try investing yourself in something as far away from your work as possible."

"Like what?"

Again the stranger shrugged. "Pottery? Find a girl with poor personal boundaries? I don't know, the idea is for you to pick something."

"I'll consider your wisdom, stranger. May I ask you a question?"

"Wouldn't be fair if I said no after all that."

"What are you?

"A drunk old man who's misplaced."

"No, *what* are you?"

The stranger checked his canteen again. "I'm a lot of things you don't have words for."

Sraac remained silent.

"Didn't think you'd like that answer either. I don't know, call me an Umbral. Probably won't set off any alarms." The stranger staggered to his feet. "Aga Anzillux is due east of here, right?"

"Lux is southeast, Khepresh is to the northeast."

"Right. Well, it's been a nice a little chat. Best of luck."

Sraac nodded. "May Anu Sidoth watch over you."

"In my years, I've found that the lucky ones go unnoticed by the gods." The stranger wandered out into the desert, headed west.

Mont approached Sraac, bow in hand. "Shall I shoot him, sir?"

"I won't condemn the act."

Mont drew an arrow. The stranger was twenty paces out, a clean kill. Before Mont loosed his arrow his arm went flailing back, arrow still between his fingers. The bow snapped forward and reverberated in his hand. Sraac looked over. Dangling from the bow tip was its string, its loop frayed and torn.

"Have you not bothered maintaining your gear?" Sraac used an even tone.

"I replaced the string before we reached Xent." Mont looked like he could feel the glare behind Sraac's mask.

"Don't let it happen again." Sraac rose to his feet. "I want us ahead of the Ecrecian by sunset. If you need anything, do it quick."

"I can take a group southwest. Pressure their flank while you run them down," said Doz.

"No. They wouldn't risk the loose sands unless they had a plan. We'll cut across the Devil's Bowl. If they're headed for Lux that'll put us a day ahead."

He was met by silent stares. The Devil's Bowl, Anu Shurpu as the Elders called it, was a cursed place. It was said that it appeared in an instant, striking all who witnessed it blind. All that remained was a crater of pale green quartz fused from heat. Any scholar brave enough to study it succumbed to illness within a decade. The curse waned with time. The last death was over a century ago. The dunes had since reclaimed the bowl. These days, just the rim would be visible above the sand.

Still, the superstition was enough to give the rest of his party pause.

"What do you fear more, a superstitious old hole, or a god you know is vengeful?"

The Otomi fell back into step. Men gorged on whatever rations they could. Khazra plunged his tail into the sand, pulling it back with a lizard skewered on the tip. The chimera put their backs to everyone else. Sraac heard the wet tearing of flesh from bone.

Mont pointed to the stranger shrinking in the distance. "What about him?"

The madman made a strange amount of sense in his ramblings. Making up a name for his species on the spot may have been a cause for concern. He was heading away from anything of consequence.

"Leave him. If Sidoth desires his death the dunes are more

than able to accommodate. Praise Anu Sidoth."

Thazgarr scratched at his chin. The noon sun reflected an orange tone against the sands. The dunes were steep in this part of the wastes, not unlike the mountains he'd seen as a boy. They kept the wagon low, avoiding the peaks and anything that might spot them.

The Ecrecian was sleeping in the back. He'd muttered something about skin-walkers at breakfast before passing out. The unnatural beasts were cowards, attacking the blind and unconscious. Had the Ecrecian's paranoia not got the better of him, they all may have awoken as vacant fleshy masks for dark things. Again, wit, cowardice, and discipline overcame strength.

These skin-walkers must be exceptionally fearful. Warriors of his tribe claimed the foul creatures would continue a hunt even with pierced hearts. Perhaps this was an aspect unique of the skin-walkers in the wastes. "Dylus, you said something about your lands also having skin-walkers. Tell me of them."

Dylus put a finger to his chin. "Not much to go on, I guess. Sometimes people who go out into the rough come back different… wrong. Like they forgot how simple things work. They'll pick things up fast but there's always that adjustment period. After a while, they try and convince people to leave town with them—hunting trips and the like. It's nothing out of the ordinary until you think about it. Once people start asking questions they disappear for good. That's what I've heard."

"Have you ever witnessed one yourself?" asked Thazgarr.

"I've never seen a live one. Not exactly. When I was a boy a child went missing in the mangroves. A search party went out looking for him. The next day they brought back a body but it wasn't the boy. Said it was following them through the trees before they shot it. It had a lanky body covered with bone spurs, wore a wooden half mask where its eyes should be. They tried to pull the mask off but the damn thing wouldn't budge. They strung the thing over the doorway of the pub like a trophy, or a warning. They put another volley of lead in the thing for good measure. Next morning, it was missing."

It matched the creatures elders warned Thazgarr of as a

boy. "Teeth like a wolf's?"

Dylus shook his head. "When they pried the mouth open it had rows of tiny dagger teeth going all the way down its throat, like a leatherback."

"What's a leatherback?"

It's a breed of sea turtle with a horrifying maw of teeth."

Thazgarr nodded. "What is a sea turtle?"

Dylus raised an eyebrow. "Why are you fascinated with the terrors of a far-off continent?"

"Our skin-walkers are durable. If the Ecrecian scared one off, what does that mean about them?"

"That they're weaker?"

"But why would they be weaker?"

"They don't like sand?" said Dylus

"Nature. They're deprived of nature. It must weaken their sorceries."

Dylus ran his fingers through his hair, freeing a bit of trapped sand. "Thazgarr, I fail to see how identifying the proportionate strengths of a skin-walkers will benefit us."

"What do you know of sorcery?"

"That if I had it, I'd be living a life of nothing but silk, wine, and warm flesh."

"My elders warned of the things that granted such knowledge—dark, wrathful things. The weakened skin-walker, perhaps it means there's a way to deprive the scaled devils of their sorcery."

Dylus blinked. "Are you still on about that whole killing all the snake people thing? You are a daft cunt."

"Perhaps I am." Thazgarr itched at his chin. Sand and sweat clung to the hairy thicket.

"Chin hairs getting not fun?"

"Awful. My people weren't bred for heat."

"I grabbed something for that back in town." Dylus crawled back into the wagon bed. He returned with a pot and strips of fabric. "For everything that's shit about this pile of sand they do know how to make a good wax." Dylus poured the wax into the strip and handed it to Thazgarr, gesturing for him to apply it to his beard.

Thazgarr smeared the concoction across his face. If the exile spoke the truth, the wax would be the simplest way of free himself from his soaking tangle of a beard. The stubble had been tolerable to a point, but once his beard began to curl and wicked with sweat, the tangle had to go. "Are you sure this is how it's done?"

Dylus pressed a piece of paper to the wax. "Don't think about it. Just yank before your chin realizes what's happening."

Thazgarr tried not to dwell too much on that last part. He took the edge of the wax strip and pulled. The wax wasn't unlike having the hot knife pressed into his shoulder. The pain subsided as it came. The exposed swath of his chin pulsed, red and sore, cold with fresh exposure to the air. Small bits of wax clung to his face.

Thazgarr looked at the wax strip, which resembled a dead vermin. Half a dozen strips later and the back of the wagon look like it belonged to a fur trapper. With a wipe down, his jaw hung clean in the desert breeze, mismatched in color from the rest of his bronzed skin. Grains of sand stung the fresh skin.

"So, what do you think?" asked Dylus.

Thazgarr nodded in approval. "Less trouble than the brew of animal fat and oil the westerners use."

Dylus smiled. "Can't cut your face open on wax."

"It's impractical. To carry all that shit for a clean face… Sharp knife and some warm water is all you need," said Ricard.

"And leave a fresh notch in my flesh every time I look a little scruffy? Wax is the civilized man's way of grooming. Waxed myself clean not a day ago, not a cut nor burn," said Dylus.

"You still have your beard," said Thazgarr.

There was a pause, and then for some reason Ricard started giggling. "Bad move. In this heat your sweat's all gonna trickle through your ass and into the seat of your pants. You made yourself a shit flume."

Dylus scowled. Both men had points. The wax was quick and thorough but would leave one exposed to uncontrolled circumstance. The blade was more practical, precise. But it had to remain sharp, otherwise, a miscalculated movement would cut the wielder. It was also much slower, much less gratifying than tearing off a mass of unwanted growths at their roots.

There had to be some ground between safety and satisfaction.

The flow of the dunes had shifted. Whether through the churning winds or since unseen force the paths flowed west to east. If they wanted to keep south, they'd have to start crossing over high dunes.

The cart bobbed in a rhythmic fashion. Thazgarr imagined the sensation of riding aboard the ships he'd seen on occasion. In their time his people only risked a handful of trips to the sea, hoping to collect its bounties. But in these wastes, there were no bounties on the faux waves, only a sickening feeling. Thazgarr decided to go on foot for a while.

Walking was by no means desirable. Only preferable to spewing precious water into the sands. Climbing the dunes was a labor. Until now the even terrain of the gullies spoiled them, Thazgarr included. It was a far cry from the jagged hills surrounding the Ebonthorn. The last time Thazgarr did any meaningful climbing was at the oasis. The sand gave way beneath his bulk. Full strides would take him at most half of what they would on flat ground. The only respite was the slide into the next trench.

Thazgarr shook the sand from his boots. "How much longer to the river?"

Ricard shrugged. "Coyotes pushed us back into the dunes. If the terrain stays like this, another day or two."

Thazgarr looked off in the horizon of trackless dunes. A tall peak stood out among the others. Thazgarr started in that direction. "I'll find us some good flat dirt."

With more than a little effort, he plodded up the hill. From the peak he watched the sea of sand that surrounded him roil. Layers of grain sheared from the dune face and danced in the air and set back down on another mound. The process played out hundreds of times a minute as if it were an elaborate dance. Funnels of brown and orange swirled together, creating shimmering towers of gold cast against the sunlight. Moments after the ephemeral treasures manifested they'd scatter back into the wind only for another to take its place. For such an alien, hateful place the wastes had its moments.

At the edge of Thazgarr's vision was Kadar's River, visible through the dancing sands. It was massive, big enough to accommodate the handful of sea-ships he had seen in his youth. The long stretch of gusty sand between Thazgarr and the river howled as if it were challenging him.

A few miles out to the west, visible over another tall dune, was a red patch, a swath of rock or clay. Whatever it might have been it was flat. If they took that path they could reach the river before nightfall.

Thazgarr slowed to a walk a few strides away from the caravan. "There's a clear path to the west."

Before Ricard could answer their horse reared in panic. In the corner of his eye, Thazgarr spotted something moving beneath the sands. Before he could say anything the horse charged. Ricard pulled the horse to the right before it plowed through Thazgarr.

The wild man hurled himself into the back of the wagon as it passed. He rolled over the side and landed on something soft. Willem let out a tirade of confused curses, struggling beneath Thazgarr's bulk. "Rats!" he shouted. A strip of Thazgarr's beard stuck to his hands.

"Stay down, Ecrecian!" Thazgarr grabbed Willem's spear and faced the back of the wagon.

The wagon made good pace in the trench. The wind at his back. It would have been refreshing if it weren't for the grains of sand stinging his neck.

Behind the wagon, sands bulged, too big for a python, too small for a subterra. A chitinous creature sprung from the dunes snapping at the wagon. It plunged back under the sand. The beast had a body of armored segments, like a string of barrels. Countless twitching appendages wrapped around the body pushing it forward regardless of orientation. The jaw split into four flaps at the center, each lined with hooked teeth. There was the vague outline of a cranium and snout mixed in among the teeth. The beast had no discernible eyes.

Dylus stumbled over to Thazgarr with his bow. "Why is it only after us now?"

"Must have thought the wagon was a basilisk. Caught on

when Thaz scouted ahead," shouted Ricard.

"Clever bitch." Dylus loosed an arrow into the sand. The shaft plunged into the sand and snapped.

Thazgarr readied the spear. "Wait for it to surface."

The creature breached again. Thazgarr lunged the spear forward. His foot slid across the wagon. The treasures from the temple shifted under him. The spear went high and missed the head. The beast sank its teeth into the wagon's rear.

Wood cracked and popped as the beast tore away part of the cargo bed. Splinters blasted in Thazgarr's face. A pair of boxes fell off the back and went spinning end over end into the sand.

The wagon hit a bump and sent Thazgarr tumbling toward the hole. He crashed in the bed, splintered wood ground into his chest. His head whipped, striking against the wagon's axle.

He flailed around for something to grab hold of. His hand found some cold piece of metal sitting in the bed. Careful not to catch his mane in the axle, Thazgarr pulled himself up. Back on mostly solid wood, Thazgarr looked to see what his hand rested on. The piercing blue eyes of the silver dog head stared at him.

Thazgarr rose to his feet. Spear in one hand, silver burst in the other. He could pitch the statue again in the hopes that it would smash the thing under its fickle weight. But the beast was agile. Should he miss he likely wouldn't have a chance to recover the strange treasure. He placed the statue behind him, in the front corner of the cargo. Thazgarr thrust the spear forward again, ready to kill.

Every time the beast rose he gouged at it, forcing it back under the sand. Fresh wounds riddled the creature's maw. Sand stuck to the fresh blood. The beast's skull must have been thick. Piercing the brain would be a challenge.

Thazgarr changed his grip. Next time he'd let the beast in close and bring all his weight with the spear.

The sand behind the wagon was calm. Had it given up? "Where is it?"

"Left!" someone shouted.

Up in the dunes the sand bulge writhed alongside parallel with the wagon.

Solid ground was close—one more hill. If the horse could

hold out a little longer he'd be rid of this damned beast.

"Will someone please tell me what the shit is going on?" shouted Willem.

Before anyone could answer, the beast breached from the dunes. Its arc was high and it's body fat. It plunged forward at the wagon.

Thazgarr's mind sharpened to a razor's edge as he took in every detail around him. The beast seemed to hang in the air, moving for the horse. Sand splashed across its hide. Its teeth sparkled in the sunlight.

Everything was painfully slow. Thazgarr felt like he was underwater as he pulled Ricard from the driver's bench.

Its teeth sheared through the horse and back into the sands. The next segment of chitin crashed into the wagon. It catapulted the wagon's cargo forward into the dunes. Thazgarr counted the others, assorted weapons, and the remaining loot among the debris. The flight was still in that same adrenaline slowed pace where he could do nothing but wait.

Willem had flipped upside down and was tearing at his blindfold. Ricard's face had contorted in a warped scream, twisted by the unnatural angle of his flight. Dylus was wide-eyed, flying with his hands at his sides like a javelin.

Finally, Thazgarr felt his back hit the sand. Things seemed to resume their regular pace.

Dylus had landed head first, half buried in the dune. Ricard was digging him out. That left Will.

The legionnaire pulled off his blindfold. The blacks of his eye were wide, unresponsive. His face contorted in pain before clamping his eyes shut again.

Thazgarr pulled Will to his feet and thrust his spear back in his hand. He faced the Ecrecian in the right direction. "There's solid ground over the dune."

Willem took off without so much as a nod. Dylus followed behind him.

Loose goods and wreckage littered the sands around Thazgarr. Anything that wasn't crushed was at most a stone's throw away. He grabbed all the gear he could, his war club, the crossbow, and the idol, and slung them across his back.

Ricard frantically dug through the wreck trying to salvage something.

The beast pulled the remains of the horse underground, a snack for a beast of that size. It wouldn't be long before it returned.

The beast had no eyes. The chances it relied on scent was also unlikely since it was subterranean. That left it with few other reliable ways to track them but feeling them through the sand.

Thazgarr grabbed a pair of the remaining crates, one under his arm, the other balanced on his shoulder. He turned to Ricard. "Grab a crate!"

"Are you mad? There's no way we can carry all this away from that thing."

"No matter what we do something won't make it!"

The little man shrugged and grabbed a box.

Thazgarr bounded up the hill, each stride taking him closer to the peak. Will and Dylus disappeared over the crest, more panicked screaming followed. Thazgarr looked back in time to see the creature disappear back under the dunes. It hadn't caused that panic—not yet.

The dune leveled out enough for Thazgarr to look over the side. Before him was more a sheer drop than a slope. Through a trick of perspective, the red rocks were a farther drop than Thazgarr anticipated.

There was no skid trail. The others must have plummeted over the side. They were still moving, though they wouldn't be happy. A problem for a different time.

Thazgarr tossed his crates over the ledge and hopped over the edge, Ricard doing the same. After a fall that was a little too long for comfort, the sand curved enough to accommodate an awkward run, more fall than a sprint.

One of the three crates shattered where it landed. The other two caught the sand on their corners and bounced. The momentum of their fall shifted forward with the slope. Now they were barreling forward, rolling right past Dylus and Willem.

The sand slope tapered back into the ground where he and Ricard caught up with the others.

Willem heard his footfalls. There was a scowl on his face.

"Send a blind man running off a cliff!"

"Keep moving."

The four of them made a mad dash for the rocks, six counting the pair of crates tumbling along with them. One in three odds this would work. The red stone was close.

The beast breached, swallowing a crate whole and disappearing back under the sand.

Thazgarr let a grin slip when he leaped onto the rocks, the others close behind him. They were even lucky enough to still have the last crate, a simple recovery once the beast gave up.

They came to rest a few dozen strides from the edge of the stone. The rocks burned hot as a skillet in the desert sun. But nothing would be attacking them through it.

The creature breached from the sand. It came crashing just short of the group, forcing them another dozen strides away.

The pale thing flailed in rage, it's legs useless on solid gorund. If it was as susceptible to heat it would be regretting its decision.

Those who were able drew their bows. The beast thrashed head to tail as shafts peppered its flesh, leaving cracks in the stone.

Thazgarr fired one last bolt, to no effect. The beast's hide was too think for the feeble shaft to penetrate anything vital. Thazgarr dropped the crossbow and grabbed his club.

The beast was a single raging cord of muscle, but it still had a skull and a brain. It flailed at random, thrashing itself against the burning stone. With a little study, a rhythm emerged. If he could avoid the tail he might have a chance to strike its head on the back-swing. It was all a matter of if he could swing hard enough.

Thazgarr took a step forward. Something was slowing his progress. A pair of hands locked around his arm. He pushed forward. Another pair wrapped around his other arm.

"Let it go," someone said.

Thazgarr pushed forward. "It must die!"

"It's not even a serpent, it has legs."

"It's close enough."

An elbow hooked around his neck and began to squeeze. A cloth of some sort chafed at his neck. "Thaz, if you go near that thing you will fucking die. It will crush you and send everything inside of you spraying from one of two places."

Thazgarr dragged everyone another step forward. The weight wouldn't have been a problem a few days ago. His body was in tatters from nonstop use. His burning muscles faltered. He tensed his neck against the chokehold but the pressure continued. He fell to his knees. Everything was going dark.

The beast had managed to flail its way back to the dunes. The wounded beast sank back under the sands. Had it not been for the other's betrayal, He could have killed it.

The sbeast was but a blur sliding into the dunes. Gone.

With his last moments of consciousness, Thazgarr let out a blood-curdling roar. He felt cold streaks running down his face. His rage only met with silence, and he collapsed to the ground as the blackness took him.

For what felt like days Thessalia felt nothing. A black void with only the faint sensation of existence. There was a spark and she could finally see herself in the darkness.

Thessalia became aware of every cell within her body. Every hair, drop of blood, every spark of energy that flowed through her form. In an instant her every nerve caught fire, growing, expanding. It was tearing her open and grafting new pieces onto her spirit. It felt as though her chest was spreading into a pair of thunderous wings, reaching out into the beyond. A wave of energy washed across her phantom form. Her mind, body, and soul aligned into what had become the center of a pulsating web of cosmic awareness. Then, as this new awareness emerged, she receded back into the abyss.

The hilt of a dagger emerged from the dark. Absent any other options Thessalia grabbed hold of the blade. Light rushed back her surroundings.

She found herself standing in a tavern opposite a man with deep blue skin and luminous purple eyes. In one hand she held a scroll, in the other, the knife plunged into his heart. He seemed accepting of the wound. With little more than a push, he fell limp to the floor, his blood soaking into the wood panels. Thessalia bolted for the nearest doorway.

She shouldered her way through the door, blinded by the sun. She was standing on the deck of a ship now. The waves were a pale blue mirroring the sky with no clear boundary between the two. A salt-scented wind blew through her hair.

Miles away waves crashed against the jaws of a mountainous skull, the Sky Tyrant's grave.

The gentle rocking of the ship put her at ease. The whole scene was like a vibrant parallel to the trackless and churning dunes of her native lands. For a moment Thessalia felt a strange longing for this place. Homesick for something she never actually had.

She heard a voice call out. She turned and the ship was gone. She found herself kneeling atop a stone pillar, waves swirling around her. Howling thunder split the air above. The swells would crush her, yet she felt no fear. She clasped a copper staff in her hands, only they weren't her hands. They were pale like her own, but they had callused confidence in them, forged through a lifetime of use.

From end to end, the staff had the diameter of a large coin, each end narrowing to a sharpened point. Foreign runes covered the staff, giving it a peculiar texture. An immense power flowed through it. Despite the staff's countless engravings and raised inlays, it felt comfortable within those hands. Every finger fell into a snug grove as if the staff was crafted for them.

The swell came crashing down, sending her cascading into a dark blue abyss. Currents pulled her every which way. Every manner of sea life real or imagined passed her by. There was no sense orientation, no bubbles escaped when she exhaled in a bid to find which way was up. Despite every violent swell, the hands clung to the staff, refusing to lose it to the currents.

As her lungs were ready to burst she spotted a black orb many times the size of what a whale would be. Then another, a third, fourth. Glinting black orbs continued to appear along with a gaping maw in the seafloor. The maw unleashed a cloud of hot ash that blotted out the sea. Already on the verge of drowning, she sucked in the slurry of seawater and ash. She wretched and choked in the blackness, flailing until she struck sand.

Thessalia lurched forward on to her hands and knees,

spitting out the vile concoction. She hacked and winced, draining every ounce of fluid from her lungs. When she regained her breath she noticed the thick tail of a Damu'yhig in front of her. Looming over her was the muscled silhouette of her father.

The ornate woven metal and leather of a slave collar tightened around her neck. Her father reached over and hooked a finger in the collar, dragging her into the basalt ziggurat of Lux.

There she suffered an endless stream of indignities. Petty tasks such as organizing alchemicals faded to sacrificial bloodlettings. He ran experiments on how the various concoctions of rare herbs and venoms affected the mind. Father was tireless in inflicting exploratory horrors on the body that she occupied. Was this sadistic vigor a detached curiosity, or something more?

Thessalia dangled from a chain, the stranger's pale hands red and bloody against the metal. A single toe dragged across the floor looking for purchase to ease the strain on their arms. The smell of waste was thick in the air. Beneath her ran a rudimentary canal filled with waste. It also occurred to her that she was occupying a man's body.

He was an excellent specimen, regardless of his species. What her father had done was akin to smashing a work of art for his own petty gain. Her ears itched. Thessalia closed her eyes, hoping to hurry along to the next part of this bizarre torment.

A gentle hand caressed their face, a mixture of pity and something else. The hand slid past their face and weaved its way into the thick wavy locks of this form's hair. Part of Thessalia wanted to recoil. For her many threats and boasts she'd never actually known the flesh of another in an intimate way. But this body relished every bit of it.

A slender tongue traced across their lips, probing every little detail. With little resistance, the tongue slid right into their mouth. The tongue rolled across their own, its forked tip exploring all the way to the edge of their throat. The nimble appendage toyed with their own, probing, savoring every taste. A set of needle-sharp teeth bit the corner of their lip, drawing blood. The tongue withdrew and licked the blood clean before probing toward their neck.

A clawed thumb massaged the pointed tip of their ears.

Thessalia felt burning desire spread through the stranger's body. His need and hers were becoming one.

They embraced the lithe form opposite her and pulled it into an embrace. Their hands explored every curve of the body before them. A tail caressing their legs and braced against the small of their back.

Two became one. Thessalia whimpered as the tail tightened. Their body and its partner undulated together with a playful rhythm.

Thessalia did everything she could to keep the stranger's eyes closed. The voice that whispered filthy ideas in their ear was too familiar.

Still, waves of pleasure rolled over her. She'd lose control. The rhythm increased. Claws dug into their back. She tried to pull away, the pleasure overpowered all reason. The stranger's face mashed against a heaving breast. The sweet taste of flesh drifted along their tongue. In a last ditch effort to escape this corrupted pleasure, Thessalia bit down. Their bodies went rigid, passion overtaking them, spilling over.

The stranger's eyes went wide. Leaving Thessalia with the sight of her mother writhing in ecstasy. Thessalia averted her eyes whichever way she could. Unfortunately, her mother's bedchamber had a mirrored ceiling.

At her knees lay her mother, heavy of breath and with a bleeding breast. Her own gaze was met by an unnaturally pale kasair with night-black hair. Thessalia forced their eyes shut again and pushed herself off the bed.

She plummeted into a mound of sand. She was back at the mouth of Ilupagru, but she was still the pale one.

The kasair's expedition was much like her own, give or take a few turns. The Pale kasair traveled a different path, one she didn't recognize.

They set the copper staff aside and took a seat along the wall. For the longest time they sat there Thessalia felt tears stain their faces. For whatever trials of this man's life she'd lived she could only guess at what drove him to tears now. Hopeless regret… What changed that it would break him now?

From somewhere the Pale kasair produced a knife and

plunged it into their throat. It felt like someone holding frozen metal to her neck. Blood bubbled in their throat and pooled in their mouth. With their dying breath they whispered something garbled in blood Thessalia could understand. "Feh ah uh." Their vision darkened to nothing. There was only cold.

Thessalia felt the cold stone pressed to her face. She tried pushing herself to her feet remembering the sordid condition of her arm a moment too late. The slash along her wrist had closed, no immediate danger of bleeding out, but back to starving to death. Was that the work of the mercury beast? No signs remained of that particular assailant. A curious thing it was.

Her eyes adjusted to the dark and she spotted the outline of a glass vial laying in front of her. She half-heartedly muttered at the vial setting it alight with a ruby red glow. She was in an octagonal hallway.

The light washed over the curves of a skeleton laying against the opposite wall. Absent the physical or mental strength to recoil Thessalia studied the bones. Draped in the tatters of a stained green and gold tunic, the bones lay still. The skull had long since fallen into its own lap, resting atop the rusted remains of the dagger. Still clutched between its arm bones was the copper staff, still brilliant as it was on that pillar in the sea.

Thessalia took the skull in her hands and traced the lines of its features. High cheekbones, a harsh jawline, all familiar from a lifetime of daily routines.

She undid her headdress and her black hair unfurled into smooth locks. Her dagger-pointed ears shivering in the cool air. She rested her father's skull against her own and began to weep.

CHAPTER
26

"Wine?" offered Ricard.

"I'll take water," said Willem.

"Last of the water went with the cart. The box we saved was all wine, that and one of the gauntlets."

Willem was already blind and dehydrated. Thazgarr hadn't caved in the back of his head yet but that likely wasn't too far off. He waved his hand around until he found the wineskin. He took a long sip of the bitter liquid. "How do they even have wine here? We've been all over and I haven't seen so much as a bush."

Ricard slurped at the wine. "Pomegranates I'd guess. That or imports, not like the cities aren't already littered with kasairan goods."

"The kasair have a direct line to the serpent-men?"

"It's more of a 'we won't stop you from selling us nice things as long as you're quiet about it' type arrangement. The Damu'yhig might speak ill of the ash nymphs out loud, but I'm sure that behind closed doors…" Ricard paused "We'll go to Bottleneck sometime, it's a port town on the east coast. You'll see what I mean."

Willem didn't have to see. It was the same in Ecrecia. The nobles and the rich all pushed to keep the kasair at arm's length. But if you were to peel back a privileged sleeve there'd be plenty of kasair finery dangling from the arm beneath. Willem took a long drag off the wineskin.

"Port towns bring any bad memories?" said Ricard.

"Just thinking of all the time and manpower the Legions could save by slipping the kasair some coin. Deliver us right to the Lux's front gates. The Legion over-complicates everything."

"Seemed all right when I passed by… free food and steel."

"It's not free, they say it's an investment, and they expect to see dividends." Willem took another sip of wine. "They call us the coal that fuels the empire. I doubt half the nobility even knows how coal works."

"You're being dramatic."

"Every morning someone would wake with our centurion's pistol in their face. He'd pull the trigger then whisper 'Not today.' Then he would go about his business."

"That's interesting. How was he not regularly beaten?"

"Well, the thing about that is that he was. If someone managed to hit him before he pulled the trigger he rewarded them. Hit him after the striker fell and there was hell to pay."

"Which were you?"

"Neither. First few times I didn't react. It seemed random until I realized there was a pattern. He never went to the same block of tents twice before completing a cycle. Based on who got latrine duty for assaulting him I was able to work out a schedule of where and when he might strike. After a few sleepless nights, I got the drop on him."

"Bet he didn't like that." Ricard made another slurping sound, drinking more wine.

"That was the last time I woke up with a gun in my face. The next day he transferred me into the vanguard, so no, he didn't."

"I don't know about that," said Ricard.

"Then why would he bring me all the way out here?"

"He thought you could make it out here."

Willem scowled. "Everyone in the cohort, including him, is

dead."

"You're not. Seems like he had a better estimate of you than you did. For a group you seem to have so much spite for, you seem bothered by them all being dead."

Willem scowled in Ricard's general direction. "How much longer until we reach the river?"

"Not long. I was going to keep quiet until you fell in but you've had a bad enough day. Now I have a better idea."

Willem nodded, thinking back on the sensation of tumbling down a hill blind. "How's Thaz?"

"Still looks pissed. Hasn't stopped fiddling with that statute since we started walking."

"Better than fiddling with the club." He was confident Thazgarr would wait for his sight to heal before attempting some type of revenge. Best not to entice him.

The two men walked in silence for a while.

"So what's the empire like?" asked Ricard.

Willem wondered if Ricard was trying to deflect. "I thought you said you've seen the Legion before."

"Only out in the colonies, never been past the mountains. Always got excited when the Legion came marching through with new toys. Never could take my eyes off them."

"Ricard does seem like a western name," said Willem. "I'd hardly call it an empire after we lost the western continent. More a loose collection of colonies centered around a well-fortified city."

"And the protectorate!" said Dylus.

"You're only a protectorate because you're too damn stubborn to listen to directions." Willem turned back to Ricard. "Perfect example."

Willem felt Ricard's hand push against his chest.

Underfoot there was a tremble in the stone. A sound like thunder echoed in the distance. If it were actual rain there'd be a cool breeze along with it. Willem readied his spear.

A hand pushed his spear to his side. "You won't need that," said Ricard.

The thundering grew louder. A great many hooves. They sounded different on stone. Sand muffled the sound. They would blend into each other, creating the illusion of a single force prowling the dunes. On stone, every step was crisp and singular among the many. Wild chaos that could change at any moment. "Riders or a stampede?"

"Horsemen," said Ricard.

The clattering thunder of hooves drowned out anything else Ricard might have said. The noise surrounded Willem. It hammered at his ears. From what he could guess the horsemen were encircling them.

The clatter faded back into nothing. The clicking of a single set of hooves came from in front of him.

"Was your trip to Xent not profitable, my friends?" said a familiar voice. Akhil.

Based on Thazgarr's exchange, Willem surmised that he responded to strength. Not the best since he was wandering the desert blind and empty-handed. Best to throw in some catharsis.

"After a great deal of effort, the city was good to us. Our trip back through the wastes, not so much. I imagine there's a… something out there that's pleased with itself right now." Willem leaned on the haft of his spear for effect.

There was a pause, then laughter. "Come back to camp with us. We'll feed you for the price of the story," said Akhil.

The meal consisted of rice and a type of skewered meat. Willem assumed some local reptile breed. The meat was bitter but full bodied and dripping with fat. The tribesman passed around skins of potent grain alcohol. Willem never managed to swallow more than a trickle of the burning fluid when a bottle came to him.

Dylus kept the camp enthralled with the story of how he blinded the basilisk. The Strahlian had a way with words. Details got a little fuzzy when he got to the part where the Kestrels captured him. He threw in a sword fight to replace slaughtering the rebels.

Drunken revelry surrounded Willem. Discordant cheers and songs rang across the plains. There were songs about old victories against the serpent-men. Songs about killing invading Westerners. Songs about treasures hidden out in the wastes, ready for people to find them. Barring the songs about slaying legionnaires it was a pleasurable evening.

Willem had missed this.

There was the spitting sound followed by heat and a loud *fwoosh*. Willem rolled back off his seat to the ground, clutching his satchel. He wasn't sure how close the fire actually got but it felt like enough to worry about his black powder. Cheers and applause broke out. Was it some feat of sorcery?

"Fire spit, fire spit," cheered the group.

A party trick. Willem released the death grip he had on his bag. Was it the powder he was so cautious of or was it the bounty? It had to be a small fortune he was carrying, but not one he had any understanding of. Was the blood money something he could even spend?

The wastelanders seemed to care little for coin but in Ecrecia they'd stab him for a fraction of the gold he carried. He'd need to figure out the actual value of what he carried. Did anyone outside the wastes even take serpent-man gold? Exchanging the gold for liquid assets was his best option. But to move that much gold he would need a trade hub—another city.

Dealing with another one of the serpent-men's cities was the last thing Willem wanted to do right now. The wastes were no vast improvement. Other than periods of boredom, its only appeal was the absence of the burning dead smell.

Akhil's voice came from the spot next to him. "Everything to your liking, my friend?

Willem nodded.

"If I may be so bold, your Thazgarr seems troubled.

Willem shrugged. "I may have choked him out to keep him from getting crushed by the thing with the legs. It cost him his chance to cave its skull in. He's taking it personal."

"He is passionate about killing scale-skins that one."

"I don't understand him. He didn't come out here to die, but every time he sees a deadly situation he dives into it face first."

"Perhaps it's not that he doesn't value his life, but that he values something more than it. Take my people for example, do you think us incapable of a domestic life inside the walls?"

"No. It seems a choice."

"Safety, while it has a certain appeal, leads to some hollow days. Thaz will forgive you with time. But I doubt he'd do anything different should a similar situation arrive."

"I'll never understand wastelanders," said Willem.

"It's not for everyone." Akhil took a seat next to him. "We're sending rafts to Lux in the morning, trade away some of our extra meat. It's easier than walking."

Willem thought for a moment. "As bad a taste as Xent left in my mouth that's still the best offer I've heard in a long while."

The last place Willem wanted to be right now was another of the serpent-men's cities. Of course, that's where the nearest port would be. Still, better to be traveling with a few dozen men, especially in his current state. He would just have to keep his head low.

Chants of "one more time" and "again" rang out.

"The crowd wants an encore." Akhil's voice disappeared back into the crowd along with a chugging sound.

Cheers erupted as Willem felt heat along his face. His hand jumped to his powder horn again. The powder was too valuable to discard. But without a proper way of using it, the inherent danger continued to outweigh its value.

It was unlikely that he'd find a working flintlock Anywhere out here. And any place he did would also have more powder. There had to be a way to make use of it.

The grenade he rigged worked well enough, but those had other problems. Unreliable fuses, misshaped clay. He couldn't assume cobbled together parts would keep working.

"Ricard, you there?"

To Willem's right there was a sound of affirmation mixed with chewing.

"You mentioned something about crafting the other day. Have any experience with metalworking?"

Ricard swallowed. "A little here and there, I saw a forge on our way into camp."

"How drunk are you right now?"

"I can still walk upright," said the small man.

"Good enough. Still have that gauntlet?"

"Yeah. Why?" Ricard's voice was laced with suspicion and a hint of excitement.

"I have an idea you'll like. If it works I'll cut you in on the final product."

"Deal."

The feast was a generous offering in Thazgarr's eyes. It pained him to abstain from such bountiful helpings of meat and drink, especially today. But more important matters won out.

Thazgarr parted the flap of a tent. Inside sat an old man. He was by no means frail but age had still taken its toll. The tight cords of muscle along his body bulged with veins. He was bald, yet he sported a thick white beard that would put men half his age to shame. His defined chest existed at odds with rounded gut. The sound of cracking bones accompanied his every move. He'd made full use that body in his time.

Thazgarr cocked his head sideways. "I am told you're the tribe's spiritual adviser."

"Do I not meet your expectations, stranger?"

Thazgarr shrugged. "Where I hail from the spiritual leaders were… puny."

"The body and spirit are a reflection of each other. Neglect one and the other suffers. So how may I guide you, child?"

Thazgarr nodded in approval. "What do you know of gods?"

"It's said by some that there are more gods than stars in the sky. Any arbitrary force can have a god associated with it. I have no great archives or cathedral, but if the matter is of consequence I may have some guidance."

Thazgarr set a piece of papyrus between him and the elder. He opened it to reveal the rubbing Dylus had taken before they left Xent. "My friend witnessed a manifestation of this thing."

The elder's eyes widened. "This is an old god, very old and very wrathful. The visage you lay before me is that of the Weeping Saint."

Thazgarr folded his arms. "The eyeball was neither weeping nor saintly."

"The true meaning of the tears are unknown. It's how they describe the Eye's emissions, a common feature in its depictions." The elder traced his finger along the rubbing. The oval seemed to be shedding a type of ethereal tears, fire or smoke, like Thazgarr's dream.

"What else can you tell me?"

"Little. The Weeping Saint has no hymns or gospels, only simple declarations." The elder's hand drifted from the Eye to the runic script beneath. "I haven't the slightest idea what's actually written here. My predecessor said it is the simple promise of flame."

"So the spiteful little thing demands veneration under the fear of its wrath. I fail to see why anyone would bow before such a power," said Thazgarr.

"There's no such worship, barely acknowledgment. The saint makes few demands and claims even fewer followers. The only time the Weeping Saint permits acknowledgment of its existence is to placate the curious, like yourself."

"The entity wishes no one know it, yet it manifests before men, dancing through their minds. Again I fail to see how it is a saint."

The elder shrugged. "More generous interpretations characterize the saint as a protector deity, quietly dealing with threats beyond our understanding. Does the term 'outsider' hold any significance to your people?"

Thazgarr didn't understand why but his hairs stood on end. His head went light and he felt the coldest he had in weeks.

"You don't consciously understand, but that fear is ingrained in your blood. I like to think that means the saint is succeeding in its crusade. The last thing its scriptures permits me to tell you is that there are a great many things beneath the moon, and that its a miracle of mercy they escape our notice. Look hard enough and you might find something, but once you see it it cannot be unseen. And worse yet it will see you. And that completes this sermon of the Weeping Saint." The old man snatched the rubbing, crinkled it up in his mouth and swallowed it. "Is there anything else I can help you with child?" he said without so much as an acknowledgment.

Thazgarr decided not to comment on the old man eating the papyrus. "What do you know of Sidoth?"

The elder finished swallowing. "Nothing beyond the

common knowledge, punishable heresies and the like. Sidoth's Children deem all besides them beneath their father's wisdom. You'd have to find one of theirs if you want anything meaningful."

Thazgarr exhaled. "About what I expected." The Damu'yhig were obtuse for how fixated they were with their gods.

"Then how about this?" Thazgarr placed the silver idol down in front of him. He was confident the priest couldn't devour it.

"A local interpretation of one of the Death Wardens. Xohloto'bas if I remember. The idea of a Death Warden is self-explanatory, I assume."

"I didn't think death needed wardening. Does this Xohloto'bas employ priests the same way Sidoth does?"

"Child, when my counsel is sought out it's intended as spiritual guidance for people. Not guidance on the spirits. Is there a personal matter you'd wish to discuss?"

"No." Thazgarr grabbed his idol and turned to leave.

"Sidoth's Children have hurt a great many who walk this desert. A great many more destroy themselves lashing out. Taking revenge on Sidoth is like trying to kill a river. Swing your sword at the current all you want, even if you don't drown you'll only end up tired, sore, and standing in a river."

"Thank you for your insight on the ways of the gods, old man." Thazgarr stepped out of the tent.

Thazgarr watched as the feast raged on at the center of camp. Dozens of shadows danced in the firelight cheering and singing. On the periphery were the sounds of subtler debauchery. It was reminiscent of his own people.

Thazgarr looked at the stars. In the better part of a day his entire life had unraveled. Everything he had ever known was gone. Wandering the wastes with people he barely knew was the closest thing he had to normal. How much longer would that last? Once they reached a port? A faraway land beyond the sea was appealing in a strange way. A place far away from this cursed land and its memories. It would be a fresh new frontier to plunder.

Thazgarr's stomach burned. If he abandoned his vendetta here the memory of his people would fade into nothing. The scaled devils would repeat their atrocities over and over again unopposed.

Abandoning his quest would be no less a cowardice than if he had fled from the attack himself. That was cowardice he couldn't survive.

Not that he could survive too well on his own. Had he managed to tense his neck a little harder he may have dragged the other three to their deaths. Time and time again he wandered too close to death. He needed someone to aim him correctly, otherwise his would be short-lived revenge.

Again Thazgarr's hand drifted to the idol. The elder avoided his last question: if this aspect of death empowered his followers, gifted them with sorcery. The idol, or what it represented, seemed to have a strange fondness for Thazgarr. It could sympathize with his hatred for the serpent-men, though that would be an optimistic view. More likely it valued him as a possible tool, a way to further spread its domain. To spread death.

Muscle won petty squabbles but the sorceries won wars. For what he desired, Thazgarr couldn't think of a better patron on his path than death itself. But the god's aid had been spontaneous and at its own volition—if it was even real—rather than his mind twisting in upon itself. Tapping into such a force at will would take a great deal of time and discipline. This elder would be of no help. He'd have to find to a place of lore. The frail scholars lurked in cities. Perhaps this Lux would have a death cult hidden among the temples of Sidoth.

CHAPTER
27

The damn moon was full. It bathed the whole ziggurat with turquoise light. Arri wanted as little light as possible but she didn't have that kind of time. A patrol was bound to find the prints from her last visit sooner or later and that would only mean more coldbloods.

Arri swapped out her leathers for patterned canvas and a matching head wrap. She applied grease to her weapons to dull their sheen. Once they spotted her the coldbloods would eventually overrun even her.

The plan had started simple. Loop to the rear, and hop the wall. Then set the oil pots in a single pass and disappear into the river before the blaze started.

With all the dunes exposed beneath the moon she'd need cover to obscure her silhouette. The only option was the foliage along the river. Crawling through the floodplain was awful. Seasonal floods softened the ground and with every movement, more mud clung to Arri's form.

Every few feet the sled snagged on something new. Each snag threatened to send the dozen some odd pots of oil clattering across the ground. Arri wasted more time than she'd have liked bartering with different merchants. That way the scale-skins couldn't trace the pots to a single source. The only commonality was that each piece of clay had a wide neck. Plenty of surface area for the oil sloshing within.

Oil was another bottleneck. Lamps hadn't caught with Lux's public yet so good sources were on the scarce side. Jack had some leftover cooking oil, but that only got her partway there. For the rest, it was back to bartering, a fair deal harder than buying pots without raising a few eyebrows. The bulk of the oil came from a den of ill repute. Arri would have died of embarrassment if the owner asked what she planned to do with so much oil. They were kind enough to throw in some candles with marked burn times, though.

Despite the rattling pots, Arri made it to the wall without incident.

Arri retrieved a length of rope from the sled. She'd tarred it and fastened each end with a hook. She tied one end of the rope to her waist, hooking the other end to the straps of the sled. With the same grace with which she'd navigate the riggings of a ship, she was up the wall.

The opposite end of the field was dotted with torchlight. Bronze colored reflections danced along the walls. On the near side the coldbloods abandoned their posts to huddle around a brazier.

Arri took the rope in her hands and pulled. In smooth, even lengths, she hoisted her sled. A moment later she lowered it into the garden the same way, guards none the wiser. Arri undid the rope at her waist and wedged the hook into the wall. She brought her leg over the wall and slid into the garden.

Arri was on the move the moment her boots touched the ground. Basket in hand she darted into greenery, a menagerie of exotic vices. A quarter way into the field Arri buried the first oil pot.

The sheer volume of poppies still baffled her. Joined with the other plants this field could keep the entire city in a stupor for months. Why bother burning it? Even if they exported the lion's share they'd still be poisoning themselves better than the Ashborne ever could. Must be a control thing, just like all the Ashborne's other minutiae.

Arri grabbed the longest candle and a tinderbox of Ecrecian make. Inside was a bundle of pine dipped in wax then rolled in red powder. When Arri struck the tinder along the side of the box it sparked bright before calming to a dull red ember.

Arri touched the ember to the candle, a moment later a purple flame was licking at the wick. Gently, she placed the candle in the oil pot. If she'd timed the burn right it would be about ten minutes before the flame hit the oil, just enough time to set the others.

Arri crammed the ember back in its box for later. Despite their bullshit, the Ecrecians made some decent toys. Arri pulled some leaves over the pot and headed deeper into the field.

She repeated the process over and over again, each pot set with a shorter candle than the last. Timed correctly the flames would erupt in unison leaving the coldbloods little hope of fighting them.

Twice a coldblood wandered too close for her liking, its boot tearing through the mud. With every pass, their rumored ability to see heat became more suspect. It would see heat soon enough, though.

Two pots left. Arri pushed her way through a particularly thick section of brush. She found herself gazing into a pair of bright green eyes. Crouching opposite her was a coldblood chewing on a piece of cactus, its pupils wide. Juice dripping from its mouth.

The two stared at each other a moment. Did the coldblood think it was hallucinating?

The coldblood sprang to its feet and started running, Arri's hopes going with it.

Arri took off after it. Her hand moved for a pistol on impulse before she remembered where she was. Its armor was too thick for a knife throw. That left one option. Arri drew one of her swords.

The coldblood stumbled through the field, its armor clattering. The mud was working against it. With a running start, Arri lunged at the coldblood, burying her knee in its back. The pair came crashing to the ground. Arri buried her cutlass deep in the coldblood's skull, so deep that mud stuck to the blade when she pulled it free.

Guttural hissing cascaded across the field. Torches bobbed in the darkness. Coldbloods in every direction. There was activity on the plateau, likely archers.

Arri dropped back into a low crouch. The coldbloods would thin out into smaller groups, two or three per torch. Manageable, but it would draw more attention. She could make a dash for the wall, but that would put her at risk of getting speared.

Her best option was the rope, unfortunately, the bulk of the coldbloods were between her and it.

Arri doubled back to where she first saw the coldblood. The last two oil pots were where she left them. She dumped the pots and grabbed the ember.

The torches bobbed between the greenery, closer every moment.

Arri steadied her breathing. She slathered another handful of mud across herself, enjoying one last bit of cool air.

Torch fire peeked through the leaves. Gouts of flame crested over the field. Arri dropped the ember and drew her swords.

The ember ignited a blaze behind her. In the light, six coldbloods stood before her, shielding their eyes. Arri plunged each of her swords into a coldblood throat. She pulled her blades back, slashing them across an upraised arm, severing it.

She brought the blades into a horizontal slash at a torchbearer's head.

This one had a helm, same as the other torchbearer. The coldblood bowled over, a pair of gashes in the helm.

The fifth coldblood managed to thrust his spear.

Arri parried it to the side, stomped on its knee, then slashed the back of its neck. Its head slumped forward, hanging from a strand of flesh, spurts of fluid coming from the spinal cord.

The one with the dented helm rose, the other torchbearer at its side. Both drew their blades. Dented helm lunged first.

Arri thrust her cutlass forward.

It made no effort to dodge, taking both blades to the gut.

The coldblood embraced Arri, clutching her in a death grip. A bloody smile beneath the visor. The other torchbearer moved in for the kill.

Arri eyes were wide with terror. She thrashed desperately to free herself from dented helm's grip to no avail.

The other torchbearer moved to her side for a clean strike.

Arri couldn't escape, but the coat of mud afforded her some play. She waited.

The torchbearer stepped in close and aligned his blade with her throat.

Arri drew a pistol and shoved it into the torchbearer's visor, pulling the trigger. The helm rang as the lead ball ricocheted inside. Blood and brain poured through the helm onto its neck. Arri felt relieved.

Dented helm head-butted her.

There was a flash. Arri fell back into the mud her ears ringing.

Dented helm brought their head down again.

Arri felt warmth wash over her face.

Dented helm raised his head a third time.

Arri wedged her elbow in the crook of his neck. With her other hand, she grabbed the hilt of her sword and started twisting. Blood poured onto her stomach. She wedged her knee between them, and finally rolled the prick off her.

Arri planted her boot on Dented helm's gut and ripped her swords out. "And fuckin' stay down." Her forehead had opened, blood was leaking into her eye.

Cries for water sounded throughout the field. Not long after confused screams and pillars of flame. They weren't expecting a grease fire.

But Arri didn't expect to still inside it either. The flames were near, air giving way to smoke.

The south end of the field was a wall of flame growing with the ignition of every oil pot. The coldbloods were probably smart enough to get out of that things way. Arri sprinted toward the fire.

The gap between flames narrowed with every step. Arri cut right. With any luck, she'd emerge right by the rope. Soon this would be over.

She felt happy, then she didn't care, then the flames turned purple and started speaking. A man made of cascading jewels wandered into her path, hardly giving her a second glance.

Arri managed a passing glance at some of the plants she'd been burning. In hindsight, it was a bad idea to cut through the smoke.

Arri came bursting through a bush. Stray bulbs bounced across the ground. A loose branch tore away her hood. She'd guessed right about where the rope was. Unfortunately, between her and the rope stood a pack of coldbloods gliding through a sea of crystalline rainbows.

This would all be for nothing if the Damu'yhig found out who was behind it. Polished ring mail, green cloaks… it was the pricks from Bottleneck. That meant at least five of them were real.

Arri brushed her blood-soaked bangs away from her eyes. Five shots left.

The coldbloods charged, khopeshes drawn.

Arri drew a pistol in each hand. Her first shot struck one in the chest.

The coldblood's mail rippled and tore. It stumbled but didn't fall.

She put her next shot through its knee. That did the trick.

Arri dropped her pistols. They all looked like they were moving underwater. It felt like an eternity before she laid hands on another pair of pistols. Shots three and four were clean hits. Bone flew from the back of each coldblood's head. The first set of pistols hit the dirt.

The coldbloods were only steps away.

The next pistol was covered in mud. Arri pulled the trigger —nothing.

The coldblood looking down the barrel flinched.

She pitched the gun at the other one. That bought her enough time to draw the dagger from her belt and fling it. The knife spun end over end, piercing the eye of the closest coldblood.

It tumbled to the ground screaming.

Arri stutter-stepped backward, reaching for her swords.

The last coldblood lunged forward, slashing at her throat.

Arri whipped her head back. The khopesh nicked the tip of her nose—no, it sliced clean through the bridge. Cut a bit of cheek, too. Blood poured from the wound, flooding her nostrils.

The coldblood slammed its shoulder into Arri's chest. The momentum brought them to the ground inches from the blaze, the coldblood on top.

Arri had the wind knocked from her. Every breath she took cut short by mucusy viscera. Blood flowed free from her forehead into her eyes. Swords were out of reach. Not counting the armor the coldblood had an easy fifty pounds on her.

The coldblood rested its khopesh against her cheek. Its words came out slow under the effects of the smoke. "I said I'd carve your ears from your skull. No reason to stop there."

Arri felt her heart beat against her chest. It was the only thing that seemed to be moving at an appropriate speed. She wondered how the Crow treated the souls of failures. Those who laid down their lives only to be throttled by a serpent-man who couldn't tell a pistol from a sword hilt.

Arri reached for the last pistol hanging on her baldric. She jammed it against the coldblood's chin and cranked the striker back.

The coldblood snatched the pistol in its free hand pulling it away from his vitals.

Arri worked her other hand free and grabbed the gun. The game was simple, the first one to look at the business end losses. Arri's two hands were more than a match for the coldblood's one. Slowly she pushed the muzzle back toward it.

The coldblood abandoned its khopesh to grab the barrel, regaining control. The barrel came to rest between Arri's eyes. Unfamiliar with the device the coldblood fumbled for the trigger. The hammer clicked.

Arri flinched, even knowing that bullet was embedded in a coldblood's helmet.

The coldblood looked at her in confusion.

Arri snatched the khopesh and slammed its hilt into its owner's temple.

The shock was enough to send him reeling.

Arri pushed with every bit of strength in her body. The

coldblood toppled. Arri rolled on top of it and brought the sword down on its neck. She leaned on the blade with all her weight. A moment of struggle later, the khopesh sunk deep enough to hit an artery.

The lift was descending with more guards. The jewel man was watching her from the edge of the burning field, blinking in and out of existence.

Arri snapped to her feet. She spared a moment to gather her weapons and finish the coldbloods she'd maimed, the next she was over the wall.

Braziers roared to life along the plateau's edge. Random arrows struck the flood plain in the hopes of hitting something.

Arri hugged to the wall and made her way to the river. Once she reached the edge she peeled off her bloodstained camouflage and tossed it into the river.

A cry rang along the plateau and arrows rained down on the cloak.

With her final diversion, Arri disappeared into the river.

CHAPTER
28

Thessalia had lost track of how long she'd stayed curled up along the wall, hours, days, it didn't matter. She cradled her father's skull in her arms, his staff resting against the wall. The sum of her birthright was within her grasp.

There was no clear order to her feelings. Each conflicting emotion bled into the next.

Relief softened the shame of her illegitimacy. She didn't share the intermingling of familial blood that seemed to have poisoned Nysra's mind. Though it didn't help that Nysra was correct in her suspicions. There was also the presumptive dread that Nysra's other ravings might be valid.

The visions tainted everything involving her mother. Years of warmth and unconditional love were hopelessly intertwined with vicarious carnal memories. This was further exasperated by her father's unyielding lust still burned into her mind.

Speaking of which, her father, the pale one… The compressed vision of his life, despite its unsavory details, left her with a detached fascination. Unlike her uncle, it was a father she could be proud of. She wondered what place beneath the moon he could have offered her if they'd escaped this cruel place.

The lands he walked seemed grand ones. Something she could never have within these winding walls of basalt and gneiss. Here she was musing about a fantastical life she'd never see. Grief crept back in as she remembered he abandoned her to die in this alien pit.

The grief that overwhelmed him in his final moments swept over her. Whatever had driven him to take his own life was still a blank. The dreams, while vivid, left too many gaps. It wasn't that those memories didn't exist, their impact still shaped the man her father seemed to be. At least the version she felt. Rather they were obscure, unable to surface without the proper guidance.

In the last few hours, the barriers between her father's feelings and her own had barely held. In a twisted way, her father now lived again, through her. It was easy to parse more esoteric matters, matters that she had no way of knowing, sailing and the like. But in their common ground, the point where one of them began and the other ended was a mystery.

Thessalia wasn't even sure if she'd always hated her uncle the way she did now. His relationship with her actual father didn't help.

It didn't matter now. Barring any other trickery from Ilupagru she was miles underground. Every path only went deeper.

Thessalia turned the rusted blade over in her hand. It didn't seem that difficult when her father did it. A shock of cold followed by a few moments of discomfort. Arguably it was a more merciful fate than anything else this place would offer her. Her body ached from days of walking, her throat was sore from breathing dust.

Still, questions danced through her mind. What was this place? What would compel someone to delve so far into this hateful place? What was her father trying to spit out with his dying words?

Thessalia raised the old blade, mimicking her father's grip as best she could. Her hand quivered. Taking the act upon herself was far more difficult than experiencing it. She steadied her breathing, closed her eyes, and tilted her head back.

"Feh ah uh."

Thessalia was overtaken by the vision of herself holding an

infant pale as ice. Warmth and guilt washed over her in equal parts. The only thing that mattered was this child's survival. A desperate hope crept into them.

Thessalia dropped the knife. Her father must have came here for her sake. Dying with her name on his lips. And here she was about to squander his sacrifice.

"Damn it all." Thessalia rose and shook a layer of dust off her robes. She grabbed her father's skull and tucked it under her arm, nestling it between the folds of her robe.

She turned to the direction the mercury beast left her facing. Ilupagru must have left her that way for a reason. An attempt to spite its will would result in some form of retaliation. Best to humor it.

Thessalia took a step forward then lurched to a halt remembering her father's staff. She took the copper shaft in her good hand. The metal was warm to the touch. She wrapped her fingers around the grooved metal, every edge familiar, inviting.

The angles of the hallway grew harsher the deeper she went. What started as a twisting octagonal path shed its sides one by one. It started as a gentle transition from one surface to another. But with every shed layer, the path became more difficult. Broad steps turned into deft hoops when she reached five sides. The square section was simple enough, fixed with a wide step as the new segment of hall twisted beneath her.

She wondered if the passage was bending, or if this was another distortion of physics to obscure her path.

When she reached the triangular segment she was shimmying, a leg braced on either side of the stone. The passage ceased coiling at an upward curve.

Thessalia felt like she was going to vomit. She wondered exactly how Ilupagru would continue this particular gimmick.

The triangular passage opened into a black abyss. The only thing visible under the light of her blood vial was a narrow path hanging over nothing. Thessalia prodded the walkway with her staff. Despite the lack of any visible support, the walkway was completely solid.

Thessalia stepped out onto the path and looked back upon the structure she emerged from. Light washed over the surface, revealing a wall of obsidian etched with runes. Her light didn't reach either edge of the pillar, leaving its actual scale to her imagination.

Thessalia wondered how many people had set eyes on such a feat of architecture in the last millennia. The pillars were far beyond anything they were capable of today.

She continued along the black walkways. Distinguishing the edges from the void beneath was a challenge. Fortunately, the paths were rigid, only shifting in ninety-degree angles. In the coming hours, Thessalia made a total of three turns, each corresponding with the edge of another pillar.

The path led her to a set of stairs protruding from a pillar. Down she went. The steps were wide enough to fit a single person, no more. The lack of any railing left Thessalia hugging the side of the pillar.

After descending the length of a pillar Thessalia found the respite of a landing. She collapsed to her knees ready to kiss the floor. Her feet throbbed in pain, blisters forming along her heels. She leaned back against the wall to rest.

Her back squashed against something soft. She reeled forward on her knees, her head hanging over the void. In a move befitting a swashbuckler she rolled onto her back, knife drawn.

Rather than some cruel beast, she met with another of the mercury filled umbilicals. The waxy gray vine pulsated with a rhythmic thump. The alien vine clung to the side of the pillar well out of view. The other end disappeared into the darkness below. Thessalia left it alone, not wanting to antagonize the beast that resided within.

Another path waited before Thessalia. This one snaked deeper into the void beneath, wild and free from the rigidity of the pillars above. Thessalia stepped out onto the path over the void.

She looked back at the pillar and went wide-eyed when she saw nothing beneath it. There was only an empty space where countless tons of stone should have been.

The endless black beneath her was unnerving. But the absence of any load-bearing structures unsettled her even more. She wondered what force kept the temple above aloft. Was some unfathomable sorcery shouldering the miles of stone above? The idea gave her chills.

Sorcery was fickle by nature. The slightest tampering could bring the temple down on her head. She imagined the face Nysra would make plummeting to her death under such unnatural circumstances. It was amusing. Thessalia welcomed any catharsis she could.

She turned another bend in the walkway. The chamber was a much simpler trick, a cavern modestly carved from obsidian. With pillars blended in the dark, a path could be wound in ways to keep travelers from getting too close a look. It was a sophisticated structure for such an old place.

Of course, that begets the question of who built it. Thessalia had two answers, both troubling. One possibility was that her ancestors were responsible. Such powerful sorcery meant they were falling from a much higher peak than she imagined.

The second was that it was someone else, an older race that achieved far greater potential. Ilupagru had either curbed her people's abilities or outright upstaged then. Something she'd have to fix if she survived.

It occurred to Thessalia that she might have traveled deeper into this pit than anyone else. Certainly deeper than anyone who'd ever returned. She wondered how deep Thule delved to retrieve his art of flesh crafting or any of his other bizarre gifts. It could have been a secret of that shrieking head.

Thessalia felt foolish thinking about how many corners she'd left unchecked. Any number of the treasures above could have provided her a means of escape. She rolled her father's staff between her fingers. The feeling vanished.

The familiarity of the staff was deeper than just the way it felt in her hands. It had a warmth to it that offered some semblance of security in this deadly place. The runes etched across its surface were of a foreign dialect she wasn't familiar with. Yet it felt as if their meaning was on the tip of her tongue, a meaning that carried weight, at least to her father. How much had her mother kept from her?

The walkway wound around for another hundred steps or so before ending in a circular platform. Unlike the last several miles of the walkway, the platform hung from a set of heavy chains. The platform swayed back and forth as Thessalia stepped onto it. It was large, larger than the floor space of her chambers even.

Thessalia walked the perimeter only to find there were no connecting paths. Was this the place she was being herded to? She was at a loss until she noticed something glinting out in the void.

The pale light that hung from her neck caught hundreds of star-like reflections in the dark. Dozens of thick woven umbilicals sweating beads of mercury swayed in the darkness. Each weave pulsated, moving fluids one way or another.

Thessalia did some brief calculations in her head. Each weave had more than twenty distinct umbilicals. Some of the thicker weaves looked closer to fifty or sixty umbilicals. If each plant was like the one she found earlier, a pair of tubules, one flowing each way, the bulbs should have been everywhere. Exactly how far did the things reach?

Thessalia's line of thought was cut short by a tempest blowing into the abyss. The force brought Thessalia to her knees, grasping for something to anchor herself.

The tempest ceased for a moment then reversed. The linens of Thessalia's robes beat against the wind. The air was moist and warm, with an undertone of decay. A low pitched groan, like rocks shearing against each other, came with the wind.

The chains went taut as the winds lifted the platform. Again the tempest ceased and the platform fell, rattling and bouncing about.

Thessalia did everything she could to avoid screaming in panic. The breeze she'd followed, the winding path hoping for an exit, it was breath. The shallow breaths of some titan slumbering deep beneath the sands.

Hundreds of things between her and this abomination could have struck her dead. Yet here she stood. "What do you want from me?" she whispered.

Her staff burned hot in her hand. She felt the sensation of pins and needles wash across her form, her hairs standing on end.

Thessalia studied the boiling metal in her hand. She was right on the edge of remembering the runes. If she had the right word the rest would come. Something that could spite this eras-old beast.

A three-fingered hand emerged from the darkness, a hand so huge Thessalia could sit on one of its fingernails. The rest of the arm followed the hand. Rotted patches of necrotized flesh dripped from the limb. With every movement exposed patches of bone tore wider. Mercury flowed free from the wounds, raining on the platform.

Thessalia endured the cold burn of the metal spraying across her face.

The arm lurched forward, the fingertip headed straight for Thessalia.

With the fear of something greater than herself something clicked. The rune etched above her knuckle made sense. The phrase was simple, poetic even.

Thessalia thrust her staff toward the arm. "Become the storm," she whispered.

From her feet to her fingertips it felt like every bit of her lit aflame. The sensation poured through her hand and into the staff. Layer by layer the runes came alight, the sequence moving to the tip of the staff.

A blinding light erupted from the staff. A bolt of lightning arced from the tip accompanied by a deafening crash. Thessalia's arm went numb. She felt a warmth on her face as blood poured from her nose.

The bolt struck the creature's finger and rippled along the surface. The hand shriveled and scattered into a torrent of sand that beat down on her.

The sand sent her spiraling head over heels, fighting to keep some sense of orientation. Sand flooded her nose and ears, scraped at her cheeks. The sand pulled her in every direction, every change in flow whipping her about like a doll.

The movement finally stopped. Thessalia took a moment to steady herself. Spit pooled at the back of her throat, she was facing right side up.

She clawed at the sand, trying to dig herself out. Wave after wave of sand washed over her. Bit by bit she managed to burrow upwards. When she resurfaced, sand clung to her black locks. Thessalia managed to pull herself free, gasping for air. She stood atop the mound in total blackness.

Thessalia took a moment to shake herself free of excess sand. No sign of the titan remained. Only the sand and the endless black.

Light cut across the distance. Orange light rolled across the sand, the sky a rich gold. Shadows glided across the landscape, familiar plant shapes bobbing in the wind.

Thessalia allowed herself a moment of respite to take in the tranquility. She reverted to her bloodthirsty scowl. "I see through your trickery. Show yourself!"

Two pits of sand collapsed in front of her, side by side. A third narrow pit between the two. Behind her, the sand opened into a toothy grin.

Thessalia glared at the skull's mock eye sockets. "Slay me if you must. I grow impatient with these petty games." Her voice sounded wrong, high pitched.

The toothy maw behind her must have widened. She lost her footing. The jaws were closing in on her.

A single light shined on Thessalia. She clutched at her staff. It felt heavy, awkward even. She clutched the copper. She gave herself a once over and realized she was inhabiting the form of her childhood self. She was hardly old enough to stand.

Surrounding her was a sand miniature of Lux crafted with astonishing detail. In front of her was the temple in all its splendor.

Thessalia put her heel through the temple's roof. She wasn't putting any deep thought into her actions. She grew tired of this pretentious game.

Before Thessalia could continue the temple expanded, becoming the only thing she saw. Walls of sand rushed past her, growing with every instant. The temple restored to its appropriate size, Thessalia now stood in the crater.

Skulls littered the ground—hundreds, thousands. The skulls were multiplying, flooding her. The only thing Thessalia could see now were the skulls, dark outlines packed around her.

Thessalia clung to her father's skull, unwilling to lose it to the mass. The skulls pressed in against her own bones, it wouldn't be long now. The pressure began to hurt. There was a *crunch* behind her. The pressure at her back released.

Thessalia fell back onto something solid. Skulls spilled over her. Orange light licked at the gaps between the bones.

Once she was sure there wouldn't be another shift in perspective, Thessalia raised her head. She was back in the crypts. Skulls lined every bit of the wall, save for the area she fell out of.

Everything seemed back to normal. Thessalia ran a hand over herself to make sure everything had returned to the proper proportions. She winced, again remembering her elbow's condition a moment too late. Her shoes were still missing, the copper staff was on the ground next to her, and she was clutching a kasairan skull. So at least some of that actually happened.

Thessalia leaned over to the wall. While skulls littered the floor, layers more still obscured the wall. A wisp of cold, rotting air danced across her nose.

Thessalia recoiled, leveling her staff at the wall. Nothing happened. Her new treasures in hand, she staggered down the hall.

How much of that did it plan? Was Ilupagru exploiting Nysra's haphazard assassination attempt? Had that alien place found a way to compel her? What did it want? And did it succeed? Questions she'd never have answered buzzed in her head.

Thessalia reached the ground level, stumbling into the main hall. Half-breeds and servants looked on in silence, too unnerved to comment, yet too cautious to look away. She realized the spectacle she must have been.

She snatched an orange from a passing tray. The servant made no protest. The juice burned the cuts in her mouth. It was the sweetest thing she'd ever eaten

Thessalia pointed at the first one to make eye contact. "You! Where's my assistant?"

The boy bowed his head. "She left the city with your eldest sister not a few hours ago."

That bitch. Even in death her sister couldn't let her be. "Where were they headed?" she asked, taking a drink from another passing servant.

"West."

She staggered to the nearest skylight. The moon was days ahead of schedule. The Sorcerer's Moon would transpire in hours. How long had she been missing?

"Shit," she muttered under her breath.

CHAPTER
29

Willem pulled at his blindfold. "Let's try this again."

"Hang on."

Willem felt Ricard reorient him.

"Best to not face toward the sun this time."

"Fair point." Willem undid his blindfold.

Before Willem was a massive pair of blurry jaws towering over on him. He screamed and leaped back, reaching for any weapon he could.

Laughter erupted all around him.

Willem looked around in confusion. As the rest of beast came into focus Willem realized it hung from massive cast iron hooks. Swaths of flesh were missing from the creature, butchered like livestock. His attention fell to a rudimentary arrow stuck in the beast's eye socket.

Akhil slapped Willem on the shoulder. "The basilisk was no easy prey, but with enough patience and a workable blind spot the meat was well worth the risk."

Willem's jaw hung limp for a moment. "You managed to kill that thing?"

"I only severed a tendon or two. Cenri struck the killing blow." Akhil waved to one of his riders, who returned the gesture then went back to preparing their horses.

Willem eyed dozens of arrows and slash marks decorating the basilisk's hide. "Hit and run tactics."

"And not a single death."

Willem nodded in approval. "Was this the meat from last night?"

"You and yours took the eye and knee. It's only fair you get to enjoy the meat." Akhil hoisted a bag over his shoulder. "Now gather your things. The caravan is leaving soon." Akhil jogged to a wagon.

Willem took another moment to appreciate the basilisk corpse swinging in the wind. Any time the Legion faced a basilisk, wild or heavy cavalry, it resulted in a handful of dead. Men sheared in half by its massive jaws or trampled beneath its feet. Regardless of how many bullets or spears pierced their flesh they'd always take some toll.

No deaths. A handful of riders faced this behemoth and they all lived to feast on it.

"You want this back?" Ricard passed Willem the powder horn.

"Sure." Willem took the horn and tossed it in his bag.

The convoy consisted of a dozen some odd wagons filled with supplies for trade. Water, herbs, and smoked basilisk meat all plenty. The first few wagons hauled treated wood of unknown origin. No less than a pair of archers accompanied each cart.

When they reached Kadar's river there was a flurry of motion as they bound the spare wood into rafts. Anyone not loading supplies tested the water worthiness of the crafts. Not a single hand remained idle. The wagoners agreed on a return time and bid the convoy farewell.

The river itself was massive. At points, Willem was sure he could loose an arrow and still not reach the other side. An Ecrecian ironclad could cruise these waters with room to spare. This begged the question of why they hadn't. Willem didn't concern himself with this too much. He'd come to accept that the reasons for a great many things was beyond rational answer.

The raft glided along the water. He watched as all sorts of creatures swam by, investigating the raft. The water was unnaturally clear, unlike the waterways in Vestinus. There the assorted runoffs from factories gave the rivers a number of hues.

Dylus leaned over the side, admiring the native breeds of fish and eel.

Willem took a seat next to him. "With any luck, the next port won't be on fire. We keep quiet, slip a trader some gold, and we'll be off this miserable continent within the week.

"Where'd you plan on going?"

"Figured I'd go back to the colonies with you."

"Protectorate," Dylus corrected.

"Semantics. You go back to whatever luxurious little power struggle you were making moves in. I can stand three to five strides behind you and keep you from getting black bagged again. Then we both live in comfort for the next fifty years arguing about trivial bullshit."

Dylus shrugged. "I do like the ring of that homewrecking cunt with a bodyguard. Still seems like a lot of effort on your end for some spare change."

"What?"

"I fuck men good and they give me nice things. I thought I was being open about that before."

"So you're a whore."

Dylus shook his head. "They're paying me for my time and company. The sex is completely coincidental." Dylus raised an eyebrow. "What did you think I was?"

"I thought you were some kind of noble angling for a better title," said Willem.

Dylus squinted. "What kind of cross-eyed fuckin' idiocy made you think I had a goddamn title?

"The first week out here you were citing baronial law and wearing a pelt that cost more money than I'd ever seen."

"You think the nobles go out looking to fuck uneducated cunts wearing nothing but rags?"

Willem clenched his teeth.

"Bit of a rockier start than you might have been hoping for. But once I've had a bath we'll be fleecing rich cunts with poor morals like that.”

"How secure are Strahl's ports?"

"Goddamn magic trick they got me through without so much as a squinted eye. It's why I'm certain a lord had a hand in it."

"No one owes you a single favor?"

"Thazgarr couldn't pull out the stick in the port authority's ass."

"How dangerous are the surrounding waters?"

"Couldn't pay me all the gold in the Strahl to set foot on anything smaller than a galleon in those waters." Dylus furrowed his brow. "Any reason you're concerned about our border security all of a sudden?"

Willem scowled. "Ever hear about what the Ecrecian Legion does to deserters?"

"Stuff of fuckin' nightmares. Basis for what we say skin-walkers do to naughty children who torture pets or get each other pregnant. Don't see that affects us."

Willem shot Dylus an even stare.

Dylus's eyes darted to the bandage on Willem's arm. A look of comprehension followed. "Ah… yeah, you're right fucked. Not a soul beneath the moon rich enough to decline that kind of reward."

"Not even on a bribe?"

"Not in snake gold."

Willem rolled onto his back. "Well, what do you think then, kasair or vampires?"

"Kasair culture is an acquired taste. Better in the long run if you aren't too squeamish. Make use of that gold at least. Still, they're on good enough terms with your boys to cash in on you if they found out, so get used to wearing sleeves. Valok-Nur… Personally, I couldn't stomach the blood tithe."

Willem watched the moon drift across the sky, parallel to the sun. "You had one thing right. I'm fucked."

"Any reason you couldn't set up shop here?"

Willem tilted his head to Dylus. "You remember the last few days right?"

"Place is a pile of shit no doubt. But with a bag full of gold and a city not under siege, I'd gamble that it might be bearable."

"In a country that'll firebomb its own people without a second thought."

"That much worse than one that wants you flayed?"

Willem scowled. "I understand why. For all I know out here I'd get volunteered for a mass beheading because the wind didn't blow the right way."

"Ritual beheadings are done to the north, in Khepresh," Akhil said.

Dylus looked to Akhil, then back to Willem. "Well, stay away from there I guess."

Willem's scowl endured. "So I'm not beheaded. What language do they speak? What's the number system? What if some sorcerer decides that my foreign ass has an exotic appeal?"

"For someone who put so much effort into getting away from the Legions, you keep finding reasons to go crawling back."

"That was before Xent."

"Was it worse than whatever sent you running from the Legion?"

"It was the same damn thing!" Willem snapped. "The damned scale-skins gassed the cohort! They got the attention of their real gods and conjured a cloud of poison so hundreds of men could choke to death on their own lungs! Hundreds dead."

Willem took a breath. "And then we helped them do it again."

Dylus sat there for a moment. "I can understand not wanting to hide underneath that nose." Dylus pulled out a knife and started scraping at his nails.

Thazgarr sat cross-legged at the center of a raft. He cradled the idol in his lap lest its fickle weight capsize the vessel.

"My friend," Akhil said, hanging over Thazgarr, his eyes locked on the snake skull pauldron adorning his shoulder, "you don't want the serpent-men to catch you with that in Lux. They are very particular in how they treat their dead kin."

"How particular?"

"Murderously."

"I will take heed, friend."

"Hopefully Ricard is as agreeable." Akhil disappeared behind a crate.

Thazgarr stepped over to the side of the raft, undoing the leather straps on his shoulder. He took the skull in his free hand and held it over the water. Before he let go his eyes locked with the empty sockets of the once-cobra.

He tried to let go but something in him refused. The only courtesy they paid to his dead was leaving them in a rotting pile. And they expected him to honor their wildlife? To yield to their will?

Thazgarr envisioned himself at the gates of Lux caving in the head of a serpent-man with the skull. Then another. Then being overrun.

His thoughts drifted again to the pale beast. He could have killed it, at the cost of himself. Now instead it would live, grow stronger, become another leviathan beneath the sands. One of which was too many.

The skull seemed to mock Thazgarr with its rictus grin.

"I'll not die for something as petty as you."

The skull slid between his fingers. With a faint splash, the skull dropped into the water. It glided along the raft for a moment before disappearing into a cloud of silt.

The Ecrecian was still sulking, and would likely be that way until they reached port. Best to act now.

"A word, Ecrecian."

"Fine, Thaz, I'm sorry I choked you out before you could get crushed. If another opportunity arises between here and Lux I won't get in your way."

"The contrary, Ecrecian. I invite you to do that again."

Willem's scowl deepened. "I'm not in the mood for this."

"You have the wisdom of a warrior well past your years."

"The Legion beat some discipline into me. It's not anything special."

"And that discipline has kept us alive."

"To what end?"

Thazgarr looked baffled. "Revenge. Your talk with the foreigner…"

"You heard…"

"Everyone heard. Hide from it as do, you have a lust for revenge."

"That's what you got from that?"

Thazgarr shrugged. "Fear is a response to pain the same as anger, it's only fed differently. I overfed the one, you the other."

"So I'm afraid then?"

Thazgarr nodded. "Overly so."

"Have you actually seen one of their highborn yet? Because you're failing to appreciate how wide the gap is between us and the sorcerers."

"You did a fine job slaying the saint."

"The what?" Willem looked confused.

"The eye creature."

"I don't even want to know why you know that." Willem looked out over the river, then his attention returned to Thazgarr. "I want you to imagine something for me. Picture a night of violent spite fucking between you and that cobra on your shoulder. Picture what the offspring of such a night would look like. Now, how many were your tribe when they died?"

"Dozens."

"Okay, now I want you to imagine… let's say ten of your tribes. A single sorcerer could wave a hand and they'd all be dead before they hit the ground. They have hundreds of those things."

"You give them too much praise. You saw the Damu'yhig's head on Xent's battlements the same as I. Sorcery aside they're flesh and bone, the same as us. Some well-placed metal is all it would take."

"You can't know if that was a sorcerer for sure," Willem said.

"Why was it alone then?"

Willem had a curious look.

"Sidoth's thralls were confident or desperate enough to leave a city in the claws of a single Damu'yhig. This could mean four things. His sorcery was feared and respected, and yet he still lays dead. It may also mean Sidoth's Children are at odds with one another, setting each other up to fail for their own gain."

Willem was listening now.

"The third possibility is that his sorcery was meager. They

were unwilling to send a more powerful vassal. Thus their sorcerers haven't the numbers you believe they do."

"And the last possibility?"

"A great deal of their power is an illusion. Ruling by the fear of what it's thought they're capable of rather than their own ability. Massive labors made to look like child's play."

"I know what I saw," Willem said.

"Tell me of the death of your Legion."

Willem spared no detail in his retelling. A group of Akhil's men gathered, enthralled by the tale of the subterra breach. They marveled at the idea of a vessel that traveled the air, despite the crash. There was even laughter when he mentioned stealing his leader's horse.

But Thazgarr noticed something else. When he got to the sorcerer and his archers there was a spark of bloodlust in the boy's eye. It was faint, smothered by fear, but burning. Fueled right he could kindle it into something useful.

While he waited for the group to disperse Thazgarr poured over every detail of Willem's story. "How do you know it was only the one sorcerer?"

"I spotted him lighting some kind of green incense through a spyglass. There weren't any other signs of smoke."

"What if it was only a signal? You didn't know of the archers until they were in your camp. Others could have been hiding from view. And if the gas was that potent why bother even bringing archers? If they were there for protection they'd have been between your riders and their master. Though if they killed the riders there would be no one left to spread the news of your crushing defeat."

Willem went to speak but fell silent. This process repeated twice more before he managed to ask, "Why are you so damned smart all of a sudden?"

Thazgarr grinned. "Men are less guarded around the simple."

"Then why do you need me?"

"I'm not incapable of the same battle prowess as you. I developed the more practical aspects first."

"You—"

Before Willem could finish his clever remark an arrow pierced his back. He fell forward into Thazgarr's arms.

Cries of "Ambush!" echoed across the rafts. Thazgarr grabbed Willem and hauled him between a pair of crates.

Arrows struck the deck in rhythm with the beats of Thazgarr's chest. Confused shouting rang out as men tried to find their assailants. Soon more injured fell behind the crates.

Thazgarr loaded his crossbow and sprung from cover. Hooded figures bobbed in and out of view behind the raised dunes that ran parallel to the river. At regular intervals, they would rise above the dunes, loose an arrow, and then retreat back to safety.

One rose across from Thazgarr, bow drawn.

Thazgarr fired his crossbow. The bolt went high but it was enough to send the archer ducking back behind cover. Thazgarr did the same.

He re-cocked the device and slid in another bolt. The process took far longer than hurling a javelin.

Willem lay against the raft, the arrow still sticking from his back. Thazgarr reached to pull the arrow out only to have Willem swat him away, shouting at him to leave it in.

Ricard came crashing over the side of the crates. Dylus was nowhere in sight. Ricard rifled through his bag and pulled out a pair of arrows with strange looking heads.

Sraac loosed another arrow. The tribesmen whose eye he pierced rolled off the raft and into the water. A plume of blood flowed from the wound as eels and fish swarmed the free meal.

It was a clever move doubling back across the dunes to enlist the aid of a local tribe. No sane traveler would risk crossing over the deep runs where the sand leviathans roam. Somehow the Ecrecian and his troop managed it.

That's why Sraac made a point of shooting him first. A moving target with solid cover was less than ideal. Covered high ground was a more than acceptable trade-off.

Once the channel narrowed whoever remained would be easy pickings. Sraac jogged to the next clear spot and nocked an arrow. He rose to loose it but when he cleared the dunes he spotted a golden glint flying in his direction. It fell short of its mark so he paid it little mind. He loosed his own arrow as it struck the sand.

A wave of force knocked him on his back with a thunderous *crack*. His ears were ringing and he felt like he was being stabbed all over. The side of his face was in horrible pain, all he could taste was metal and blood.

He braced himself on his elbows. Two others were hit. Doz was dragging himself away, the other lay face down in the sand.

Deep red stains formed beneath his own surcoat. He looked to the left and spotted a piece of jagged brass sticking out of the sand.

Before he could grab the brass for further investigation a gloved pair of hands grabbed him. Mont was dragging him away from the river.

Sraac struggled to get back on his feet but the hold was firm.

"You're bleeding out," he said.

Sraac thrashed, to no avail. "Kill them first!" The words slurred, his face twisted in horrible pain as he spoke.

"You won't last long enough."

He was too weak to protest. Before he could make a coherent argument Mont had torn open his shirt. He doused Sraac's wounds with some foul smelling concoction of animal fat and honey. His wounds were bound in tight strips of linen, making it difficult to breathe.

Mont hesitated for a moment before removing Sraac's mask. The left side had a massive tear running its length. The flap of skin that danced on Sraac's gave him reason to believe a similar wound was on his face.

Mont rolled Sraac onto his side to keep the blood from pooling in the back of his throat. Sraac felt the tremors of Mont's boots as he returned to the line. Rivulets of blood pooled in the dirt in front of him. The blood taste cleared, leaving only the metal.

He reached inside his mouth with a quivering hand. Hidden among the warm chunky viscera was something smooth, cool to the touch. Sraac was able to remove the piece of metal with the same ease that it had when it ripped through his cheek.

Glinting between his fingers was a golden pyramid, one of the many he promised the Kestrels. It's three sides were each sharpened to a razor's edge. He turned the coin over in his hand to the visage of Kadar stained with his own blood.

Sraac dropped the coin. He calculated just how many ways, physical and symbolic, the Ecrecian had managed to spite him. Sraac did what he could to strike the man dead. If Sidoth, Kadar, or any of the others had even the slightest bit of integrity they'd drag that Ecrecian's soul into the deepest pit of their domain.

At the edge of his vision, Sraac saw a red light washing over the horizon. Was this what uncontrollable rage felt like? Was the blood loss too great and this is what it felt like to die? His eyes drifted to the sky. It was no such personal matter, it was only a Sorcerer's Moon. The reflection of that bloody stain that marked the sky above.

He'd been so focused on recovering Xent he completely lost track of time. His blood only carried enough of Sidoth's divinity to cause slight discomfort. At least the moon would boost his half-breed's latent talents enough to assure victory.

Another explosion went off.

A blood-curdling howl echoed somewhere behind him. Khazra.

The Beast Mother was a sensitive topic among the Damu'yhig. First identified by an envoy to Strahl, serpent-men were her among her worshipers. The rest were mixtures of man and beast of all types.

The host of theological implications kept the new bloodlines at arm's length. Regardless of the abilities, aberrants among the chimera left their legitimacy in question. Sraac was not one to deprive himself of such resources. Praise Anu Sidoth.

"You had sorcery this whole time?" shouted Thazgarr.

"Ecrecian alchemy. Ask Willem." Ricard loosed the third of the bronze thunder arrows. No fire or noise followed. "Dud."

The first arrow was the most successful. The scale-skins were cautious now. The second only took one more.

"How many more do we have?" Thazgarr asked.

"Dozens!" Ricard raised a single finger.

The remaining archers were focusing on their raft alone.

The sheer volume of arrow shafts sticking from Thazgarr's cover gave it the look of a thick bush. From what he could tell the other rafts were using the opportunity to fortify their own cover.

Willem was laying on his gut, the blood in his wound seemed to be clotting well enough. Dylus and Akhil had scrambled behind the crates, Thazgarr wasn't exactly sure when. Also, the sky had turned red.

The other rafts began a counter attack. The rhythmic beating of arrowheads against his cover relented. Those who were able yanked arrows from the crate and started loosing them back at their owners. Through the combined efforts of the three rafts they were able to suppress the ambush. For now.

"Land, and overwhelm them on foot!" shouted Akhil.

The polemen ran from cover and started jamming their rods into the riverbed. With each push, the rafts edged closer to shore. Thazgarr grabbed his war club. His shoulder wasn't healed but he'd still be off far more use on dry land than behind the crates. Bronze blades unsheathed in preparation to take the hill.

The shore was no more than a stone's throw away when a guttural roar came from the other side of the dune. A lone figure came bounding over the hill with unnatural speed. A flowing brown cloak obscured its form.

A pair of the archers at the front raft focused on the mad assailant and loosed their arrows.

The arrow placement was perfect, each a kill shot. Something twitched beneath the assailant's cloak. The arrows shattered in the air fractions of a second before striking.

Thazgarr squinted. The sun did him no favors in studying the assailant's movements.

Without breaking stride the cloak flourished and a pair of broad darts flew from beneath it. The first dart pierced an archer's bicep, the second only grazed its target. Both archers dropped their bows. The muscles around their wounds twitched wildly. Poison.

Thazgarr shouted something at them in the commotion. They didn't notice.

The raft was still a way offshore. The assailant's suicide charge would likely take another man or two but would be a vain charge into the shallows. Thazgarr loosened his grip.

That was before the assailant reached the edge of the water, coiled into a low stance, and lunged into the air. Sand sprayed into the air, leaving behind a pit deep as a man's knee.

Thazgarr watched in awe as the figure launched farther than a natural being had any right to, legs swinging forward in the air, squeezing every inch of distance from the leap to land on the edge of the raft. The raw force of the impact forced the raft back ten steps. The right side lurched into the air opposite the assailant. As the raft looked ready to flip the high end rocked back. Crates scraped across the deck. Everyone was scrambling to regain their balance. That's when the assailant dived into their midst.

Thazgarr struggled to try to catch even a glimmer of the assailant's blade. It had to be something small the way it danced between the tribesmen's khopeshes. Blood arced in every conceivable angle. A few tribesmen fell over the side, darts embedded in their skulls.

Confusion and range seemed the key to the assailant's strategy. If it came to a melee Thazgarr would have to leverage his reach to counter the speed of his opponent's blade. That was only after he closed the gap provided by the darts. He cocked his crossbow on the off chance.

Slaughter was an accurate description of the first raft. Though Thazgarr thought butchering a more appropriate term. A steady stream of meaty chunks filled the air above. Men fell to the deck skewered by blades clutched in their own severed limbs.

Cutting down the last of the tribesmen, the assailant came back into view. Someone tore the hood away in their death grip, revealing a slender feminine face. Rows of shallow scars marked her cheeks, a few fresh cuts mixed in. She ran her bloody fingers through a thick mane of deep red hair.

It was then that Thazgarr noticed she wasn't carrying a blade. Rather, her fingers ended in a heavy set of claws sharpened finer than any knife.

A semi-intact tribesman laying at her feet lashed out, hoping to slash a tendon.

Before the blade struck, a scaly appendage thick with muscle lashed out from her back. The tribesman's blade, as well as his fingers, went tumbling into the river, each with its own splash.

The tail ended in some kind of chitinous blade bristling with her throwing darts. Barbs.

She plunged the tail into the tribesman's lower back and hauled him to his knees. She locked her jaws around the man's face, one hand on his forehead and the other against his shoulder. With a series of wet snaps, she tore his jaw from his face, clutching it in her own.

Muscle and tendon rolled back, exposing the man's remaining teeth and tongue to the air.

The woman spat her victim's jaw into the river and let out another bloodthirsty howl. In the moonlight, her bared teeth looked closer to a lion's fangs.

"Chimera!" Dylus shouted. "Manticore blood!"

Thazgarr watched in disgust then leveled his crossbow and fired.

The bolt flew straight only to have the skewered tribesman pulled in front of it.

Thazgarr reloaded his crossbow, never looking away from the manticore. She had a hateful glare in her eye, one he imagined like his own when his bloodlust was interrupted.

Thazgarr pulled the trigger. Before the bolt left his crossbow the body was already hurtling toward him. He dropped the crossbow and reached for his club. He hesitated. The manticore put the corpse between them for a reason.

Instead, he opened his arms and embraced the corpse. The flesh hit Thazgarr with enough force to knock him back a step. Blood cascaded over his chest gushing from the corpse's wounds. As he regained his footing he felt a salvo of light jabs against his chest. A quick glance revealed a trio of barbs sticking from the corpse's back. Had he swatted away the corpse they'd have pierced between his ribs.

A pair of arrows flew past Thazgarr. In a blur of motion, the manticore swatted the arrows away with her tail.

"How many arrows can we volley at once?" said Thazgarr.

Akhil nocked an arrow. "Not enough. The back raft is only barely keeping their archers at bay."

Ricard did the same, nocking the last of his bronze-tipped arrows.

The manticore's eyes snapped to Akhil. Her scowl deepened.

Thazgarr risked a sideways glance at Akhil and noted the ornate fur sticking out of his bag. "That's the pelt we bartered to you, correct?

"Makes me quite popular on harsh nights. Good trade. Why?"

Before he could respond the manticore coiled and lunged at the raft. The force tore the bonds of her raft to shreds. Straw and wood spread out across the river.

Thazgarr sidestepped between Akhil and the manticore. He pulled the corpse in front of him an instant before feeling the rhythmic thumping of more barbs.

If the poor tribesman Thazgarr was using as a shield wasn't dead before, he was now.

The venom pulsing through him caused massive, violent convulsions. His limbs flailed in every direction, snapping joints under their force. Whatever blood he had left was spraying from his wounds. Thazgarr gritted his teeth as a fingerless hand slapped against his face.

At the edge of his vision, Thazgarr saw Ricard loose his arrow. No noise followed, only a look of disbelief on Ricard's face.

Thazgarr felt someone yank him backward. The manticore's tail blasted through his shield's chest, occupying the spot he stood not a moment ago.

The raft lurched forward when the manticore landed. Fortunately, with a much thinner crew, everyone kept their balance.

The manticore was no more than a few steps away. Clasped between her claws was the thunder arrow. The other ready for battle, ready to carve. She swung her tail backward and hurled the corpse into the river. With another whip, she cleared her tail of gore.

The others drew their swords. Thazgarr heard the creak of Dylus's bow behind him. Finally, Thazgarr drew his war club.

The manticore lunged forward, thrusting her tail at Thazgarr's heart.

Thazgarr swung a low to high strike and knocked away the blade. Instead of aiming for a killing blow Thazgarr focused on attacking her blades. Her free claw and tail whipped back and forth between the three of them. A single missed parry would mean death for all three.

The manticore's stamina seemed to have no end. He couldn't say the same for them, or their gear.

He fought with singularly devastating strikes, not glancing blows or parries. Deep gashes were forming along his club. Soon the gashes would turn to splinters, then shards.

An arrow whizzed between him and Akhil. The manticore knocked the shaft away, but it was enough to disrupt her pattern. Thazgarr brought his club overhead for a finishing blow, swinging at her skull. Before he connected the manticore raised the bronze thunder arrow overhead. Thazgarr managed to divert his strike, settling for a blow to her shoulder.

There was a heavy *crack*, like a tree branch had shattered.

The manticore reeled back in agony. Her arm hung limp at her side. Tears flowed from her eyes in a mixture of rage and pain. She looked at the three of them and her blood stained lips curled into a smile.

Akhil's leg started twitching. Dark spots formed along the leg of his pants, the stain wider and darker with every beat of his heart.

The manticore brought her tail her face. It was hardly noticeable under the light of the moon. Along the edge of the blade-like appendage was a trickle of blood. The manticore looked Thazgarr dead in the eyes as she ran her tongue along the blade's edge.

Akhil's leg gave out beneath him.

Dylus dragged him back, shouting something about a tourniquet.

The manticore pushed her offensive. She abandoned finesse in favor of heavy, deliberate tail swipes.

Each blow was easy to predict but they rattled Thazgarr's bones. With every strike he and Ricard lost more ground.

The manticore beat them back to the middle of the raft.

Thazgarr weaved between a pair of overturned crates.

Sweat poured from his body. The manticore's strength matched the beast from the souq while dwarfing its speed. It would only be a handful of swings before she overpowered him.

The tail was the problem, dangerous but over-relied on, that's where he needed to make an opening. Thazgarr dived behind one of the boxes. He contorted his body into a position between an acrobat and someone trying too hard to attract a mate.

Basilisk meat slid across the deck. The manticore thrust her tail through the box.

The tail passed above his chest, a hair higher and it would have landed. He wrapped himself around the muscular appendage in a death grip. He planted his boot on the blade where it met scales.

The tail was strong enough to handle a maimed wastelander like a toy. How would it handle a thick-bodied wild man and a crate of basilisk meat?

"Now!" Thazgarr shouted.

Ricard charged the manticore, sword drawn.

The box made a dull whining sound as it scrapped across the deck. The blade beneath Thazgarr's boot carved a deep gash in the deck as it dragged along the wood. His other boot, braced against the deck, left a long scuff mark.

Ricard was closing the gap. He was going to make it.

The raft lurched to a halt, caught on the debris of the front raft, and everyone stumbled. Then the rear raft crashed into them, and anyone still standing tumbled to the deck.

The manticore made another agonized roar, must have landed on her bad shoulder.

The tail sprung back to life. It dragged Thazgarr along the deck, headed straight for Ricard.

Ricard raised his sword the moment before getting struck by the tail's midsection. The manticore kept pushing until she knocked Ricard off the raft.

Thazgarr lost his grip on the backswing and rolled to the deck. His club was nowhere in sight.

The manticore stood opposite Thazgarr, finally breathing heavy. Ricard's sword was run through her tail. Without breaking sight, she brought the blade to her jaw and bit its hilt. The manticore's face twisted in pain as she pulled her tail free. Blood spurted from the wound. She let the blade fall to the deck, kicking it into the river without hesitation.

The manticore glared at Thazgarr, rolling the bronze orb in her good hand.

Thazgarr scanned the remains of the raft for something he could use as a weapon. He was careful not to look away from the manticore, lest he give her an opening.

To his left, beneath the remains of a shattered crate, he spotted a gleam of silver. It was pure, even under the dull red light of the moon.

The manticore brought the orb back past her shoulder and pitched it.

Thazgarr dived. For the wreckage, the orb whizzed past his ear. A shock went through his left side, his ear rang. He plunged his hand into the wreckage. Splinters pierced flesh as he wrapped his hands around warm metal.

He yanked it from the debris. The bust of Xohloto'bas' bared its teeth. Thazgarr clutched the idol by its ear.

The manticore cracked her knuckles against her chin and lunged at Thazgarr.

The idol was weightless. Thazgarr swung it like he would a short blade. Sparks lit the air as the manticore beat against the idol. With a single arm, no barbs, and an injured tail this fight might be winnable.

With every exchange of blows, the idol grew warmer, building into a searing heat. There was no burning flesh smell, no pain like the rock, only the warmth, and a certain rigidity.

The manticore over swung and listed to her left.

Thazgarr planted his feet, he took the idol in both hands, brought it over his shoulder, and swung it at her ribs. A cold, metallic howl pierced the air.

The manticore raised her arm to block her torso. The base of the idol slammed into her forearm and bicep. The impact sent her flying. She bounced across the deck and into the river with a splash.

The idol felt ice cold in Thazgarr's hands. His heart was racing. Every drop of blood in his body felt alive.

Dylus poked his head out from behind a crate. "The fuck was that shit!?" he shouted.

Thazgarr looked back. The rear raft was in charred pieces. Those that survived the blast were clambering into their raft.

A hooded figure came over the hill and loosed an arrow.

Thazgarr leaped behind a crate as the barrage resumed, arrows pelting every inch of the raft.

Arri propped her feet up on her desk. Everything hurt. Breathing was hell. But this far into the day without the scale-skins making a scene it meant she was in the clear. She poured herself a glass of majaun. A concoction of wine, rum, and honey left to soak with roots from the Northern Isles. With a drink swirling in her hand and a binder fit for bludgeoning in her lap, she got to work. The ledgers seemed in order, no overt fuckery on Howellin's part.

Without warning the ship rocked hard to starboard. The majaun bottle tipped from her desk and shattered across the floor. On instinct, Arri grabbed her desk and braced for impact. The ship swayed once more before settling. On any other day, she wouldn't have batted an eye, but docked in the middle of Bottleneck this was cause for concern.

There was a commotion on deck.

Arri grabbed her pistol and booted open her cabin door. She stomped onto the deck. "Who the fuck is rocking my ship?"

The crew was in a flurry of action, re-securing crates. "Rouge wave, Captain," shouted the quartermaster.

They were in the middle of an estuary.

Arri climbed to the upper deck. All the other ships moored at Bottleneck were in a state of chaos. A dozen docks were smashed by ship hulls. The rogue wave could still be seen up-river, overpowering the current. It wasn't her problem now.

She shoved the pistol into her belt and returned to her quarters. Her copy of the ordainment orders was covered in glass. She brushed the shards aside and her finger came to rest on an interesting sub-header. "Mother fucker."

Beyond Lux's outskirts, a cumbersome rig sat lopsided

along the river. Nysra paid extra to have the cranes moved out to the hillside under the cover of night. Threaded along the rotted old booms were a pair of chains fit for pulling ships. At the end of each chain was a hook dug into the whale heart, ready to drop it into the river.

The border between stone and dunes was ambiguous at best. Her servants worked tirelessly, clearing and re-clearing sand from the runic array.

The array was a temporary fixture, so Nysra opted to paint it on the rock, easier than engraving. The base was a paste of shredded man hearts mixed in with phosphorus, ergot extract, and cobra semen. The shape of the array was an overlapping pair of three pointed stars inside of an oblong hexagon. Runic symbols lined the perimeter.

She marked the upper star with symbols representing the first of Sidoth's children. Kadar, the desired summon, she placed on the outermost corner.

Opposite Kadar, on the far point of the other star, was a shallow bronze pan filled with her blood. The other two points of the star were a variable. The most accepted practice was to mark them with the standing masters of Lux and Khepresh. The Sar Emush and Ul Kyzagmi respectively. Another variation was to mark the points with the summoner's parents. A notation of their bloodline.

Theocratic upstarts debated the Beast Mother as a viable point since her discovery. Without a counter deity to balance the second star this was generally avoided.

A small copper brazier sat at the array's center, stuffed with soft fibers soaked in scented oils. Nested at its center was a blackened shard of wood of unknown origin. That coal collared wood was as expensive as the crane and heart combined.

Nysra leaned against her mock altar. A raised stone slab between the whale heart and the summoning array. An impatient look crept across her face as she watched the light of the Sorcerer's Moon nearing in the distance. Bandits were raising a convoy a mile or so up river, nothing of consequence.

She fiddled with the gold plates of her necklace. Unsure of the appropriate amount of exposed nipple for beseeching a demigod.

She glanced over at her sister's minion tied to the altar, dressed in white ceremonial linens. "Why was she so fond of you?"

"Loyalty, I imagine."

"I could understand that. How much have I offered you to strangle her in her sleep?"

"I've not kept a running tally, but the offer from earlier this year included land and a title."

Nysra nodded. "Now that begets the question of what compels such loyalty? A plot of land among your own people would be preferable to running that hateful little harpy's errands."

The women scowled "When we were girls Lady Thessalia made it a point to explain what a scapegoat is. As well as your fondness for them."

"She did put a good deal of effort into you. Literate humans are few and far between, much less among the collard. And it's more than that." Nysra ran her nails along the woman's navel. "She dressed you better, she taught you to speak better, you have more teeth than three of my slaves put together. My sister declined countless offers well beyond your value. Did she ever tell you that?"

The girl looked away.

She grabbed the woman's face and forced it back to her own. "That's impolite, dear girl," Nysra chided. "Whatever reasons my sister had for grooming you died with her. You, however, are very much alive, and without a master. Were you loyal out of fear? Did you enjoy the luxuries she offered over the life of a commoner?"

The women's eyes flared. "I'd nev—"

She backhanded the insolent girl. "I know she taught you the dire consequences of interrupting. Now, where was I?" Nysra straightened her jewelry. "My stock of servants, while plentiful, are lacking in some ways." Nysra tilted the women's face toward a guard gazing vacantly into the desert. "If I don't need to sacrifice you to Kadar, would you see any appeal in becoming my servant?"

The girl glared at Nysra, a dark bruise forming on her face. She held her tongue."

Nysra smiled. "A fast learner. You're here more as a contingency if the heart isn't sufficient. The documentation of these rituals is dreadful."

"You'd risk taking in a servant you'd sooner use as a sacrifice?"

"Hence my inquiry into the nature of your loyalty. My offer is one no sane being in your position could decline, not considering their own self-interest. But if your loyalty was of a more… abstract nature…"

"What do you actually offer me?"

"A means to join us."

The girl gave a look of non-comprehension.

"The actual means by which Sidoth and his first brood grant us sorcery is rather nebulous. It may be as simple as a wave of the hand or the granting of a boon. The generational thinning of sorcery has led me to believe the process is more…" Nysra searched for the right word… "intimate, less rewarding in a personal sense."

The girl's voice quivered. "You ask me to serve as surrogate for a god?"

"I'm inviting you to help me preserve their blood. When a sorcerer renews their bloodline it's only a matter of time before it's polluted. Within a century, ambitious and clever half-breeds drag us back into mediocrity. But with a breeding pair that ceases to be a problem. Unfettered by dilution beyond our own blood, we could mother a bloodline unlike any seen since the first days."

The girl stared at Nysra for a moment, a twinge of terror in her eye.

"They'd worship you as the bearer of the greatest sorcerer in ages, not counting whatever I produce."

"So that's why you choose me, enough dilution to assure your own child's superiority."

Nysra giggled. "Simple girl, I'm not so petty-minded. You're also the last bit of my sister's memory I have left to defile."

The girl seemed to consider the offer. Not that she had much of a choice.

The light of the Sorcerer's Moon drew closer. Its red light washing over them.

Her pale skin took on a pink hue in the alien light. Her blood burned in her veins, yearning to unleash its sorcery. The gold chains wrapped around her chest nipped at her most sensitive flesh, setting it alight with sensation, frustrating and enticing.

"Make this quick." With a wave of her hand, she signaled the crane operators.

Wood and metal screamed as the crane swung the whale heart out over the river. With the pull of a metal rod the chains released. Wood splintered and scraped under the stress. The heart plummeted into the river, landing with a massive splash. Another length of chain twice as long as Nysra disappeared beneath the water with it. With another pull of the lever, the chain locked in place. The crane's boom bowed and cracked, a deep crevice now running its length.

One of Nysra assistants—she wasn't sure which underneath the hood—lit the brazier at the center of the array. The assorted oils caught fire first, burning in a miasma of blues and greens. A moment later a gold light overpowered the smoke as the wood caught aflame. Under the firelight, they began a low hissing chant.

Nysra drew a dagger from her waistband. The flat blade was cast from copper, a viper carved from jade made the hilt, ending in a cobra head pommel. A piece intended more for ceremony than treachery. "As much as I'd love to have patience, we don't have time."

The girl's eyes darted about, taking in every detail of the situation. "And this offer stands as I'm not deemed a vital sacrifice?"

Nysra smiled. "If it isn't vital that you die I'll swear it on the honor of my bloodline."

The girl looked out into the desert. "After the mistress's first bottle of wine, she'd often speak of you."

Nysra tilted her head.

"She goes on about your petty, thoughtless, often poorly thought out schemes. How you squandered every gift from birth. If she'd received a third of your abilities she'd have Lux under her thumb within a decade. She'd even keep you as a puppet ruler. For the longest time I thought the wine was making her dramatic" The girl locked eyes with Nysra. "Without her standing between us now I say she was kind in her description."

Nysra held back a snarl. The girl would not get the best of her. "So be it," she said, feigning disinterest the best she could.

Nysra raised her dagger high and aimed for the girl's heart.

She was about to thrust her dagger when one of her assistants sprang to her feet.

A pale pair of hands came from beneath the robe, accompanied by a copper staff. A rippling bolt of energy arched from the tip of the staff to her own dagger.

The lighting stabbed at her hand, lighting it aflame. The glowing dagger seared the flesh of her hand. The energy dancing through her muscles undermined any attempt to release the dagger. The flesh above her wrist shriveled, black and smoking. Her rings and bracelets were stuck to her charred husk of a hand. A delicate latticework of burns like ivy weaved across her arm all the way to her shoulder.

Nysra screamed. She dived to the ground, plunging her burnt limb into the sand. When she was confident it would no longer burst into flames—as confident as she could be—she pulled it from the sand.

Whatever movement her hand was capable of sent waves of pain jolting throughout her arm where it still had feeling. Her fingers were stuck to the dagger. Any attempt to pry it away tore away her charred flesh, igniting the pain anew.

Nysra coiled herself behind the altar slab and listened. Chaotic shouting and crackling boomed through the air. One of the other bloodlines must have subverted her ranks. No matter. The assassin had failed and would be overtaken once the element of surprise was lost. The noise died. Nysra rose to face the treachery.

The stones were littered with burning heaps of cloth and meat, some still writhing. The sentinels each lay dead, their armor blackened from the inside out.

A single figure stood basking in the moonlight. Black hair flowed in the wind, dagger edged ears like horns, ivory white skin, bright red in the moonlight. The features coalesced to form the visage of a blood thirsty devil.

The figure turned to have Nysra, one pupil blown to an

empty black. "Dear sister."

The smell of ozone and burning hair washed over Thessalia. The once irritation of that beautiful blood stained moon light was now so much more. Basking in the afterglow of this new sorcery, she questioned everything she knew of the art.

The coppers and golds decorating Nysra's servants attracted the lightning. With only Nysra left she could take her time. The look on her face was well worth not smiting her outright. Thessalia slipped her dislocated elbow back into her robe. No sense in displaying how much Nysra had actually done.

"What deception is this?" Nysra shouted.

"Your incompetence is no deception. Trying to kill me was the kindest thing you've ever done. Thessalia glanced over at the runic array. "You inverted the symbols for insight and wisdom. Ironic."

She reached over and took a finger full of the mixture and brushed it across her tongue, bittersweet. "You used cheap ergot. And did the hearts come from sickly old men who wasted their lives in brothels?"

Nysra sneered. "You dare mock me?"

"You've left me no reason to hide it."

One of Nysra's still flaming minions rolled onto the runes, setting the whole array ablaze.

Thessalia sniffed twice. "Phosphorus?"

"To oxidize the cobra semen." Nysra was shaking in rage.

"Quaint." Thessalia fought back the urge to wretch. "Did you understand the necessity of the whale heart, or were you guessing at how to use it."

"I'll not let a half-breed lecture me in sorcery!" Nysra took a deep breath, the angry chanting of an acid transmutation rumbled in her throat.

Thessalia tipped her staff forward and released a thread-sized arc of lightning. Her own body tightened at the release.

Nysra went rigid as the energy danced across her chains. A half-formed gout of acid leaked from her mouth as she collapsed.

Thessalia strolled over to the altar. With Nysra's every attempt to rise, she was again felled. With every arc of lightning, warmth flowed through Thessalia. She wound around the altar and glanced at her convulsing sister. "None of that struck you I trust, Anissa."

"A few raised hairs, Mistress," she said, reverting to her even tone."

"I'll have you collect a few books on the workings of thunderstorms when we return to Lux." Thessalia turned her attention back to Nysra. She placed the tip of her staff to her sister's forehead once the convulsions started to subside.

Nysra looked at her in disgust. "You really are a devil child."

"Maybe. You're the one that let it out."

"Father will have your head for this."

"Your father, our uncle, would risk no such embarrassment."

Nysra held up her burnt hand. "You defaced his favorite. He'll squeeze the life from your body."

"Have you ever given any thought to why you're his favorite?"

"Only I match his sorcery."

"That would have been a good guess a day ago, but no. The answer is much simpler. Your the only one he's certain is his."

Nysra's eyes hardened.

"It's true my lineage is less than irrefutable." Thessalia cleared some sand from her ear. "But it was only ever questioned because I lacked tangible sorcery. If Father kills me now, he validates every rumor ever whispered. Of course, then the other Elders will question the legitimacy of all our siblings. The polite fiction that is our family breaks. They'll pluck at every loose thread from outside and within. Soon, all that'll be left of us will be tatters. Do you think Father will risk all that over your fingernails?"

Nysra was silent—only for a moment, unfortunately. "What did you see down there?" she said through clenched teeth.

This was a vital moment. The answer to such a question needed to be both eloquent and vaguely ominous. Done correctly it could instill Nysra with a lifelong fear of her. Fear of what she might be capable of, freedom from her schemes.

Thessalia smiled. "Something—"

Before she could finish the chains started clunking against each other. The first crane's pulley snapped, the chain went plummeting into the river. The second crane's boom snapped, tumbling with it, crashing end over end against rocks into the Kadar.

Thessalia glanced over at it, realizing her mistake a moment too late. A wall of scaly flesh hit her stomach, knocking the wind from her. The staff flew from her hand, landing out of reach. The coils of Nysra's tail tangled around her and began to squeeze.

Thessalia let out agonized cry. Her dislocated elbow ground against itself.

Nysra only tightened her grip further.

Thessalia could only take the shallowest of breaths. Fleshy coils twitched and tightened around her, tightening in any conceivable way. Thessalia felt as though her veins were going to pop.

Nysra pulled herself on top of Thessalia. She set her dagger, still fused to her hand, to Thessalia's throat. "What was down there? Tell me and I'll end you quick. No vagaries, no pseudo-spiritual bullshit. What gave you this power."

With the last of her air, Thessalia whimpered her answer.

"Again, louder!"

Thessalia's surroundings blurred. The outline of Anissa hung over the altar, shouting something at her. The coil around her chest loosened enough for her to take a breath. Everything snapped back into focus.

Nysra's copper dagger gleamed in the light. "Speak, damn you!"

Thessalia bit the dagger. Energy surged through her body. It felt as if she were sweating acid through every pore. The power welled in her core and shot through her throat, along her tongue, and through the blade.

The bolt traveled through Nysra arm, warping flesh as it traveled. Nysra flung herself back, flailing in every direction. By some immeasurable stroke of luck Nysra's muscles contracted in a way that didn't crush her.

Thessalia scrambled to her feet. She felt like she'd vomited a pure salt. No time to find her staff. She leaped on her sister's back and went for her dagger. Thessalia grabbed the weapon as best she could, two fingers hooked around the hilt, the rest on the blade.

Nysra was regaining control of her muscles again. Random spasms turned into coordinated resistance. She twisted the blade in any possible way to keep it from her sister.

Blood poured from Thessalia's hand. She threw her legs over her sister's torso, jamming her bad elbow against the back of Nysra's neck for leverage.

There was a peeling sound mixed with Nysra's screams.

Thessalia fell back, her head hitting the altar. She felt the dagger in her hand along with burnt flesh.

Nysra doubled over in pain, the muscle and bone of her hand exposed to the sandy winds.

Thessalia lunged at her sister, again landing on her back. Nysra collapsed to the ground. Thessalia drove her knees into her sister's shoulders. She pulled Nysra's head back by her hair and stuck the dagger to the base of her skull.

Nysra froze.

Both of them were gasping for air, gazing over the ledge at the Kadar.

Nysra went limp. "Someone will make you pay for this."

"God."

"It will take far less than a god to smite you."

"No, in the void beneath I think what I found was a god."

"You believe Anu Sidoth was beneath us this whole time? You are mad."

"Not Sidoth, something else."

"A mad heretic at that."

Thessalia drove the pommel of her new dagger into the remains of Nysra's thumb. Nysra's claw shattered all the way to the tip of the thumb.

Thessalia brought the knife to her sister's throat and whispered in her ear. "It might be the wrong god that loves me, but no god loves you."

After all of today's pain and frustration, only now did

Nysra's eyes finally well with tears.

Thessalia ran her tongue along Nysra's cheek, her forked tongue savoring every drop. It was as if the salty fluid quenched years of some primal thirst. She watched her sister's face twist in disgust and horror. "I finally understand why you like doing that so much."

A breeze came from the river and for the first time in years, Thessalia enjoyed the wind blowing through her hair. "Now, dear sister, when you get back to Lux, I'd advised you isolate yourself for a while. I'd actually rather keep the money I offered for your head if I'm going to live anyway."

"You're going to spare me?"

"That depends entirely on you. What are you going to tell anyone who asks about your arm?"

Nysra groaned. "It was because of my own incompetent sorcery."

"No. You're going to tell them exactly what happened. You tell them that this is what happens when someone wrongs me. Do leave out the part about Ilupagru, though. I doubt either of us wants our peers getting any ideas."

"I accept."

"I want to hear you swear it."

"I swear to Sidoth," Nysra said.

"You were trying to conjure Kadar. Swear to him too."

"I swear to Kadar, Vythera, Amon Thule… I swear to whoever you want."

"Good." A wide grin crept across Thessalia's face.

Anissa let out a panicked yelp.

Thessalia gave her servant the briefest glance to assure her safety. "You're breathing in fumes from the ergot, Anissa. Think of pleasant things and you'll be swarmed by those instead." She looked back at Nysra. "Now, where were we?"

Nysra was dumbstruck, staring out at the river, mouth agape.

Thessalia looked up. Despite her newfound confidence from not a moment ago she couldn't help but be awestruck.

Upriver, mixed among raft debris and confused bandits, a massive, thick-armed cobra emerged from the water.

Willem leaned against a crate, the bleeding had stopped but the arrow still stuck from his back. He squinted, trying to focus on the massive figure casting a shadow over the raft. If the panicked prayers of his assailants where correct it was Kadar, the Hooded Death standing before them.

Kadar towered well over fifty feet tall, not counting whatever part of him hid beneath the water. For some reason Kadar was holding a massive heart under his arm, taking bites of it like an apple.

Willem expected the demigod to tear them to shreds. Yet all he did was stand there watching them, eating his heart.

Thazgarr gazed up at the beast. His club slipped from his hand, and the wild man fell back on to the deck. That was one problem avoided.

The wild man had done more than his share to protect them. All Willem could do was lay there and bleed.

A low rumble came from the demigod's mouth. "Well?" Chunks of meat sprayed across the deck.

The voice didn't hurt his ears the way the assorted explosions did. None the less, a prolonged conversation with Kadar would do his hearing no favors.

Kadar looked at them expectantly. "Mortals. With the amount of sacrifice transpiring on my river this last day, there is no conceivable way one of you wasn't trying to summon me. Patience is one of my few finite qualities. Speak your intent."

"Tribute," said Dylus, brushing a stray piece of heart meat from his shoulder. "We're here to pay tribute to the grand and mighty Kadar. We dedicate this battle and the lives spent to you, the aspect of war!"

Kadar's eyes shifted. Willem wracked his brain trying to interpret the facial expressions of the god.

"Master Kadar!" One of the assailants charged over the hill. "This heathen tries to deceive you. They desire the destruction of—"

Before the man could finish an emerald green fluid enveloped him. The man hardly had time to scream as he crumbled into a pile of bones.

Kadar's attention returned to Dylus. "You may continue your dedication."

Dylus took a deep bow and resumed.

Willem stood dumbfounded, watching the dedication.

Dylus went on at length about how glorious the being standing before him was. There was praise, poetry, he even broke into song at one point. His throat hoarse, Dylus took a bow.

Kadar seemed to calculate something in his head.

Will searched for whatever protection he could. Such a cruel being couldn't be placated that easily.

The demigod nodded. "I deem your tribute worthy. What boon do you seek?"

The words left Willem's mouth before even he realized. "Safe passage."

Kadar glanced over at him.

"We wish for safe passage along your river," he repeated.

Kadar's gaze fell on Willem now. "Did I ask you, mortal? You were more than content to keep silent until the prospect of a reward arose. And such a petty one at that."

Ricard's voice rang out from over the side of the raft. "I want sorcery."

"And sorcery for the short one," said Willem.

Kadar leaned forward. His face hovered over Willem's, just far enough to maintain a semblance of eye contact. "And now you make demands. Do you speak for these men?"

"Only in matters of dire importance." Willem wanted to run, to be anywhere other than standing right there. His back burned, his body ached. Fear would only provoke the god.

"Then what would you say for them if I devoured you all here and now?

Willem fought the urge to drop to his knees, to compromise. He tightened his fist. "I'd tell them to try and spear you in the eye. Try to leave a memorable scar."

"And now you threaten me." Kadar bared his teeth, the smell of rotten meat rolled over Willem.

"I imagine threats are much more commonplace in war than groveling."

"Only dull prey begs for death." Kadar's irises bent at

unnatural angles.

Willem felt a tingle in his neck, a warm mist of Kadar's breath licked at his face. Despite his dire situation his mind managed to wander. He saw the subterra, the gas attack, that child's charred remains. It was like the last week's events played back to him in the fashion of a stage play. Along with passing feelings, fear, hopelessness, anger.

Kadar's tongue, dripping in green ichor slid from between its jaws. The forked appendage radiated a warmth rivaling the hottest days in this wasteland.

The tongue slipped in and out of Willem's vision. It never touched him, but he could tell it was coiling around him. Still, Willem locked eyes with the beast hanging over his head, never blinking, never averting his gaze.

Willem felt another sharp pain in his back. The pain vanished, along with the dull burning sensation.

Kadar's tongue retreated back to its master, the arrow wrapped in its tip.

Kadar laughed. The demigod was laughing at them. "I expect you to be very amusing. You'll have your safe passage."

"Do not disappoint me, mortal," said the booming voice.

Sraac limped toward the river. Discipline must have broken without him. Kadar himself was compelling him to action. That or he was delirious from blood loss.

Sraac hauled himself over the dune, passing the other two caught in the explosion. Doz still had shallow breath, Kriss was missing part of their skull.

That's when he saw Kadar in all his splendor. Emerald green scales shining in the sun. Kadar's head was the size of a carriage, sporting milk white fangs and eyes like rubies. Even without the hole in his face, Sraac would have been speechless.

Not a moment later, Kadar disappeared back into the river. Every living soul stood awestruck. The red shimmer of the Sorcerer's Moon faded. The sky returned to a cool blue.

Mont drew his bow, the others followed.

Sraac let out a breath. Two or three more salvos and he could put this behind him. Then he saw the Ecrecian, still standing. The arrow he'd put in his back was gone. "Finish it," he muttered.

Mont's leg dropped beneath the sands, his arrow flew off into the river. A python embedded its teeth in his thigh. He let out a confused scream when a pair of pythons dragged him to the ground, burying their teeth in his neck and dragged him under the sand.

The other five met the same fate, dragged screaming into gouts of sand and writhing serpent flesh.

Sraac felt his heart pounding. What deception was this? How had they offended their god so grievously? He dropped to his knees exhausted, waiting for the pythons to take him to his comrades. None came.

The Ecrecian and his caravan dislodged their raft and were back on the river. The Ecrecian stood at the edge of the raft, facing Sraac. He brought his arm forward, a single finger raised. The raft shrank into the distance, straight for Lux.

Sraac sat there trying to understand what happened in that handful of minutes he was out. How had things gone so wrong? No answers came.

Khazra stepped onto the river bank, wrapped in her soaking cloak. She stood doubled over, coughing water, but she was breathing.

Sraac stumbled down the dune, falling every few steps. "What happened?"

Khazra straightened her posture. She stood half a head taller than Sraac. Her leonine features faded with the moonlight. "He hit me with a statue." Her arms hung limp at her sides, tangled in her cloak.

"No, the avatar."

"I was underwater by that point. Its attention was on the raft. What about that?" Khazra motioned with her head to the mound of molten bone and acid.

Pain surged through Sraac's abdomen. This was too much to process. "We need to get to Lux. Can you ride?"

Khazra winced. "Left shoulder's fucked. Haven't checked the other side, but something's wrong."

Sraac peeled back her cloak. The look of disgust on his

face was only matched by the one of horror in hers.

Everything beneath her right elbow was a desiccated husk. Gray flesh stretching over bone. Blackened skin was spreading toward the bicep.

Without Mont, there wasn't much he could do. Sraac tore off his sleeve and fashioned a sling for her broken arm. He bound his other sleeve around the desiccated one, much the same way humans did for snake bites. He didn't know if it would actually do anything to slow the corruption but he needed to try. Losing everyone was still worse than losing almost everyone.

"Horses, now."

The pair hobbled up the hill a step at a time. Sraac hitched together a pair of horses before placing Doz over the back of his. He helped Khazra next. She was shaky but could use her tail for balance.

With a flick of the reins, they were off.

None of this made sense. When did the Ecrecian get his hands on alchemicals? And that was nothing compared to hiding a sorcerer in his ranks, only fielding them as a last resort.

There were too many details to parse through. He hadn't even touched on his god slaying his followers at the behest of an invader. Then for some arcane reason leaving the three of them alive.

Sraac replayed the god's words in his head. *Do not disappoint me, mortal.* He thought Kadar was speaking to him, unlikely as that sounded now. Had the Ecrecian achieved favor with Kadar through some arcane means? Did he discover some abstract methodology foreign to the Damu'yhig?

Him, the rebels, kasair, and now the Ecrecian. Sraac longed for some type of rational symmetry to define the last few days, but there was none. Chaotic wills clashing into each other was the only description. Irrational acts sparking others to irrational acts.

Sraac looked at his surcoat. The black spots were growing. His wounds were reopening.

He looked back at the others. "We'll find help soon."

Khazra nodded.

Nothing from Doz. His entire leg was red and soaking wet. A piece of shrapnel must have hit an artery, opened once they were moving.

The pair rode for what must have been hours. If they dumped Doz's body they'd make better time. But Sraac couldn't leave him out here after what happened to the others. Not that he could anyway, that kind of strain would reopen the rest of his own wounds.

Every awkward step his horse took over the dunes opened his wounds a little wider. Dozens of tiny openings along his torso, none more than a finger's length away from connecting to another. Stains crept across his surcoat, black patches overtaking the blue.

Sraac was closer to laying on his horse now, his face pressed to the animal's mane. Khazra was still holding herself upright, but there was a look of sickness to her.

Structures were coming into focus, a sentry tower on the west end of Lux.

Sraac turned to face Khazra and something gave out. Sraac's eyes lost focus. The last thing he felt was his head hitting the sand.

CHAPTER
30

The Ashborne made a habit of keeping their trading houses close to water. Easier for plunder, or "salvage" as they called it, to disappear amongst the liquid capital. Howellin's was no exception. Arri kicked in the door to his office.

Smug little cunt was at his desk sipping tea. He glanced up, feigning surprise. "Captain Adfir, what's happened to your nose is unforgivable. If you wish, I can introduce you to a witchman with a talent for the restorative arts. It's the least I can do."

Arri slammed the contract on his desk, the wood almost buckling under its weight.

She'd underlined the offending language with the knife stabbed through the page. "The fuck is this shit about an indefinite retainership?" The mangled state of her nose made her voice nasal, every word grating to her ears.

Howellin gently placed his tea on the desk. With practiced grace, he pulled the knife from the mess of papers. He pulled a book from his shelf. It was bound in leather with the silhouette of the Crow burned into cover. The tome looked older than both of them put together.

He opened the tome to a page marked with a number of gashes like the one Arri left in her own contract. "The old bylaws were a bit more draconian, a necessary byproduct of the times. Regarding field promotions, ordained captains are obligated to follow the orders of their region's field commander. Such will be the case until the Admiralty Board deems the disputed territory secure. You needn't worry, though, the rest of the rights and privileges of captainhood still apply."

"As long as I'm stuck playin' in your fuckin' pond."

Howellin shrugged. "I wouldn't say the captains didn't have a reason for secularizing their appointments."

"And that's why yah didn't fuckin' say it."

Howellin crossed his legs across the corner of his desk. "Semantics. Politicking with snakes has required a certain finesse." Howellin tossed the knife back to her. "On occasion, it also requires an elegant form of savagery. It's only natural that I'd use what I have in abundance to gain something I need. I can't only rely on myself after all."

"That's a roundabout fuckin' way a sayin' you wanted a new dog."

Howellin spread his arms wide. "I know talent when I see it, Captain."

"Keep yer fuckin' captain appointment then. Getting elected admiral wouldn't be worth your bullshit." Arri made her way to the door.

"I'll have you know that abandoning an ordainment is grounds for excommunication."

Arri froze. "Yer bluffing."

"When you agreed to this arrangement you took an oath. And when you succeeded the Ashen Crow recognized you as its loyal vassal."

Arri drew a pistol. "Bullshit!"

"You can kill me, maybe even kill the courier before the news reaches the flotilla. But you'd know, you and the Crow would always know. Is that handful of years worth more than the eternity your soul will spend trapped at the bottom of a glacier? Countless lifetimes feeling nothing but cold? Millennia watching the abyss? Waiting for the things at the bottom to awaken and swallow everything beneath the moon. That's not the kind of thing you cut your way out of."

Arri's trigger finger twitched.

"Or shoot your way out, if I must be literal."

Arri felt her vial of ash warm against her chest. The prick had her. Arri holstered her weapon. "You said this is only until we oust the Damu'yhig, right?"

"Correct," said Howellin.

"I'll deal with that."

"Thank you for seeing reason, Captain."

Arri walked back over to Howellin. She prodded at the tip of her knife with her finger. "So what constitutes a lawful order?"

"A lawful order is defined as one with the intent to forward the interests of the Ashborne Fleet. It's that simple."

"So I only need to listen to yah when it's for the good of the fleet."

Howellin smiled. 'If you must be cynical about it."

"Lotta wiggle room there." Arri plunged the knife through Howellin's left hand, pinning him to the table."

Howellin cried out in pain. "What part of that wasn't clear?"

"Stow it." Arri backhanded him. "You haven't picked up a sword once in yer goddamn life. As long as you can sign your papers as you do, and lo and behold your signin' hand is pristine as ever, I haven't broken shit. And as for a formal excommunication, you'll need a good fuckin' reason."

"You think this isn't good enough?"

Arri twisted the knife, silencing him. "For a rational fuckin' person, for someone who cares about appearances the way you do, not even close." Arri took a seat on his desk. "It's like yah said back in Bottleneck. We're both out here because of the appealingly small list of people who can give us shit. Excluding the locals, for me there's you, and for you, there's no one. The moment you're responsible for the first excommunication in decades that's all gone. Sure, it'd fuck me in every conceivable position, no one able to give you so much as a confused shrug." Arri leaned over, resting her elbow on the knife.

Howellin groaned in pain.

Arri brought her lips to Howellin's ear, her voice a whisper. "But they'd all be thinkin' it."

"What?"

"You're the de facto ambassador to the scale skins. What'll it look like if you go crying to the Crow because your knife hand got a little uppity? Only takes a lil blood to bring the sharks."

Howellin was silent, a scowl across his face.

Arri hopped off the desk. "I spose that'll set the tone for this partnership better than any formal shit. I'll be at Jack's when yeh need me."

Howellin rose to his feet only to recoil back, the knife pinning him in place. "It is a fucking sin that you aren't at the helm of a dreadnaught."

"Yes, it fuckin' is." Arri slammed the door behind her. A moment later the door rattled. Sounded like the pommel of her knife. She had to listen to a prick who couldn't even throw a goddamn knife right.

Arri took a spot along the pier, her feet hanging over the side. This'd be her home for the foreseeable future. A hot breeze hit her face. Sand stuck to her wounds, little mounds clinging at the faintest hint of moisture. Arri ran her thumb along the contour of her nose past the eye. She couldn't leave this place until she owned it. Oddly poetic.

A piece of food drifted into Arri's line of sight. A local dish consisting of spiced beef shavings and vegetables stuffed in bread. Beneath it was a familiar hand, weathered by age.

Arri took the sandwich and said, "Have at it." She braced herself for the chiding of her life.

Jack took a seat next to Arri. "Yeah, you fucked up. Try and do learn for next time I guess."

"Next time?" Arri frowned. "The scales ain't rollin' over anytime soon. I'll be fuckin' ash long before there's a next time."

"You'll figure something out."

"Got plenty of time." Arri thought on all the faces she wouldn't see for a while. "Mom's gonna feel ashamed, if she isn't right fuckin' pissed that is."

"You'll board that ship when you come to."

Arri squeezed her hand into a fist.

"If I had a silver for every hole your mother dug herself into we'd be having this talk… well, we'd be here. I'd just have a nice pair of boots."

"Like what?"

Jack scratched his head. "She'd have my head and balls on a stick for telling you this."

"Well go on then. You can't leave that hanging."

Jack took a deep breath. "I'd been under your mother about five years at this point."

Arri made a face.

"Hush. Anyway, we're moving some wine from Valok-Nur. We make port along the southern coast and wouldn't you know the town was host to a doomsday cult. Not one of those highbrow robes and daggers cult, this was a carving patterns in your body, smearing shit on the walls cult."

Arri nodded. "The usual fare."

"It'd be simple enough if it weren't for your mother being pregnant. So shit goes sideways, the whole town's ready to eat us and carve flutes from our bones. Then one of them notices the baby bump. That's when your mother gets the idea. She starts proclaiming she's the vessel for their god's reincarnation. Kept that song and dance going for three months before we escaped. We didn't speak the language, had to figure the religion out through body art and shit murals but she pulled it off. Mother to the god of a batshit cult. And that's how your brother Aric was born."

Arri fought hard and failed to hold back her grin. "Please tell me she kept the whole aloof mistress thing up."

"She had a throne made of driftwood at the local pub."

The image of her swollen mother commanding a taproom of cross-eyed farmers sent her over the edge. Arri broke into laughter.

"That's the Arri I like to see. But seriously, if your mother finds out I told you about the cult I start giving Glasha bottles of sand.

At that moment, overthrowing the serpent-men didn't seem so impossible. Arri took a bite of the shawarma. There were worse places to get stuck working for someone you hated.

CHAPTER
31

Thessalia slid past the curtain to her mother's chambers. The room was deep, with four pairs of columns. A green and gold carpet at the center. The desired effect was to put visitors on edge. It gave them enough time to second guess themselves as Mother waited for them to approach. Had Mother been waiting there it would have worked.

The setting sun shined through the balcony doorway, its rays orange against the polished carnelian floors.

Mother was out on the balcony, a goblet carved of white marble dangling between her fingers. Her pale skin was orange in the sunlight.

Thessalia peeked around the corner. "How was your trip?"

She turned her head, the serpentine tendrils of her hair rolled across her shoulders. "You needn't worry. The westerners won't return for at least a year or two." Her angled features cast a shadow over her face. "It's unlike you to concern yourself with matters outside the temple. Why did you actually come?"

Thessalia took a deep breath. "In your absence, Nysra challenged my legitimacy."

"I'll speak to her on your behalf. Besmirching her own bloodline, the petulance."

"Thank you, but it's more than that. I want to know about the pale kasair."

Mother bobbled her goblet, spilling a pungent wine. "What did she tell you?"

"Nothing beyond the usual remarks." Thessalia shrunk. "But some older things came to my attention."

Mother set her goblet down and slithered over to Thessalia. She stood well over two heads taller, putting her bust at eye level.

Thessalia looked away, sickened by the way Father's memory stirred her stomach.

Mother guided Thessalia's face back to her own with a clawed digit. "Before your time your father acquired an exotic servant. There is nothing else to the matter. Nysra is seeding truth within her lies to make you doubt yourself."

"But mother—"

A hand whipped across Thessalia's cheek. She tasted blood.

"That will be the end of it." Mother leaned in and whispered, "Your father is unsure, not unwilling to take action."

Tears pooled in Thessalia's eyes. "Yes, Mother." Thessalia was confident she could deal with whatever her uncle might try. Yet she couldn't find it in itself to drag her mother through such hardship. "I'll not take any more of your time." Thessalia turned to leave only to feel her mother's arms wrap her in an embrace.

Her mother's fingers caressed the top of her head. "Sweet child. Anyone would be proud to call you their own."

Thessalia slid back into the hallway. Anissa was waiting for her, staff in hand, skull under her arm. "I trust it went well, Mistress?"

Thessalia took her staff back. "More than expected, less than hoped. Mother struck me. That was a first."

"Shall I schedule time with a physician?"

"No need, that pain is of the soul." Thessalia brushed a lock of hair over her ear. "Though I was concussed a few times. Schedule it."

"Yes, Mistress."

"I'd also like you to reset my elbow before my bath."

"It will be done."

"And I want you to join me."

"Mistress?" Anissa went redder that a still-beating heart."

"What? We'll be going to the city tomorrow. I'll not have you mistaken for a commoner."

Anissa had a confused look on her face.

"I desire closed toe shoes, the leather kind worn by savages and westerners.

"Mistress."

"And I'm also going to require some rings, something conductive. It'd also be in your best interest to stop wearing metal."

"Mistress." Anissa's voice was raising.

"We'll find you some nice silks, too."

"Mistress, what actually happened these last few days?!" Anissa was shaking. "You're assumed dead for a week. Your sister tries to recruit me as a sister wife for a demigod. And now you return from the dead with sorcery I've never seen." Anissa was breathing heavily. "And now all this. What's happening to?"

The enthusiasm faded from Thessalia eyes. "I'm not sure myself. I'm not even sure how much of it was real." She gestured to her elbow. "Whatever dwells there, it's more than a place. It has its own will—more than one even." Thessalia traced her thumb along the runes of her staff. "I want to believe this sorcery is something of my father, a birthright lingering in my veins. For all I know it's a vestige of the entity slumbering beneath us. I wish I had more answers, for both of us."

"Please, this is all so much," Anissa said.

"All I can offer is my best guess." Thessalia motioned with her hand, beckoning Anissa to follow.

Anissa returned to her side. She chose her words carefully. "How are you in such good health after a week without food or water?"

"It felt like little more than a day to me. Something could affect gravity. It isn't too far an assumption that it could tamper with the flow of time, too."

Anissa nodded. "Do you really think you found a god?"

"In truth, no." Thessalia rolled her shoulders. "But I don't have a better word to define what I saw, how far it was above us, above everything else beneath the moon. A god is the closest thing I can think of. Regardless, it isn't something I wish to antagonize, nor entice."

Anissa looked like a wave of cold air had washed over her. "That actually was another thing, Mistress. Nysra mentioned that Kadar may not actually bolster sorcery. Rather he may act as sire to produce a child of exceptional gifts."

"Ah, that's what you meant when you mentioned sister wives." Thessalia nodded. "It is a theory on how the ritual works, and not the most appealing one."

"And this was something you were prepared to accept?"

Thessalia shrugged. "Mother has done it plenty of times. Of course, there'd still be drawbacks. I'd still need to find a decoy mate and convince him it's his. There'd still be a decade of teaching the little shit before it yielded dividends. In hindsight, this foreign sorcery might be the better deal once I find a way to legitimize it."

"Mistress, I apologize for my insolence but you're dodging the question."

Thessalia blinked. "I covered the entire duration of the process, I fail to see what part you find confusing." As the realization struck Thessalia a wicked grin crept across her face. "Does the idea of me copulating with a demigod make you uncomfortable?

"Mistress?" Red was creeping back across Anissa's face.

"My lithe little form on that stone altar, back arched, squirming between Kadar's arms in delight as he ravishes me. His tongue sliding across—"

Anissa clamped her eyes shut. "Mistress, I would never!"

"Then you must be envious. You wanted Kadar for yourself. Do you think your charm surpasses my own?"

"No, Mistress." Anissa shook her head back and forth.

Thessalia smiled. "Then you wished to share him. Being sister wives wasn't what disgusted you, it was that it would have been with my bitch of a sister. Well, rest easy, if you were so enraptured by Kadar I'd gladly share him if we ever get the chance to conjure him again. There's no way he'd resist our combined charm."

Anissa finally broke. "Yes, Mistress, this makes me uncomfortable!"

"Wasn't that so much simpler, dear?" Thessalia patted Anissa's head.

The poor girl finally seemed to calm. "You also seem to have taken some embarrassment, Mistress."

"It's my complexion. It leaves little room to hide such things."

Thessalia smiled to hide the gruesome image in her mind. If Kadar was anatomically accurate at the size they'd seen him at, she winced at the thought. Regardless, it seemed to be enough to placate Anissa.

"I have one more question, Mistress."

"Have I not tortured you enough today?" said Thessalia.

"All I'm asking is what we're going to do about your father."

"I imagine we can buy a shelf tomorrow."

"Your father, Mistress. I doubt he's taking Nysra's maiming lightly."

Thessalia stepped off the ramp to the ground floor. A balisk hide scroll tube hung from the doorway of her apartment. "Shall we find out?"

Thessalia took the scroll tube in her hands. She tipped it to one side and shook out a rolled papyrus, tightly bound in gold and green linen strings. Thessalia dug the nail of her index finger into the strings, undoing the knot. The letter rolled open.

A part of Thessalia was expecting some elaborate veiled promise of her destruction written in blood. Instead, she found a single line of text quilled with cheap black ink.

Thessalia's eyes glazed over the letter. " 'This is a formal notice of reprimand for raising your hand against your sister. Signed: The scribe of A'rssenak Thaxiss.' The bastard couldn't even be bothered to write it himself." Thessalia glanced back over at to Anissa "Remind me to get a frame for this tomorrow."

Anissa looked awestruck. "That's it?"

Thessalia slid the scroll back in its tube. "From him. Nysra herself will likely lash out again at some point. I'll have to prepare for that." Thessalia reached for the doorknob and glanced over at Anissa. "Put copper floor inlays on the list too."

Anissa's face twisted. Before she could say anything Thessalia had already opened the door. The room was completely empty.

"Anissa… where are my things?"

"The contract you told me to place on Nysra's head needed to be excessive. The Shifting Blade has a higher opinion of your sister than you do."

Thessalia took a deep breath. "I'm choosing to interpret this as unwavering loyalty."

"Thank you, Mistress."

Sraac awoke to dim candlelight and a brown stone ceiling. He was in a wooden cot with a thumb's width of padding, more comfortable than anything he'd slept on in weeks. It seemed to be a private room, no sign of Khazra or anyone else.

Cotton threads bound his wounds shut. At his bedside sat a tray filled with bronze shrapnel. He couldn't help but notice there weren't any gold pyramids mixed in with the other fragments. As long as they weren't still in his guts he didn't care.

In stepped a warmblood draped in medical linens. "We've removed all the metal inside of you. Should you find more you're permitted access to the temple's physician."

"How's Khazra?"

The warmblood flicked his tongue in the air. "The chimera is resting. It will take some time for her arm to heal, but we have confidence."

"What was wrong with it?"

"She had a broken shoulder. Were you not the one to dress it?"

"What about the other arm."

"I beg your pardon?"

"Her right arm, the withered one." Sraac clutched the side of his cot.

"When she brought you in she only had the one arm. The other was a blackened stump. We cleared the corrupted flesh, everything beneath the shoulder had to go."

Sraac tried to sit up, only falling back as pain surged through his guts. "Get her a new one."

The lesser serpent-man scowled. "I don't believe you're supposed to know about the art of flesh crafting."

"My service to the Elder has permitted me knowledge of a great many things."

"No."

"She lost that arm in the service of our homeland."

"Ours, not hers."

Sraac felt his voice raising. "She has our blood."

"Chimera blood—a dilution of a dilution. Don't even try arguing the semantics of that Beast Mother heresy."

"Her tail had more scales than your entire body!"

"If we had to correct the deformities of every child with a swath of a noble scales, acquiring the parts alone would bleed the streets dry."

Sraac took a breath. "How am I supposed to face someone I'm responsible for and tell her that?"

The warmblood straightened his garb. "Your chimera made it clear in no uncertain terms, she has no interest in speaking to you."

Sraac rolled his head back. "So that's it then." He'd lost everyone.

"Your master is waiting out in the hall. Now, if you'll excuse me I have apothecary orders that need filling."

Without another word, the warmblood turned on his heel and left. A moment later Sraac found himself face to face with a Damu'yhig dressed in the colors of Amon Thule, the Sar Emush.

Sraac nodded, it was the closest thing to a bow he was capable of. "Elder Krait."

Krait had golden brown scales and wore a robe of black silk with soft lavender colored accents. He glanced at some parchment. "Virtually the entire city slain is what it says in my notes. Is that accurate?"

"I take full responsibility for the debacle. All I ask is that someone sees to the Ecrecian." Sraac braced himself. Krait's wrath was swift and exacting.

"Yes, a commendable effort, child."

"What?"

"It will be some time before we need to set another example quite like that."

"But it will set back food production for months. The kasair—"

"A matter if petty logistics already in the works. You needn't worry about it."

There was no sense in trying to argue with an Elder. "Then once I've healed I ask for the opportunity to follow up on the Ecrecian."

"There are more pressing matters. In your absence, a saboteur burned the Gardens of Phantasms."

"But those where novelty crops, poppies, and ergot. The Ecrecian is a threat to the entire city."

"You will not belittle the destruction of our property, Cutter of Men." Tremors ran along Krait's hand, faint but noticeable. "At your earliest convenience assemble a new team and investigate the matter."

"It will be done, Elder."

"Good." Krait slithered out into the hall.

Sraac caught a glimpse of a figure joining Krait, who wore a red waistcoat and a ghost white ponytail. It was too dark to makes out any other details.

He spent the following hours starting at the ceiling. A city's worth of production capacity was gone. Kasair and Ecrecians were free to move about his city bleeding it dry. And his team lay dead at the hands of his own god. And somehow this failure was "commendable"?

Sraac clenched his fist. Enemies surrounded him, their poison already flowing through the veins of his homeland. But now he knew the face of the greatest foe in their midst. It was one that blades, arrows even, couldn't stop. Willful incompetence.

Sraac basked in his heretical thoughts. If the foreigners didn't destroy them the Elders would do it themselves. Victims softened by their own ancestors. Every time Sraac failed to question them was another step along the path of destruction.

CHAPTER
32

Willem cracked his back. The spot hit by the arrow had warped and discolored but he was otherwise functional. According to Akhil, that color was a sign of a fast-acting poison used by the Damu'yhig. He'd felt it crawling through his veins during the ambush, yet here he stood. Kadar probably had something to do with that.

Regardless of how kind the deity had been, the encounter still gave Willem chills. "Don't disappoint me, mortal." Kadar's parting words. What could he want from Willem? Little about the incident made sense. A demigod turned on his own people for a song and dance. It was possible the serpent-men didn't hold as much sway with their gods as Willem thought. Like Thazgarr said, fear could be as powerful sorcery, if not more so.

Lux towered over him, a mountain to the left, a sandstone maze to the right. The proverbial lips covering the serpent-men's teeth, his enemy's capital. Countless countrymen of his died before ever seeing the walls, and it was right there for the taking.

Willem heard a dragging sound. Akhil limped over to him. "Finding someone to take you the rest of the way down river shouldn't be too hard, my friend. I would offer, but…" Akhil gestured away his leg. Everything beneath his tourniquet still pulsated red.

"It'd be unfair to ask more of you, Akhil."

Willem stepped off the raft. People were going about their business like it was any other port. People shouted back and fourth in the trade tongue. The food and style of dress were different, otherwise it could have been any port in Ecrecia, right down to the kasairan girl unloading a barge full of the gods knew what.

Willem wasn't sure what he expected to be different. The Legion spoke of Lux as if it was actually made of serpents. Spare the armor-clad serpent-men and it was downright normal.

Dylus stepped onto the dock. "Shouldn't be too hard to find a ferry."

"About that," said Willem. "It might be a good idea to bunker down here for a few days and recuperate."

Dylus shrugged. "Couldn't hurt to sample the local fair. Get a feel for what this place is like outside of open revolt. Still have that bag of gold?"

Willem shook his satchel. It was a fair bit lighter after making the grenades but still the most gold he'd ever had by far. Exactly how much it'd be worth outside the Serpent Wastes was questionable. It'd be a shame if it had to go to waste.

"Still think there were plenty of other pointy bits you could have mixed in with the bombs," said Ricard.

"We'll make due," said Willem. "Any luck with that sorcery?"

Richard shrugged. "You'll be the first person I tell."

The pier flexed under Thazgarr's weight as he stepped off the raft. Hanging at his side was a patchwork leather bag, the ears of his idol poking through the top. He clutched his war club, still splintered and red.

Willem eyed the wild man. "Thaz, is this going to be a problem?"

"All the serpent-men must die, eventually."

"Good enough."

Beyond the gate stood Lux. There Willem stood, the lone legionnaire in the heart of his enemy's homeland.

Time to get started.

COMMING SOON

GOD OF THE HOWLING STORM

A TEMPEST OF ASH AND STEEL

DEVIL IN THE BURNING SANDS

DAY OF THE MIDNIGHT SUN

www.ingramcontent.com/pod-product-compliance
Lightning Source LLC
Chambersburg PA
CBHW021105110726

47900CB00007B/2040